For Michael and Christina Barrett, with love.

Thanks to Ali, Christine, Sayeh and Yvette for their encouragement and Anna for her French and Italian.

Limerick County Library
30012 00511572 9

rtae Luimni

# THE INCONSTANT HUSBAND

Also by Susan Barrett

*Fixing Shadows*

WITHDRAWN FROM STOCK

# THE INCONSTANT HUSBAND

Susan Barrett

LIMERICK
COUNTY LIBRARY
00511572
AFH

Copyright © 2006 Susan Barrett

The right of Susan Barrett to be identified as the Author of the Work has been asserted by her in accordance with the Copyright, Designs and Patents Act 1988.

First published in Great Britain in 2006
by HEADLINE REVIEW
An imprint of Headline Publishing Group

1

Apart from any use permitted under UK copyright law, this publication may only be reproduced, stored, or transmitted, in any form, or by any means, with prior permission in writing of the publishers or, in the case of reprographic production, in accordance with the terms of licences issued by the Copyright Licensing Agency.

All characters in this publication are fictitious and any resemblance to real persons, living or dead, is purely coincidental.

Cataloguing in Publication Data is available from the British Library

Hardback 0 7553 2177 4 (ISBN-10)
Hardback 978 0 7553 2177 3 (ISBN-13)

Typeset in Bembo by Avon DataSet Ltd,
Bidford-on-Avon, Warwickshire

Printed and bound in Great Britain by
Clays Ltd, St Ives plc

Headline's policy is to use papers that are natural, renewable and recyclable products and made from wood grown in sustainable forests. The logging and manufacturing processes are expected to conform to the environmental regulations of the country of origin.

HEADLINE PUBLISHING GROUP
A division of Hodder Headline
338 Euston Road
London NW1 3BH

www.reviewbooks.co.uk
www.hodderheadline.com

# The First Chapter

Once more she dreamed of that first entrance, made through the open window of the drawing room. A tall stranger with red-gold hair, he'd passed over the sill, aimless as a butterfly that drifts in from the garden, alarming as a Viking bent on rapine.

'Tennis?' he lightly inquired as he landed. Rose considered whether she should stand and scream or just run. Perhaps because he appeared disguised in white flannels on a mundane May afternoon and not as a furtive ruffian with a cosh (or a blood axe), she stayed put to see what he might do next. Having apparently forgotten the pretext of tennis and untroubled that his break-in had a witness, he sized up the room before crossing to the mantelpiece to select a pretty shepherdess from among the clutter displayed there. As he assessed it, Rose found her tongue, saying, in as commanding a voice as she could manage, 'Please put that back.'

'Do you care for it?' inquired the burglar.

Truthfully, she'd never considered it. It was just one of the many sentimental nonsenses her mother dotted about every horizontal surface. But she knew that possessions were to be defended.

'One can't just walk in and take things, you know,' she primly stated, ignoring his question.

He smiled at that, and asked, 'Can't one?' as though this was news to him. And the unlikeliness of it all made Rose laugh. Or was it from fright?

Laughing too, he pretended to slip the figurine into his pocket. As she moved forward to rescue it from him, he grabbed her hand and pulled her nearer, saying with theatrical relish, 'Anyway, *she's* not what I came looking for.'

Startled, Rose decided that now she must certainly scream, but he'd already released her to resume his pilfering. Again she was fascinated, as he speculatively picked up and replaced the little articles that told of Mapus's narrow life and concerns – a cranberry glass perfume bottle, the blue cow from her Swiss bridal trip, the pill box that held Rose's baby curls. He ran a thumb around the rim of a chipped cup before delicately replacing it among the rest.

'All junk, no?' he commented, as though they colluded over what was worth taking.

'No, it's not!' she replied, stung.

The discerning thief looked again, 'You think not?' He raised an eyebrow as though, hard to imagine how, he might have missed something among the jumbled mementos.

'Well, I don't know. I never thought. But I'm sure that one was terribly expensive,' she hazarded, pointing at the figurine that he still loosely held, surprised to find herself urging it upon him.

'Expensive, yes,' he conceded. 'It's Meissen. But do you believe it's worth anything?' Since she had not a word more to say in its defence he went on, 'Hasn't it become just like all the rest here: invisible to everyone, apart from the drudge whose job it's been to dust 'em all for a century or two? Pick it up, flick it, replace it, next to the china thimble, present from Scarborough. "Oh, my aching back!"' Matching action to words he reached to the mantelpiece to return the figurine, but misjudged it so that the little shepherdess toppled into the hearth where she quite comprehensively smashed. He picked up the pieces and chucked them into the coal bucket, saying, 'All is junk in the end.' Perhaps seeing how shocked she was he added, 'One less for poor old Barbara and her *arthur-itis*.'

'It's Mona, actually . . . and I do hope she won't get into trouble over it.' She tried to sound disapproving.

'We'll see if anyone notices. Bet they don't.'

Rose was excited, troubled. Had he meant to be so wantonly destructive? Even if it had been an accident, his calm dismissal was equally disturbing. She'd never witnessed anything so daring, so naughty, in her whole life. A new world opened up before her of quite deliberately not doing the right thing – and getting away with it.

He took a step closer, as though he would say, or do, more. Rose held her ground, willing to find out what might happen next.

'There you are, you pup!'

Cousin Edith marched into the room, banging the door and putting the capricious moment to flight. Edy, too, Rose observed, was attired for tennis but had contrived a headpiece from fringed oriental fabric to show that, though she was plain, she was modish. She addressed the handsome housebreaker, who'd flopped down into her father's chair, throwing long legs over one arm, and gave him a familiar little punch on the shoulder. Rose noticed that he didn't hold back in punching her in return.

'For pity's sake stop mooching and start spooning. The idea was that you were sent in advance to seduce Cousin Rose,' she paused in order to toss her cousin a wicked look, 'to our purpose.' Edith insinuated her arm round Rose's waist. 'Rose, my ownest, if he won't ask it I will: we may use your tennis court, mayn't we?'

'Of course,' she replied, perversely disappointed that her intruder had come only as the harbinger of harmless family games.

Following behind was Edy's brother Guy, who kissed Rose,

saying, 'Child, excuse this unannounced visit and our unconventional house guest—'

'Who, because he is an artist, believes he must be rude,' Edy interposed, wresting back bragging rights.

'Hate to contradict, but I'm never rude, always charming,' he languidly interrupted. Rose noticed that, behind his steepled fingers, his eyes were closed. And right now, she thought, he's just bored.

'Anyway,' he briefly opened his eyes to smile at her, 'it was Cousin Rose insisted I skip the niceties and engage with her on a higher level.'

Pleased, Rose speculated that, if this was indeed what they had been doing, he hadn't found it boring.

'Engage in smashing up the ornaments, I see,' Guy snorted, retrieving the incriminating shepherdess's head from among the coals.

'Useful or beautiful – that's all I ask,' was the weary response from the chair.

'My dear old creature, as an absolute by which to live, isn't that harsh on all the rest of us who can only aspire to be middling at either?' grumbled Guy as he deposited the head amongst blushing china cherries in a china basket and hid the lot behind the wedding bouquet preserved within its tall glass dome.

'Our lad is one of those who believe the only china one should own is the type one has to strive to live up to. You know the kind of thing,' Edy remarked, very pleased with herself for the witticism. Although she had not the vaguest idea what this might mean, what Rose did understand from their over-excited performance was quite how enchanted both were with their new friend. Evidently Guy and Edy considered that they had landed themselves a live bohemian, here in South Yorkshire. But his apparently random course in from the garden had led to her.

'Edith.' The celebrity stirred himself to unfold elegant limbs and, feinting a serve with an imaginary tennis racket, tossed back at her, 'You should beware of making glib assumptions, or hadn't you heard, mediocrity always caricatures genius?'

Edy gave Rose a little conspiratorial squeeze, as though to say, only listen to how clever we are! Then exclaimed, 'Hark at the man! Always charming? My eye! I bet the scoundrel hasn't even introduced himself, has he, Rose darling?'

'Darling Rose, I'm Patrick,' he said.

That 'darling' flooded her cheeks with charming pink.

All that exceptionally warm afternoon they played on the new grass court, and by the time they stopped for lemonade, Rose Seaton's heart was stolen away by the man who came in at windows and didn't care for soppy souvenirs. As the two girls sat side by side on their deckchairs, she whispered to Edy to tell all about her house guest, and Edy, full of him, was happy to comply.

'He pretends not, but his people are stinkingly wealthy and well connected – sugar, or snuff, or something else quaint and eighteenth century,' she spurted. 'Goodness knows how many black men died to pay for the marvellous façade of the ancestral pile.'

Yes, yes, Rose thought, but more important than all that, is he a bachelor?

'What he'll gladly admit to,' went on her cousin, 'is that he's on the verge of excommunication, I mean disinheritance. And that's why he came back to England, straight from his Parisian atelier, resolved to patch things up with his governor, who is, as I say, rich as a Jew.'

'Why isn't he staying with his people then?' Rose whispered, trying to ascertain the one necessary fact of his domestic arrangements without appearing too eager.

'See, here's the thing, Rosie, the affecting reconciliation didn't go to plan. You know, "Never darken these doors again!" thundered the merciless patriarch. So penny 'orrible, you wouldn't believe! And since he has no home to call his own and no wife to succour him, until the air clears the poor lamb's billeted with us at Fell Top.'

Glad to discover that Patrick was dispossessed of every prop including a wife, Rose exclaimed, 'Oh, I'm sure I should rather be in Paris.'

Edy had the good grace to laugh, saying, with authority, 'Paris is quite *out* these days. It's the industrial wasteland that's the coming thing in artistic circles. So Patrick, bless him, couldn't say no to exposing himself to the slough of despond *chez nous*.'

The two girls looked up to regard Patrick, glamorous in this setting of rhododendrons and green lawns.

'Darling, we live plum in the middle of the wreckage of nature and man. It must be faced!' Edy declared cheerfully.

'Are you talking about old man Pat?' Guy, coming over to the two girls, attempted to sit on his small sister's lap.

'Get off, you oaf, you'll smash the chair! Sit on your billy, like a good boy, and shut up.'

Guy complaisantly pulled out his large, silk handkerchief and placed it on the grass so that he could be seated at the feet of the two girls in their deckchairs. He shouted over to Patrick, who was batting tennis balls into the net, 'Hi, Pat! Come and defend the sex, old man. My sister is belittling me and defaming you to your lover.'

'It's true though, isn't it, darling?' Edith called, squinting into the sun. 'Dear old Dad stands in the way of youthful ambition.'

Patrick came over to them with his easy, swinging stride, saying, 'Oh, don't go on, Edy.' He kissed her squat hand and said, in the whine of a tetchy shop girl, 'It gives me such *chronic* brain fag.'

'Don't you think the girl you're going to marry wants to know her future husband's origins and prospects?' Edy smirked at Rose who, feeling herself found out, looked uncomfortably at her shoes.

'My dear Miss Seaton,' Patrick pointedly addressed Rose, 'please ignore this bourgeois young woman who, being home-educated and a natural blonde, knows nothing of the workings of the real world.'

He *was* rude, even if the drawling, indolent way he talked diffused the harshness of what he said. Rose expected her insulted cousin to burst into a boiling rage, but not a bit of it. Edith shouted with glee, 'Well, I like that, carrots! Come, Rose dear, we'll leave the men to their pontifications. We girls,' she said facetiously over her shoulder, 'have an urgent appointment with a mirror and a powder puff,' and retreated, drawing Rose unwillingly behind.

Edith, having the gift of sarcasm, could scathe as few others, but it seemed to Rose that Patrick McKinley could teach her a thing or two about the liberties that genius can casually assume.

# Chapter 2

She shouldn't have been there at all, mooning alone in the drawing room.

Nearly eighteen, rightly Rose should have been launched to hunt upon the London scene had it not been for her Papus's antipathy to the soft south and the mechanics of matchmaking. Rose's father, Robert Seaton, was of a mind that healthy young persons need only be shown each other for satisfactory alliances to result. He maintained that one might as profitably throw eligible young ladies and gentlemen indiscriminately together into a steep-sided pit as corral them with strangers in some hot and unhealthy ballroom. The end result would be the same: all would eventually struggle free in matched couples. Why, his own wife hadn't been obliged to polka or leave the county to bag her catch and he'd not be put to the needless expense of it for Rose. Truth be told, the expense weighed heavier with Robert at this time than did his mistrust of such jollifications. Of course he did not intend literally to confine his daughter to a pit but he had commanded that her South Yorkshire home would be her only setting. Any local young man worth his salt must seek out a prize such as his Rose. And, to his mind, only a *local* young man would do: one whose pedigree was writ proudly here, in the north, and in manufacturing.

Nevertheless, despite the useless outlay of funds, Robert Seaton had indulged his only child and wife with an allowance for new everything, complacent in the orthodoxy that the instinct to adornment was as natural to woman as the instinct to tangle wool was in the kitten. Besides, it kept them from worse meddling.

Elizabeth-Jane had confidently undertaken the task of equipping her daughter for the sacred rite. Off had come the protective glass dome and training had commenced to fit Rose into a hand's breadth corset and to dance a quadrille. Elizabeth-Jane had squinted over the illustrations in *Myra's Journal* and happily harassed the shop girls at Cockayne's and Walshe's to clothe the newly marriageable shape. The symbolic putting up of hair and the letting down of hems seemed to Elizabeth-Jane to complete her daughter's successful matriculation from schoolroom to nuptial bedroom. And, such was her pleasure in the business of transforming her little lass into the estate of wife (at last the opportunity to indulge her impulse to shop), that she would have run on in this manner even to the ordering of the wedding trousseau. All without a *bona fide* suitor let alone an actual groom, in prospect.

For here was the rub. Not only had the trainee wife, equipped by seamstress and milliner, nowhere glamorous to steer her hats the size of cartwheels or to drag her new hems, but her heart, primed, hair-triggered, by the expectation that now it would love, had no target upon which to fix.

Meetings had been contrived with the unclaimed youth of their acquaintance and she'd arranged for Rose to be invited to call at those households known to harbour the species. But, truth be told, she'd been disappointed with the choice. Limited, by her husband's directive, to the sons of the people they knew and those whose fathers prospered in manufacturing, the show of home-grown sons-in-law did not inspire. Here was Eric, a second cousin, who would have been quite presentable but for his wall eye. Mr Helaby's lad, Ernest, Robert Seaton had vetoed on the grounds of his mother's insanity. Leslie was too silly, Frederick too dull and Reggie plain peculiar. Sad to say, Robert Seaton's theory on home-grown courtship did not take into account the fact that the pick of the local youth did not themselves practise it.

The only young man who might have passed for a suitor was Thomas Newton, a lad to whom Rose had first been introduced when he'd put parts of a milk pudding down her neck at a children's party. Because she was a nicely brought up little girl she'd tried her best not to spoil the birthday tea by fussing and so had decided to bear the cold slime that slid down her back. He'd been disappointed in his fun and she had futilely loathed him back.

However, this Thomas Newton was generally judged to have grown into a sound enough young fellow. Robert approved of his family (a solid dynasty of button manufacturers) and he was conveniently to hand since he did not waste his time either up at the university or down in London. Elizabeth-Jane had taken tea with nice Mrs Newton, Robert had gone for a turn or two around the Crimean monument at Moorhead in company with Mr Newton. Thomas had called upon Rose, she'd visited his mother and gone riding with his sisters and had been introduced to his rather grand aunt. Everyone concerned was happy that an understanding now existed between Seaton and Newton. Rose, too, had tried to be pleased because she knew her duty to Mapus and Papus; besides, wasn't it every good girl's wish to be a wife? Nevertheless, his admiration had, at times, seemed harder to submit to than had the business of the blancmange down the collar. Rose's unease had only grown as they'd passed each staging post along the inevitable plod of Thomas's wooing towards matrimony. Too soon, hanging over her head like a gathering storm, the marriage proposal itself threatened.

Only the previous week, seated together in the arbour at the end of the garden, Mapus close at hand, encouraging but not too obtrusive, Rose had felt the looming prospect of that declaration.

On that occasion she'd managed to deflect him but it was only a matter of time before the question was asked that, once uttered, could never be unsaid, and a love offered that she could not return. Rose suspected her time would be up on 21 May 1897. For on this notable day Queen Victoria was coming to town to celebrate her diamond jubilee and, since Mapus had hinted that Rose might have a reason of her own to commemorate it, she had dreaded this date as the one appointed by Thomas to mark another historical event, her acceptance of him.

An arrangement had long been in place for Thomas to escort her into the city to view the parade and jubilee celebrations. Later they'd rendezvous with her parents for an early dinner. And somewhere in between, she supposed, Thomas would find his opportunity to kneel, a play petitioner at her feet, and request his prize. She knew that once, however unenthusiastically, she would have surrendered it to him. For, until Patrick Michael McKinley broke in through the drawing-room window, Thomas Newton had been her fate.

# Chapter 3

Came the royal red letter day and Rose went into Sheffield to visit the Queen a deal more thrilled at the prospect of spying Patrick McKinley there than Her Majesty. And she carried with her the awful anticipation that 21 May would mark a momentous turning point in her life.

Who knew what the Queen's expectations were for this her first, and last, visit to Sheffield. Among its citizenry there was a grumbling, pride-filled undertone of, 'Why send to London when you can get what you want, and twice as good, in Sheffield?' It was certainly felt as a snub that the Queen's visit came a full forty years after she'd first been up to Leeds.

Nevertheless, splendid triumphal arches were raised, patriotic garlands, banners and bunting hung out, and the royal route lined with as loyal a horde as Her Majesty could wish for. People thronged the barriers and every window to wave flags and shout themselves hoarse, so that Rose and Thomas had to push their way to the stand at Fargate where he'd paid for seats. Thomas had liked the sound of the 'Grand Seating Stand' and imagined himself and Rose raised up in positions of isolated privilege away from the mob. However, they found that they were as jostled and deafened here as were the common people who only stood. Once installed, Thomas was further put out of sorts to learn from his neighbour that the sharp Sheffielder who'd raised this structure for the paying public had knocked down any unsold seats that morning.

'Did you hear that? This fellow says he paid only a shilling for his and I'll be . . . if I didn't part with a guinea apiece! It's a poor show, crammed together anyhow, and with the worst types.' He extended his elbow to dig his cheap neighbour illustratively in the ribs.

Rose privately considered the stand very fine, offering as it did an elevated prospect from which to spot people one knew (or would like to know better) among the crush. Even more advantageous, it provided absolutely no opportunity for dropping to one's knee and offering a ring.

'Please don't go on so, Thomas,' she said. 'Only think, here are we on the sidelines of history.'

'That's as maybe,' he grumbled. 'However, I suppose a man's the right to expect what he's paid out for.'

Rose ignored Thomas looking in vain for the Fell House party. They had evidently not been swindled into taking seats here. She thought of her irascible parent, Councillor Robert Seaton, already long accommodated in the official stand in Pinstone Street, among those notables similarly invited to witness the official opening of the new town hall. No doubt he, too, grew ever crosser, obliged to wait upon the grandmother of Empire without benefit of luncheon or tea. He'd grumbled before he'd left that morning, 'Due on the dot o' five and all over, bar the shouting, be seven, but I'm forced to give my whole day over to it!' She wryly considered that he'd been trapped there from the fore-noon, with no other entertainment than the tootling of the military band, and idle hours spent in contemplation of the expensive Stoke stone frontage of the new town hall. Neither would have improved his temper.

Rose and Thomas in their inferior spot had no view of the historic moment when the magnificent town hall, in all its allegorical swank, was at last formally opened. Thus, they could not feel cheated that the Queen hadn't deigned to set foot on Yorkshire soil to conduct her bit of business but, as if by remote command from within the royal carriage, merely turned a little key in its lock to convey the electric current that caused the massive doors of the town hall to slide effortlessly aside. But they were duly thrilled by the tremendous parade of mounted lifeguard that eventually heralded Her Majesty's lightning round of the city. For truly, sixty years practising pomp and pageantry resulted in a display thrilling enough to satisfy the crowd's appetite for spectacle, whether they sat expensively, stood, lolled or leaned out precariously at upper windows. The Queen's men pranced past in a glittering stream, two by two, breastplates, helmets and swords jangling and clashing in the sunshine.

'Every man jack of 'em, horses and all, brought up from Cockney land by rail,' informed Thomas, out of the corner of his mouth. Gingered up by all this masculine dash, Rose, along with everyone else in their stand, craned forward, making the structure creak, to witness the eventual entrance of the phenomenon absolute monarch of one-quarter of the globe's population. However, the curtain-raiser proved more impressive than the main attraction. Rose saw for herself that the royal carriage contained a stout, elderly body cased in black. Why, she's nothing but a little albino mole wearing a bonnet and carrying a parasol, she remarked to herself, disappointed. Here presented, then, for one afternoon only: Britannia, the mighty Queen, Empress over land and sea – sans crown, sans jewels, sans mystery!

Aware that Thomas was trying to be heard over the tumult, she turned to him, her heart full of trepidation. Surely not now! But he only shouted into her ear, 'Let's get away before this mob realises the show's over,' and was already roughly clearing a way for them to descend. Leaving the generality to follow on behind the carriage in its progress to Norfolk Park, there to take in a choir of fifty thousand children primed to 'strike loud notes of triumph', they set off through the crowd, avoiding the steaming souvenirs left by the London visitors, for the restaurant of the

Albany Hotel, which had judiciously remained open to profit from the festivities. As they jostled on their way, Thomas ostentatiously shielding her from outrages, she looked out for Patrick among the monarchist multitude. If she'd known him better she wouldn't have bothered.

In the dining room, Robert Seaton was not apoplectic; quite to the contrary, he was chuckling still from the conversation he'd had with one of his fellow councillors that had confirmed his verdict that electricity was good only for chicanery and cheap effects. Electricity was his particular bugbear.

'Muscle power was the only force behind those blinkin' doors!' he said, by way of greeting. 'Forget little keys on blue velvet cushions – that fool electric wire did nowt but light a bulb to signal three brutes hiding in there to push 'em open from inside. I had it all from Carr.'

'Well, I'm supposing it makes no difference to Her Majesty how the town hall doors were opened,' replied his equable wife, distracted from checking Rose's ring finger and her face for telltale glows.

'But it does to me. It does to me. I can tell you, it chuffs me!' he said and laughed heartily. 'Electrickery! It'll come to nothing.'

Hidden by the tablecloth, Thomas sought Rose's agile hand while, across it, he blandly addressed his future pa-in-law.

'Our great-grandchildren,' he gloated at Rose, and her heart seemed to falter in her chest, 'will regard electricity as a very commonplace miracle.'

Robert snorted, dismissive of the pup, and turned away to seek out his ally Carr among the other diners. Grimly, doggedly, Thomas continued his pursuit of Rose's hand. They tussled under the table, she always slipping away from his grip until he was forced to give it up and look sulkily into his menu.

'Can you credit it – sixty years she's ruled over us,' clucked Elizabeth-Jane, making conversation to fill the unaccountable vacuum. 'Eh, but she must have seen some changes in her time:

indoor privies, motor vehicles, telephones, lasses riding on bicycles – quite apart from electricity . . .' She nodded significantly in her husband's direction. 'It must break her mother's heart to see how things have gone to the bad.'

Her husband grunted his general assent and then, having seen for himself that there was nothing to hang around for, and anxious to escape more of his wife's maundering, excused himself to join Carr and his party.

Elizabeth-Jane turned her benign attention upon Thomas, asserting comfortably, 'I'm sure we're all with Her Majesty in mistrusting this mania for *improvements* and *advancements* in everything. There're that many works in the city centre at present, one can't walk a yard without falling down some hole.'

Thomas protested at this vision but Elizabeth-Jane, mildly reproving, held up her hand. 'If the streets aren't got up for laying telephone cables, they're pulling down the Duke's fancy gas lamps (which, to my mind, just went up) to make way for the new electric trams. And why can't the people be content with horse-drawn, I ask you? Nothing but fads and crazes!'

Judging that having run out of steam and breath, she would now turn to the other matter of the day, Rose contrived to set her mother off again, with only the smallest of well-placed jogs.

'Won't you tell us how things were better in the past, Mapus?'

Elizabeth-Jane, rarely invited to reminisce, smiled at her daughter and indulged herself.

'Why, in my day, Rose pet, Sheffield was more of a big, homely village with each person acquainted with every other, and interested with that other's concerns.'

Rose affected the expression of someone who listens quietly but attentively to good sense and Mapus, encouraged, continued along this pleasant anecdotal byway.

'A lady could come to town to purchase something quite small – say a packet of glass-headed pins – and the shopkeeper, I mean the proprietor himself, pet, would come out to the street with samples – no need to leave the carriage. And in those days a lady never expected to carry *money*.' She said this last in a significant stage whisper, as though she uttered an expletive. 'It was simply never mentioned. Why, when I was a lass, I hadn't the slightest idea of it.'

'Hopelessly old-fashioned.' Thomas smirked, unpleasantly, still out of temper with Rose.

'Very proper,' Elizabeth-Jane countered, not to be put off her stroke, 'To my mind this city's turned into a great, swollen beehive abuzz with factory workers and other scoundrels who've forgot their proper place and swarm about full of rebellion and discontent!'

Thomas huffed and made Elizabeth-Jane a little hotter. It occurred to Rose that she might drive Mapus's prejudices and Thomas's contrariness in tandem until they were both safely miles from the topic of marriage proposals.

'But Mapus, aren't childhood memories blurred by nostalgia? Perhaps one simply forgets the bad.'

Elizabeth-Jane rose to the bait. 'Not at all! I remember just how it was and I'm sure I can't be blamed for preferring the old picturesqueness there used to be hereabouts – the narrow streets and shops with their old-fashioned fronts and the little workshops busy on every corner. None of your great hulks of factories . . .'

'Paradise lost!' slid in sardonic Thomas. 'Those old places were a disgrace: wood-built frames, wattle and daub façades falling into the street – quite right they should be swept away.'

'Thatched roofs, little allotments here and there, and the lasses going to the wells to fetch back water,' Elizabeth-Jane persisted.

'And cholera to sicken their children,' he mocked.

Rose noted Mapus's flushed and disconcerted face. Thomas clearly hadn't grown out of his predilection for publicly discomfiting females. Rose who had previously been drilled in only doing, or saying, the right thing, recalled her recent thrilling education at the hands of Patrick in pre-meditated acts of wrongdoing, and took the opportunity to lob in her own sly incendiary. 'But surely, Thomas, seeing the Queen Empress personally fills you with patriotism and reverence for tradition and the past?'

'The old girl is grand enough in herself, I suppose,' he expansively informed the ladies, 'but I can't be doing with hitching myself to a dusty old epoch that was half played out before I was born, or to its monuments.'

Whether he was sneeringly referring to the Queen, the Duke of Norfolk's fancy gas lamps, or Elizabeth-Jane herself was not clear. But it was apparent to Rose that he'd done for himself with those 'monuments'. She seemed to hear the *pouf* as he was blown out of the water.

Arrogant Thomas, who noticed nothing, obligingly finished the job himself. 'I'll always be one for progress over glass-headed pins!'

Thus Elizabeth-Jane was made to realise that she could not be doing with Thomas Newton. There was something sharp and disrespectful – worse, something unfilial – about him. She looked at her innocent daughter and thanked the heavens that, not a second too soon, she'd seen through him. It had been a near escape.

At the end of that notable day Thomas returned from the jubilee parade, question unpopped, engagement ring still in its box and his diary entry for 21 May 1897 eloquently crossed through. As for Rose, she was released to speed home, hot on the heels of true love.

# Chapter 4

The Whit Walks were the next event in Rose's social calendar that would have to stand in for the whirl of the London scene, although this time without benefit of actual royalty, or indeed the official escort. It was a summer Whitsuntide this year, Easter having fallen so late, and so these church pageants, traditional in their part of South Yorkshire, occurred on a beautiful day in June. Rose hoped that the sunshine and the show might tempt the unconventional Mr McKinley into the open and kindly volunteered to help Mapus in her charitable provision of refreshments for the holiday. For, having waited in vain for an invitation to visit her cousins at Fell Top, and being timid of issuing her own, she plotted other opportunities to put herself in the way of Patrick. Though she might have wished for a more elegant and conventional setting than this pastoral of public games and sports, this was where her beau must discover her.

The Whit Walkers ended their parades in the park where they embarked upon their Whitsun ale, meaning picnicking and the playing of cricket matches and children's games – a right down good spree. Dressed in their Sunday best, holding banners aloft, they trooped in the sunshine and arrived full of goodwill and ready for their fun. Rose, stationed behind a trestle table equipped with a tea urn, looked in vain for the unsettling Patrick

McKinley among the festal crowd. It seemed the only reward for her charitable impulse would be the opportunity to spend all afternoon serving parkin to parishioners – and in particular, to the young men who singled her out, among all the other helpful, gracious ladies, to pour their tea for them. The lovely Rose Seaton, in her new season's frock, stood there feeling that, perhaps even more than the refreshments on display, she was what her stall had to offer. Striking an attitude of dignified unconsciousness, she poured and smiled, and glumly observed how, under the blue eye of summer, the young girls in their carefree liberty, garlanded in flowers and dressed in sacrificial white, stripped off stockings and shoes and danced together in rings upon the new grass.

A dark-browed, high-coloured man she'd noticed looking at her with a curiously intent expression resolutely approached, carrying his teacup in one hand and wiping his moustache dry with the other. She prepared to be politely aloof.

'Miss Seaton?' he ventured.

Put at a disadvantage, Rose acknowledged that it was indeed she. But who was he? Obviously a local man, and neatly turned out and well-spoken, but she had no recollection of ever having met him. Just in time she recognised him: Harold Webb, brother of her childhood friend Marion, and an employee of her father. How embarrassing to have to steer a course between deference as the younger sister's friend and condescension suitable to the boss's daughter. But Harold did not shy from this social minefield. Choosing to employ humour, he said, 'I thought I knew you, though you've changed a great deal since you used to play at dollies' tea parties with my sister.'

'How do you do, Mr Webb. As you see, I've graduated from paint water to real tea,' she replied, adopting the same tone.

He looked at her approvingly and she noted that he had changed too: he'd developed into a rather fine young man, tall, with longish, thick black hair.

'Are you here with Marion?' she asked, looking hopefully past his shoulder. She was not that grown that she knew how to banter solo with a man. Particularly one who'd last greeted her with a pat upon the head.

'Oh no, she is a little poorly at present and must stop indoors.' He did not sound particularly sorry about this.

'Then you're to give her my love and hopes that she'll soon be fit again to enjoy this lovely weather,' Rose said and, without intending it, put an end to their only topic of mutual interest. She realised with a sinking heart that she'd also used up the weather. Evidently Harold did not feel the want of his sister as a conversational aid. Surveying the trooping crowds, he pointed to a couple of urchins. 'Do you see those little lads?' Evidently not official participants, in their shabby weekday clothes, she saw they'd attached themselves to the end of the Boys' Brigade procession, and carried aloft a broom to substitute for a proper banner.

'So pleased with themselves with that brush!' She laughed, relieved. It was easy to chatter about the peculiarities of other people.

'No doubt they think themselves as deserving as all the rest when it comes to free buns.' He smiled at her over the rim of his teacup.

She was about to remark on the unfortunate lady who'd trodden on a bit of bunting and was dragging it along behind her when he abruptly asked, 'Won't you come and look at some of the sport? They're setting out deckchairs by the pavilion right this minute.' He flushed darker as he risked the invitation. But Rose, overtaken by her eagerness to get out from behind that stupid stall and walk about in the sunshine, did not stop to think whether she did right to accept. She was already loosening her apron strings when she glanced up, unconsciously smiling, and saw Patrick in a tomato-red unfitted shirt worn without a tie. She saw him notice her, and Harold, and he winked mischievously. Then, a handsome Pan, he turned away to lead the country maidens in their loose-limbed dance. Rose suddenly felt that she could hate Harold Webb.

00511572



LIMERICK
COUNTY LIBRARY

'Thank you, Mr Webb, but I think I should stop here,' she said, prim and discouraging in her mortification, and she stepped back behind her stall. Harold looked sharply in the direction of the girls, and Patrick in that shirt, unmissable among the white lace frocks.

'Just as you please Miss Seaton.'

Dismissed but on his dignity, he gave her a stiff little smile, accompanied by a stiff little bow, and walked purposefully away.

Well, she thought. He doesn't know how to behave, not one little bit.

All that long afternoon, Rose twinkled over the teacups and cheered the cricket in vain, as shining Patrick flashed hither and thither in the sunlight like a goldfish in a green pond, apparently oblivious of her, the neglected nymph of the tea urn.

# Chapter 5

The missed opportunity of the Whit Walks was succeeded by days of dreary vigil by the living-room window. Uncomprehending Mapus's sensible prescription for brooding was fresh air and light company but Rose, unwilling to desert her post, apparently preferred to asphyxiate herself upon books and daydreams.

She was dully eating breakfast with Papus and Mapus when a servant announced a caller from Fell Top at last. Miss Seaton.

'Dear's sake, what does the girl want at this time of day?'

But Rose had rushed already from the room to greet her least favourite cousin with a kiss.

'We heard from your ma that you'd got the mobs,' said Edy with her usual charm. 'So Pat and Guy sent me over here to dig you out. Though,' she said, looking at her cousin's vivid face, 'you seem cheerful enough to me.'

Rose's heart was light, reckless, blithe: Patrick, the golden, divine, breath-stealing Patrick had called for her! Or, as good as.

Rose, a tall lily, looked upon her low weedy cousin and noted that she'd come dressed in an old faded curtain with a droopy low belt made from its own cord. The thought of what use Edy might have put the curtain rings to, as well as excitement, made her laugh out loud.

'If it isn't the girl of the age!' she commented unwisely.

'What? Oh, don't you mock me, it's just comfortable and unrestricting,' Edy tetchily replied. 'And shockingly expensive, it came from Liberty in London.' Edy looked at her cousin, still in her dressing robe, and gave her a malicious little pinch on the upper arm. 'Anyway, you'd better look lively and get yourself dressed, that is if you want to come with.'

'Where are we going?' Rose asked, suddenly unsure of herself now that the longed-for moment had arrived.

'For a hike across country, dear heart,' replied her cousin, showing off her new sandals.

'I'll call for Joan,' said Rose, running off to change.

As the cousins stepped into the summer morning she saw him, still far off, and thought he looked carefree, as one who understands that it's always so much nicer to be expected than to arrive. He strolled up to her, graceful in a moss-green suit of loose knit woollen weave that was perfectly matched to Edy's vegetable-dyed sack. Rose was made horribly aware of her neat and conventional walking costume of skirt, blouse and bolero jacket, topped by the ubiquitous straw boater. He stood before her larger than in daydreams and twice as vivid, chewing on a grass stem. She thought she must faint.

'My one, perfect rose,' he greeted her.

Colour bloomed instantly in her cheeks.

'It's so hot today!' she said in her confusion, flapping her hand in front of her betraying face.

'Didn't I spot you at the church pageant thing,' he asked, 'looking charming in a cross-over pinny?'

'Oh that,' she said with false gaiety. 'I was only helping out for a bit behind the refreshments stall. I could have left it at any time.'

'Indeed? I was wondering if I dare ask you to desert, but that saturnine chap of yours scared me off.'

'Mr Webb?' She blushed even hotter. 'He's really nobody, just the son of a local farmer.'

'What a shame then for you to have missed out. It was lovely frolicking in the sunshine. I intend never again to dance indoors.'

'Really, you mustn't concern yourself. I'm sure I had just as much pleasure in watching,' she said, unconsoled.

'I'm so glad.'

His polite condescension made her feel utterly inconsequential. Then he smiled, pressed her hand and called for the other two to get a move on, before striding off in advance of the party.

Walking down through the woodland that lay below Rose's home, the company passed between ash and oak, birch, rowan, alder and elm and the broad, strangely grown coppice stools: neglected remains of the industrialisation of these woods by the Seaton estate in a time before coal was king. Where the wood's dense canopy had been most recently opened up by falling giants, elderberry grew and foxgloves and beds of nettles and wood pimpernel thrived and Rose saw only that Patrick's hair seemed to kindle as he strode, always ahead, through the patchy sunlight.

They skirted a clearing where the gamekeeper's isolated cottage stood and startled a noisy jay that had been sitting on his garden gate, in open defiance of its enemy. Rose walked along bearing a heavy smiling mask upon her bruised and tender face, but kindly Guy, who seemed to understand that she suffered, dawdled behind with her, making conversation so that she would not have to.

They'd been going for ten minutes when Patrick ambushed Guy from behind a tree, pushing his portly friend to the ground where they briefly tussled on the wood's loosely littered floor. They soon left off, laughing and red in the face, Patrick's rough green suit snared in rusty leaves and Guy pleased as a puppy, his sad cousin forgotten. Now the two men continued along together and she overheard Guy telling Patrick the history of these woods: gift of the Duke of Somerset, together with twelve quick does to stock them. Even from a distance his extravagant gesticulations told how happy he was to have won Patrick to himself.

At the boundary of the ancestral wood they entered a neglected hinterland of rough, tussocky grass and gorse that led down to a lane running alongside cultivated fields. Rose, in her narrow skirt, tottered behind the rest, leaning upon her furled parasol, but Edy plunged recklessly ahead, sandals aflap, and disappeared down the incline, calling, 'Well, chase me, girls!' Rose saw that she charged straight into Patrick who only saved her from falling by grabbing hold. Then, arms still round each other, they set off, singing, down the lane. They must have gone on too far, or sung too loud, for when Rose gave a pale little cry and sat down theatrically upon a hillock rubbing at her ankle, it was Guy who hurried back to pull her to her feet and hook her onto his rough tweed arm.

So, two by two and arm in arm, they marched down the little lane between hedgerows that, now it was June, were full of flowering dog rose and fragrant woodbine, the verges deep with shimmering grasses and buttercups and moon daisies, and poppies that had escaped from field edges.

Patrick was singing, 'Tar-ra-ra-boom-der-ay!' swiping at the banks with a stick he'd cut for himself, in time to the music. Edy joined him in the chorus, loud enough to startle the birds. Then he launched into 'Her long, tall feller', tucking Edith under his arm and employing his best cockney: ''Im just a long string bean of a feller and 'er the 'ottest little radish of the bunch!'

She played up to the theatricals, looking up at him and wagging her finger.

They entered the mining village of Eckersby, whose Scandinavian name was recorded in the Domesday Book, just before eleven, told by the striking of bells from the church that the Normans built. On past farm labourers' cottages dating from feudal times and the massive medieval tithe barn to the rows of raw, red-brick houses of the modern era, which accommodated the miners and their families, imported to work Eckersby Main, the Seaton pit. Patrick began to improvise to the tune of *If It Wasn't For The 'Ouses In Between,*

> 'Oh, it was surely once a wery pretty country
> And Ilkley to the northward could be seen
> And by hangin' off the tree tops
> You might catch a glimpse of Cleethorpes
> If it wasn't for the eyesores stood between.'

Rose felt obscurely embarrassed that at least some of this industrial despoliation was the work of her own relations. At the canal towpath that ran along behind the miners' cottages, Patrick took Rose's arm, so that Edith was left to Guy. Rose began to feel that she, too, might enjoy the outing.

They came across a couple of larking children, too young for school, who were trailing homemade boats on pieces of string through the canal water.

'Where's the pithead?' Patrick asked, looking past the children who played among the dandelions to the cow meadows on the far canal bank. 'I thought Eckersby Main was at Eckersby.'

'Not so far from here,' supplied Guy. 'Along the towpath, beyond those trees.'

'Too far for a hot day,' said Edy firmly. 'Anyway, if it's proper industrial hellishness you're after, wouldn't you be better off going into the city?'

'In Sheffield the pigeons fly backwards to keep the dirt from getting in their eyes,' commented Guy, who was pulling the seed heads off the longer grasses and throwing them at his sister's back so that they stuck where she couldn't reach them.

'Sounds horrible.'

'Curious then that you want to see it, since it might so easily be avoided,' said Edy, now frantic as a dog with fleas.

'To be honest I would rather avoid it. It depresses me to see how ugly we've made the world. How irretrievably spoiled it is.'

'Out of sight, out of mind,' said Edy, turning her back so that Rose could pick off the rest of the grass seeds.

Patrick was not content to let the matter drop. 'Artists have a duty to look, though,' he said, perhaps trying to persuade himself. 'There is as much truth in ugliness as there is in beauty.'

'Well, I choose beauty,' said Guy. 'Modern life is too full of ugly, necessary things for me to want to stick them up on my drawing-room wall and look at 'em.' Rose detected how uncomfortable it made him to cross Patrick.

'Don't misunderstand me, I'm for beauty,' Patrick said. 'More than most! But I can't just stick my head in the sand and pretend I live in the best of all possible worlds.'

'Well, I think it's perfectly livable,' Edy replied.

'And I'd like to sweep the whole thing clean and start again!'

Patrick sounded heated and Guy tried to make a joke of it, saying, 'Quite a job, starting the whole thing over from scratch.'

Patrick laughed and they all relaxed. 'I won't. I'll start with . . . a chair. A chair that is beautiful in its utility. And when I've perfected a chair then I'll tackle my own life and invent a new way of living that's simple and creative and good.'

'Puritan Pat,' said Edy. 'I think not! You already lead the kind of life that suits you to a T.'

'You mean that of the sybarite and sponger?' he replied, suddenly harsh again. 'I'm sick of it and sick of myself.'

The whole party was now wary and on edge. Guy patted his friend calmingly on the shoulder but Patrick shrugged him off.

'Come on, Pat, let's go home,' said Edy, equally appeasing.

'I think I shall go on,' he answered.

Rose felt the tears start in her eyes.

'Look,' Edy appealed to him, 'Rose's feet are killing her. You wouldn't lame her for the sake of a silly principle and a pithead, would you?'

She poked Rose in the back, who heard herself bleat, 'I should like to go home now.'

'There you are!'

Patrick looked full at Rose and said, 'Of course, you must! I am sorry for your poor feet,' and made her feel even more miserable and defeated.

Guy, ever solicitous, got them off the hook by announcing, 'Good gracious, my dears, I've been a bore, making you come so far and trot so fast along the way.' He turned to Patrick. 'Old man, perhaps it would be best if you went on by yourself and I'll arrange for a trap or some other conveyance to carry the girls back in time for luncheon.'

Patrick took Rose's hand and squeezed it briefly before strolling off, in the opposite direction to the stand of poplars that hid the colliery. He trod the thin path worn by the horses and men who hauled the coal barges as delicately as a tightrope and waved his switch in farewell as he went.

They went to Webb's Farm, home to Marion and her brother Harold, which was conveniently located for the taking of refreshment after a long walk on a hot day. Rose bit back her tears. She'd made the wrong decision. All was lost. She should have gone on with him, gone on with him forever side by side. Why ever had she chosen comfort and food when she could have been labouring along next to him, hungry and thirsty in her heavy, tight clothes and boots?

As they went down the farm drive, flanked by a cow pasture on either side, they came upon the younger Master Webb leading a docile Jersey heifer by its nose.

''Ow do, Miss Seaton, Mr Seaton,' William greeted them. 'My sister Marion's at 'ome. She'll be ever so pleased to see you, Miss Rose, it's been that long.'

'What are you doing with that cow?' asked Rose to cover her embarrassment at apparently having neglected her friend.

'Eh? I'm trainin' 'er to walk t'alter, for the county agricultural show, miss. I tek 'er for a ramble every day.'

The heifer, losing patience and, no doubt, anxious to continue with her training, or to reach the lush grass which grew at the path's edge, pulled her escort away.

'Sitha!' saluted William amiably as he followed behind the ambling beast.

'How droll. 'odge with his 'ound!' said Edy a little too loudly for Rose's comfort.

As they approached the farmhouse, the invalid Miss Webb was to be heard playing Schumann on the piano. She greeted them all and seemed particularly pleased to see Rose, even though it had been a good two years since last they'd met. She left the piano stool and, leaning upon it for support with one hand, held out the other to Rose, saying, 'How kind you are to call. My brother Harold will be so sorry to have missed you. He told me how much he enjoyed meeting you on the common the other day.'

Having welcomed cold tea and declined bread and cheese, the young visitors spent what was judged to be sufficient time complimenting Mrs Webb on her perennials and Miss Webb on her *Frauenlieb und Leben* to be considered polite before they accepted the offer of the trap to drive them all back down the laden summer lanes to home and luncheon.

Looking for her maid Joan to sponge and powder her damp neck and back and help her dress for the midday meal, Rose was put in a worse temper to find the girl making sheep's eyes at the Fell Top second footman. Back, once again, safe, beneath her glass dome Rose thought how terribly stupid and young love made one.

# Chapter 6

Waiting at Moorhead, where the trams from the western suburbs turned round, Rose and Edy diverted themselves in observing that today every couple that passed through that busy junction was a comic mismatch. All at odds they went by arm in arm, jolly apple-dumplings husbanded by dour cricket bats, the nervous carrot-nibblers wived by ruddy carnivores.

'See that girl with the ugly, old man?' Edy gestured indiscreetly at the delicate young matron whose arm was taken, as though in triumph, by her elderly spouse who stalked on thin shanks. 'Too horribilino! Think how dreadful strong the parental opposition must have been to make her marry him, eh?' she said, winking at Rose. Rose speculated that whatever the force that yokes, shackles or splices those whom common sense would never have brought together under the same roof must indeed be formidable. But despite her cousin's cynicism Rose preferred to believe that the power that united even the most incomprehensible pairs was love.

They'd come into Sheffield earlier that afternoon, supposedly to rendezvous with Guy who, the story went, was treating them to a symphony concert. Rose had been barely able to suppress her giggly panic at the deception all the way through tea with Papus in his nearby offices. For when Patrick had proposed this unwise outing to the Empire Palace Theatre to see Vesta Tilley, it had seemed to Rose her chance to put right the missed opportunity on the towpath, and if today's adventure required lies and recklessness, so be it. Here she was, poking fun at the passers-by, a little hysterical from excitement and fear, waiting for Patrick to claim her.

'Watch out, girls!'

Here he was, leaping from the back of a tram, just when they despaired of him. At the same moment the cousins had to look to their skirts as a water cart swished past spraying the cobbles to keep down dust.

Edy, made cross by wet feet, remarked irritably, 'I can't understand why we should be made to wait for you in the street, rather than at Roberts!'

'That's the thing,' replied Patrick, acknowledging Rose with a smile. 'Rather than going straight to the restaurant I thought you lasses could show me a bit of the local colour.'

'Darling, there is no colour in Sheffield, apart from the rosy glow of the steel mills,' answered Edy.

Patrick laughed and Rose, who struggled to find something, anything, to contribute, said pluckily, 'I should love to explore.' She'd not make the same mistake twice.

Edy shot a look at her. 'Must you side with him?'

Though she wished that he had made a distinction, Patrick took the arm of each, smiled equally on each, and said, 'Come on then, let's walk up an appetite. Now, how did that song from the Japanese scene at the bazaar in *The Shop Girl* go?'

As they marched resolutely west down Union Street and away from the more familiar and salubrious part of town, he belted out, 'Tokyo, Tokyo, stoneyo brokeo . . .' drowning out Edy's complaint that they went too fast for her little legs.

At the end of the last verse, when a silence overtook them, Rose wished that it could be her who filled it with something clever or at least amusingly rude. How she regretted her lack of ready repartee which served her cousin so well in place of conversation. She seemed only able to comment upon what she saw and state the obvious. Looking around herself for a subject, Rose realised they'd arrived at a quarter where cheap boot shops, cash tailors, and corner brewers predominated and that they were increasingly at the mercy of the black-faced girls who shouldered past in their heavy work clothes and the glancing men who turned to stare at them. 'We've come miles from the theatre. Shouldn't we turn back?' she inquired nervously.

Idiot, she'd done it again! Instead of following boldly she was girlishly shying away.

Patrick obediently pulled up short to wheel them about, but Rose, impulsively, desperately, struck off down South Street, saying, 'I'm sure we've still plenty of time and, anyway, we can always catch a tram. Let's try down here, it looks exciting.' Edy groaned, however she and Patrick followed behind as Rose recklessly led them past the tripe and butcher's shops, shabby penny bazaars and economy hatters, deeper and deeper into the unknown. At last they came to Brunswick Chapel, all rather giddy from that mad dash. Now was Patrick's turn to dare them.

'This is rather grand. What lies behind it?' he asked.

Gingerly they made their way past the elegant building to discover in the untidy muddle of alleys, entries and jennels that lay behind it the ugly, hidden face of their city's pride and prosperity. Here dwelt and worked her smiths, hammermen, grinders and metal workers and from among these squalid workshops and forges and grinding hulls that coughed black plumes of smoke from their forest of chimneys, the name of Sheffield was sent out into the world. Rose gripped Patrick's arm. She knew that it was not right for them to be here but she was determined not to be the one to say so. She would hold on tight to her masculine protector and do her best to enjoy the risky ride, for he surely wouldn't let her come to harm.

'Do you notice how many of the little tykes wear eyepatches?' observed Patrick. He sounded as detached as an anthropologist.

'Grit, I suppose – flying off the grinding wheels and likewise,' replied Edy, consciously impassive.

'Poor little children, most of them don't wear clogs, let alone boots,' Rose whispered back.

Though she was shocked by this unexpected blast of raw poverty, Rose's sympathy wilted under the jeers and taunts of the barefoot boys. Patrick and Edy, too, hesitated. How Rose wished they were quietly at Roberts enjoying their pre-theatre dinner. But fired still by bravado, the tourists pressed on until they came into a primitive court of back-to-back cottages where washing was strung across from house to house and waste water drained into shallow gutters let through the paving flags. Mercifully, now that it was summer, these were not overflowing, but still the stench of humans and their animals, as well as the din and scorching smell of small-scale home manufacturing, affronted their ears and noses.

Rose saw that almost every window glass was broken, the only attempt at repair being to stuff them up with rags and paper, making even closer and blacker the kennels in which the capital of cutlery's workers fitted penknife blades or put incomparably fine edges on razor blades and surgical instruments. She watched, fascinated, as one shadowy craftsman, in his flat cap and apron, sat hunched over his wheel, incessantly grinding scissor blades in the gloom. Then, with a prick of fear, she suddenly felt trapped in this fetid cul-de-sac where they were at the mercy of its natives: the hard-faced women in their tribal red headscarves and heavy aprons and surly, loafing men. One of these, who wore a topcoat that, incomprehensibly, had the sleeves cut off, like the cannibal chief parading the missionary's mutilated jacket, made to approach them. Perhaps he meant to welcome them to this hostile shore, perhaps to warn them off it. With an involuntary squeak of panic, Rose ran for it. When she looked back to check that Edy and Patrick followed, she met the man's sly grin.

When, panting, they regained the safety of South Street, Edy (perhaps made sharper by their near escape) demanded of Patrick, 'There you are – Sheffield. And I hope you found it inspiring!'

He did not reply at once, then, sounding ill-at-ease, said, 'No. Nothing that is that meaningless inspires.'

'I never knew that common people must live and work in such misery,' Rose said simply. 'It's shaming.' And, now that they were safely delivered, she meant it.

'Contemptible! Incomprehensible!' dismissed Edy, who could not be doing with any more artistic angst or sentiment.

Patrick, however, no longer in the mood for teasing, replied bleakly, 'Not incomprehensible, Edy. I understand it well enough to know that I hate it. But it's the future, isn't it? Unthinking brutes chained to machines, working at the pace of those machines, to convert the world's bounty into valueless things all the other unthinking brutes have been taught to covet.'

Edy huffed. 'However, my dears, life is too short to weep over the exploitation and ugliness there is behind every horn-handled carving knife, isn't it?'

'It's what convinces me I must go a different way myself.' Patrick concluded.

He looked so discouraged that Rose worried that this outing would end as disastrously as had their country walk.

She linked her arm through his and said as cheerfully as she could, 'Hurry up! We don't want to miss the show – all those new songs to learn!'

Evening was coming on. Lanterns flared beneath the canopies of the rabbit-meat and pottery costers' stalls and shop boys were putting up shutters as the three hastened back towards Charles Street and that complacent zone of shiny plate-glass arcades and street lamps and dashing cabs. Too late now for a pre-show supper, for already theatre-goers trooped into the splendid new Empire Palace Theatre of Varieties, past the posters advertising Miss Tilley, 'the greatest favourite now before the public appearing here, previous to her third triumphant tour of the USA'. Presumably Miss Tilley thought this provincial engagement worth the candle now that the Queen had opened Sheffield up to civilisation.

Patrick, still rather quiet and preoccupied, sat himself in the stalls between Rose and Edy, to await the entrance of the music hall favourite. Rose was very conscious of his leg next to her own as the lights went down. He turned to her and said, over the opening bars of the overture, 'Rose darling, you mustn't mind me. Time to time a black crow sits on my shoulder.' He reached for her hand in the dark and held it, stroking the palm. 'But I know that you're the one, my beautiful little Rose, shall put it to flight.'

The curtains opened and, though the blaze of light that came from the stage illuminated the audience, he did not let go of her hand but retained it casually in his, as though it belonged to him. Rose could hardly breathe.

The marvellous manifestation of an afternoonified man about town, complete with cane, top hat and gloves, was an illusion of masculine dandyism somewhat marred by the unexpected soprano voice in which Miss Tilley sang. However, the frisson of having the London idol here, before their very eyes, resulted in a stamping, shouting ovation that surprised even that old trooper. Contortionist Ena Bertoldi, the anatomical wonder from the London Alhambra, earned the audience's restrained appreciation for the ease and graceful freedom of her movements. However, they were ready to roar again at the antics of Oscar Hampson, the negro comedian, black as any miner. And through it all, while Rose laughed and gasped and wondered in unison with the crowd, her whole attention was fixed upon her hand held loosely in his.

At the end of the riotous evening, Patrick whispered to her, 'I feel it still, perched upon my shoulder. I'm sorry.' And when the girls returned from the cloakroom, they could not find him. Patrick, it seemed, had disappeared into the night. Trying to keep the panic down, Rose said, 'I haven't any money. Have you, Edy?'

Must romance always vacillate exhaustingly between these sharpening sensations of unease and bliss, engagement and neglect? She felt her heart to be a fish, reeled in tight and close, only to be let run on a slackened line, until the whole, teasing process of being played began again.

'Where *is* the man, drat him? But look over there, isn't that your friend, what's his name, brother to the lassitudinarian?'

'You mean Marion Webb's brother, Harold?' Rose was obscurely unsettled that Harold Webb should find her at a disadvantage.

'It is! It's Mr Webb. Hi, Mr Webb,' Edy called, flapping her handkerchief.

Harold diffidently approached the two girls and, tipping his hat to both, inquired, 'Miss Seaton, and . . . Miss Seaton. May I be of assistance?'

'Oh wonderful Mr Webb, how clever of you to be here just when we need you.'

Harold looked taken aback and replied, 'I came for the concert at the City Hall.'

Ignoring this, Edy said, 'We are in need of rescue,' batting her sparse eyelashes at him. 'We've been deserted and abandoned by a scoundrel and seek salvation. D'you think you can help?'

'Really, Edy,' Rose rebuked. 'Patrick would never just abandon us!' Then, to Harold Webb, 'We have somehow become separated from our escort. If you would be so kind as to find us a cab and stand the fare, my father will be pleased to send over the money tomorrow.'

Despite her managing tone, Rose was close to tears, perplexed at having failed, again, to keep up with Patrick.

'I think it will be difficult to find a cab with all these people about, but if you ladies would care to wait inside the foyer I'll try my best to hail one,' he replied.

After a few minutes a hansom was hailed and Rose and Edy were handed in, so ending their little adventure. Once safely installed, Edy turned to her cousin and, clasping her hands to her breast, said, 'Our hero!'

Jogging home to face the music, Rose considered, crestfallen, that she obviously hadn't put Patrick's crow to flight after all. Heartsick, she put it down to her inability, having attracted a man, to keep him interested. She obviously lacked the art of fascination.

# Chapter 7

Having arrived back at home disastrously late and in a public conveyance, Rose saw nothing for it but to make a clean breast and ask for three further crimes to be taken into consideration: the musical entertainment substitution, the escort switch and the shameless importuning of an inferior young man. Exposure and swift punishment must be the only outcome. However, Robert Seaton's impulse to imprison his daughter in her room, on bread and water, was snagged by the necessity of her courteously repaying Harold Webb. He might be a farmer's son but he was worthy of respect. The lad had worked in the accounting department of Seaton and Gast for seven years, since leaving school, continuing his education in commercial law and book-keeping at night school. Robert had great hopes of young Webb running rings around those clever legal dogs who worried him at present. For if rats made ratters inevitable, wasn't it better to have your own, home-bred ratter on the end of a chain?

Instead a drive with the groom over to the Webb Farm, to settle her debt that very afternoon, when Harold would be home from his Saturday morning's work in person, was imposed. Rose marvelled how, once again, she'd done wrong and got away with it – though perhaps not scot-free. She could not relish the prospect of abasing herself before Harold Webb in his benevolence.

She went the long way round to the farmhouse. And, having jumped down from her carriage, dawdled with the little Webbs, Rosalind and Florence, whom she found standing in the orchard, calling, 'Com 'ere, Duster, com 'ere, Emerald and Camomile, right this minute!'

Rose went to the fence and leaned over to inquire about these absconding duchesses.

'Eh, they're our chickens, miss,' said the elder, curtseying and picking up her pet hen to show.

Rose stroked their chickens' warm puffy back feathers and half wished she could have stayed to climb apple trees and play at taws.

Let in by the house servant, Rose thought how comfortable and homely was the wide hall with its faded runner that lifted with the draught from the door over stone flags. A vase of garden roses slipped their petals onto the polished oak chest, like pale lilies mirrored in a black lake. She glanced into the kitchen, which opened off the hall, and saw that this must be a baking day as Mrs Webb was rolling out on the kitchen table.

'Good afternoon, Miss Seaton. Please excuse my brat,' said she, flustered, wiping her hands on her apron to shake hands with the visitor. 'You mustn't mind us, just tek us as you find us.'

'Excuse me, Mrs Webb.'

'You'll be wanting the young people, no doubt,' she continued, changing her mind about shaking hands as she saw her own would not be free of flour and butter without a thorough washing, and her guest wore kid gloves. 'You'll find 'em both in the parlour, my dear. You know the way, I suppose.' She smiled at the elegant lady visitor, who used to ramble through her husband's fields and follow behind her helping to feed the bantams she kept for egg money.

Outside the parlour door, Rose was surprised to hear, from

within, the sound of a pleasant baritone voice, accompanied by the piano, singing, 'I dreamt I dwelt in marble halls.'

She knocked and entered the light-filled room, where she expected to find Marion and her brother Harold at the piano. But both were seated on the sofa, though the song continued.

'Oh, I thought I had disturbed you singing,' she said stupidly.

'Rose!' Marion greeted her with surprised pleasure, raising her hand while Harold leapt to his feet to salute her and halt the voice in its pleading refrain, 'that you love me still the same . . .'

Sounding discomforted, he said, 'I'm afraid that my voice is not worth the listening to, so I hired a gramophone to stop my sister pestering me to sing for her.'

What an unaccountably surly man he was!

Marion patted the place next to her. 'Please, come and sit by me. Harry was just this minute telling me that you met in the city last evening.'

Rose noticed that he blushed, as did she, to remember why she had been sent here, but sensitive Marion, having looked from one to the other and seen that this was not a topic for airing, quickly changed tack.

'How rude of me, running on and I haven't even offered you tea!'

Harold took this opportunity to exit to the kitchen for an extra cup.

'If he can't sing, surely he can draw,' Marion said to Rose. 'He won't like me showing them, but only look at these,' and she handed over the drawings that she'd been in the process of mounting at the little work table set by her elbow. Rose gratefully received them, happy to be distracted from the shortcomings of the previous night. She sat in silent contemplation of the many delicate sketches of a single, perfect, pheasant's tail feather until, on hearing her brother come back into the room, Marion remarked, evidently for his benefit, 'I don't know why Harold doesn't put all his energies and passion into his painting and drawing, instead of columns of numbers and law books. He has such a talent.'

'I find equal beauty in numbers, Marion. Besides, I lack the means to indulge my creativity, quite apart from coming from the wrong stock. Common folk, such as we, make artisans not artists.'

His disobliging words made Rose suspect he bullied his poor gentle sister into flattery.

'My brother is proud to number himself among the workers,' commented Marion, not noticeably crushed.

'I *am* a working man, Marion.'

He still sounded cross but, Rose was pleased to see, Marion stood up to his temper.

'Fiddle-de-de!' she teased. 'Harry, you know you're no'but a mardy lad, one of 'em surface folk who know nothing of wining coal.'

But he was having none of it. 'The stark fact that I must work to earn my living makes me one whether or not I use my muscles in the process,' he replied, still on his dignity, still a little over-emphatic.

'There now, I've gone and offended thee,' Marion soothed, 'and I didn't mean to, Harry dear. Let's not fratch.' And Rose saw how, by recalling him to his childhood self, Marion had done the trick of disarming him. She followed up, now a little exasperated with the big silly, 'And yet, Harry, you make these delicate, beautiful drawings and you appreciate classical music and,' she turned to Rose, 'the books!'

'Just as you say, Marion – lily white and soft handed,' Harold acknowledged, softened to grudging humour. 'A pipsqueak as wouldn't last a day doing a proper man's toil.' He came over to her and put his hand on her shoulder and rubbed her back.

Marion sighed and relaxed, saying, 'And what sympathetic magic is it that you use to know just when I need my back rubbing?'

It was apparent that it was not antipathy but springs of understanding and love that ran deep between brother and sister.

She was proud of him, even a little protective. Though it seemed to Rose perverse that Marion chose to draw attention to her brother's refinements in taste, and his accomplishments, when Harold's redeeming quality was this loving care for his invalid sister.

Got off the hook of his pride, Harold went on, in a more playful tone, 'But then, Marion, isn't my proper calling to labour upon the land rather than beneath it?'

'Harry, you know that our William is better suited to taking over from my father. He hasn't your brain.'

'Or my wheezing chest.'

'He is a big boy for his age, isn't he?' put in Rose. 'I met him taking his beast for a walk the other day when I called upon Marion, and I shouldn't have recognised him, he's grown that much.'

'Harry and I got the artistic leanings and the delicate health and William all the brawn,' commented Marion cheerfully.

'Yes, William will make a fine figure of a man,' said Harold, returning to his own unfittedness. Strange, for Rose perceived he was quite as well made and possibly a head taller than his brother – though half as sunny-natured.

'Wasn't that the day you came to call with Mr and Miss Seaton from Fell Top?' asked Marion, turning her smile on Rose.

'Yes, we'd gone for a walk with their house guest, Mr McKinley, to show him Eckersby . . . Though he did not come on here.' She was flustered by even this casual mention of Patrick.

'The chap in the red shirt, I presume,' remarked Harold, sour again.

Momentarily Rose could not think what he meant, for hadn't Patrick been dressed all in green when they'd walked through the woods to Eckersby? Then she remembered.

'Yes, of course, you saw each other at the Whit Walks.'

Harold acknowledged this with a curt nod and then said, almost nastily, 'Was the elusive Mr McKinley ever sighted again after he became separated from his party at the theatre?'

Rose looked at her hands. He'd seemed so much friendlier when they'd talked that day on the common. She answered him, a little on her dignity herself now. 'You've reminded me what it was that brought me here to see you. I came to return the cab fare you were so kind to lend me.' She tried to put the coins into his palm but he would have none of it.

'Don't think of it, any gentleman's duty,' he said, affecting an affront she found most unattractive. 'Who could be blackguard enough to desert a damsel in need?'

'Well, I can't go home with it. You must put it towards another phonogram cylinder.' And Rose stood to take her leave, placing the coins on the table at Marion's side.

As she walked away from the farmhouse to the waiting dog cart, Rose heard again the gramophone's plaintive refrain, 'I dreamt I dwelt in marble halls', yearning from the half-opened window. 'I had riches too great to count, could boast of a high ancestral name . . .' And thought, what a sad song to play over and over on such a sunny afternoon, almost as though poor Marion was unhappy in love with someone beyond her reach. Recalling a vivid image of Patrick bright in sunlight, Rose felt some sympathy for her friend.

# Chapter 8

Now the mid-point of summer was nearly over-stepped, the violet yielded to the sweetpea and it seemed to Rose that she tasted the fruits of a dejection that sunshine and birdsong make exquisitely poignant. At seventeen she and the summer alike squandered their fresh charms on the endless round of empty days. How *was* she to get through the remainder of her disappointed life?

Then a card was delivered from cousins Guy and Edy by that second footman whom, she noted, improved the inconvenience of his every hike across country between the two houses by making up to her maid Joan. He brought an invitation to an 'at home', which had the exciting addition of 'dancing' in the bottom corner. Once more, summer held the promise of youth and life before the drab diminution of inevitable autumn, ageing and death that, only yesterday, had lain ahead. So this was to be her first ball. At last her proper coming out, her flowering, for surely *he* must be there. No occasion for stupid aesthetic disputes, and no Harold Webb to get in the way. For hadn't Patrick held her hand in the dark and as good as said that she was the one for him?

The entertainment was to be *un ballo in masquera*. From Edy she discovered that Patrick would indeed be there, returned to good humour by the promise of this party, of which he would be the chief architect. Having learned that they were to dress as characters from *commedia dell'arte*, Rose bagged Columbine for herself.

But first she must persuade Papus that she should be allowed to go since it would only be a very little, family party, attended by local people (she took care not to mention Patrick's presence) and with no dancing to speak of. Then only a couple of days to arrange for a costume fit to be seen at the event of the season, the county, her whole life!

When she tentatively presented herself to Papus for his judgement, accoutred like a ballet dancer in a short, white silk dress, which showed her lower legs somewhat, complete with tambourine and black half-mask, her father grunted, 'What is it you're going dressed up as, the spirit of pneumonia?' But, perhaps because his cousin Albert, and not he himself, would be put to the expense of this ball, he could not find it in his heart to object. So he concluded with, 'Very pretty, pet,' and gave her a nostalgic look. Rose, relieved, gushed, 'Really, Papus, it's only a lingerie dress adapted a bit.'

Thus she'd contrived it, contrived her launch upon the season of love and romance!

On the evening of the ball, Guy drove over to collect her in his automotor, got up as Pagliaccio, the clown, in baggy white tunic and trousers, with a sad, powdered face. She was waiting, wrapped in her mother's white fur.

'What a stunner!'

'Oh, Guy, don't.'

They drove off, across country for a little while, speeding past a group of miners who walked homewards from the pit through fields, troglodyte beasts they moved stiffly in their thick, grimed pit clothes, white eyelids flashing in black faces, incongruous amid the lavish green of mid-summer. Guy didn't say much, only looked over at her and whistled through his teeth. They turned off at the Seatons' gatehouse where Mrs Breedy was waiting to open the gates for them. Guy pulled a handful of change from his pocket to throw to her children. They drew to a stop at the top of the drive, letting the motor stand and pant like a blown horse.

'I'll take the Audibert and Lavirotte round to the stables. I expect you know the way to the front door?' said he and she jumped out to let him drive off.

It was still early and the façade of Fell Top House was closed up and blank-looking, giving Rose the unpleasant sensation that she was not expected, or wanted. She was, timidly, approaching the front door to knock (an enterprise she could not remember ever before having to perform for herself), when Edy appeared from round the side of the house, in a pompadour and a foul mood.

'Hullo, Columbine.'

'Edy! You look splendid, what a fizzing gown! Or should I say Lady Inamorata? Your servant, ma'am,' said Rose, bowing to her mistress. Edy's bad moods must be humoured.

'Pretty dull, ain't it – landed with a part that has no character to speak of but being in love. Since you nabbed Columbine, my only other choice was that ugly old gossip La Ruffiana, which suits even worse!'

Rose chose not to comment. Instead she said, 'Well, you look darling.' Then, trying to appear unconcerned, asked, 'Will your *inamorato* be Mr McKinley?'

Just then Patrick, who had somehow crept behind and up onto the wide, stone balustrade that swept to the front door, surprised them by leaping down. He was dressed in a close-fitting tunic, laced at the front, and tights in variegated red, green and blue diamonds. His small, black felt skull cap and a half-mask of a cat-like mien gave him the look of a satiric sensualist. Sure as a cat he landed, feet in fourth attitude, knees slightly bent. Rose caught her breath; she'd never before appreciated that a man might be beautiful.

'Who's this, Edy?' he asked mischievously, pointing with the little wooden sword he carried. 'I'm certain it was a dove I sent for, not this small, toddling polar bear with a pretty face.'

'Good evening, Mr McKinley.' She looked away from him in confusion. 'It's me.'

He took her hand to kiss it and looked intently into her face. 'Ah, now I see, for underneath the fur is Columbine and underneath Columbine is darling Rose.'

He did make her blush.

'I'll take it off as soon as we go inside. My father wouldn't let me come unless I wore it for the motor car.'

'Then I'm afraid you'll have to stay as a bear, we shan't be removing inside. The party's to be in the garden, dancing on the terrace and drinkables and eatables in the conservatory,' said Pagliaccio who had appeared from the back of the house, hands in pockets, smoking a cigarette. 'Give it over, ducky, and I'll get a maid to carry it indoors.'

Rose surrendered her mother's fur to Patrick, and exposed her bare arms and ankles to him and to the midsummer night air.

'Now then,' said he appreciatively. 'That's how we like it – live and natural!'

'You sound like a turn at the pantomime,' remarked Edy, huffily.

'What is life but a pantomime, dear Edy?'

'Cut it, you two,' from Guy, good-naturedly, as he offered Rose his arm to escort her. She noticed that Patrick abandoned her mother's ermine to the balustrade where it lay forlornly limp.

They turned the corner of the house to discover the scene being set for the most glamorous, the most unconventional, most magical ball ever to be held. The terrace, which ran the whole length of the house, was designated the dance floor. It had been covered with boards, over which thick canvas was still being stretched and tacked in place by a couple of workmen on their knees. Other muscular young men were in the process of wrestling the grand piano into position near the small orchestra of German musicians seated on gilt chairs under a magnolia tree, who tuned their instruments in anticipation of its arrival, and Fell Top's tallest footman (she recognised him as Joan's swain) was hanging out oriental paper lanterns on strings stretched overhead. Patrick danced away to a huge canvas that curtained the conservatory windows. Like a theatrical backcloth it was painted in bold, impressionistic strokes to resemble an antique Italian square, with rustic well and tavern.

'He painted it, that's why he's so interested in making sure it hangs true,' said Edy, walking Rose over to have a closer look. 'He *is* a genius, you know,' she whispered out of the corner of her mouth.

The heavy canvas was tugged into hanging straight and it became apparent that a door-sized oblong had been cut away within the frame of the tavern door. Rose saw that it matched exactly one of the conservatory's own doors and the two stepped through from the busy terrace into hot shadows and the looming presence of giant palms. Backlit, the canvas now showed the Italian square in reverse, somehow lopsided and rather sinister. Guy stuck his head through the opening into the interior, inverse world. 'You can't lurk in here, girls. It'll be ages yet. What say you we lessen the tedium of anticipation with some champagne cup and a stroll?'

The four wandered away from the terrace and down lawns that sloped to the lake. This was the long evening of the spring equinox, when dusk surrenders to night reluctantly, to rise again as dawn after only a very little dip into absolute black. Rose, glass in hand, conscious of her flimsy, pretty dress, felt that she too stood at a magic switching point. Purple loosestrife and yellow irises stood, half drowned, at the lake's margins, and the gnats hung, bright motes, in the light let through willow leaves. They walked out along the boathouse deck and the pondy smell breathed out by shallow water mingled with the spice of sun-baked wooden boards. As they sipped their champagne, house martins skimmed the warm air rising and the blunt brown shapes of fish hung in the cool shadows beneath their feet.

'I can hardly breathe, it's so close,' said Edy, putting her hand to her chest.

'Shouldn't wear your corsets so tight,' commented Patrick flippantly.

'Old man, I warn you: mention my sister's underpinnings again and I'll have to land you one,' drawled Guy, flicking his cigarette end into the water.

'Well, I'm sure I didn't choose to adopt this ridiculous, dressing-up-box rig!' she palpitated angrily within her constraints.

'Your wasp waist is making you waspish, Edy,' Patrick observed.

She snapped back, 'Waspish! I'm a paragon of forbearance. Anyway, it's you men who demand irrational figures. You can hardly keep your eyes off Rose's trim waist!'

'Not I. I consider an hourglass figure unnatural and if not natural then not beautiful. It makes a young lady look as though she will snap in half at the middle.'

Edy puffed.

'The fashion-plate ideal,' Patrick continued laconically. 'Thrust out before so that she appears to be leaning forward to gaze over a generous balcony while behind presenting a shelf upon which one might display a row of silver photo frames. Indecent really.'

'Hypocrite! I seem to remember your spontaneous epithet was live and *natural*,' said Guy, protective of his discomposed cousin.

'Quite right, Pagliaccio. Fashion may be an affront to nature, but Rose's beauty is eternal: she's as beautiful as sweet, as young as beautiful, soft as young, gay as soft and innocent as gay as someone said first, it's just the tricking out I object to.'

Though he smiled at her, the ingénue had another reason to regret the agony attendant upon achieving that perfect fifteen-inch circumference. She'd felt so beautiful, so sophisticated, and now she saw that she was still only a very young girl with muddied feet, wearing a silly costume, over a too-tight corset and her hair coming down.

'You're too intense for your own good,' Guy said easily. 'If you want to flatter a lady I've found it more effective to find her perfect, not just good in parts. Come to me, Rose. Cousin Guy knows how to pitch the woo. Anyway, isn't it time we lay in wait for our guests, Pat? You're the stage manager.'

Patrick led them back to the terrace and through the opening in the stage cloth into the close, dim conservatory. Now giggly with anticipation, they looked out onto the prepared terrace. Peasant girls arrived first, from those countries where the poor employ silk and satin to achieve just the right effect of simplicity. These were joined by a gaggle straight from the court of the sixteenth Louis. Then some little Japanese girls hobbled on, followed by a pair of disconsolate goddesses and a pasteboard Queen of Hearts (who was to discover before the night was done that she could not sit). Like Noah's animals they made their entrances mostly in pairs, so that gallants in bandoliers, peg trousers and wide sash belts partnered the peasants, and powdered wigs squired the ladies from the French court. However, not a few of the young men (as is their way) had made no more effort with their toggery than the wearing of a flamboyant buttonhole or an opera cloak over conventional evening dress.

After the guests had made their own introductions – they had known each other since infancy – Patrick gave Rose's elbow a squeeze and said, 'Come on, enough spying, time to make our entrance.'

They stepped through the doorway into the village square set and everyone applauded.

Clearing his throat for attention and gesturing theatrically, Guy proclaimed, 'Lovers stand forth, with you we will begin.' He turned to Rose and then Patrick, and taking her by the hand brought her forward. 'You will be fair Columbine—'

'And I, your Harlequin,' interjected Patrick, claiming Rose's free hand.

Guy continued, now presenting his cross sister. 'Here is our

Inamorata. We'll call her Isabella. Let her evening's mission be to find her fortunate fellah . . .'

'Shut up, Guy,' said Edy, whacking him with her fan, to the amusement of the assemblage.

'Quite right, your ladyship,' Patrick intervened. 'Now, you there, you've always been a *Guy*, so play the clown,' he improvised, provoking more laughs. 'And Pagliaccio, no stabbing me and Columbine before the curtain's down.'

'Oh, jolly good,' said Guy flatly. 'Enough of our preamble.'

At a sign from him, two footmen pulled on ropes which sent the painted canvas rolling upwards like a shop blind to reveal the magical conservatory, now full of light and informal groupings of chairs and small bamboo tables, and banked about by hothouse flowers.

'Welcome, all. Now on with the music, and on with the ball!'

The brilliant young people stepped onto the terrace as the little orchestra of four struck up with the first quadrille. Harlequin took his Columbine, just as Nanki-Poo claimed his Yum Yum and every courtier his lady-in-waiting, as well as some other, less felicitous pairings. These multiplied as the evening progressed, for every young man was aware of his duty by every young lady, whether well matched to his attire or not.

After supper the dancing recommenced, young people being unconcerned that middle-aged German musicians might experience fatigue while they are still mad to exert themselves. By three the next morning the ball could be fairly judged a thumping success and it was left to the hardiest among them, fortified with hot coffee and bullion, to prove that seven hours of pleasure never killed anyone – although the slaves to music might have been observed to grow paler under the strain.

How splendid, how fine, Rose felt, singled out by Patrick for more dances than was polite, and at the midnight supper table loaded with the evening's refreshments, he had made her take her first raw oysters, slipping them off the shell and into her mouth so that they slid down her half unwilling throat. He'd poured her too many glasses of champagne and whispered arch, outrageous things into her hot ear. And Rose yielded to him, thrilled that at last she was initiated into the dangerous glamour of the grown-ups' world.

After the last dance the two clever lovers slipped away, alone, to the lake. They stood where they had stood before, in that same half-light. But now all was changed. He held her hand and solemnly intoned, ''Tis almost morning,' as though he put it in quotation marks.

And Rose suddenly appreciated that the birds' urgent chorus told that this was dawn, not dusk. Unnoticed by her, the year had slipped past its solstice, and this new morning marked the midsummer after which each succeeding day would grow a little shorter than the last.

Seeming to pick up on her reverie, he said, 'It feels like the end of an era, doesn't it? Our over-ripe civilisation on the turn.'

They looked back towards the wreckage of the terrace where only those few remained that could not bear to let the fun stop. Ruination had followed that decadent excess, beautiful food all gobbled up, flowers crushed underfoot, musicians silenced, and John, the footman, slowly extinguishing the paper lanterns one by one.

'Only imagine, later on this very day, somewhere in London, our most noble Queen Empress will be watching her jubilee fireworks with a crowd of courtiers and nobs and Indian princes and African chieftains – all rigged up for their own fancy dress ball. And there she will be, in the middle of all that pomp and panoply, the Widow of Windsor!'

She laughed, remembering the mole in her carriage, and he moved closer.

'And won't all of us take a complacent look back over our shoulders at those sixty years and give a huge communal sigh,' he sighed, and she felt his hot breath on her cheek, 'so very satisfied with the long road we have travelled down together . . .'

Rose surrendered to the delicious melancholy of his words

and leaned into his chest. Aware of the nearness of his body beneath his too thin clothes, she shivered. As though to warm her, he ran his hands lightly up and down her sides, hardly touching, but so close that he excited the fine hairs on her arms. The sense of her own powerful desirability made her vulnerable. Like a flower unfolded in the secret night, she stood full blown, and voluptuously yielding. There would be no going back.

He breathed again, long and slow, then tilted her face to his, and whispered, 'Here are we, suspended between past and future.'

'At the turning point,' she responded.

'But every end holds the promise of a new beginning,' Patrick murmured, very close, 'and I'm all for new beginnings.' He moved nearer to kiss.

'Hulloo, you there!' Edy called out as she stamped along the deck to them. 'Such fun, Belmont's cigar has caught on fire his cotton-wool moustache!'

They pulled apart before their lips could meet, and sharp Edy saw that disengagement.

'I do believe our Pat *does* have a rave on little Cousin Rose!'

Edy's grating voice returned Rose to herself, awakened from seduction's lullaby.

'Enough flirtatious colloquials, my lad,' Edy ordered. 'Reggie's gone to get his banjo and we're all going to have a jolly sing.'

Marching off ahead of them, towards the remains of the ball, she did not overhear Patrick's surreptitious whisper, 'This bud of love, by summer's ripening breath, may prove a beauteous flower when next we meet.'

# Chapter 9

The next day Rose slept until noon. When Joan was sent in, with tea and toast on a tray, she awoke to the knowledge that today her life stood on the very cusp of becoming marvellous.

Still in bed, she looked through her little library and tracked the 'bud of love' to Capulet's orchard, act two, where the lovers secretly met after a dance at dawn in an enchanted garden, reluctantly part in delicious anticipation of 'when next we meet'. She shouted urgently for Joan to help her dress. And quickly! Then she arranged herself by the window that overlooked the drive to the house, to be discovered looking prettily intellectual with a book. Engaged upon reading a single paragraph which was without sense and without end, Rose prepared to be caught unawares by the tall, brilliant caller.

No one called and nothing happened. Disappointed excitement only when a note was delivered from Fell Top by Joan's John – Guy sent his compliments and inquired whether she had enjoyed herself and wasn't too tired by her exertions of the previous night. Far from it, she thought crossly, she was awakened. Awakened to an awareness of new sensations that touched her with almost too fine a point. But life carried on, as ever, sleepy and dull. It seemed she was to be no Juliet.

A day passed and then another and still he kept her waiting, tantalised. Suspense was a female affliction familiar to Rose from her wide study of literary romance, as well as life. She'd learned from both that men had lives and women waited. So she kept her vigil. It was some comfort that, having followed numerous heroines through their page-turning tribulations, she also knew that as the pages turned, so love's glad denouement hurried ever closer. However, despite her plucky confidence that tears and patience must have their reward, it was an added snub to Rose that Joan and her tall John's courtship proceeded at a spanking pace. No exquisite dangling for Joan. Rose decided that, for her maid's sake, the thing must be got out in the open and thoroughly tested.

Narrowly observing Joan's face in the dressing-table mirror as she dressed her hair, Rose saw none of the signs of true love. Eyes bright, mouth firm around the hairpins, Joan went about her business without a single sigh.

'Has John called on you often since the midsummer ball?'

Joan, startled that she should be cross-examined, and so early in the day, replied defensively, 'Eh? No, miss, for 'e cannot allus get away. 'E 'as 'is own duties to perform, tha knows.' Then she admitted (for it was only Miss being nosy), 'Mind, 'e invents all manner of excuses to slip over 'ere. Between ourselves, he can't stay away!'

Rose sniffed at that. Surely this indiscriminate visiting back and forth proved nothing.

'He certainly seems keen,' she grudged.

'Oh, 'e's keen, right enough,' agreed Joan, pleased with herself.

'Then we've to pray for more messages from Fell Top, have we?' she remarked pettishly.

'That we 'ave, miss. The more invites to balls an' teas an' tennis parties, the better.'

Rose looked sharply into the mirror to see if Joan cheeked her but the girl reflected there wore a soft, inward smile of satisfaction. It made Rose want to slap her.

'Well, I think you're very unwise to believe that just because a man calls a couple of times there's any future in it,' she said crossly.

'Oh, miss! I don't know 'ow you can say such a thing!' Joan, in a huff, put down the brush, leaving a long strand of sectioned hair to dangle ludicrously in front of Rose's nose.

Despite themselves, they both looked in the mirror and laughed at this vision.

'I'm sorry, Joan,' Rose said, blowing the lock clear. 'I don't know what's put me in this temper. It must be the heat. Now then, I'll try to be good if you'll tell me how you know John's love is true.'

And, since she couldn't resist a gossip, Joan forgave and pinned the fallen strand in place.

'As fer true love, miss, I couldn't yet rightly say if it were or if it weren't.' She was still a little on her dignity, but not for long. ''Owever, 'e did give me a little locket, belonged to 'is own dear mother. Said it were mine fer keeps, no returns.'

'And you accepted it?'

'Well, miss, it says in "Answers to Correspondence" in my *Girl's Own* that any love token given privately to an unengaged lady by a man should be politely returned. And any young man 'oo offers one betrays 'is low breedin' and dishonourable intentions.'

'Oh dear,' said Rose sympathetically, although she thought a locket a vulgar offering in comparison to Shakespeare at dawn.

'But I can't see as it does any 'arm, mesen,' said Joan, who was evidently immune to the sanctions of literature. She reached into her pocket and triumphantly brought out the trinket to show Rose.

'Well then, we must continue to pray for invitations from Fell Top.'

Time was all she needed. Indeed time was all she had, an infinity of it, while she waited for Patrick to sweep her off her feet.

'Will you look at this, Elizabeth-Jane,' remarked Robert Seaton, gesturing at the London Crime and Litigation column in his *Sheffield Weekly Independent*, then denying her the chance to do so, read out loud. 'A man chloroformed on a train and then robbed, and here – a stockbroker goes and shoots himself in another train, and look, a respectable woman jumps to her death off a balcony. There's no end to it and all typical of London. Bedlam let loose. Toffs and swells with no proper occupation and the ordinary folk rabble-rousing until all hours. Mark me, where there's wealth without occupation, there's vice and there's despair. And who pays for their fine mansions and their opera? Why, the honest manufacturing towns of the north. Who brews their beer for 'em, weaves their cloth, digs their coals and sharpens their knives for 'em? Why, the north again, the north. Even our slums beat London's for squalor!'

Elizabeth-Jane knew from experience that her husband's rants required little endorsement; indeed his opinions were so well worn she scarcely felt obliged to listen. What made her put down her sewing was a far graver matter than this confirmation of distant London's woes.

'Rose is in such a fit of the dumps. I don't know what to make of it.'

'Nothing wrong with the lass, she's blooming,' her husband replied shortly. But the pointed turning of his page did not put her off.

'Well, I don't know how you can say that, Robert. She's quite fallen off in flesh and has no colour to speak of.'

'Tek her to dentist.'

'I do believe it's her heart not her teeth that ails her.'

This made him look up from his paper, even though his eye was caught on an advertisement for an electric range, an abomination that would usually have caused eruptions.

'Has this summat to do wi' that theatrical young man – guest at my cousin's? What do they call him?'

'Mr McKinney, or McKinley, or some such. All I rightly know of him is he was invited for a Saturday to Monday by the young folk at Fell Top and has stopped on ever since,' she replied, tentatively airing her anxieties.

Again putting up his paper against her, Robert said dismissively, 'Lord knows, Albert's children cultivate every kind of scoundrel and southener.'

Elizabeth-Jane, for whom no shadow had hitherto darkened a long and harmless life, held her tongue. Married from the schoolroom (a fact in which she took pride), she'd ever since fulfilled the role of wife and mother without hitch, without equivocation. And, when the time had come for Rose to effect the nuptial transaction, she'd seized the reins and driven her off to market confident in a happy outcome. But it now appeared that she'd mistaken the way, gone too far, misread the directions. For the only domestic custom she'd attracted had been that time-wasting dud, Thomas Newton. Elizabeth-Jane had begun to harbour the prickly notion that perhaps Sheffield was indeed too limited a showplace for the proper display of her masterwork, her Rose. And, having dressed the window to attract gentlemen browsers, how in conscience could she dismiss Mr McKinley just because he was passing trade rather than by appointment? Especially since Rose seemed to have set her cap in that direction.

Out loud she ventured, perhaps as much for her own benefit as for her husband's, 'I believe that his people are very respectable.' Robert grunted at that. 'They hardly go up to London at all.'

Aroused by mention of the metropolis, Robert responded, 'London, you say?'

She dissembled. 'Oh, I hear they have only a *very* small house in Mayfair.'

'And do his people mek anything, are they in business?'

Now that she properly had his attention, she found she did not want it.

'Goodness, yes, I believe so,' she replied, evasive. Then, 'Robert . . .' He looked up at that; the use of proper names between them was usually kept for company or arguments. 'There's no harm in seeing the fellow.'

Then, knowing her husband as she did, Elizabeth Jane selected her exit line. 'I must see about luncheon, I haven't an idea in my head what to order,' and wisely left him to argue himself round to her point of view.

'All I say is, people should remember what it is that puts the food on their table!' he shouted after her. It was a refrain of his. He might have added, 'And what cooks the food.'

For Robert Seaton's main line was in the production of cast-iron stove grates. He might have preferred to style himself gentleman farmer but since he made his money as a manufacturer, even if only on a smallish scale, he would defend industry and, in particular, northern industrialists to the death. Privately he comforted himself that he had inherited his wealth and it was his own father who'd blackened his hands in the getting of it.

The fate of men such as his parent, a second son, might have been a commission in the army or a living in a parsonage, like all those generations of second sons before him. But William Seaton had found himself a business partner in Mr Walter Gast, an immigrant of German origin and possessed of the zeal to self-improvement that is the mainspring of the incomer. Mr Gast had grown a small independent foundry and cutlery merchant's business from his beginnings as a silver buffer. William, who had a house to mortgage and some land to sell, bought himself a partnership with the enterprising German and these two had gone into the business of supplying items of domestic cast ironwork at a time when the demand for cheap mass-produced appliances took off.

They'd started in a small way manufacturing rainwater guttering, drainpipes, gullies, gratings, shovels and spades, trowels and hinges. William, not being one to sit on his hands, had discreetly commissioned a geological survey of the Seaton ancestral lands at his own expense. With the knowledge that the scion of the Seatons squatted neglectfully upon mineral wealth, he'd approached his elder brother with the suggestion that, for a small percentage of profits, Henry should allow a part of his land to be mined for coal and iron ore. The deal was done, a new blast furnace built, and there followed a pleasing upturn in profits. Now Seaton and Gast did well enough: turning out bedsteads, kitchen boilers, chimneypieces, register fronts, foot-scrapers, garden rakes, sad irons, tailors' and hatters' irons, toy irons (at 2d each), clothes posts, railings, spittoons, clock and sash window weights, truck wheels and anvils. And the rapid expansion in the population combined with further industrial innovations gave them just the leg-up they needed to expand again. Here in the north, as well as nationally, the need was for manufactured goods, which Seaton and Gast were perfectly placed to supply. William, always with one ear cocked, heard that all those new industrial workers, crowded into their new towns, cried out for housing, and what did all those houses need, each and every one, but stove grates?

If these modest, mass-produced appliances provided their bread and butter, then the diversification into the huge engines destined for hotels and country houses heralded the banquet years for Seaton and Gast. The original of these mighty metal beasts was dubbed the Sheffield Hephaestus, and its boast was that it could 'roast, steam and bake for a family of five to fifty individuals and afford a constant supply of hot water'. It was represented at the Great Exhibition of 1851 and sold, appropriately, like hot cakes. In the following decades the sire gave rise to a dynasty of other famous ranges: Arges, Brontes and Steropes (Brightness, Thunder and Lightning – named for Hephaestus' three Cyclops workmen) all improved. The firm's lavishly illustrated catalogue was their breed book and they were even lent out, on licence, to other manufacturers rather as though on stud. Hand in hand with the spirit of the age, Seaton and Gast fed the industrial beast as it fed them, and they prospered.

Proud of their enterprise as they were, they were even prouder that their sons, Robert and the younger Walter, were freed from the necessity of vulgarising themselves with the hands-on business of getting brass. The two young men would turn up every day at the offices in Moorhead, where they'd flirt with the girls in the front office and go out to lunch.

So, on William's death, Robert found himself in part possession of a thundering great factory which privately he feared. After a year of miserably turning up to sharpen his pens, he'd at last contrived a way of putting his own stamp on the old firm. He sank all his creativity, and a deal of his share of the profits, into the building and furnishing of a fine new residence for himself, in which as many of the appurtenances as are usually contrived in cast iron, and some which even the most militant metallurgical brain might struggle to imagine, could be put to the test before being set before the buying public. Thus, Elizabeth-Jane's dressing table was weighed with a cast-iron perfume holder and brush set and her wrists with cast-iron bracelets. Young Rose slept in a cast-iron cot, rode on a rocking horse contrived from cast iron, and the footmen struggled with cast-iron louvred shutters on the ground floor windows and the maids with ornamental cast-iron teapots (a huge concession these, being of Japanese manufacture) in the parlour.

Altogether, Robert's gentlemanly seat was a splendid advertisement for that heavy, over-decorated, bombastic style of middle-period Victoriana. Robert looked about himself and was satisfied. However, if these novelty lines did well enough when they were novel, now that it was gone two decades since electric light had been introduced and the same since mild steel was made cheap and malleable by the Bessemer process, they no longer sold. For years his partner, Walter junior, had grumbled that they must modernise or go under, but Robert could not allow that he was in the wrong and had kept dogged faith with the old lines and the old patterns. And thus the proud firm of Seaton and Gast continued disastrously long in the single-minded manufacture of all that was unworkable, obsolete or simply old-fashioned.

It was only recently that Robert had clearly understood that the mechanism given over to him, tightly coiled and well greased, was nearly run down and realised he had not a notion how he might wind it up tight again. The son of the coming man grudgingly admitted to himself that nowadays he himself might best be described as passed-over and that what the old firm needed, urgently, was fresh blood. Latterly he'd decided that a likely chappie might be poached ideally from another manufacturing dynasty. Not any chappie, for he'd need a bit of vision as well as some of the old man's nous. In other words, Robert Seaton acknowledged that he was in need of a son-in-law. However, of the potential candidates, young Newton was evidently out of the running (he could not be sorry for that; the lad was a fool) and despite Elizabeth-Jane's credulity, this Mayfair McKinley could safely be discounted as a snob and a swell.

An uncomfortable bubble of bile rose in Robert's chest. He thumped himself there and thought sourly that, apart from giving him indigestion, this matchmaking palaver confirmed that his wife couldn't be trusted to make a proper a fist of it. He'd heard that the young man belonging to his friend Shaw, the owner of Pyracmon Mill, was home from the university and had been put to a spell of work in the office. Robert decided that Oxford might be excused if this lad, properly put through his paces, could prove his mettle as son-in-law material. Time had come to make shift and land the suitor himself.

Somewhat encouraged by this thought, Robert turned back to his paper and the consolation to be found in strangers' ruin and despair.

# *Chapter 10*

Joan dashed open the bedroom curtains to let the bolts of another blazing July morning slap on to Rose's pillow.

'I wish you wouldn't.'

'Miss Rose!' her maid reproved. 'I don't know as 'ow you can lay abed on such a fine morning.'

Rose pulled the bedclothes over her head to shut it out. What possible interest had she in mornings?

'Come on, miss, I've drawn your bath and laid out your costume and, look, there's your cup of tea gone cold as stone. Your father *'as* been carrying on . . .' She moved around the room tutting and humming beneath her breath as she set it to rights. Seeing that there was no rousing the lie-abed, Joan came and sat by her mistress and cajoled, 'Shall we 'ave some more of *Diana Tempest*, miss? I've turned down the page at chapter fourteen ready for you.' She shook the shape under the bedclothes and tried to reveal more of Rose than her topknot. At last she stuck in her head and whispered into the dark, hot space under the covers, 'Go on, tha knows tha wants to.'

Rose groaned, sat up and took the opened book into her hands while Joan made herself comfortable next to her, leaning back against the companion pillow.

'*It was the middle of July. The season had reached the climax which precedes a collapse. The heat was intense*,' Rose read, without expression. '*The pace had been too great to last. The rich sane were already on their way to Scotch moor or Norwegian river; the rich insane and the poor remained, and people with daughters – assiduously entertaining the dwindling numbers of the "uncertain, coy and hard-to-please jeunesse dorée of the present day". There were some great weddings fixed for the end of July, proving that marriage was not extinct – prospective weddings which, like iron rivets, held the crumbling fabric of the season together. "I wish I were married," said Di—*'

'Eh! I wish *I* were married,' sighed Joan.

Rose ignored her and read on. ' "*I wish I had a rich, kind husband. I would not mind if he parted his hair down the middle, or even if he came down to breakfast in slippers, if only he would give me everything I wanted.*" '

'Men can always be changed,' said Joan authoritatively. 'But you must tek care to marry 'em properly first, lest they tek fright and bolt.'

'I wish you'd stop interrupting. Anyway, wouldn't you be better off finding a husband you didn't have to modify as soon as you've led him from the altar?'

'Whatever give you that idea, miss? If a girl saves 'erself in expectation of a man who needs no work on 'im, likely she'll die an old maid. An' I allus vowed I must marry someone afore I turn a day over twenty-seven.'

'Why marry at all? You have a comfortable position here, haven't you, naughty Joan? Nothing to do all day but boss me and, you know, if you kept a husband he'd be twice as much trouble to you.'

Joan was scandalised. 'You expec' me to carry on workin' and slavin' 'ere till I'm all used up an' dried up, fit only fer workhouse?'

'Now, now, Joan. It shan't come to that. Anyway, you have a lovely tall beau to sweep you away from all this.' Rose settled more comfortably against her pillows. 'Now tell me what alterations John requires to turn him into a serviceable husband.'

'My John is as near perfect as makes no difference,' replied Joan snootily. 'Just a little bit of tinkering 'ere and there is all that's needed. Though I can see no prospect of me marrying 'im.'

'"One of the hard-to-please *jeunesse dorée* of the present day", are we, Joan?'

'I 'ave no notion of what that language might mean, as you well know, miss, and so I don't see why you bother to tease me wi' it.'

Joan looked so affronted that Rose put her arm round her shoulders and coaxed, 'Why can there be no prospect of marriage for you and John? You love him, he loves you. You are perfection in every degree and his faults are correctable.'

'Miss Rose, John's no'but second footman,' Joan said, as though this explained everything.

Rose snorted. 'His rank is not high enough?'

In an altered, serious voice, Joan explained, ''E cannot marry me, no more than I can marry 'im. 'E cannot support a wife, leave alone afford lodgings on his wage.'

'But Joan, there's surely the prospect of advancement?'

'If he were to climb all the way up the ladder to butler 'e'd likely never be in a position to marry.'

'Even then?'

'Who keeps a married butler, miss? No, the only chance for the two of us is to scrimp an' save an' wait till we are both grown old and past work an' then we may starve together.' Joan burst into tears. 'Servants cannot afford to marry servants, miss,' she sobbed. 'It cannot be worked.'

Rose closed the book, the better to comfort Joan. Enough of the contrived trials and tribulations in the lives of witty young ladies who always find themselves well and securely hitched by the last page.

★ ★ ★

Later that airless day Rose called upon Edy at Fell Top. She went with no particular perturbation because her cousin had invited her (by way of keen John) to keep her company while 'both the boys' were out of the way.

Perhaps because of the heat, Edy had chosen to wear another of her rational robes, this one in a faded antique terracotta, smocked and decorated with sage-green leaves and amber-gold daffodils. Never a beauty, she actually suited this soft, loose drapery better than the S bend of contemporary fashion, her lack of bust and buttocks rendering that padded matronly perfection unachievable. Edy had an undernourished child's narrow body and sinewy limbs though she, daughter of wealth, ate like a horse and had no daily occupation or exercise beyond what energies she squandered in teasing and gossip. Her hair, too, would not conform to the ideal bouffant, being rather pale and fluffy, like a chick's. It never seemed to grow beyond a couple of inches and, positioned in a shaft of full sun, filtered light like the aureole of a dandelion clock, giving her the guileless look of an infant.

'How *does* one survive this climate?'

Rose smiled and said, 'You could ask for the blinds to be lowered.'

'And sit about in the dark, darling one?'

'I read this morning that it's only the poor and the rich insane that stop at home in England in July,' Rose commented.

'Couldn't you just *yearn* for Switzerland, though?' asked Edy languidly. 'Think of it, to turn ice pilgrim, find a nice glacier upon which to recline, naked, and laugh at all the fat tourists with their alpenstocks and haversacks and their spiked shoes and capes and smoked-glass spectacles. Wouldn't that be a scream?' Edy gave a delicious shiver as though she felt the ice against her back.

Rose only replied, 'I'd rather stay here.'

Her cousin looked at her slyly. 'Ah, we both know it's not insanity keeps you and me from straying out of this dull corner of a duller county.' She dug Rose in the ribs. 'Don't look as though butter wouldn't, you cat. You know who I mean. And what is it, do you suppose, keeps *him* here when he itches to be off and started on his new, improved life?'

Rose couldn't stop herself. 'Really?' she asked. 'Does he really care for me?'

Her cousin gauged her out of the corner of her eye. 'Who else?'

'But didn't you tell me he only stopped on in Yorkshire because he wants to be reconciled with his father?'

'*Needs* to be reconciled, darling heart. Ideal lives come expensive nowadays. Our poor Pat has a thousand and one topping ideas for building his artistic Arcadia on England's green and pleasant, all he lacks is the funds to realise them, remember; "Tokio, Tokio, Stoneyo Brokeo"!'

'So it's not just me that keeps him here, is it?' Rose said, trying not to show her disappointment.

'Rosie, you goose. Can't you see that since he's been here he's felt an even greater need to stay put and win over Dad? Love is the spur!'

Rose said only, 'Oh, I see.' And swallowed the soft smile of pure joy she was wary of trusting to her cousin.

'He will be great, you know. It's just such a trial that money matters curb him at present. I only wish I could help him myself, but what little I have is all tied up in trusts and land and suchlike.'

'I'm sure he doesn't need a fortune on my account,' Rose responded, eager to embrace the happy prospect that Edith had dangled before her.

Edy took her hand and drew her close, the better to patronise. 'No, of course, ducky, for you shall have a handsome settlement from your own fond papa.' Then she dropped Rose's hand and chided, 'Only consider, darling. How can he, in all conscience, gather rosebuds when he has nothing to offer himself?'

The melting smile became a sharp obstacle that lodged in Rose's throat and brought tears pricking to her eyes.

'Yes, it all comes down to a matter of masculine pride,' went on Edy, matter-of-factly. 'Pride and economics.'

Was their only prospect of happiness to scrimp and save and starve together? To be a Joan and John?

'What are we to do then?' Rose asked, in a small, fretful voice.

Edith looked out of the window at the blazing day. 'What *are* we to do?' She paused as though mulling over the solution but only remarked in a flat voice, 'I suppose we must be reconciled to losing him.'

With horrible prescience, Rose demanded, 'Edy, do you know something?'

Her cousin looked away, as though unwilling to reply.

'He's planning to go right now, isn't he?'

'Off on the morrow.'

Rose's heart sprang in her chest and Edy, seeing that she'd had the desired effect, added, 'One last-ditch appeal to his old man.' Dramatising the scene to her own satisfaction, she took her cousin's hand once more in her own and clasped it to her chest in a pose that imitated extreme identification with her pain.

Rose wished that she'd been spared the insupportable weight of this foreknowledge.

That sultry afternoon Rose could not bear to remain at home. She needed diversion from the tormenting thought that her whole future might be decided by that impending interview with the merciless patriarch. Also she dreaded her own father's roar; these days he was in a permanent state of colic. So, despite the heat, she rode out with the groom and ended up, without intending to, at Webb's Farm.

Marion's shrouded, old-fashioned sitting room gave what coolness there was to be had on that blazing day and her gentle company offered relief from a mind stoked by care. The two girls were alone in the house. Mrs Webb was gone to town, the little sisters were paddling in the stream and William was off walking the fields with his father. But Marion mentioned none of these absences on receiving her hot and bothered caller.

'You've just missed my brother, Harold,' she exclaimed, as though this might have been the first thought on Rose's mind. 'Your paths might have crossed, for I believe he came back from his work early for an appointment with your father.'

'Have I?' said Rose, without interest. Seeing the discarded book at her friend's side, she asked, 'What is this you're reading, Marion?'

'Oh.' She laughed. 'Another of Harry's books. He's set me quite a curriculum in reading. This is his latest fad: H.G. Wells's *Time Machine*. Have you read it?'

'No. I'm afraid I've squandered half my morning on Miss Mary Cholmondeley.'

'You mean the dashing Diana,' said Marion, smiling. 'I wish I could be left to choose my own books, ones with no future shocks or self-improvement in them. Harry the pragmatist looks for the answer to everything in science and machines and self-disciplined study while I would much prefer to seek it in romances.'

Rose looked at her friend. *Was* there some romantic intrigue here?

Marion, having started upon the subject of Harold, was determined to persevere with it. 'I shouldn't complain about him. For Harold is a dear brother to me, though I confess it hurts me to see him tending to me, an 'elpless case when he has a bright future life of his own to live, did he but know it.'

Rose, who was more of a mind to examine the trials of love, said, 'Marion dear, you are not a helpless case! Harold is kind and he does what he can to make your life more congenial because he loves you. But another, even dearer one who know that his bright future is entwined with your own will replace him one day.'

Marion looked away from her friend for a while as though to master an inconvenient emotion. 'Women such as I am may never marry,' she said simply.

'Of course you may! Marion, you're a beautiful, good, charming woman—'

'With a lame leg and no stamina for life. Rose, since the age of two I've lived my life upon a sofa and watched the world through a window. And in my tedious experience of living with disease, despite the prevailing view, I do not find it promotes a becoming frailty. My illness does not make me spiritual or poetic or even prophetic. It certainly does not make me interesting to men!'

'Still, there are men of sense who surely value someone who is gentle and clever over the stupid but robust,' said Rose with perhaps more conviction than she actually felt.

'I believe that most men would consider it sensible to opt for the silly "stunna". Two legs and vivacity usually win the day.'

But Rose would not concede the point. Having started upon it, she must force her friend to allow that only marriage made women happy and fulfilled.

'There will be somebody who can appreciate you as a woman and with whom you may enjoy the contentment of married life.'

'Dear Rose, perhaps there is indeed such a man. However, it is not the man but the woman within me that I doubt. This body may be that of a mature woman but it hides a child that cowers from pain. For me another's touch means ice rubbed on my back, and mercury ointment, and blistering, and iron leg braces and steel corsets. Why would any man want to burden himself with an invalid who fears his hand? I cannot be a proper wife for any man, I cannot bear a child – it frightens me too much that it would kill me or that I'd not be a proper mother to it, which I could not bear. No, I accepted long ago that I must not deceive myself with hope for a normal, married life. That is, if I must not sacrifice tranquillity.'

Rose remained silent, shamed. Then, not knowing what she might say to make amends, she stroked her friend's sleeve and confessed, 'I've obviously no talent for it,' and continued, untruthfully, 'In the long run I'd surely be happier forgetting about men.'

'Dear Rose, I know you are mistaken in that,' Marion replied, smiling. 'You may intend never to marry any man but some man will nevertheless marry you!'

By the time Rose returned home, the shadows were blue. Jogging slowly up the drive, she was surprised to see a tall figure walking jauntily back down it from her home. Coming closer she saw that it was Harold Webb, and remembered that Marion had said he'd gone to call upon her father.

He tipped his hat to her, a wide grin plastered over his face. 'Evenin', Miss Seaton.'

'Evening, Mr Webb. Hasn't it been a hot one?'

Was he whistling as he marched off home?

Wandering around her own quiet, afternoon house, everything was just as it should be: Papus in his study, no doubt counting out his money, Mapus in the parlour, and Joan, quite probably, in the garden plotting with John. Not a single ripple on the millpond of family life.

It wasn't until Rose went into Mapus that she discovered quite how momentous the object lobbed into that hot, still afternoon had been. 'You'll never guess who your pa was interviewing not an hour past?'

'Harold Webb. I saw him.'

Rose was surprised that her mother should think it important enough to mention.

Elizabeth-Jane blurted out, 'Your Mr McKinley,' happy to be the bearer of this interesting news.

Put in a spin that the dreadful interview she'd dodged half the day had been taking place here and with her own merciless patriarch, Rose demanded, 'What did Papus do to him?'

Mapus, startled, replied, 'Gracious, I couldn't rightly say, my pet. However,' she was quick to conciliate, 'they were together in your father's study for such a time they drank up all of the Madeira, so Mona told me when she'd been in after to tidy away.'

Silly Mapus could add nothing else of use to the bare fact of him having come, talked and left again. Anxious to encourage, Elizabeth-Jane could only surmise, 'I do believe I heard them laughing, or at least I heard Mr McKinley laughing, when I chanced to pass by the window, so it can't have gone too badly, can it?'

# Chapter 11

Robert Seaton had been surprised at the announcement of that caller. He knew the name, of course: the young man with the Londonish tendencies who had put Elizabeth-Jane in a tizzy and was somehow mixed up in that bad business of the theatre outing. Lucky for him then, that Robert, being one of that breed that never ask an Englishman where he comes from – if he's Yorkshire he'll have told you and if he's not he'll be embarrassed to – had already had it from Carr that McKinley senior was a big noise in the north of the county. On account of which pedigree he'd not shown this McKinley the door straight-off. No, he'd give the laddie his fair chance, to properly sniff out his intentions.

But, before a word had been uttered, his inclination to go easy had hardened into belligerence. The young man wore no necktie and his boots were unpolished.

'Mr Seaton, sir,' the appellant uttered, in a drawling southern accent that only confirmed the initial, unfavourable, assessment.

'Young man,' he replied gruffly and, as courtesy dictated, invited the wastrel to sit.

He noted that McKinley lounged where he should properly have been stiff with respectful apprehension. And, instead of allowing his host to make the opening remark, the tyke started up, unbid, on his account, 'It seemed timely that I should present myself, before more damage might be done my good name . . .'

He broke off, smiling.

'You've been 'ow long at my cousin's place?' Robert asked, having none of his smarm. Short temper bringing out the Yorkshire.

'The whole summer, I believe,' came the imprudent reply, accompanied by another smirk.

'The whole summer?' Robert mused and then inquired disingenuously, 'Now, where is it that your own people have their seat?'

McKinley looked momentarily baffled. 'Why, here in Yorkshire.'

Robert raised an eyebrow. 'And they've not missed you all this long time?'

'I shouldn't expect so. I've always been away so much, at school and . . . abroad.' He faltered, as though he spotted the trap, but then rallied, sure of his ability to charm. 'I've been such a stranger there these last years I believe my own father would mistake me for an intruder, probably call for the gamekeeper with his gun if he caught me coming unexpected down the drive!'

At this, Robert's hackles rose higher still and his colour deepened. But the young scoundrel continued on in the same vein.

'I've lived mostly independent of my people from the age of eighteen. To be honest with you,' he confided, making Robert wince, 'since I left school I've been racketing about the place – London, Paris, the Holy Land for a time, making a go of life on my own account.' He looked down at his worn shoes, his expression self-satisfied, and Robert perceived that he'd intended, by this account, to impress the old man with his marvellous get up and go. Then he caught the puppy eyeing up his decanters. Robert gave a tiny gesture of invitation – he'd as well hang him for a sheep as a lamb – but was nevertheless scandalised when McKinley went ahead and helped himself to a good glassful of his Madeira.

He sipped and spoke. 'Mr Seaton, sir, you should know that my peregrinations are now at an end. I've resolved to put into practice some of my ideas for living and working that have been informed by my travels. It is high time I settled to taking life seriously.'

'What line of work is it that you now turn your serious attention to, lad?' Robert asked disingenuously.

'I am an artist.'

The puppy announced it as though he expected congratulation!

'I can't claim to make my fortune from it,' he leaned forward towards Robert, who withdrew further into his chair, 'but, sir, nowadays isn't money so much less important than ideas? I mean, in a civilised and evolved society, such as ours, shouldn't money be put in its proper place – to serve man's quest after truth and beauty?'

From the depths of his chair the old industrialist rumbled like a blast furnace put under insupportable pressure. 'As you've no inclination for money-making yourself, I'm supposing your father is happy to fund your *ideas* with his *money*?'

McKinley had the decency to look discomposed. 'I must admit to recent differences between us on that account.' He tried a smile. 'I am intending, imminently, to go and make my peace.'

Robert nodded, as though reassured, then leaned forward suddenly and shot back, 'But, in meantime, you came 'ere to sound me out about letting you 'ave some o' mine?'

He had the satisfaction of seeing McKinley flinch.

'Mr Seaton, I have no idea what you mean.'

'I mean, young man, you've set your sights on my daughter, Rose.'

'I wouldn't be as bold as that, Mr Seaton. As I say, this visit was to introduce myself in person rather than have you hear something spoken of me that might have done my reputation harm.'

Robert looked at him with his baleful eye, to communicate that if that had been his intention, he'd failed in it.

'Oh, I've 'eard plenty about you, young man!' He glared at him. 'But it's what I've got from your own lips today has done the damage.'

Patrick rose gracefully from the chair. He held out his hand and, smiling, said, 'I shall be going. Thank you so much for the Madeira, it was delicious.'

The cheek of him!

At the door – which, Robert noticed, he took no hurry in reaching – he turned and said, 'I'm sorry that we appear to have got off on the wrong foot. You'll like me more when you get to know me.'

'I doubt that.'

And Patrick McKinley was gone from the room. Robert chose to interpret the exit in terms of having seen him off.

In anticipation of his next interview, the one he had been expecting, it had been necessary to finish the last of the Madeira to swill the taste of Patrick McKinley from his palate. But Robert was still rather red and emphatic when he received the next young man, Harold Webb, who had arranged to visit with some of his new designs for fire surrounds.

Robert was pleased to see that this lad had the decency to look thoroughly uncomfortable in his presence. His lack of fluency was calming to Robert and the Yorkshire vowels easy upon his ear, just as the solid, manly, graceless frame was restful on the eye.

Thus he was inclined to give Webb his head, rather than bite it straight off. Harold spread out the drawings which favoured the undisciplined vegetable and flower motifs of the Continent. And Robert, who favoured decoration that was old-fashioned, English and sternly repetitious nevertheless condescended to look through them.

'You've done well,' Robert said after a while, surprised by the delicacy of the drawing. 'Though I cannot see that these will suit our customers.'

'Sir,' Harold Webb ventured uneasily, 'may we not win new ones with these new lines?'

'Fair point, Webb. I'll keep 'em by me for further consideration.' He tapped Harold encouragingly on the knee. 'I can't say fairer than that now, can I?'

Harold looked surprised.

'How's the commercial law coming along?' Robert asked benignly.

'Very well, sir.'

Though he waited for the lad to expand on this, he seemed tongue-tied and Robert liked him all the better for that. Then, there being nothing more to say and since men did not exchange pleasantries for the sake of it, Robert rose to usher his caller from the room.

'Well done, lad. Tha's done well,' he said by way of farewell and surprised Harold into a smile. His step was lively as he strode back along the gravel drive that only an hour before he'd ventured down fearing rockets.

By the close of that smouldering day in July, Rose's romantic expectations had been blown open, exploded, smashed beyond repair, although what she'd found on returning from her visit to Marion was only tranquillity. Papus was not in a rage, not in a stamping, thumping fury but, rather, fond and tipsy, and Mapus, anxious to forestall another to-do between father and daughter, full of vague reassurance.

It wasn't until Rose visited Fell Top the following day that she discovered quite how momentous the cryptic events of yesterday had been. Patrick McKinley had gone, dropped out of her life like a stone down a well. Edy could furnish no information other than her theory that a fit of artistic melancholy had driven him away.

'Edy, what *exactly* did he say before he left?' Rose interrogated her cousin. 'Do try to remember how he seemed. Was he angry or just sad?'

'Oh, pretty black, I'd say,' she said unhelpfully. 'Maybe he went back to his people, as intended. I really haven't a notion.'

'I don't understand it. Mother said he looked perfectly calm when he left my father,' protested Rose, thinking of the overheard laughter and the empty Madeira decanter. 'Whatever could have happened to have made him that miserable?'

Edy stirred herself. 'Dear heart, don't you see, he doesn't need a reason. For someone sensitive as Patrick to have a reason for his unhappiness would be vulgar. To be melancholy without a reason is a sure sign of his genius. Misery shows imagination, don't you agree?'

Edy may have been pleased with her conceit but for her, too, his loss was a blow. Despite her subtlest stratagems, she'd let slip her bohemian. Even Guy seemed, if that were possible, at a looser end than normal. And whether Patrick had gone to stay in his Yorkshire home expressly to seek rapprochement and the chance to marry or was just driven away by an existential black crow, none of them were any the wiser.

Her brief season having apparently drawn to its premature close and with no prospect of Switzerland, Rose reconciled herself to dull days spent at home with Mapus and Papus. Her only diversions were calls to Fell Top and a curious outing to a steel mill. For some reason Papus took it into his head that the most sultry of late summer days would be wonderfully appropriate for her first sight of a furnace. They drove over to Pyracmon Steel Works where she was encouraged to look into the pit of hell and was introduced to a dull dog called Christopher Shaw. Almost fainting with the heat, she had nothing to say to him nor he to her and so they drove home again, her father, perhaps equally affected by the flaring day, now in a worse temper.

And so, as the evenings drew in, Rose resumed that elegant pottering with paintbrush, needle or guitar designed to occupy rich young ladies who are left upon the shelf.

# Chapter 12

September came at last but still the long summer endured without relief. Only the council of the swallows, who ranged themselves on every rooftop, twittered that the season was nearly done for, that it was time to escape the coming of the next. They gathered and agreed on flight, calling, 'To the south, to the south!' Earthbound Rose was gathering blackberries, popping the spoils into her mouth as she foraged, and had strayed far from home along the dusty country lanes. She continued to reach into the brambles for the black fruit even as a light rain began to fall, so fine that at first the droplets hadn't the substance to land but seemed to swirl and dance in a dampening haze around her. Then the rain decided to drop rather than float and a proper torrent began. By the time she was running back home, blackberry basket hooked over an arm, holding her hat on with one hand and her skirts up with the other, it was stinging and sharp as stair rods. She came upon an oak tree and her heart beat in alarm to see the figure of a man smoking and loitering underneath. She resolved not to look but to run on and hope to escape his attention.

'Rose darling!' called the man. 'Stop and shelter. There's no lightning, we'll be safe here until this rain lets up.'

'Mr McKinley, is it? Have you come back to Fell Top?' She

was flustered that he should turn up again, without word, without warning.

'I came to visit you.' He let the statement hang before continuing, 'I was caught out by this rain. Heaviest rainfall for weeks.'

'It is siling down,' she agreed and then tried to formalise this strange meeting, saying primly, 'Father is at his business, but Mother will be pleased to invite you to lunch, I'm sure.'

He smiled down at her and repeated, 'I came for you.'

If there was a sensible response to this, Rose did not know it. But there was a world of longing in her unadorned 'oh'.

They stood together in the rain a moment, before he said, laughing and shaking off the raindrops, 'Whatever became of "summer's ripening breath"?'

'It was a most wonderful party,' she blurted, seeing the lake at dawn and her Romeo dressed in spangles.

'Yes, I suppose it was.' He sounded a little uncertain. 'Though the parties I enjoy most are the future ones that happen in my head. I like the planning and the anticipation but the reality is generally a letdown, don't you find?'

She could only shake her head.

'Reality is never quite . . . perfect,' he mused. 'That's the problem with it.'

She couldn't bear to hear him diminish that magical evening, make it a drab and disappointing thing.

'Well, I thought it was perfect,' she said, too vehemently.

He looked at her closely, shivering in her summer frock, and said, 'Put my coat over your shoulders.'

As he put his arms round her to wrap her in the coat, Rose's heart seemed to squeeze into her throat with his nearness and the masculine smell of his damp, wool coat and the tobacco he'd been smoking. The intimacy gave her courage to ask the question that had tormented her all these weeks. 'Where were you?'

Smiling sadly, he pulled her nearer to him by the lapels of his coat. 'Rambling,' he said, and used both hands to tilt her face to his, so gently that she hardly noticed that it was not by her own volition. He paused, and she felt the same voluptuous appointment with danger that she'd felt in the garden after the ball. 'I called upon my people.'

He seemed to look straight down into her heart, and she shivered to receive him there, warm and tender and vulnerable. She was mesmerised by the intent gaze of the predator, robbed of the power to resist, or dissemble.

'You're reconciled?'

He, flinching from that question, broke the trance. 'I think not, no.'

Released, she took a step back and was surprised to find herself there, under the tree with him.

'I need only be reconciled with you, darling Rose,' he lulled. 'My heart's true home, where my only fortune is lodged.' He eased her closer to him again and she came gladly, willingly. 'Rose, I have been engaged upon quite another plan—'

'You were such a long time away,' she interrupted, hardly listening.

'Darling Rose, do I ask too much?'

'I don't understand what you expect of me.'

He stroked her hair. 'For now, only to trust. Just that.'

Sight and sound of the outside world was dulled by the curtain of rain that enclosed their little universe. He pulled her to him to kiss her at last. The kiss that, for so long, had waited to be given and received. She was so utterly relaxed that he seemed to melt into her, blend himself with her so that she tasted with his mouth, felt her own body under his hands and, when he sighed, breathed the spice of mutiny and treasure islands. They stood together, loosely clasped, becalmed inside the ring of pattering rain.

Now that some form of pact had been sealed, he spoke quickly. 'I've been making travel arrangements.' Rose stiffened but he soothed again, bringing her back to him. 'Ones that involve you. But . . .' He stopped and looked directly at her. 'Rose, will you be brave enough to follow wherever this will lead us?'

Her sparkling eyes broadcast her willingness and he kissed her hands in gratitude.

'Leave all to me, Rose. Only wait a little longer and—' He suddenly jerked away from her, pulled by a rough hand.

'Miss Seaton!' Under the tree, his hair slick with the wet, stood Harold Webb. He was breathing hard, wheezing a little, from his run through the rain. He looked challengingly at Patrick, bristling for a fight, but controlled his breath and his temper as well as he could, to address Rose. 'Might I be of assistance here?'

All she could summon was a little gasp of shock which made Harold even more assertive. Face set, he pushed Patrick roughly by the shoulder and demanded, 'What's your game, mister?'

Rose, appalled, found her tongue. 'Stop that! This is my friend Mr McKinley.'

Harold, inflamed by undischarged aggression, could not hold off from sneering, 'Mr McKinley, we meet at last!'

'Charmed,' smiled Patrick, taking Harold's unwilling hand to shake it and divert some of his rival's dander into civilities. Harold remained gruff and stiff-legged, readied to attack.

'You have the advantage of me,' Patrick continued, standing with his arms hanging loosely at his sides, ostentatiously off his guard. 'You are . . . ?'

'Harold Webb.'

Patrick affected bafflement, forcing Harold to expose his inferiority.

'From Webb's Farm that lies yonder.'

'Ah, I have you now.'

Harold, momentarily abashed, took a step back and turned his attention upon Rose. 'Miss Seaton, the rain is easing off. Will you step over to the house with me? It's not too far and we may dry and warm ourselves there. You must be starved.' He used this familiar dialect word for 'cold' like reassuring code that stood between them and the outsider, Patrick McKinley.

'Dear Mr Webb, *would* you be so kind as to escort Miss Seaton?' With an easy smile, Patrick graciously gave way before the paltry challenge of his rival, so sure of himself, of her, that further engagement was superfluous. He took her hand in farewell. 'Rose, will you excuse me? I fancy walking on a while, now this cloudburst is passing over.'

She looked at him, disappointed that he would leave her here with Harold.

'Won't you, darling?' he said persuasively. Harold flinched at the casual, retaliatory use of that word. 'I know you may be perfectly trusted to the care of Mr Webb.'

He kissed her hand and, swinging his jacket over a shoulder, set off down the lane which now steamed under the dazzling burst of sunlight that had succeeded the rain. Without breaking step, and unseen by Harold, he turned once to give her the most tremendous stage wink and pull a grimace at Harold's ramrod back. She answered with a little nod and a trembling smile, and watched as he strolled elegantly away, his hand raised in easy salute, not looking back to the two who now stood close, but disengaged, under the dripping tree.

They walked to the farm, which was only across a couple of fields, finding conversation difficult. Rose was taken under the charge of Mrs Webb and Marion, while William was sent off to her own home to let them know that she was safe, and was invited to lunch at the farmhouse.

During the meal, which was served by the indoor girl and Mrs Webb, Marion remarked to her brother, 'Harry, you must cultivate this hobby you have of rescuing Rose from peril. Since you have taken it upon yourself to be her knight, we have seen so much more of her.'

Harold turned a thunderous red. 'I think she must learn to take more care, and spot for herself dangers upon the horizon.'

'For Rose, of course, can outrun a weather front!' Marion joked.

Though Marion pleaded with her to stay and keep her company that afternoon, Rose was made too jittery by the secret exchange beneath the sheltering tree and must return home to think through, in peace, the exciting development of the kiss, the implication of 'travel plans', and the wicked complicity of that wink.

# Chapter 13

She waited, as she'd been instructed by a secret note smuggled into her hand by Joan, in the gazebo at the end of the garden. She was surrounded by the luggage that Joan (whose expertise in the management of an elopement had been gleaned from their study of the society novel) had helped her to pack. That note had been a thrilling call for bravado, a challenge to grasp hold of her life and to live it recklessly, splendidly, selfishly. Harold Webb would see if she couldn't handle danger!

But now, as she sat chilling inside that decorative cast-iron cage, Rose considered consequences. It really was an awfully big undertaking to desert the certainty of parents and home for a lover she barely knew and, she hardly dared admit, who frightened her a little. Might there still be time to run for it?

'Pssst, Rose.'

'Edy?'

'Come with me, there's a cab waiting further along the drive.' Her cousin's whisper grated. Rose could not make sense of what Edy said and her impulse was to dissemble.

'Edy, I was just sitting in the garden making the most of this beautiful late summer's evening.'

'Come on, show a leg. We can't mooch around here

appreciating the gnats. The cab's waiting for us and it can't be long before you'll be missed.'

'Where's Patrick?' she asked, stupidly.

'Oh, don't you worry about Patrick, he's meeting us at the station with three tickets to London.'

'Three?'

'Yes, so come on, do, the train won't wait. I say,' she looked at the pile of luggage, 'you've obviously never done a flit before. Quick and light on the feet is the form, I believe. Just take what you can lug and follow me.'

Rose hesitated and then stepped away from duty, respectability, security, and the bulk of her luggage, and into the path of the tornado.

And that was how she came to be in a scarlet first-class carriage of the Midland Railway's London train with a carpet bag containing three novels, a cast-iron framed photograph of her parents and a paper twist of mint humbugs to quell travel sickness. Her duenna, she noticed, had had the prescience to have had her own substantial, initialled travelling cases stowed for her upon the luggage rack over her head by a porter. Edy's luggage, no doubt, would be equipped with all the necessities, almost as though she'd had the time to plan for this impulsive flit across the Channel.

'Where is Patrick? He is coming, isn't he?' asked Rose, a sudden panic overtaking her that Patrick, having substituted Edy in the flight from the garden, had decided his presence might be de trop, two being usually sufficient to carry off an elopement.

'Of course, you ninny!' said Edy, so excited that the veins in the middle of each cheek were suffused with red corpuscles. 'Ain't you pleased to have me as your travelling companion?' she went on with sufficient menace to keep Rose from shouting, 'No! no! no!'

Then, just as the last of the mailbags was loaded and it seemed that he must miss them, Patrick was there, a soft bag over his shoulder, nonchalant, debonair, somehow indifferent to the enormity of his crime. Didn't he consider that he was a thief and seducer? He didn't beg her forgiveness or fall down before her in gratitude but merely said, 'Hello, darling Rose, so you came,' and, despite the smile and the light kiss, these crumbs of endearment sounded detached, even ironic. But in her tantalised heart she knew that he had won her with just this cool assurance.

'Patrick! You dog, aren't you even going to hold her tiny hand and look beseechingly into her twinned, limpid pools?' asked Edy greedily.

'Oh, I thought I'd leave that until after you'd dozed off, or got bored of the show and run back home,' he said, with an edge of cruelty that made even Edy pause.

So she galloped south to London, source of all sin and her own voluntary ruin – how appropriate the scarlet of that carriage. To one side of her a gaudy sunset played out and on the other night had already brought down curtains. After hours of rushing shadows, dreary railway towns and a desultory meal in the dining car, the demon engine, losing patience with level progress, alternated between excavating through tunnels and cuttings, and rope-walking at a level with chimney pots and panted, at last, into St Pancras station. Rose looked up through the steam and the black smoke that poisoned the palate with sulphur, into the huge vault above, where cast-iron ribs spanned the roof, and felt a pang for her own home.

At the St Pancras Hotel, where they would pass what remained of the night, Patrick requested a double room for her and Edy and a single-bedded one for himself. They loaded themselves into the lift with all Edy's luggage and a sleepy hotel *piccolo*. As they separated for the night, Patrick called pleasantly after them, 'If I were you I'd get a call for five tomorrow morning. We must cab it to the station at Liverpool Street in time for the early train to Tilbury Dock to be sure of the paddle steamer for Boulogne. It only runs Thursday to Saturday so we mustn't miss it or we'll be stuck here kicking our heels. Five, mind, no later, or you'll find yourselves left behind.' He smiled and retreated down the long hotel corridor carpet to claim his bachelor cell. She seemed forever to watch him thus, strolling lightly away from her.

And so Rose spent her 'bridal' night in a stuffy railway hotel room that smelled of cold bacon fat and dusty drapery, listening to her cousin snoring in the bed beside her. That last remark of Patrick's, she thought to herself, suggested that Edy and she were extra travellers who'd attached themselves to his trip, tolerated hangers-on who were only welcome if they kept up. Then she wondered at how familiar he was with the escape route across the Channel. How many times had he caught an early cab to Liverpool Street in order to make the connection to Boulogne? With this uneasy thought, she fell asleep.

The first daytime view Rose had of the capital was of that early, dozing, bluish-grey morning London, when even in the Euston Road there was still the butterfly touch of dawn. Dew was suspended on railings and the world paused to hear a blackbird sing in a plane tree. But as they crossed the city by hackney cab, so the arcing course of another London day was launched and any reminder of the natural world was put to flight by the rising tide of human bustle and business and traffic. Like pertinacious, mechanical salmon swimming upstream, omnibuses, wagons, handcarts, drays, carters, cabs and carriages jostled and skirmished all around them, making collision and broken bones inevitable. Rose held on to the strap and thought tearfully of Mapus and Papus stricken at news of their only daughter's death. But somehow she escaped retribution and they slithered through the morning race to land safely at Liverpool Street station where there was time for coffee and a saunter before their train left to carry them to the new docks at Tilbury.

The crossing on the neat little paddle steamer, *Marguerite*, left Edy and Rose wretched with seasickness, despite Joan's mint humbugs. Patrick stayed hour after hour, untroubled, on deck to contemplate the churning grey Channel and smoke his cigar – the smell of which quarantined him even from avid Edy.

During the arduous journey to Paris, Patrick conversed very little with the two cousins; never anything less than considerate and chivalrous, he'd organised their journey rather like a very obliging travel guide. But this chivalry in protecting Rose's honour until they were safely married was rather disconcerting, since it seemed to keep him from kissing her or reassuring her that he loved her and that she'd done the right thing in leaving father and mother's protection to follow him. She must only trust for, of course, he knew best how to arrange everything. No doubt true romance would begin once they were married and her chaperone dismissed back across the Channel; in the meantime her elopement felt more like a cheap holiday spent in the company of a stranger and a scold.

They passed another night in a hotel that, even though it was French, was as dingy and noisy as any English one. Rose and Edy again shared a room and, as they lay side by side, listening to the late-night noises of the port, Rose said, 'I do hope we shall be able to get a licence to marry quickly.'

'Not too quick, my duck. I'm so dying to visit Paris's dressmakers and milliners and, goes without saying, its marvels.'

'I suppose I'll need to buy some new costumes myself. I've only the stained old thing I travelled in,' Rose acknowledged. She forbore to mention the many other outfits that had been left behind in the garden at Edy's command.

'Yes, rather *jeune femme*, isn't it?' commented Edy, perhaps remembering how her unsophisticated cousin had teased her for her foray into rational dress. Then, getting in another dig, 'I believe we shall re-invent you as a high-art maiden, straight out of a modern painting. But, then again, perhaps not.' She craned her head to look critically at Rose. 'I fear you can't be made to droop sufficiently and you do *bloom* rather.'

Rose bit her tongue and then, there being no one else in the world to ask, ventured, 'Do you think Patrick thinks of me as just a silly young girl? You do think he loves me, don't you?'

'Oh, like crazy, I'd say,' answered Edy. And Rose was silenced by the hollow, indifferent ring of her cousin's affirmation.

'And won't we have fun in Roma!' Edy continued. 'I'm simply dying to see all those wicked classical profiles made flesh. Just us three romping through Europe . . .'

Rose let her quiet tears run down to soak her hard, French bolster.

The next day the three travellers boarded a train of the Chemin de Fer du Nord for a rattle through the French countryside, with its French cows and farmhouses and forests, disembarking at the Gare du Nord to step at last into bright Paris day. Here, too, were omnibuses, wagons, carts, drays and cabs but sparkling water flowed in the gutters, the sun shone and Rose saw her surroundings through holiday eyes which will always make passing people appear more fashionable and more fascinating, waiters busier, sky bluer and future brighter. Despite everything she was still a very young girl and it would have taken more than fatigue and hunger to stop her heart from rising of its own account at this breath of freedom and foreign air. The uncrushable enthusiasm of callow youth would out. And, surely now that they were done with uncomfortable train rides, nasty hotels and queasy sea crossings, the proper adventure of her life could begin.

With the first whiff of French cigarette smoke and garlic in his nose, Patrick seemed to awake and notice her for the first time as she knew herself to be: hollow-eyed with weariness, clothes greasy and dirty from travel and bad hotel food. She thought she saw something inside him turn away.

'I'll drop you girls off at a little hotel I know nearby,' he said, rubbing his hands with the expression of someone who grows suddenly kind in the near prospect of relieving himself of a tiresome relative. 'I'm sure you could both do with a rest and a wash.'

He solicitously handed them into a cab.

'But where will you go?' Rose asked, desperate that he would desert them again, as he'd done outside the theatre.

'Oh, just about. I have some business to attend to. I'll be sure to pick you girls up around seven and we'll go for supper in the finest restaurant in Paris. Will that suit?' he said bluffly as though that gave him leave to escape duty and answer the call of the glamorous city.

It was only a short hop to the Hotel du Nord; they might have walked the route but for Edy's impedimenta. After exchanging a few words with the concierge, Edy and Rose were duly deposited and Patrick skipped out of the door and off into that intriguing, golden, Parisian day.

Edy and Rose stood, smiling uncertainly at Madame behind the desk, until it became clear that in order to secure the keys to their rooms and a porter for their luggage, money was expected to change hands.

'Jolly utter behaviour! Lucky I had time to get some of the necessary before we left,' said Edy, rummaging for cash.

Rose had followed Patrick across the Channel, had dared to embark upon her life's biggest adventure because he'd asked it, and now he'd abandoned her, dropped her off like so much left luggage. How could she have so disastrously misinterpreted the promise of that kiss in the rain?

# Chapter 14

A week went past in the world's wickedest capital, brought to the point of licentious ripeness in its *fin de siècle* years, yet Rose persisted innocent as a schoolgirl. Days and days in the dull hotel near the Gare du Nord and never a sign from Patrick that nuptials were being organised or an onward journey planned. His polite indifference might have given her parents cause to hope. Indeed, caught between Edy's bossing and Patrick's distraction, Rose was protected, managed, maintained as ever, and harboured the familiar suspicion that plans concerning her were being made above her head.

Each morning, the three of them breakfasted together and the only conversation to be heard over that dour table was the fitful observations exchanged by the two 'grown-ups'. Every day Papa Patrick went off, like a regular man of business, not to return from his mysterious occupation until the evening when he disappeared back behind his newspaper and his abstraction. Left to their own devices, Rose accompanied eager Mama Edy to the Parisian sights and the Parisian *couturiers célèbres*, where she waited patiently on fragile gilt chairs as her cousin was fitted for her.new costumes and hats and shoes (away with sandals and earth tones) or, submissive to her cousin's directions, was fitted for her own. All paid for, humiliatingly, from Edy's purse. Edy did enjoy having the upper hand. Rose considered glumly that her cousin had probably engineered this escape across the Channel with Patrick's connivance. But if the purpose of the visit wasn't debauchery but shopping, then who chaperoned whom?

After nearly a week of trailing, Rose took sufficient courage in her French to give her cousin the slip and partake of the solitary tourist's melancholy freedom to explore unhindered by purpose or companions. The Indian autumn persisted warm enough for her to remain for the greater part of the day out of doors; indeed she had neither the money nor inclination to seek out covered places of entertainment or culture. Instead she spent the morning traipsing along the boulevards and wandering by the river and through the public parks and gardens of Paris. And in the early afternoon she sat in a particular little patch of green, where children came with their nursemaids to chase the pigeons or run through fallen leaves, and pondered what she must do next.

She returned to the usual torture of *dîner en famille*, half resolved to send a telegram to her parents, throwing herself upon their mercy and pleading for rescue, to find Patrick and Edy, waiting for her in the *salle à manger*.

'Edy, you will please excuse us. I must speak to Rose alone,' said Patrick, without looking at her.

'Well, I think that I should come with you. I am her relation, you know – which is more than you can claim for yourself, vile seducer,' replied Edy, full of glee after her day of boulevarding.

'I'd like you to stay here,' answered Patrick firmly.

And so she did. Thank God.

He took Rose off to a small drawing room, where the hotel guests adjourned after their meals, a place of slopped coffee and cold cigar smoke. Because the lamps were not yet lit here, he led her by the hand through the dank semi-dark to sit by the dead fire. She disengaged the hand he held and laid it tenderly on her lap like an injured bird that needed comfort.

'Rose darling, we must talk.'

She did not reply; she did not trust herself to do so without betraying all that pent-up disappointment.

He went on, 'I know that it's been days and days and that I have neglected you . . .'

Righteous hurt welled up, and she began to sob.

'My darling Rose. I did not intend it to be so. Indeed I did not!' He reached for her but she cowered elaborately away from his touch.

'You brought me here to ignore me and now I can't ever go home, or anywhere else. And for what?'

'But Rose I'm not *such* a thumping villain, am I? Haven't I behaved honourably by you? I hope your own mother couldn't accuse me—' he interrupted, perhaps surprised by her venom.

'Not even properly ruined!' she spat back.

The vile seducer, amused at that, sat back in his chair, reviled, it seemed, more for the omission than the commission of that dastardly crime.

'Why did you let me come at all if you didn't want me?'

'Rose, I didn't force you. You came of your own free will.'

'You are supposed to honour and protect, to guide, to revere – to give me everything I want.' She ran out of husbandly virtues.

'Why does playing the game have to be so impossibly difficult?' he said, half to himself, and she burst into a fresh spate of sobs and accusations. He became tender and beseeching. 'But I *do* want you, darling Rose, and I do revere and all the rest,' he said, kneeling on the vile and spongy carpet, and then he had the sense to say what she needed to hear. 'I love you. I love you, I love you.' He looked up soulfully into her shiny, dripping face until at last she abated a little.

'Now, that feels better, doesn't it?' he said and, ignoring her feeble struggle to break free of him, stood her up and took her into his arms.

'You didn't just come to Paris because Edy wanted to?' she mumbled into his chest, suddenly exhausted.

He laughed outright at that.

'Rose, didn't I tell you that there's a plan? And Edith played her part in it. But, dear creature, it was all about, only ever about, you and me. Didn't you come because you knew that and you trusted me enough to pack your bags and get yourself to the railway station?' He tried to raise her face to his but she resisted, aware of her pink nose and eyes. 'And didn't you trust me enough to follow all the way to this godforsaken hotel, with never a question, my brave girl?'

Despite herself she felt gratified that he considered that what she had done had been brave – not, as she suspected, horribly ill-considered and weak. She gave a self-righteous sniff.

'Which was quite the right thing to do because, as I say, there *was* always a plan at the back of it.'

'But what is the plan?'

'I heard that my mother was to be here, in Paris,' he began. 'It is with her that I have been engaged since we came.'

'Just with her? Every day?' she said, in her confusion sounding as though she was accusing him of something.

'The greater part,' he replied defensively. 'It's taken time to rebuild family ties, you understand, it's been years . . .'

'But I thought the rift with your parents was unbridgable,' she said in a small, damp voice.

'In my sire's case, that seems to be so,' he said. 'However, and I should whisper it even here,' looking theatrically around the empty room, 'dear Mama is a divorced lady and so quite independent of Papa McKinley's decrees and, luckily, also of his cash.'

'Why did you wait a week to tell me this?' she said, sounding sulky, though his renewed attention had made her light-headed, as if she had been forced to hold her breath for ages and, having been given access to oxygen, had gulped it down too greedily for fear it might be taken away again.

'Dear Rose, I was afraid you'd consider her to be not quite respectable.' Rose gave a watery smile and Patrick, encouraged, went on. 'To the facts then: to add to my poor ma's vices, she is an American, an heiress of shipping, or cattle or bauxite, I forget which – anyway, some useful commodity. Thus she was imported to be married off to the old man and invigorate with fresh blood and finances my withering branch of olde England.' Before she could duck away he gave her a kiss.

'Got you!' he said, smacking his lips, and continued more jauntily, 'But having provided the heir and the spare, myself,' he smiled, 'Mama being financially independent, as well as a fascinating original, soon hopped the ancestral twig. And now, like the wandering albatross, alone she circles the continental resorts. Round and round she flies – Geneva to Paris, Paris to Rome and back again, like so much of the American diaspora in search of culture, meaning, youth.'

'Did she remarry, a Mr Van der Decken?' Rose endeavoured to sound sensible and wished she had a handkerchief.

'Oh, that's only been her title since she reinvented herself as the heroine of her own life story. I can only imagine, since she has adopted a rather florid path to travel, not to mention a ceaseless one, she nicked it from the captain of the *Flying Dutchman*. You know the legend: "I will continue! I will not surrender!"'

Rose tried to hold on to the thread of what he was proposing. 'I'm to meet her then?'

'That is the plan.' He pulled her closer to him, running on, in the full flush of his enthusiasm. 'I've arranged for you to call upon the ageless one tomorrow morning. Oh, but won't she be charmed by you, my darling!'

'How shall I charm her?' interrupted Rose nervously, trying to keep up with him.

'That, my darling, will be unavoidable! Mrs Van der D will be so charmed, she won't know what hit her.'

'Why should everything depend upon your mother's approval of me? You're the long lost son.'

'Darling, don't you see, all we need is the very tiniest shaving of bauxite, just a pair of baby longhorns and then we'll be set, all our problems sorted, and we may properly start out together.'

'Please don't joke,' she said, in agony.

He took her hands in his, and said, sober now, 'I'm really not joking. You are the one to win her over to the cause. The ex-Mrs McKinley believes it impossible to underestimate the folly of the male. I know she considers I've squandered all my advantages – she's probably right about that but, I pray, she'll forgive and forget my crimes for your sweet sake. My mother has a tremendous sympathy for young girls in peril.'

'Mightn't she consider that you are the one who put me in peril?'

'Jaded man-haters are secretly the world's greatest romantics.' He pulled her closer and she did not hide her face from him.

'Especially when it frustrates the patriarchs.'

They were standing very still and close in the darkened room.

'Rose,' he whispered, 'you can't know how hard it has been to keep myself from you all this long time, every day to have you so close and yet beyond reach.'

Just as he began to kiss her in earnest a hotel servant came to light the lamps and they sprang guiltily apart as though their love was truly forbidden.

That night, in her single bed, Rose was no longer the schoolgirl out of her depth. Patrick and she were once more those star-crossed lovers, for whom love grew more poignant, more desperate, more romantic because of the parental barriers thrown in their way. She fell asleep full of nervous anticipation for tomorrow's interview.

At breakfast she was buoyed by the pleasure of informing Cousin Edith that Patrick and she would spend the day exclusively together. Today she and he would be the co-conspirators. But, after lunching together in a jolly brasserie, on their walk to the swankiest hotel in the swanky arrondissement, she became increasingly tense and silent. I must be bold enough to help myself now, Rose thought to herself. I must do this because poor Patrick is too proud to ask me to marry without money of his own to support us. It is right, it is the only way, and it must be gone through with. And then, when it has been done, Patrick will be in a position to properly ask Papus for my hand. Everything will come right in the end.

They paused in the hotel foyer at the foot of a mile of red-carpeted stairs and he gave her arm a squeeze and whispered, 'Just shares in one of her smallest, rustiest steamers,' and they began their toil upwards to the albatross's eyrie.

Rose, in her new Paris gown, was introduced into the private sitting room of the fascinating original, who awaited her, perched upon a taut silk sofa. Though she'd apparently already lived a couple of double lives, Mrs Van der Decken looked to have suffered no consequences but for an over-bright and sceptical eye and an excellent taste in dress. She was brisk with Patrick, as he had warned her she would be. 'Be off, waster. Everything I need to know I'll find right here. Come, sit by me, my child,' she beckoned to Rose.

'Dreadful boy! He does amuse me,' she said, aiming the sceptical eye after him. 'Reminds me of myself – always gazing, longingly over the paddock fence.' She focused it now on Rose, adding, 'A bit of a bolter, my son.'

Rose, aware that she was there to plead the merits of constancy, replied, 'But Patrick's sick of that old, rootless life. He truly wants to settle.'

'Why, sure he does!' Mrs Van der Decken was overtaken by sudden laughter so violent that it caused her to hold on to Rose's arm for support with one hand while putting the other to her bubbling chest. Rose braced herself, worried that they'd slide together off that over-ripe upholstery and onto the floor.

When she'd recovered herself, Patrick's mother inquired, 'And you, Miss Rose? Which are you, a settler or one of us bolters?'

Rose, feeling herself on surer ground, replied feelingly, 'I should like to be married, of course!'

Her examiner repressed more erupting bubbles, her expression betraying their sour taste, and remarked, 'I settled. It is what we women do, isn't it, settle for lives we did not choose?'

Aware that the interview had once more skidded off course, Rose steeled herself to get it securely back.

'We *both* so much want to marry . . .'

Mrs Van der Decken patted the hand she still held as though in sympathy.

'But since Patrick's expectations of his father have come to nothing . . . I mean, since . . .' Rose stuttered to a halt, not knowing which was ruder, to make mention of the husband to the wife he had divorced, or to discuss his money.

'Ah, the *expectations*!' said Mrs Van der Decken, who was happily above such scruples. 'Ten years I served in concubinage to that man and what did *I* get out of it?' Rose was too startled to speculate. However, the question was evidently rhetorical for Mrs Van der Decken answered herself. 'An oaf for a husband, two children who didn't know or need me and a weak chest – oh, and the finest Palladian mansion in the county, so I'm told. Getting free of all that was the best thing I ever did.'

Rose couldn't help but ask, appalled, 'Weren't you sad to leave your children behind?'

'My two little boys? No, for children are never really one's to own. They toddled off to school like good little English boys and what was I to do – watch them turn into daddy from afar? My dear, they would have passed me on the street and not recognised me. I do believe they only knew I was Mother because good old Nanny told them so. It really was the simplest thing to shrug 'em off!'

Rose looked at her feet. She did not understand how to engage in this heartless, world-weary badinage.

'A shocking bad example of my sex, I know. A rotten wife and a worse mother,' Mrs Van der Decken added in mock contrition.

'Oh, no! I didn't mean to suggest that,' said, Rose, tears pricking.

The unnatural woman took pity on her. 'Little girl, you are too young to know anything of what it is to be either.'

'But I would so like to be both,' answered miserable Rose.

'And, I have no doubt, you shall,' Mrs Van der Decken replied briskly.

'Isn't that what happens when you love someone?'

'Ah, love!' She took Rose's hand and pressed it, saying, not without compassion, 'You'll let me give you this bit of advice, Miss Rose, one it took me long years of unhappiness to learn: better to take your own name, as I did, and make your own way through the world without sentimental attachments.'

'But I love him,' she repeated, startled into desperate bravado. 'I don't want my own life, I only want to be with him!'

Mrs Van der Decken paused to consider before saying, 'Well then, since love matches are quite outside my experience, what else can I offer you but my good wishes?'

'There is something else,' said Rose, increasingly desperate to argue her cause before she was dismissed.

Mrs Van der Decken asked almost kindly, 'And what may that be?'

'You can allow Patrick the money to marry upon,' she blurted, risking all.

Mrs Van der Decken returned her hand to her as though something slightly soiled by use. 'You shall not like to hear this, Rose, but I have no intention of subbing my son.'

Rose, determined not to cry, demanded, 'How can you be so cruel?'

Mrs Van der Decken corrected sharply, 'To the contrary, dear, I believe I do him the greater kindness of keeping him on a short leash. Money goes to his head.'

Despairing, Rose almost wailed, 'But if we can't marry, what shall I do? Where shall I go?'

'You will not return to your father's house?'

Rose mutely shook her head, at which Mrs Van der Decken seemed to approve with a tiny nod of hers.

'Then do as I advise, dear, take off and live your own life.'

Her complacency now seemed wilful to Rose who said hotly, 'Can't you understand, I have no money to live on!'

'You have absolutely no money of your own?' Mrs Van der Decken sounded slightly scandalised. She looked judiciously at Rose who, in her distress, was finding it increasingly difficult to keep her place on the slippery material of the fat little sofa. 'All the more reason to stay clear of Patrick and, though I hate to say it, to stick to Papa.'

Rose nearly yelled out in her exasperation, 'But I love him!'

'Love is love, my dear, but money is the thing,' Mrs Van der Decken patiently returned. 'Without it we women are nothing and can become nothing. Put simply, even if I allow the waster my money, you still will have none *and* you will be married. We are really no further forward, are we?'

Rose could make no reply through the lump in her throat.

'So, you understand, I cannot condone it,' concluded Mrs Van der Decken, not unpleasantly.

Realising that she'd get no further along this treacherous path, Rose stood to take her leave.

'But you can't prevent it,' she remarked flatly.

'Quite true, my dear,' Mrs Van der Decken answered her, with regret. 'As I say, there is nothing in the world that I, or anyone else, can do to stop you young women from offering yourselves up in sacrifice once you've set your hearts on it. So I must bid you good luck.'

They shook hands and Rose unsteadily descended the red mile and stepped out, blinking, into the hazy light of autumn afternoon. She'd arranged with Patrick that, since the length of the interview was unguessable, they should rendezvous at a nearby park. Full of her failure, she went there to meet him.

# Chapter 15

It was to the same little park in which Rose had sat by herself and contemplated her uncertain future that she now went. Once again she sat and watched the governesses and the courting pigeons and considered that since Patrick had reassured her that he loved her, she was perhaps even more miserable and confused.

An older lady, decked in mourning, stayed by her for a while to feed the pigeons and they exchanged a smile. She wondered what the time might be. The nearest church clock was out of view of the park and she dared not consult it for fear of missing Patrick, whenever he might come. A man dressed all in brown approached with the obvious intention of sitting next to her. Anxious not to appear what she was, a lone, unprotected woman who waited for someone or something, she stood and walked deliberately away and paced a circular route along the gravel paths, all the while keeping the appointed bench in view until the man left. And still the governesses scolded and still the birds hopped and still Rose waited.

A pretty, graceful young woman with a heavy mass of copper hair and a pale, oval face, who, like her, apparently had nowhere to go and no one to talk to, appeared by her side. The French girl indicated that she sought permission to walk along beside her.

'*Si vous désirez,*' said Rose hesitatingly.

'Thank you, miss,' replied the other, matching her step to Rose's.

'You speak English?' asked Rose, eager to connect with another anonymous soul in this friendless world.

'But of course,' was the reply. 'My mother was an Englishwoman.'

'But how did you know I'm English? Not by my dress for I had everything made for me here in Paris – unless it was by my accent, which I know is poor.' Rose had so lost confidence in herself that she blushed before this self-assured young lady.

'*Pas du tout!*' said the beautiful girl, reaching out to take Rose's arm in her own, in a friendly, unaffected way, as they walked on.

Close to, Rose saw that her costume was rather worn at the elbows and the stuff from which it was made already too thin for the season. But her profile was beautiful and her thick, coiled hair was a glory: glossy as the horse chestnuts that the children collected around them. It suggested luxuriousness and breeding all by itself.

'My maman was an expensive English governess – just like this, I think,' said the handsome girl, indicating the brisk young woman who was rounding up her charges, making them all hold on to a ribbon so she could march them home from their airing in the park.

'She met my papa and they married, poor lady, for I do not think she was bred to be the wife of a French artist.'

'But how romantic.'

The girl smiled. 'Here in Paris, you know, art is only work.'

Now that dusk had closed in around them, the nursemaids departed and the birds taken to the trees to find their roosting places, other types began to occupy the park: the pale girls who worked in shops and the clerks who courted them come to enjoy the last of the short day before they, too, should set off for home. Had she really waited here so long?

The beautiful girl, tucking her arm more snugly into her own, went on, 'My mother missed always the English life, the *good form*!'

'She never returned there?'

'Oh no, for she was orphan with no friends or relations. When she left England she was all alone in the world,' the girl replied with emphasis.

'Goodness, how sad, never to see one's home country again,' Rose responded, with more empathy than she might have felt had she not been wondering precisely whether she'd see Yorkshire and parents again.

'But you must not be sorry for *ma mère*. In those days she was happy to have her own family,' she said, dropping all her aitches. 'In these days *mon père* had a little success and he was always painting, always singing.'

She sang vigorously in imitation:

*'Dans la grande ville de Paris,*
*Dans la grande ville de Paris,*
*Il y a des bourgeois bien nourris . . .'*

swinging Rose's arm in time to the tune.

*'Vive le son, vive le son,*
*Vive le son de l'explosion!'*

She finished with éclat, making Rose laugh for the first time since she'd arrived in Paris.

Smiling, the French girl continued, 'And I fed my caged birds and sang, "Baa, baa black ship, 'ave you any whirl",' she employed an exaggerated accent, 'because I am the, how do you say it, the *outcome* of a French seditionist and a nice English lady. *Quelle confusion!*' The lovely girl stopped walking to shake Rose by the hand and introduce herself. 'Veronique La Vigne – you see, my first name means *fidélité*, and my second that I cling like the vine.' She held firm to Rose's hand and squeezed it rather tightly to illustrate.

'So nice to meet you, Mademoiselle La Vigne. I am Rose Seaton. I think that my names have no romantic meanings, either first or last, and I know that my family history is utterly unremarkable. My mother and father are just very ordinary, dull people who never went anywhere or did anything interesting . . .'

It occurred to Rose that she had never before had the opportunity to talk candidly with another who knew nothing of her and was in no position to judge. Having started to speak in the same light tone as her new friend, it was with surprise that Rose realised that she was crying.

'But you are unhappy, poor Rose?' asked Veronique, beginning to shiver in her thin costume. 'Did you lose Papa and Maman? Are you, too, all alone in the world?'

'I didn't lose them, they lost me – or rather I lost myself. Oh, Veronique, I wish I could go home!'

'But you *can* go home, my dear. You *must* go home to Mother and Father!' exclaimed her excitable new friend.

'No, I can't, I can't,' answered Rose, just as vehemently as she had earlier that day protested to Mrs Van der Decken that she could not survive without them.

'What can it be that stops you? Not *une aventure amoureuse* like Maman?'

Rose could only shake her head in mute misery.

Veronique continued decisively, 'Come with me, we will go to a café and drink chocolate to cheer ourselves. It is too cold to talk in this English governess park.'

Rose looked about her and saw that it was already dusk, the time that the French called *entre chien et loup*, between the dog and the wolf. The shop girls had fled before the more flamboyantly dressed women, whose working shift was just begun and whose followers' attentions had a more certain outcome, and Rose was frightened to remain alone among the flower beds these packs hunted.

They walked a short distance to a café where Veronique was

greeted by the patron and were seated and their chocolate brought to them, Rose all the while anxious that she had strayed from the park. She looked distractedly out of the condensation-misted window, examining the smeary faces of the passers-by for the red-gold blur of striding Patrick. Veronique continued to talk, telling the tale of her life in her steady, tranquillising voice that invited neither response nor comment, seemingly oblivious to her new friend's unease.

'Maman and Papa and me, are we romantic? It is certain we are poor. So poor. Sometimes my papa must take his paints and his small canvas on his back and go out walking in the street, knocking at the doors of those well-to-do and offer to paint their little child, their little dog, their bowl of fruits – *n'importe quoi*. Our *boucher* and our *traiteur* and our *tabac* have more portraits in oils than walls to hang them and Maman must walk to the next arrondissement to find one that is willing to give her credit.' Veronique paused and looked at Rose from under her eyebrows, seeming to assess whether she was safely under the influence, before continuing, 'Sometimes Papa sells a big painting and then we three are happy: new clothes for Veronique, new paintbrushes and good coffee for Papa and for Maman a little more credit. *Une lumière au bout du chemin*.'

Again she paused and looked at Rose, who squeezed her hand, made to feel worldly, capable, by these delicate confidences, though she could not stop herself from looking up expectantly whenever someone new stamped in at the door of the café.

'But this street was a long one, such a long one we three never reached the light at the end of it. And so Maman must go further and further for our 'Orniman's pure English tea,' she said, making a little joke of it. 'And Papa must paint on coarse canvas and there are no seeds for my birds. The English lady's life destroyed by the selfish artist and the artist's genius dried up by the scolding woman.' Veronique stopped talking for a moment and sighed. 'How dreadful it is to have parents who hate each other.'

Rose looked guiltily away from the shop window, sharply reminding herself to consider that there were other woes in the world than her own.

'The arguments!' Veronique burst out, making the people in the café look up. '"English bourgeoise! A curse on your respectability!"' she dramatised, and answered herself in her mother's thin, querulous voice. '"You must remember, Edouard, you have a duty to your wife and your child!" For, you see, my papa had once worked in a bank but he would not give up his ambition to be an artist, to go back to that, not for nothing! *Pauvre Maman*. For, it is true, Rose, *On ne marie pas les poules avec les renards*, one cannot marry hens to foxes.' Veronique looked significantly at Rose. 'However hard the hen may try to tame him.'

Now completely involved in the unfolding tragedy of the artist, his wife and their child, Rose allowed herself to forget that she should be waiting on that pre-appointed park bench.

'One day she introduced an important man, a gallery owner, the client of her old employer. He came to see my papa and he looked at his paintings, and he looks and he looks and he makes a face like this.' Veronique pulled an expression of disgust, saying in imitation of the self-important dealer, '"Too old-fashioned, too classical, I can take nothing." Then he goes to the side of Papa's studio and finds the canvas he uses for the scrapings from his palette – all colours, no form, rubbish! But this great man puts on such a face . . .' again Veronique mimicked, this time showing delighted surprise, 'and he holds it up to the light and says, "This I may sell, this is modern! You must give me more like this one." '

Rose didn't know whether she should smile at the absurdity and was glad that she hadn't when Veronique continued, 'Papa broke that board of old paint drips on the man's ignorant head. "I am an artist, not a dog that does tricks!" Then Maman cries and says that, for this pig-headedness, we must starve all together. But he says, "Maud, to bc great an artist *must* be selfish! He must be resolute because art is more important than a child crying for bread." Ah, yes, it was always *l'art pour l'art* with Papa.' Her voice had taken on a harder edge. She concluded her cautionary tale. 'So, you see, the romantic life is not always desirable. Better the ordinary, better the dull for my poor, English maman. And for you, Rose dear.'

'What a sad story.'

'Rose, this is why you must go home while you may.'

Rose came to herself with a start, realised that it was now very dark outside the steamy windows of the cafe. How long had she been listening to this beautiful, troubled young woman? She jumped up, looking vainly for some coins with which to pay for her chocolate.

'I've stayed too long. It's too late!' Rose was embarrassed to find that tears once more welled in her eyes.

'It is never too late!' cried Veronique passionately. 'It is never too late to go home.'

Distracted, Rose repeated, 'Too late, it's too late!' and looked about herself as though she expected to find Patrick there. How had she come to be in this grubby café when she should have been waiting for him in the park? All was lost!

As she made for the door, Veronique said, 'You must not walk by yourself, I will accompany you to your 'otel.'

Together they hurried back to the Hotel du Nord and it wasn't until they parted at the door, Veronique oddly anxious to cut short the pleasantries, that Rose wondered how her new friend had led her unerringly to just the right street.

# Chapter 16

Down the hotel corridors where the scent of mice persisted beneath that of polish and back to the dreary room she shared with Edy. No sign of Patrick and, she thanked providence, no sign of her cousin. Fully clothed, Rose fell upon her bed and into a tormented slumber. And this was where Edy found her, drenched in sweat, raving about birds and park benches.

It was two days before she was well enough to come downstairs to breakfast with Patrick again. She dreaded this meeting, their first since he'd delivered her, full of expectation, to his mother and she'd botched the job of charming down the circling albatross. However, in Rose's feverish mind the subsequent crime of not waiting for him in the park had resolved itself into being the greater test, the greater failure. Sitting at the breakfast table she noticed that he looked as strained and ill as she knew herself to be.

'Darling Rose,' he said anxiously, studying her pale face. 'Are you quite well again?'

Biting her lips, she replied, full of contrition for her disobedience, 'I'm sorry I didn't wait for you.'

'Please, don't! Poor little thing alone all that time in the cold and the dark. How long did you stay?'

As though she needed him to be angry with her, to be shriven of her sins, she hastened to confess every fault. 'Have you seen your mother? Did she tell you there will be no money?'

Edy snorted and poured the tea.

He waved away the teacup and her confession, as though neither interested him, saying lightly, 'Well, now we are even, you and me – neither of us any good at talking round the previous generation. I've coped up until now without her and no doubt I will continue to cope.' And having let her off that hook too, he returned to the park. 'I simply can't understand how Gaspard didn't find you there. He had my explicit instructions to deliver a message to you that I was delayed.' He was angry now, but with this Gaspard's failure to carry out his instructions, not with her.

Rose began to protest. 'There was really no one . . .' and then, remembering the persistent man in brown who'd approached her on her bench, she dissembled. 'Nobody spoke to me on the park bench where I was waiting.'

He looked happier and said again, 'Poor little thing.'

'Aren't you going to ask him where he was? I know I would,' put in Edy through her buttered toast.

'Someone set me off on a wild goose chase,' he said vaguely. 'That's why I sent Gaspard to get you. But you're certain you didn't meet anyone there?'

'No,' replied Rose firmly. Now that she was elevated to being the victim rather than the villain of the piece, she would not risk complicating his sympathy by admitting either to having run away from the brown man or to meeting Veronique. She repeated firmly, 'I stayed the whole time in the park, just as we arranged, until it was too cold and dark to remain there and then I came back here.'

He jumped up from the table, looking relieved, and kissed her on the forehead. 'She still looks pale, doesn't she, Edy? I think you two shouldn't venture outside for a couple of days. Stay strictly indoors and keep warm.'

As Patrick made to leave them, Edy looked at her cousin,

puffed, and said, 'Well, I'll ask it if you're too soft to: where are you off again now, Patrick?'

'Never you mind,' he replied archly, covering his annoyance with a tight smile.

'I'm sure Patrick is right, it's only sensible to stay inside today,' Rose said and he smiled his approval before he left them to their own, stale company. But after days spent in that frowsty hotel bed, Rose was overtaken with the need for fresh air. Patrick may have brushed off the failed interview with Mrs Van der Decken but she could not do so. What now of the plan? She needed to be outside to think.

While Edy inspected hairpieces that had been brought to the hotel for her consideration, Rose slipped away and out into the street. But before she had time to reach the corner, Veronique was by her side, almost as though she'd been waiting for her to appear.

'Hello. How strange to meet you here,' Rose said, discomposed. Since she had lied to Patrick about having seen no one in the park, she would have preferred their odd encounter to have been their only contact, with no inconvenient expectations of continued intimacy.

Veronique kissed her firmly on both cheeks, scolding, 'Rose, you did not return home as I advised.'

'No, as you see I'm still here. I was ill, but now I'm better,' Rose replied, smiling bravely. 'And now I'm off for a little constitutional by myself.' She rather hoped that Veronique would take the hint and let her be.

But Veronique, perhaps because she was half French, did not.

'How I love a constitutional – so nice, so English!' Taking Rose firmly by the arm, she said, 'We must stroll together to my *appartement*. I live in a place you call, in English, Beautiful Town. Doesn't that sound nice? You will come to drink tea with me. But one thing you must promise – you *must* compliment me on my tea or my poor English mother will roll over in her grave.'

'Your mother is dead?'

'Yes, she died. I think she died from a disappointed heart. But come with me, Rose, and I will tell you what became of little Veronique.'

Veronique hurried Rose through the streets, all the while talking with a kind of manic gaiety that fuelled the urgency with which she forced their pace. After her feverish days in bed, Rose felt dizzy as they climbed higher and higher, mounting narrow, cobbled ways as steep as goat tracks. She realised, with concern, that they had come to one of the poorer parts of Paris where children went without shoes, the hurrying men in long overcoats wore hats and side-locks, and the cafés had inscrutable foreign names. Behind every sinister samovar there seemed to lurk a knot of anarchists, behind every window a pair of thieving eyes.

They emerged in a small square, crowded with fruit and vegetable stalls, slippery underfoot with cabbage leaves, spoiled fruit and wet straw, and came to a stop outside a slumped and dejected dwelling. The ruin suggested the rustic origins of Belleville. This square might once have been a pasture high above the city, this hut a simple stable for beasts, and the loft above a store for dry feed or hay. But like a peasant come to town to find his fortune who had stayed too long, it had fallen among towny modernisers and improvers. So, the honest country fellow had been forced to adopt an urban mien the better to blend in. The opening into the hayloft, with hoist beam still in place, had grown a dirty window, furnished on either side by broken-slatted shutters, and the much-mended stable door had clothed itself in garish advertising posters and notices. But despite dissembling still it found itself jostled and pinioned on either side by expansionist neighbours whose spreading elbows and knees squeezed so hard it must soon be crushed entirely. However, for the present, the buildings on either side helped to delay collapse, although sagging shoulders and the skewed single eye showed that collapse was inevitable.

It was via this stable, useful as a storage place for market barrows and the secret den of cats, that Veronique's loft *appartement* was reached. She chivvied her guest up the ladder that poked through an opening in the ceiling, so that what greeted the visitor upon arrival was the close sight and smell of dirty floorboards.

As her head emerged into light, Rose looked up into her destination to discover the underside of the rotting thatch which, bulging and leaky as an ancient straw mattress, served as its ceiling. The space that lay between the floorboards and this moth-eaten lid was all taken up by furniture. The bed was pushed against one wall and loaded with a tangle of assorted coverings – a laddered woollen blanket cobbled from knitted squares, a silk coverlet faded and stiffened by stains, and a fur rug that might have come from an elderly grey dog Rose smelled an odour of unwashed human, ill-disguised by the heady scent of oponopax, and observed the slovenly practices of her hostess. The half-open door of the wardrobe showed that it was here, when she could afford them, that Veronique kept her coals rather than her clothes. These were thrown over the backs of the two chairs in the room, one of the wooden kitchen variety, the other a greasy, padded throne, its gold-painted curlicues chipped to reveal white plaster. The broken deal table that stood beneath the window, and the floor around it, was loaded with pots and pans, medicine and wine bottles, cups and glasses, all still holding sticky residues, dregs and slops.

Against one wall, to demarcate the bathing quarter, was placed a folding screen from behind which showed the lip of a shallow metal bath and soap-slimed floor. Next to this facility stood Veronique's dressing table with looking glass, brush and comb set, and cut-glass perfume bottles (the only neat and pretty things in the room). Veronique passed to and fro about her dwelling, lifting up and replacing objects with such delicacy that she suggested refinement, even elegance, in what she touched. Passing to the little stove whose chimney jutted through the roof, she unselfconsciously pulled some thatch for kindling from the habitual plucking place above her head and lit the wooden splinters in the stove, blowing to make them catch. Then she absently emptied a pan of leftovers out of the window, filled it with water from a large pitcher fetched from behind the screen, and set it to boil, poised as any society hostess.

'How nice it is to entertain,' remarked the gracious lady, in an exaggerated English accent. 'But please, my dear, sit by me, at the tea table.' Veronique gestured for Rose to take a seat, which she could only do by first transferring the assorted containers it supported to the floor. Repressing a queasy notion about the various uses of the water pitcher, Rose seated herself on the chair, which was the padded one of state, and wished that she might politely have protected her skirt with her handkerchief.

The water began to pop merrily on the glowing stove and Veronique spooned fragrant tea leaves from a canister labelled 'Horniman's'; the cosy scene of their tête-à-tête was staged. Veronique smoothly resumed her tale of the snares of tying oneself to an artist.

'So, my dear Rose, as you know, *pauvre Maman*, she gave up the ghost, she died. And little Veronique had only her *cher papa* to care for her, and she to care for him. But her papa grew more mad than ever, for now he cannot sell his paintings, cannot finish his paintings, cannot paint.' She snapped her fingers, as though snuffing out a candle flame. 'And all is the fault of his own little girl.'

Veronique stood to pour boiling water over the tea leaves and Rose, oppressed by the intense young woman and this close, squalid room, glanced towards the exit hole in the floor. Veronique noticed this impulse to flee and was suddenly solicitous. 'My dear, try my poor attempt at tea. And do not laugh that I forget when to put in the milk. What is the English good form? Is it first or must it be the last?'

'Oh, I don't think it really makes any difference,' Rose said, nervous not to cross her.

'But I have no milk!'

With this exclamation, Veronique leaned from the window

and called down to the milk cart that was stationed in the little square fronting her garret. She threw down a couple of coins, wrapped in a piece of paper, and a minute later the lad wobbled up her ladder with a measure of milk which he poured into the dirty glass she held for him.

Rose accepted her tea, with its scum of milk, and wondered what her mother would say about her taking this obviously contaminated stuff. But fear of giving offence, perhaps even plain fear, demanded that she accept and swallow the offering. She sipped and smiled at her hostess and, encouraged, Veronique once more took up her tale which she seemed unable to leave go of until it was all spun out.

'This is the time when I become model to my papa. Since domesticity has stolen his genius then the robber must pay,' she said, matter-of-factly. 'So I am placed to sleep on the floor of his studio – I mean he gave me a medicine so that I will sleep all day long – and I am become a dead child from "Murder of the Innocents". In truth,' she said, putting her hand confidentially upon Rose's cowering knee, 'I am every dead child in that canvas, boys and girls, for he change my position for each one he paints. Then I must stay kneeling for days as I am Ruth who begs permission to gather wheat at the feet of Boaz. You see I must suffer for his art. Oh, my father he made me many saints and good women from the 'Oly Bible: Genevieve on her deathbed, Irene bathing the wounds of Saint Sebastian, two of the righteous women kneeling at the tomb in Jerusalem.' Veronique paused to sip from her teacup. 'But he does not like this.' She put her hand to her wonderful copper hair. 'Too red, you understand. Red hairs are not the proper colour for a saint.'

'But it's so beautiful.' Rose smiled a grimace, anxious to please so that she might be allowed to leave this dreadful tea party.

'No, Rose, red is the colour of bad women. So, I am Cleopatra on her deathbed, with the serpent and the Magdalene – kneeling again. I am Salome holding a platter with a great cabbage on it to show the weight and proportion of the head of St John.'

Veronique laughed bitterly. 'You understand, if not aching knees then aching arms for whores.'

Rose winced at the word and Veronique said, 'Isn't that how it is said in English, without the "w" – like horse, *non*?'

'I believe so,' replied Rose unwillingly.

'Yes, as I say, whores. I must to pose as whores. And am I not anyway a very bad woman, for is not the model in the artist's studio no better than these whores, a fatal woman, *une femme fatale*?' Her eyes flashed and Rose stood to leave but Veronique darted out a hand and held her by the wrist with surprising force and made her resume her seat.

'Every day I must stand or lie or sit and he paints and paints and paints over until there is nothing left but mud on his canvas and still he must paint until I cry with the cold or faint with the heat and the hunger and the loneliness! And still he continues, like a mad man. For this is what an artist is, my little Rose. He is nothing more than a monster. He must turn all to his art, whether he is a great artist or a bad, like my papa; he must create and all around are sacrifice!' She stopped then, panting with her passion. For a moment the sounds of the market below intruded into that still, charged room.

Veronique resumed, 'Then my papa, he dies. His body it already decomposes, even before it is cold. It smells dreadful, of brandy and linseed oil. And then what is to become of Veronique? No education, no trade – her only skill is to stand still and not cry very much, her only treasure is this whore's 'air. If she is not to end her days *une fille publique à vingt sous*, her profession must be as the model to artists. And artists, they like me – now my hair is the right colour for the times, *non? Toute à la mode*. And I am poor and I will do what I am bid because that is how my papa taught me to be, for men holding paintbrushes in their hands.'

Veronique was now so flaring and intent that Rose was really afraid of her, all too aware that she had let herself become trapped in this rancid room, in a poor part of Paris that she did not know, with a woman who appeared to be descending into madness.

'Here, Veronique, take this,' said Rose, trying to placate the lunatic with the offering of a valuable. 'It belonged to my mother, it's gold . . .' Perhaps robbery was the point behind the kidnap; she could think of nothing else to offer of value.

But Veronique jumped up and dashed the ring from her, saying, 'You can't pay me off. Didn't I tell you I will cling on till I die. Don't you understand, I am born and bred to play this part?' She looked haughtily down on Rose. 'I suffer!'

Rose stood too, looking desperately for an escape route.

'My pretty English rose, run home now, run home to Mummy and Daddy!' Veronique jeered in a low, threatening voice. 'Little rich girl, run as fast as you can from the fox lest it gobble you up.'

'Veronique, I think you have upset yourself remembering your childhood. I am sorry for you and I will try to get some money to help you start a new and happier life. Please,' she could not stop her voice from trembling in her fear and desperation, 'I must go now.'

And she ran from the rank lair, clattering down the ladder, through the door and out into the street of this unfamiliar part of Paris. She stumbled through the market stalls looking for an escape from the girl in the attic. But where was she? She knew that they had not walked far from the quarter of Paris in which stood the familiar Gare du Nord. If she could find the courage to ask for directions to the station, there was a chance she would recognise her way back to the hotel. But whom to ask? She came upon a large cemetery, occupied by the ghostly shapes of the unfortunates who wander where there is anonymity. She quailed at stopping one of these, and kept her head low so as not to meet the eyes of anyone and walked purposely away, trying not to look behind for a following fury with red hair.

# Chapter 17

When Rose found the Hotel du Nord, the lady with the hairpieces had gone, leaving Edy to sit before the dressing-table mirror and approve of the fringe of curls that she had glued along her hairline. Her gimlet eye found Rose in the mirror and she remarked, 'It's useless to follow him. I tried but he moved too fast for my little legs.'

'I don't know what you mean,' she replied, and indeed she didn't.

'Patrick, you idiot!' the confidential friend informed her through the hairpin that she held in her mouth. She turned to look at Rose. 'That's why I commissioned a hotel porter to track him to his hiding place.' She waited for a reaction and, when none came, went on, 'Isn't that why you scarpered after him this morning?'

No reply.

'Rose, you *have* wondered where it is he disappears off to every day, haven't you?'

'I know where he goes.'

'Really you do not,' replied her cousin.

'To his mother, Mrs Van der Decken,' responded Rose stupidly.

Edy goggled briefly at her. 'Does his mother live in a garret on the rue Jacob?' She shook her new curls at Rose. 'No? Then I rest my case.'

Cabbing it to the sixth arrondissement, they passed along the quai de Montebello, catching glimpses of the sparkling Seine between the booksellers' stalls. On this brilliant autumn midday, Paris deserved its name, City of Light. Its buildings, river, people showed themselves off to best effect, confident beneath the revealing sun. But to Rose the brightness was too stark, she shrank from it.

At the address on the rue Jacob, Edy paid off the concierge and they climbed up a winding staircase and turned the key in the lock of Patrick's atelier. The remains of his meal, a hardened crust and rind of cheese, were still on the plate and the cushions on the chair were dented by his use. Canvases were ranged about the wall, his paints, brushes and easel awaited him. All unsuspecting, Patrick had closed the door on these and the secret life he led there, so that as they opened it a shut-up ghost fled.

They saw that Patrick had been in the process of sewing his paintings into hessian covers, perhaps for transportation. Rose went closer to examine one as yet unparcelled canvas and suddenly the gash of red that she had taken for some abstract diagonal of colour on a creamy ground resolved itself into red hair that spilled like liquid metal through the teeth of a wide comb and down a sinuous back.

She took the palette knife from the easel and approached one of the shrouded paintings. She ripped through its hessian wrappings to look. Copper again. Still the model's head was turned away, as though to conceal her identity, but that blazing hair was her brand. In the next the glorious colour was muted in shadows, glowing a darker red, like the pulse of dying coals. Half hidden, half disclosed by the screen in the foreground, she knelt naked in a shallow bath, dreamily sponging the green-blue skin, pale and cool against sumptuous purple-flecked shadow and that smouldering red. Rose's eyes skidded away to a puddle of beige paint, cut in two by the edge of the canvas, and knew it for a water pitcher.

Then she showed her face to Rose. Beneath another hessian cover she sat enthroned, the queenly head inclined, as though she looked down imperiously at a courtier who knelt at her feet.

'I know her,' Rose said sadly, but before Edy could reply they heard a voice singing up the long, winding staircase. He finished with a flourish as he pushed open the door to the attic: '*Vive le son, vive le son, vive le son de l'explosion!*'

Sick with the evidence on every canvas in the studio, Rose was shocked to realise that she was smiling. So he discovered her standing there, surrounded by Veronique, and wearing the grimace of hurt a child has who's just been smacked.

'I met her,' she stated dully. She felt drained of every other emotion now but sadness.

He came cautiously over, perhaps still expecting explosions, and answered, 'I know.'

He was panting, perhaps from the long climb up to the garret. Gathering himself to say more, he noticed Edy, who was bending down to examine a painting, full of light, that showed Veronique's window on to the square.

'I might have expected to find *you* here,' he said dismissively.

Rose went over to her cousin and put her arms round her. 'Please, Edy,' she said quietly. 'Please leave us.'

And, perhaps for the first time in her life, Edy let pass the opportunity for a *mot*. She trotted across the room, docile as a lamb, and left.

They watched her leave and then he started to speak, low and steady. 'I am not a very honourable man, Rose. You probably realised this of me.'

She looked away.

'But I have tried always to behave honourably to you . . .'

His words recalled their last confrontation in the hotel drawing room where, it now seemed to her, he'd bamboozled her with talk of his tremendous probity in keeping her pure.

'I don't care about being treated honourably.' How she hated the dishonesty of that word! 'But you do owe me the truth.'

He gave her an odd, appraising look, cleared his throat and pressed on. 'You met someone yesterday I would not have had you meet – to save my feelings as well as yours.'

He paused, as though to assess whether it was safe to continue.

'Because I rejected her for your sake, she made it her business to discover where we were to meet and then tricked me into leaving you there so that she could come to you in my place and do her worst.'

'Did you ruin her? Did you ruin that poor girl's life too?' Rose asked, trying to keep control over her trembling lips.

'No, I don't believe I did, for she was a very unhappy girl when first I met her and I was a very young, unformed man.' He kept his voice flat, reasonable, as though he believed any spark might set her off.

She replied bluntly, 'You have made her unhappier still.'

'I was a very young man,' he repeated, 'one full of idealised notions of leading the bohemian life here and I thought that I was a very fine fellow, with my coterie of cynics—'

'And tarts!' she interrupted. He flinched at that flash of spirit from her.

'Whatever else she may be', he answered, 'Veronique is not one of those.'

He reached for her, or perhaps it was to relieve her of the palette knife that she still held among the folds of her dress, but she stepped back and asked, heart in throat, 'Does that mean you married her?'

He shook his head briefly. 'No. No, we are not married but, you understand, I lived a life here, or I tried to live a life, that was founded on something more honest than those tired old codes.'

She did not respond and he carried on, his voice less even. 'My artistic brothers and I had the highest, the purest ideals for ourselves in everything, nothing less than a brave new order. We came together to celebrate friendship, love, art and literature.' He smiled grimly and shook his head. 'And what did we do but sit in cafés and drink ourselves insensible and mock the hypocrisy of the petit bourgeoise. The whole thing was a sham!' He had grown passionate, the need to go gently, to disarm, forgotten. 'In the end I knew those talentless hangers-on for what they were: nothing. They were nothing, Rose, and they made nothing. And our lives celebrated nothing but debauchery and squalor.' He shook his head again, as though to shake away the memory. 'And she, she fed off it, like a big glossy fly.'

'But you did love her once?' she challenged, for the tender beauty of all those paintings could not be denied.

'I thought so,' he replied unwillingly. 'She seemed to need my love and I was flattered by that. I offered up everything for her, when I was naive enough to think that would be enough. My own father disowned me because of her and the life I led here.' He paused, as though to contemplate that sacrifice, and tried to come nearer, but she retreated again. She needed to think clearly and see the truth through this fog of pain and words.

'But now your Paris plan has all unravelled, hasn't it? Admit it, you only came back here to break off ties with her, hoping your father would relent.' She saw more clearly now. 'Meanwhile I was to charm your mother out of her money. And failing all that, you might still have a chance at me and my dowry!'

'Rose, you make me out to be an evil genius.' He tried to appear amused though she noticed that he bit his lips. 'If I did come back to settle with her, it was only because I owed her that. Even if I could not be accused of ruining her,' he laughed shortly at that notion, 'I needed to do the right thing by her.'

She turned from him.

'And as for all the rest, you must believe me, darling, my only reason for bringing you and Edy here was so that when I was clear of her and all this mess, we two could properly be together and I could ask you to marry me.'

He sounded so beseeching, so contrite, but she would not soften, she would not cry.

'You didn't feel the need to rid yourself of these, though.' She indicated the pictures, readied for shipping.

'In my blackest mood I intended to burn them all,' he replied. 'Truly I did, Rose. But to destroy my art – they are my best work.'

'They are *all* Veronique,' she said simply.

'Rose, don't just see her.'

'I can see only her.'

'Darling, think of them as arrangements of fruit upon a plate, the impression of under-ripe peaches and pale melon flesh – just colour and form.' He pulled the ripped hessian aside to reveal more of the paintings and pointed to the bather. 'Look here. This is what fascinates me, Rose, this half-inch of light coming in under the door and the effect of shadow. See how, instead of just using black, these strokes of different colours put together make them seem to crawl like real shadows.' He turned an eager face to her.

Rose, now purged of that first emotion of shocked recognition, looked again. 'But what makes them beautiful is love,' she observed sadly.

He hung his head and said almost desperately, 'But darling, I told you, that's long over. I stopped being able to paint her when I realised she was only another poisoned flower growing from this dung heap!' He seemed to crush something between his hands. 'To work seriously, to make something good, I need someone who truly arouses those feelings of love in me, someone I can feel more than pity or contempt for.' He reached out his hand for her and pleaded, 'That is you, Rose, only you. Save me from myself, darling, please.'

She would not reply, but it was because the tears stuck in her throat prevented it.

'My Rose without a thorn.'

He took the knife from her and she surrendered and came to him at last. They stood and held each other for a moment, both weeping now.

'I should go to Edy. Heaven knows what she must be thinking,' she said, breaking away.

He smiled at her. 'Darling, I will destroy all these right now.' He spoke as though this undertaking was the final, desperate pledge that would sever him from that unsatisfactory past. 'After it's done I'll come to the hotel and we'll decide together what to do next.'

Despite herself, her heart leapt with hope.

He crossed to the canvases and then, as though summoned, Rose looked again at the regal portrait of Veronique and glimpsed quite another story. For this was not a queen on her throne, but just a girl sitting on an old theatrical prop, face lit by the one whose head had just emerged through the hole in the floor, the sock she'd been darning for him neglected in her lap. Here was an intimacy she'd never known with Patrick, the evidence of an everyday love that pricked sharper than all Veronique's possessive spite.

'I love you,' he said, crossing over to the canvas, as though everything was settled.

But even those words, the ones she longed to hear, could not match the power of that view into Patrick and Veronique's shared lives. It sent Rose hurrying over to the door and away from him, down the twisting staircase and back onto the street. It seemed as though in an hour winter had arrived on the rue Jacob. Sleet now slapped the pavements and the people scattered blindly under their umbrellas. Shivering in her inadequate clothes, Rose reached her hotel bedroom and found Edy already busy among dressmakers' and milliners' black glazed boxes and pyramids of pasteboard, packing up the spoils of her Parisian shopping raid.

'I must leave – at once,' Rose announced in a voice that trembled.

Edith, well aware that the party was ended, continued steadily to pack, saying over her shoulder only, 'Had enough of frivoling? I rather thought that might be the case since we learn that old mother McKinley won't stump up.'

'I just think it's time to go home now,' Rose replied, grateful to Edith for not mentioning the showdown in the atelier.

'Not that I personally care about coin, but the fascinating Patrick is turning into rather a *digger*. Even old Edy's purse is getting dangerously light.'

'What do you mean?'

'Didn't you guess, darling? Your elopement's my treat,' replied Edy sourly. 'Since your *inamorato* hasn't a bean, young love's dream is all at my expense. So, as you may imagine, I'm getting rather short.'

Enlightenment struck Rose another blow. It seemed to her then that all her past life had been nothing but false confidences and lies.

Edy came over to her. 'Naturally a girl should look for more in her heart's music than the clink of gold and the rustle of banknotes but a little bit of private income is always a welcome thing.' She stroked Rose's forehead and said, almost kindly, 'Best write it off as experience and hie us back home again.'

They'd bundled up the evidence of their Paris jaunt, leaving the Hotel du Nord before Patrick, satisfied that he'd diffused the bomb, had time to intercept them. So Rose returned from the elopement-that-wasn't, battered but intact, by the same route of uncomfortable trains, dreary hotels and queasy sea voyage, back to her Yorkshire home and dull, ordinary, ineffably honourable Mapus and Papus.

# Chapter 18

Another November day and to the young woman who sat with book in hand, before the window that overlooked the drive, life seemed to hold exactly the same prospect of endless reverie as it had in the spring of the year, before the brief season of her 'coming out'. But those giddy weeks had brought about a revolution, for she had apparently come so far out that now there could be no going back. Rose, fresh in her youth and loveliness, was spoiled. The worm was in the bud, which condition even the hermetic glass dome that had been popped back over her head could not arrest or disguise. Exposure to the corrupt world had evidently blighted her and she might ever remain contagious to respectable society. Two months ago she had condescended to be Marion's friend and Edy had chaffed her for her ridiculous naivety. Now she was Marion's moral inferior and she endangered Edy's innocence. And so she sat and read and helped Mapus with the household and wept. She had learned, if nothing else, that renunciation is a woman's lot and only men have licence to rebel. The inconstant man may smile a wry smile and be excused his lapse, but only misery and self-blame became the compromised woman. She submitted to it because submission was the contract she had made with her parents. The terms were harsh but she had nothing left to bargain with since her season of liberty and fun hadn't brought in their proper return of a husband.

She looked up from her book and was surprised by a flimsy black, red and orange butterfly that buffeted her window.

'It is too late,' she said to it. 'Didn't you know? Summer's over, all the other butterflies are flown.'

Jumping up, Rose wandered, on restless feet, around the house, full of contemptuous pity for the self she had outlived: the nascent creature she seemed to meet around every corner, pirouetting in her childish fancy dress and tambourine. She reached her bedroom and fell upon the bed. Rose concluded that if a girl's life must be all passion or a failure, then she had failed – and barely eighteen.

Indolently, she rang the bell for Joan. Poor Joan, without her John – they could cry together.

There had been a deal of crying, and shouting, to be heard ringing around that house of iron since she'd run back to it. At first the shouting had predominated. Her father had been beside himself with an inarticulate rage, so uncontrolled that it frightened her. Days and days of it she'd endured. Though she'd cowered and wept and admitted her fault, his anger had seemed without let, without diminution. She'd hardened at last under the unremitting lash of fury and defied him: would no longer listen, no longer care that he couldn't forgive what she'd done to him. Even Mapus had dissented at the rigour of his telling-off, reasoning that Rose had committed a social misstep rather than a mortal sin. There *were* worse things in the world! For, though the mother hen was programmed to dispatch her chick from the nest, Elizabeth-Jane was still a mother hen and would cluck and chivvy and make the best of her fledgling's untidy return to it. She banished her husband to his study to crow out his masculine hurt and defiance, for she understood that time and forgiveness together mend. And, after all, hadn't the cousins' flighty trip to Paris been chiefly a shopping expedition? With McKinley safely put behind them there was, to her mind, nothing material to stop Rose from having another turn at courting next year.

But Rose was not so sanguine about her lost love. She choked herself into convulsions, at first careless of her sore throat and stinging eyes. Then she wept long and low, eking out the agony. Then, having learned the trick of it, she cried quietly and economically for hours, without damage. Latterly, like a tobacco fiend, she must daily indulge the habit, finding the facilitators of tears where she may, since the mere thought of Patrick was a stimulant dulled by over-use. Nowadays, as she sat by her window, she chose to read from books of melancholic verse or those that concerned the early deaths of infants, stimuli that left her washed up on a bank of almost pleasurable exhaustion.

Joan, her sole ally, the only one who understood, came hollow-eyed into the room, with a cursory bob.

'What is it now, miss?'

'Don't be pert. We know each other well enough to share our true feelings, don't we, Joan? I know it's a comfort to me.'

Joan sat heavily on the bed beside her and said, 'I'd rather you read about feelin's out o' that new book as talk about mine and yours.'

Rose took up at random *A Woman's Patience* and opened it but did not look at it.

'Have you still heard nothing from him?' she pressed.

Joan let out a sullen, 'No.'

'Do you know none of the other servants at Fell Top to ask about him?'

'No, miss.'

'Oh Joan,' said Rose, with a gusty sigh, 'what are we to do?' and tipped herself into tears. They cried together then. But, as they wept, Rose looked at Joan's raw misery and thought how pale and familiar her own grief had grown. She put her arm round her maid comfortingly and said, 'I'm sorry, Joan, I didn't mean to provoke you. Now, stop crying and wipe your eyes.' She went on, encouragingly, 'What shall we do to take your mind off it and cheer you up?'

Joan sniffed and Rose picked up the book and began to read.

*'You see,' said Madge Madeley to Mrs Flora Bannatyne one day, 'Connie had so much patience; she was content to trust and hope – and wait! The end of it is, she has gained all hearts – her husband's included.'*

*'Yes,' said Mrs Bannatyne thoughtfully. 'Long ago I marvelled at her indomitable patience.'*

*'Do you know, I think patience is an attribute of great characters only? A small, undisciplined nature gives way to fretfulness and complaint the moment it is thwarted.'*

But, unaccountably, literature did not salve. Rose shut the book and flung it from her so that it hit the wall.

Then both girls hugged again and laughed through their tears.

Alone in his study, Robert Seaton, holding a chipped cup in his tender hand, looked back as though across a great and mysterious gulf to another country, another age, where he had once belonged.

So many years he'd lived and all of them seemed to him now to have been unsatisfactory, insubstantial. Of what could he boast? Weakly he'd hidden his mediocrity behind the edifice of his father's achievements and bluffed a position in the world but, with little vision or enthusiasm to shore it up, his father's empire had crumbled quietly away. Now even that notable structure could no longer provide cover for his failure as a man. The spiteful phrase 'clogs to clogs' repeated in his head to tease and torment. It was his secret fear and he denied it with bombast and prideful temper.

Once only, it seemed to him now, he'd felt what it was to be a man of substance: on the day his daughter had been born, his Rose, the dearest thing in the world to him, his cause to hope.

He chuckled to remember that Carr had sent his jocular commiserations upon the announcement of the birth, and reassurances that the next must be a boy. But there'd been no next, there had been no boy, and he'd not been sorry for it. Never! He'd felt satisfied to have his little lass.

But even as a father he'd not been able to do his job right, he'd not managed to keep her forever safe in that iron-bound house he'd built around her. He'd not managed to find for her that man who understood the times and would do a better job than he at keeping this third generation from clogs. Somehow she had slipped away from him, swept off to where he could no longer reach her. He stood up and put the cup back in its place on the mantelshelf. This age does not suit me, he thought sadly to himself.

Iron Robert cried into his hands. A lifetime, his whole long lifetime, had passed him by and he'd done nothing on his own account, it seemed, but stoke up this head of impotent rage.

# Chapter 19

So the singular year of 1897 wound itself up in the usual shortening of days. But, for Rose, as they dwindled, so they pinched. Winter weather's hardening grip was matched by social bounds that keep her tight within the circumference of a diminished world. For though Mapus would do her best to re-introduce her daughter back into society, it would require the same deft observance of form as was employed by the recently bereaved. This year's end there would be no seasonal celebrations: no balls, no carol singing, no outings for Rose, only subdued clothing and quiet visits to close family.

Mapus duly proposed that her daughter's first engagement should be with Cousin Albert's wife, Emma. Appropriate, to be sure, but also a safe bet. That lady couldn't very well refuse to receive them since her own daughter had been instrumental in the Paris debacle. In fact Mapus had to draw on all her forbearance not to place a deal of blame on Edith's silly head for leading a younger girl astray; nevertheless, the senior Mrs Seaton was the perfect choice.

Rose was less certain about being paraded for her approval and indeed she was right not to expect delicacy of feeling. Emma Seaton's opening salvo was, 'So, the black sheep!' For, after all, hadn't the mother had the training of the daughter? 'Sit yourselves. I'm afraid you will have to make do with me alone. Both the youngsters are away from home at the present.' She looked quizzically at her niece to judge how she might react to this piece of news.

'Guy's shooting in the Highlands with a friend and Edy has left us to go up to Harrogate for a cure,' she amplified.

Lucky Edy, thought Rose. Her 'cure' is at a comfortable fashionable resort; mine is to be taken, with hard commons, at home.

'Still, you won't be after lively company in your condition,' speculated her hostess.

Rose must content herself with the rebellious thought that she'd done nothing worse than kiss a man, to whom she was not formally engaged, in the public rooms of a hotel, albeit a French one. She bowed her head and listened as the matrons talked on in their low, inconsequential murmur, about her and above her, using the muted, mournful tones suited to discussing the terminally ill or newly dead. They seemed to find their comfort in the age-old talk of all the earthly woes that men were heir to and that women must bear.

What precisely is it that, if I *had* committed it, would have done me such irreparable, irreversible damage, Rose thought to herself, while you two, with your wedding bands, are sanctioned by the state, blessed by society and encouraged by the church to do?

Thus she mutely defied them and the two lawful wives went on with their mild complaining and their tea, ignoring her.

The following week the circle widened a little further to re-admit Edith, back from Harrogate. Washed clean of blame and starved of gossip, Edy had issued a peremptory invitation to her unshriven cousin to call upon her for a spot of remedial teasing.

The door was opened by tall John and Rose jumped to see him standing there, buttoned up stiff in his uniform. She'd meant to have it out with him if she chanced upon him during this visit to Fell Top. Only the previous day she'd found poor Joan in the laundry cupboard weeping over that locket of his. By the look of the nasty little thing, Rose thought he probably bought them cheap by the dozen – and, she guessed, distributed them by the dozen. How dare he treat her poor Joan so? But now that he stood before her, six foot two of cool denial, she held her tongue. How could she presume? For who in the world can rightly know what passes between a man and a woman? Only the insensitive or the ill-informed meddle there, she decided, and curtly handed him her gloves.

Unbending as a poker, he showed her to the library where Edy was writing postcards from Harrogate. She looked up, pen in mouth. 'Simply hadn't the time while I was there. Anyway, no one'll be the wiser. They'll all have Yorkshire postmarks.'

'Hello, Edy,' said Rose.

'Hello, Rose,' she replied, indolently offering her a cheek. 'Poor you. I'm glad we don't share a father. D'you know how mine greeted me upon my return? "Have you been away?"' She mimicked his distracted affability. 'He simply can't be bothered with getting angry.'

Rose responded, trying to sound breezy – it was wise not to indulge in self-pity in front of her cousin. 'An explosion was only to be expected from my father, I suppose.'

'I don't know what all the upset is about, really I don't. All frightfully unnecessary and Victorian. I mean to say, *is* there a novel nowadays that doesn't feature an *enceinte* maiden of good birth?'

Rose remained impassive and Edy softened her teasing with a laugh. 'Quite apart from elopements and gay Paree, I consider that you have let the side down by staying so absolutely, resolutely, unseduced. Goodness, darling, despite every imaginable opportunity, you're probably still the most innocent girl alive in Yorkshire!'

'Quite right, Edy. I remain, as ever, depressingly unfashionable,' she answered, sounding glibber than she felt. 'Just the same, dull old me.' Though she said it, she knew it was not the truth. If not *ruined*, then she was altered beyond repair. Truly it felt as though something had been damaged deep inside her. Perhaps her heart was broken.

Edy looked around herself and, having tiptoed to the door to check no one listened at it, she whispered, 'Have you heard from him since we got back?'

Rose bit her lip, her eyes filling with those too easy, betraying tears.

'Never mind,' said Edy, trying to sound sympathetic. 'Neither have I.'

At that moment Guy came into the room, loudly blowing his nose. On seeing them start guiltily apart he stopped and affected elaborate surprise to cover his embarrassment.

'Rose, as I live and breathe! The last time I saw you must have been at that midsummer's ball we held to mark the jubilee. Was it really half a year and more ago? D'you remember?'

'Shhh!' admonished Edy, indicating the tearful Rose. 'You clot, that was when your scoundrelly friend, cause of all the fuss, first made up to the dear girl.'

'Oh, sorry,' said Guy, looking abashed. 'It's just that it really was a ripping party and you looked stunning that night. Still do,' he added, anxious not to commit another faux pas.

'I don't believe so,' said Rose, taking his hand. 'Too much crying has ruined my looks.'

'Nothing about you is ruined, Rose my love,' squawked Edy, who didn't like to go so long without being the centre of the floor and the main source of controversy and dismay. 'Pure as the driven, as I can attest before witnesses.' She put her hand to her heart and Rose blushed to be branded so. 'Anyway, as I was saying, nowadays *les aventures amoureuses* don't count a fly unless done thoroughly – one must have had an infant fathered upon one by the seducer. Mustn't one?' she inquired brightly.

* * *

In the effort to stay clear of her father, and with so few places of resort to hide herself, Rose took to wandering about the winter countryside. She went as far as the encroaching tide of Sheffield's new suburbs which lapped ever further from the mainspring, observing that, as the tram routes went out, so the dwellings went up until every green hill and prospect must soon be lost beneath a wilderness of eyesores in between. The spoiled countryside matched well her gloomy frame of mind which looked for, and found, ugliness and ruination. It seemed to Rose that the earth itself had lost its innocence and all for the sake of nasty red-brick row houses with a pub on every corner. She wondered crossly whether anyone but herself felt that there was escape and consolation in lovely old things and in natural beauty; she had conceived such an intense nostalgia for their rapid passing.

In her rambles she often walked out towards Eckersby, retracing that sentimental route through the Seaton woods, past the gamekeeper's cottage, and down the deep lane between the plenteous summer hedgerows, now impoverished by winter. On one occasion she recognised at a distance the long stride of Harold Webb coming in her direction. It recalled the last time he'd come across her walking here, when he'd nearly punched Patrick on the nose. She leapt into a ditch full of frosty leaves to avoid him and from this hiding place observed that, though he was a handsome man, in her opinion sullen black looks were inferior to Patrick's flamboyant beauty.

On her return home it was already beginning to be dusk so she cut warily across Webb's farmland to shorten the way. The farmhouse looked so still and quiet, she came closer, approaching obliquely, through the apple orchard. Like a sneak thief, she crept up to the sitting-room window. There was Marion, dozing. Rose lifted her hand to tap the glass, and stopped herself. After her weeks of seclusion, she was not yet ready for exposure to the world outside her family sphere. She could not bear to look into Marion's blameless face and wonder: does she know? Rose sprang away from the window, her heart making dry, clenched knocks inside her chest and, looking back over her shoulder to check that no one from the farmhouse had noticed her, ran straight into the broad front of Harold Webb.

'You may go in by the door, you know,' he commented drily.

'I saw that she slept and thought I'd best leave her,' Rose dissembled, breathless with the shock of being discovered and cross that he was perhaps poking fun at her.

'I'm sure you'd be a welcome diversion.'

'Oh, I couldn't. I mean I couldn't wake her.'

'I wish you would. I reckon she sleeps too much.' He sounded more natural, kinder, as he spoke of Marion's well-being.

'But she must need her rest.'

'What our Marion needs more of is to be taken out of herself. She has too much rest, and not enough company, for her own good. We all turn to brooding when we lack for human contact and conversation.'

His tender appeal made her respond generously, decisively. 'Well, I *shall* visit her,' though she felt as unsure as an anchorite invited to a court ball.

Mrs Webb met them at the door with her old familiar courtesy, the warmth of which carried Rose over the threshold and into the sitting room before she could lose momentum. Harold roused his sister, then left the two girls to their chat.

Though still a little subdued and ruffled by sleep, Marion's delight in seeing her friend again was unmistakably genuine and warm. Rose dared to hope for the unforced intimacy that had grown between them in the summer and her chance to confide at last. For, if Edy had shared in the Paris flit, the damaged heart she'd carried home with her might only be trusted to gentle Marion. But, even if they did not speak only of conventional topics, each seemed to be holding back a little, waiting for a disclosure of the other's truer feelings. Though Rose could read the sympathetic understanding in her friend's eyes that seemed to welcome openness, how could she unburden here, where she knew romantic love was not considered?

As they parted, Rose warmly promised to return soon, feeling obscurely sad that while their reunion had gone off well enough, it had done nothing to bring her relief. Realising it never could, she resolved not to call there again.

At the front door, Harold appeared and offered to drive her home in his mother's trap. She declined, saying she'd rather take the quick route, on foot, but he walked along by her side, his hand hovering somewhere near, but not quite touching, her elbow. They continued in this way uncomfortably silent until they reached the path through the woods.

'Thank you for escorting me, I've only a very short way to go now. It will be quite safe. I mean, these are our family woods and the gamekeeper will be about.' She held out her hand to shake his in farewell.

'I meant to walk with you all the way,' he said gruffly.

'There's no need for that, really. I can take care of myself quite well.'

He stretched his lips into a lofty smile under his black moustache and walked back towards the farmhouse. Rose returned to her lonely home irritated that he should always be thrusting his protection upon her.

# Chapter 20

On a crisp March morning Rose and Marion sat out together on the farmhouse veranda, each in her swaddling of blankets and rugs, like two big, placid babies put out to air.

True, she'd have been welcome to call at Fell Top and had sworn off Webb's Farm but Rose had come to realise that she was more in sympathy with Marion's wounded withdrawal from life than with her cousin's remorseless engagement with it. And though Marion's hibernation was habitual and Rose's self-imposed, these last winter months they had both surrendered to its charms, each content in her inertia. For, as is often the case with people who pass a great deal of time together, they'd grown more and more to resemble each other. Rose found that the gentle regimen and Mrs Webb's baking suited her. In short, she'd begun to enjoy ill health. And Marion learned to appreciate the delicious sedative of literature. So, as January had passed her by and now February, Rose had sunk further into quiescence and maudlin novels as though into a deep, warm, chloral sleep.

Today, as they sat out together, Rose, in dreadful betrayal of neglected Joan who pined still for her John, read aloud from Emma Jane Worboise's *Husbands and Wives*. She did not read at random. Although the girls had finally begun to talk again with their old affection and found that they shared settled opinions on everything under the sun, Rose longed for complete candour between them. In her most secret heart, she still believed that marriage and children were her destiny, not the self-denying spinsterhood Marion had reconciled herself to.

Looking up from the page she said rather pointedly, 'And so, Marion dear, we reach today's moral: "*Still it is good that every woman should have her own husband and her own home. Married life, in spite of all its cares and crosses, is by far the happiest and most blessed state for women.*" But you do not believe that, do you?' she challenged.

Marion answered her, rather guardedly, 'On the contrary, I believe marriage is a very fine thing, for others.'

'But what else should a woman be or do if she doesn't marry?'

'Women have other choices, don't they?' replied Marion, still on the defensive. 'Nowadays, since we're all advanced and emancipated, we may have careers of our own.'

The two swaddled girls looked out over the greening fields in contemplation of this idea. Rose imagined one of those unhappy women with wispy moustaches who thump at typewriters. Apparently Marion, too, shied away from the option of working for one's living, and promptly backtracked.

'However, it seems to me that even if your girl of today is blessed with a tough, first-class brain as well as robust good health,' she paused to cough, as though in illustration of her own disqualification, 'it must be said her choices are limited. She may go to the university and yet she will be denied her degree. And should your brave, clever girl qualify for the Bar, still she does not win the right to practise. Of course, superhuman determination may qualify her to work as doctor or dentist to other women. But, as for the girl of modest talent and resolve, her highest aim can be only to enter the inferior walks of a business life.'

So, back to typewriters. Rose, who suspected that she was herself of modest brain and knew for a certainty that she lacked superhuman determination, grimaced at that. No doubt this dilemma was genuine, for so they were informed by the most humourless newspapers, the most advanced books), but why ever would one choose work over love and marriage? Then it struck her that, even after months of intimacy and reading, she still could not unpack her real regrets and hopes to her friend.

'Isn't it stupid then that women are educated at all, if their education's only use is to school their daughters who in turn may not use it?' she said dismissively.

Marion, as though relieved that the queasy topic of what was to become of them was safely past, made a joke of it. 'Dear Rose, since we are daily informed that all women are unbalanced from their earliest youth and subject to intermittent physiological emergencies and irrationality ever after, perhaps the only course open to the persistently unmarried is to be shut up in mental asylums.'

'Women really are a terrible problem, aren't they?'

'It is a wonder that women are allowed to exist at all!' concluded Marion.

Rose laughed but was not satisfied. Perhaps, like the awakening world, she too felt the stir of spring today. For, if the bland diet of languishing anaesthetised a damaged heart, it was no stiffener for the moral fibre, no spur to be about the painful business of living again, and she had begun to understand that she was no longer satisfied with observing the world from a divan. Rose considered ruefully that her sisterly companion had settled upon her role of chronic ill health. But she herself had not. No, for her, marriage remained the magical future prospect in which anything might become of one. Just let fate and biology decide.

In this spirit of rebellion, she realised she was actually looking forward to talking to Harold that evening when he joined his sister after work. He at least brought something of the outside world. Marion was a dear, but the liveliest hour of the long day was his, even if it was animated by controversy.

At that day's end, while Harold sat with them as he was accustomed, Marion repeated some of the discussion they'd been having earlier about the 'woman problem'. Having listened to Marion's complaint about the impossibility of being a woman in a world engineered chiefly by, and for the advantage of, men, he replied, 'I'd say the greater question is what it means to be a man in the present age.'

They both laughed at his cussedness.

'Don't you girls see you've got it all the wrong way about? Yours is the freer, the more fortunate sex.'

'How can you say that, Harry?' Marion rebuked, happily roused to the fight, 'Women have such narrow lives. What freedom have we to choose how we live?'

'Well, Marion, it seems to me that nowadays a woman who has a brain and is not forced by absolute necessity to work has greater scope than a man to live life for its own sake. You should ask yourself, what freedom has a man, unless he is independently wealthy, but to work and strive and wear himself out in the scrimmage of some form of trade?'

Rose remembered the pleasure he found in his Saturday hobby of drawing and felt a tiny stab of sympathy for this man who must grind out his days at her father's office. But she could not allow his rhetoric to put her off.

'You men are suited to it,' she challenged. 'You know you all love to stick out your elbows and trample the world under foot in your big boots, jangling the coins in your pockets.' Her model of a man she based on her own father, someone who defined himself, it seemed to her, by his title of iron *master* and by his loud and belligerent satisfaction in it.

Harold smiled. 'Perhaps you're right, Miss Seaton. But who does he do it for? What motivates him to get ahead, fight wars, make money in a business he perhaps hates, if not the woman he loves and the reposeful home she makes for him?' He added, more quietly, 'If he's lucky enough to get her.'

'Ah, the angel in the house.' Marion guffawed. 'Harry, you're no'but a stick in the mud!'

'I know, I know,' he conceded. 'Men are. It's you women,

rushing on ahead, re-inventing the world, that make it so difficult for us poor men to keep up.'

Marion laughed. 'What possible influence do women have over the way the world's run?'

'Women are geniuses at it! They don't realise (or are too busy complaining to see it) that it's women's whims affect everything a man is, or tries to be. For good, or ill.'

'Harry, you talk a lot of rot, but I do like to be acknowledged a genius,' commented Marion.

Rose ganged up with her against him. 'And I like the choice of good *or* ill.' She went on, 'But if our *genius* is only this instinctual sway over men who, you can't deny, have all the real power, what use is there in us being taught to think beyond the hearth and the cradle? Isn't training for anything else a waste or, worse, a source of continual regret?'

He could not fail to notice the real passion with which she made her point.

His sister put in, 'Now, Harry, admit – what men really want is a woman with none of the complications of a mind of her own.'

'What men want from a woman, I should say, what they need to make the best of themselves, is an equal,' he answered.

'And that is all?'

'Childishly simple, I admit,' he said. 'You'll no doubt call me mad but I put all my faith in the love between a man and a woman who are companions, capable of sharing and supporting each other's triumphs and burdens.' He stopped and blushed a thunderous red, as though he'd let out his closest secret.

As he accompanied her to the path that led back through the woods (she never let him walk her home), they carried on the conversation, talking as easily as though they were still in Marion's parlour.

'What if a man rejects the role of money-maker?' she suggested, with a model other than her father in mind. 'What if you men were more like you say we women are, and just decided to do what you liked, lean on someone else, and let money go hang?'

'I didn't say women should only do as they pleased. You forget the necessity of the well-ordered and reposeful home.'

'Ah yes,' she answered him teasingly. 'Slippers and pipe and informed conversation.'

'We men are too selfish to devote ourselves to the comfort of others. We haven't the talent for it. Besides, someone must worry about the money side of things.'

'Money can't buy happiness,' she lightly countered.

'No. But, as they say, freedom comes from wallets.' Then he looked so searchingly at her she was forced to look away. 'I mean, it's money gives one the freedom to follow wherever it is the heart leads. Lack of it makes a life so pinched.'

Was she being rebuked for being a silly little rich girl?

'But what is most valuable in life can't always be got with money,' she replied, on her dignity. 'Love, for example.'

He stopped walking to turn and address her directly. 'No, it can't, but at least it allows a man to hope.'

They walked on in silence. Rose admitted to herself that, one way or another, means and happiness were entangled. Then, sounding less measured, Harold spoke again.

'You can't know how I have lamented that my modest birth made me ineligible . . .' he paused and summoned himself. 'I mean, lack of money stops me from achieving my dearest wish. And that has made me more sick at heart than I can tell you, Miss Seaton.' He looked at his feet, as though lost for words.

He evidently hated his work with a passion and wanted only to pursue his first love of art and design. What a dull dog, she thought impatiently; he knows exactly what it is he wants yet dares nothing. It made her feel superior to think of her own impulsive leap after happiness.

'I don't know why you don't just follow where your heart leads, money or not. I think once we find what that is, it's our duty to risk everything to get it.' Had the man no poetry in his soul?

They had reached the end of the path. She held out her hand to shake his. He took it and held it too long.

'I would so like it if we could continue to talk like this. It does give me hope—'

'I really must go,' she interrupted, removing her hand from his grip and looking away towards the sheltering woods.

He looked crushed but affected a jocular tone. 'Lucky Marion, to have her monopoly of you almost every day. I am left only the crumbs, on this too short walk.'

She smiled vaguely and, hoping to break away from him, said, 'If I manage to give you ten minutes more on love and marriage, will that satisfy you?'

'I'd take it as a good omen!' He laughed, uneasily eager. 'If we had ten minutes more of private conversation like this—'

'I'd talk just as much nonsense as I do with your sister,' she finished for him, and escaped.

Nearing her own hard home, Rose's newly awakened enthusiasm for life decided her that though her father's unforgiving temper did not make it a welcoming place, nevertheless she'd do better to choose it over Webb's Farm and the deceptive attractions of silly books and ill-health. By the time Rose called Joan to help her dress for dinner she had quite forgotten her conversation with Harold.

# Chapter 21

A few days later brought a sere, chill afternoon, which threatened rain, but Rose resolved to keep clear of home and, by so doing, avoid Papus. He was due back imminently from that swollen-headed Cottonopolis they called Manchester, which was bound to have put him in a worse mood than usual. Walking briskly, with her shawl round her, she found that the chill invigorated her. She could have walked for miles, walked forever. It was not a sensation that she remembered having felt all this long winter and she relished it. Without noticing, her feet took their familiar path to Webb's Farm and, not thinking, she turned in at the gate and let them carry her on up to the front door, upon which she knocked. Instead of Mrs Webb or the indoor girl, it was Harold who opened the door, in his shirtsleeves, surprised to a broad grin.

'I thought you were my brother,' he said, looking at her as though he still expected to find that he was mistaken and it was gangly William who stood there.

'I believe not.'

He smiled again, saying, 'You came, though. You came!' He did not stand aside for her to enter.

'Marion's in the parlour?' she prompted.

Then, remembering himself, 'Marion's not here. She's gone

with my mother to visit a poor family. In point of fact, no one is here but me, for the little girls went with them. My father will have stopped on at the market and our William is who knows where. But *you* are here,' he finished lightly and stood back so that she might come in.

'You sound very cheerful to have rid yourself of your whole family.' She stepped over the threshold and he smiled down at her and shut the door.

'I've been sorrier,' he said drily.

It occurred to her that he'd probably elected to stay behind to work on his drawings.

'Will you come into Marion's room? I know enough about the mechanics of a kettle to brew tea,' he said with an exuberance she'd never before heard in him. Evidently he did not consider it a tiresome interruption to have to offer hospitality. She knew she should politely decline and let him get on with his hobby but, as so often in her relations with conventional Harold Webb, she was aroused to devilment. She would stay and he'd have to put up with her chatter until Marion returned.

Harold lit the lamps in the little sitting room and drew down the blinds for her. No sign of his drawing materials. He came back with a tea tray which held an odd assortment of cups and saucers standing in slopped milk, which would have shamed his mother. Rose was somewhat touched by this tall man's inept attempt at hospitality. It recalled his tender treatment of Marion.

'Even though it's all to my advantage, I can't help but be a little sorry for my sister to have missed you,' he said, sitting down easily opposite her.

Ignoring the compliment, she replied, 'Curious, for whenever I come to call, Marion seems always to be expressing the same sentiment in relation to you.'

He smiled again – he seemed to be always smiling – and replied, 'Aye, Marion knows my mind.'

Rose felt compelled to speak, to break the spell of that self-satisfied grin and get them off this half-articulated subject upon which they seemed to be stuck. But, now it came to it, she had no idea what to speak of. She couldn't mention his work as that might embarrass him since he apparently hated it. Wasn't he studying at night school? He might like to talk about that.

'Are you succeeding in your studies?' she ventured, unable to recall precisely what these were.

'I am!' he answered, too animatedly, as though her thoughts chimed exactly with his own. 'And, more important, I think I have impressed even your father with my efforts in commercial law. Besides, I've been using every spare moment to look into new markets and new products. I have great expectations.'

Goodness, perhaps he didn't hate his work.

He gave her another compelling look and went on, 'You made me realise how lucky I am to live in a time when a man may progress upwards by self-improvement and that brains and gumption have rightly come to be valued above birth and name.'

She had no notion how to reply to this assertion but he did not need a prompt.

'Today, just as you say, if a man follows his heart, there's nothing he may not achieve, in business or anything else, however high he aims.'

'I suppose not,' she replied, thinking, he's dragged us back to talk of his wallet – how vulgar.

He paused and breathed through his smile and repeated, 'And my, the expectations!'

'I'm so glad to hear it,' she said, straining to hear if any of the Webb family had returned.

'Yes. After our talk the other evening, I knew there was hope if I could only be bold enough to seize it!'

'Indeed, you must be bold.' She did her best to match his enthusiasm, surprised that succeeding in business could mean so much to him.

'Rose, if you only knew how happy it makes me!'

'Yes?' she answered uncertainly, noticing that he'd used her Christian name.

Then, as though talking brought a lump to his throat, he said, 'I hardly dared to hope, but then you came, just as you said you would. You came!'

'Oh, I did, didn't I?' she replied, remembering. 'For ten minutes on love and marriage!' And it occurred to her how much easier it had been to raise these topics with Harold than it had been with her dearest friend.

At that moment William made his noisy entry, stamping his boots and breathing loudly through his nose from the exertion of running to reach home before his father's return from the conviviality of the market-day public house. Just before he opened the parlour door to greet his brother, Harold took her hand in his and whispered fervently, 'Then I have your permission to talk to your father?'

'Of course, though I'm sure you don't need to ask it of me,' she answered politely, smiling more broadly in response to his delight than felt quite natural. He seemed to be quite overwhelmed with this prospect of advancement in her father's firm.

At last she managed to break away and return home, wondering that Harold had such well-hidden emotional depths.

# Chapter 22

Rose had been back at home six months and had succeeded so well in avoiding her father that she suspected that all his residual bellicosity was safely channelled into his chief concern, the foundry. Every evening he retreated to his study to sit and smoke and brood about uppity workers and the unrestricted foreign imports that meant the uppity buying public did not purchase in the volume he demanded of them. Only when he emerged to eat a sullen supper did she have to keep out of sight. Still she fretted that his business worries would, in their turn, remind him that his lack of a son and heir was compounded by her inability as a daughter to bring in the champion son-in-law he might have expected.

It was no real surprise, then, when early one Sunday afternoon she was summoned to his study. She steeled herself for further chastisement and reproach, and entered the room.

He was seated behind a desk covered with a muddle of documents, red in the face, full of bitter self-loathing. The long, slow decline of Seaton and Gast was drawing to its terrible conclusion. What lay ahead but failure, exposure? He had allowed it to come to this. And, because he hadn't served the industrial beast well, it now demanded the dearest thing he possessed in sacrifice. The shameful thought of his own inadequacy stung his opening remark into a wounded roar. 'I suppose you know we are like to be ruined?'

Rose was so used to associating this word with her own condition that she failed to fully grasp his meaning, but bowed her head before the coming sentence.

'I've had to put the men on half time and have no notion of when things might look up again,' he continued, making things clearer.

'Even I cannot be blamed for that,' returned Rose, in her relief sounding more flippant than she intended.

He snorted, letting her insolence do its coward's work for him of firing up the self-righteous anger he could not feel in his heart.

'Mabbe not, mabbe not!'

Dear Lord, she'd played her part in it, though, boxing him into this corner. He allowed that thought to spur him to greater rage. He could not look her in the eye.

'See what you've forced me to. Brought me down to!'

'What are you forced to do, Papus?' she asked, fearful that he meant banishment.

'I cannot be grateful for it, but beggars can't be choosers.' He fabricated an accusing tone. 'He's a worthy man, God knows. If he had been born a gentleman, I mean a proper gentleman, I might have been glad to have called him son.'

'What do you mean, whose son?' she demanded, alert now that this conversation was about more than her crime.

'Given the condition you've landed yourself in,' he paused to let the crude words bite, 'no doubt your mother and me must fall down before him in gratitude that he'll even look at you.' He was almost in tears now as he mouthed the cruel repudiation that his own heart and mind rebelled against.

'Who are you talking about?' She tried to take his hand but he withdrew from her.

'Why, Harold Webb, of course. Your blasted Harold Webb!' He cracked out the syllables of that name, each one a hammer blow to his chest. 'I shall be obliged to offer him a junior partnership so *you* shall not be socially embarrassed!'

'But Papus, why should I be embarrassed?'

In his disappointment, he attacked more savagely. 'Quite right, it's me as suffers the embarrassment, me that must make a son-in-law out of Harold Webb – one of my own men!'

Rose was horrified to understand what her father was proposing. Then she began to sob.

He allowed himself to soften, to offer relief from the battering, now that the hateful performance had frightened her and blame had done its job of disguising his own humiliation.

'I'm not saying he's not a good man and there's no denying he has great plans. Let him finish his legal studies and then we'll see what he shall do to set the business on its feet again. Once you two are married, all will come right, lass.' He said it as much to comfort himself that this was the correct course and offered a hand in truce. Rose rejected it.

'Is Mr Webb absolved from asking for me himself? Of bothering to court me?' The damaged daughter had come in useful after all, had she? No wonder the iron master had passed such long evenings plotting in his study.

'Absolved from asking thee? What in heaven's name have you two been getting up to every blasted day at Webb's Farm if not courting?'

She slammed out of his study and surprised Mapus who was at that providential moment passing outside the door.

Rose shouted, 'Am I beneath consultation in this business arrangement between Harold Webb and my father?'

'Now then, now then,' stalled her mother, perplexed.

'How on earth was I to know it was in his head to marry me?'

'Well, that was your father's understanding, pet, when Mr Webb came to see him yesterday.'

'Was it indeed!'

Mapus, who had expected to follow up this momentous interview with glad congratulations, carefully reeled in the events of the previous day and found just what she needed dangling at the end of the line.

'I'm certain sure I heard him say myself, as I happened by, that you two had come to terms and you'd given him encouragement to be bold and follow his true heart and ask Papus for your hand. Well, I have to say, your pa was that surprised to hear what had been going on between you two! Nevertheless he heard the young man out and, when it came clear that you wanted it too, they agreed it between them.'

Rose stamped her foot. 'And I'm a chattel to be disposed of between two men, over their wine, like a girl from the slave market?'

Shocked, Mapus curbed her, saying, 'I'm sure it wasn't anything like that, dear. Mr Webb was ever so humble, and so pleading. He told Papus he loved you more than life itself.'

Did he really think that ridiculous, cross-purpose conversation at the farm had constituted a proposal?

'Well, he might have had the courtesy to plead with me himself. Told me outright he loved me first. It is the convention!'

'I've no doubt he will, my dear,' Mapus soothed, 'now that he has your father's blessing.'

'And I will tell him to jump off a cliff!'

'Rose,' she replied sharply. 'Harold Webb is a good, decent man and loves you very much and,' she paused to consider the delicacy of what she must say, 'there's not quite the variety of choice that once there was in the way of husbands.'

'So, I'm to have no say in the matter?' she demanded furiously and stamped up to her bedroom.

'Eh, I wish you'd never gone to foreign parts!' sighed her mother to the departing back.

She went into her husband and turned up his chap-fallen face to hers, saying, 'The lass only needs time to get over herself, Robert. And she will.'

'She must learn,' he said obstinately, still fuelled by self-loathing. 'I only mean to do what's best for her.'

'I know, I know, love.'

'This is no way a business arrangement!'

She patted his cheek. 'No way.'

'Elizabeth-Jane, Webb'll do!'

In the end, there was no getting over the fact that her husband had decided. Harold Webb would be the one for Rose

Rose escaped from the house into the woods. She marched over frosted earth that cracked beneath her feet, mouthing, 'Harold Webb, Harold Webb!' She passed the gamekeeper's cottage and saw that a curl of smoke rose from the chimney and a lamp shone at a window, even though it was but two in the afternoon, and the domesticity of this little house lost in the woods caused in her a tremendous surge of emotion that she could only identify as nostalgia. I have no one to turn to and nowhere of my own to go, she thought, and the pang was like the symptom of an illness from which one might die. But this was not nostalgia for home or the comfort of the past but for that old fairy story of love she'd once looked forward to.

On through the wood she went, in her temper pulling at and stripping the rusty dead bracken. She left the shelter of the trees and stood looking down at Webb's Farm, which was so close that she might have dropped a stone down one of its smoking chimney pots and heard the tinny trumpet call of Mrs Webb's bantam cockerel, summoning his wives.

So I'm one of the keepers of the public morality, am I, stood upon so high a pedestal that my little fall from grace creates such a racket that all the other women are reminded why they keep on balancing?

'I'll show you what a noise I can make, Harold Webb, I'll show you!' said Rose aloud and started to stride, half falling, down the slope to the farm. She saw that William was crossing the farmyard from the mistal where Janet, the house cow, was lodged. He was carrying a pail of milk warm enough still to steam. His dog Brock close at heel, he walked slope-shouldered against the wind in boots claggy with clay and cows' muck. He looked up in her direction unseeing, before going in at the kitchen door which had opened to receive him and his kit of milk. Rose stopped and panted, for she really had no idea what she would say to Harold. She'd given him no real encouragement, had she? Beyond the ridiculous assumptions he'd cobbled together from a couple of friendly chats in the lane, there had been nothing, had there? All she could remember saying to him that might have been misinterpreted was to give him that bit of advice about taking risks. Then she recalled her last meeting with him, when the rest of the family had been away from home, and he'd been so full of glee. At the time it seemed that he had chiefly talked about money and his ambition to have more of it. But, damn him, whatever she had said had been enough for him to seize the day and go to her father for permission to marry, and for her father to give it. He'd learned to be bold all right! Rose turned and went home.

Two days after her father had first informed her of his and Harold's agreement, a meeting was arranged. Perhaps two days were deemed to be sufficient for her to have got over herself. But Rose would not consent to meet him in her own home and could not bear to go to his, where she dreaded Marion's triumph at having gained her for a real sister. For Rose suspected that Marion had been involved in encouraging him to make his bid, and resolved never to forgive that betrayal. And she reasoned that since her marriage was a business deal, then the interview should properly take place at the offices of Seaton and Gast. It was the only bit of rebellion she could contrive.

Harold was already seated in an inner office when she was brought there by her father. He jumped up at the sight of his trophy, saying, 'Mr Seaton, Miss Seaton,' and shook her hand. Then they all three sat and, although she knew that he sought her eyes, Rose looked into her lap and waited for her father to institute the proceedings.

'Now then.' He slapped his knees and looked Harold, the chosen one, squarely in the eye, the very image of the bluff, commercial man. 'As you know, I've talked to the lass and she's agreeable to a six-month courtship. Isn't that so, Rose?' he asked, chafing her elbow encouragingly, but she made no response.

Harold Webb said, 'You can't know how grateful I am, sir. I only want to prove to you and Miss Seaton what a worthy son-in-law and husband,' he blushed, 'I can be.'

'When you two are married,' her father paused, and swallowed, as though this was a very hard obstacle to get past his gullet, 'you shall live at home with Mrs Seaton and me and your name will be put above the door, after mine and Gast's, you understand.'

Harold murmured his gratitude, and looked at Rose. Then the old man suddenly reached over and took him by the hand, saying, in a trembling voice, 'You *will* take good care of her for me, won't you, lad? For she's my little girl, my treasure here on earth, the best of me . . .'

Rose unfroze at that and knelt at her father's knee.

'I want only your happiness, lass. I can bear anything if I know you are taken care of.'

It was shocking to see Papus like this, so doubting. The most immutable thing in her life, sure and solid as cast iron itself, able to withstand any amount of her defiance, reduced to a terrible vulnerability. Rose felt almost frightened that what she had resisted with all her might had collapsed, and all the certainty there was in the world went with him.

# Chapter 23

It was a subdued betrothal to be followed by a discreet wedding – not so much a joyous public affirmation as the phlegmatic union of a match-made couple. No celebrations were planned for the introduction of the pair, almost as though it was a hole-in-corner business best kept private.

The young couple usually met at Rose's home, where Mapus endeavoured to be cheerful and welcoming. She did like Harold and thought him a steady influence and a well brought up young man, despite being only a farmer's son. All in all, she was more comfortable with this suitor than the Newton boy and thanked her stars that that devil, Patrick McKinley, was off the scene. She was only bothered that Rose continued to find so little joy in Harold's company. After all, you'd expect a lover to enliven his young lady, not make her palely pine. But, she reasoned, once her daughter was caught up in the excitement of wedding presents and fittings and plans for the bride journey, she'd soon cheer up. Rose was still a young girl, after all.

Every evening mother and daughter would sit in companionable silence to embroider the entwined initials R and H upon the many items of her trousseau. Rose was often made to cry by the pricking of her clumsy needle.

After a month or two of formal courtship, the pair were

encouraged to meet in private and now that it was once again springtime they were able to walk together comfortably out of doors. She noticed that still his hand trembled indecisively beneath her elbow as they perambulated side by side. He was kind, he was good and honest, he loved and venerated her and he was, undoubtedly, handsome, and for all of these she wanted to punish him.

One sunny afternoon she suggested that they walk into the woods since they'd already done a couple of circuits of the garden and the weather was very warm. They followed a path bordered by flowering blackthorn that led to the gamekeeper's cottage and beyond it to Eckersby and the farm. She went a little in advance of him, turning to remark over her shoulder, 'The last time I walked this way I came to give you a flea in your ear.'

He smiled in reply. 'Which flea was that?'

'Oh, I never delivered it. I thought better of it and turned back at the last minute.'

'What a shame,' he said comfortably. 'I don't like the thought of having been deprived of any meeting with you even if it was to scold me.'

She, too, smiled benignly. 'Don't you think I'm saving all that up, as is proper, until after we're married?'

The path descended between high, mossy banks where the new green bracken uncurled fists and clumps of wild primroses seemed to generate their own greenish light. Their heads almost on a level with the forest floor, they looked straight into bluebells, ripe and ready to burst like a low-lying drift of cobalt smoke.

'I should like to pick some bluebells to take home,' she said, trying to scramble up the bank.

He climbed up ahead of her and reached down to take hold of her hand and pull her up to him. She landed beside him, falling against him a little so that he had to steady her. This was the first time since they had been affianced that their bodies had touched each other so closely.

'I used to sam armfuls and armfuls when I was a boy and, I'm shamed to say, trample even more of 'em underfoot.'

He stepped away from her in among the flowers and she, lapped halfway up her shins, began to snap the sappy stems.

'Do you suppose that one day all the bluebell woods will have been built over and children won't have the luxury of their wanton destruction any more?'

'I suppose they'll find something else to despoil,' he replied, picking a single flower to smell and then throwing it from him. 'You do know that it's pointless to collect them, they'll only droop even if you put them in water.'

'I know. But I just like to have them – I can't stop myself. When I see a whole wood full like this I'm just mad for them.'

But she stopped her harvest and sat down in an alcove made by the roots of a great elm curtained by thick ivy. He came and stood before her, uncertain what to do, so that she reached up and pulled him down to sit beside her. In this bower the pungent, dusty odour of ivy mingled with the scent of bruised, wild mint that they had crushed.

'You may call me by my name, you know,' she said.

He tried to sound jocular. 'I'm sure I do, dear.'

'No, you don't. The day we were betrothed you greeted me as Miss Seaton and ever since you've avoided it,' she goaded.

He seemed to gather himself for the effort and said, 'Rose . . . dear,' sounding thoroughly awkward.

Full of spite, she demurely offered him her lips and he kissed her as passionlessly as he would his aunt.

'So formal,' said Rose, giving a cruel little laugh.

He turned his humiliated face from her, mumbling, 'I do want to be romantic. It's just that I get mithered and can't seem to act naturally, as I feel.'

She pulled him to her and kissed him, almost in punishment, and he responded, taking her in his arms as though she bruised easily. She held him harder, so he couldn't draw away from her and they kissed again.

When she allowed him some breath, he said fervently, 'I love you, Rose!'

They were still for a while and then, as though her kisses had taken minutes to hit their mark, he launched himself at her, murmuring, 'Oh, Rose!' and kissed and kissed. Briefly, in that moment, she forgot herself and the hard resentment she felt for him and began to open beneath his deep kisses, her hands, sticky from the bluebells, tight around his back.

Understanding the change in her, the sudden surrender, he groaned and pulled himself away.

'We can't,' he said breathless, full of embarrassment.

It was Rose's turn for humiliation; she'd given way to him, and he knew it, he'd felt it. Now she really needed to hurt him.

'Say that you don't want to. Say it!'

He blushed. 'I've imagined how it would be for so long . . . You can't know how I've wanted the day when I can hold you in my arms in a bed . . .'

She saw that this big, proud man had begun to cry, the tears running down into the soft ends of his moustache. She could not bear it and, to shock him back to common sense, said brutally, 'Why not a bluebell wood?'

'Why do you make yourself so hard, Rose, when I know you aren't? Why do you want to punish me for loving you and wanting to wed you and look after you? I love you!'

'Well, I don't love you and I never shall!'

She ran away through the trees angrier and more resentful still, and frightened too, because in that bluebell wood her body had responded to his, the pompous, conventional, impossible Harold Webb.

# Chapter 24

Rose and Joan packed again, limiting themselves to portable items suited to single flight. For this time Rose was not eloping but fleeing from marriage. And she escaped by tram.

Joan led her to the stop, kissed her goodbye and returned, weeping, to the mansion.

It took scarcely an hour for Rose to reach a world where her parents, and Harold, would never think to seek her. In that inner Sheffield suburb she descended from the tram and followed Joan's directions to the house of her paternal aunt, Mrs Jannock. It began to drizzle as she approached the door to 16 Raglan Street, one of innumerable doors standing in a row, all painted green or brown or rusty black, and knocked. A woman, obviously Joan's relation although much older and more worn than she, answered, still holding in her hands the dinner plate she'd been in the process of rubbing dry.

'Mrs Jannock, is it? I believe you let rooms?' said Rose, nervously touching her hat and holding out her hand.

The older woman stood silent for a moment, not taking the hand of the apparition standing there in its hand-stitched boots.

'If there is no room here, perhaps you'd be so good as to direct me to other respectable lodgings.'

In order to forestall full-blown sobs, Rose was now on her

dignity. Still the woman suspended answer, only rubbing the plate speculatively. Then, as Rose decided that she'd come to the wrong door, Mrs Jannock said, 'So you're Miss Rose, sent by our Joan?' Her brother's little lass was one for suchlike flighty notions that were got out of daft books and periodicals.

Rose gave a tiny nod.

'I'm sure you're welcome to any bit of 'ospitality I can offer yer,' Mrs Jannock grudged, standing aside so the pretty young troublemaker could enter.

They passed down the passage to the back kitchen where washing steamed on clothes horses set before the fire and dripped from creels hoisted to the ceiling.

Rose, lacking the courage to explain herself, said miserably, 'It's only a room to rent I'll need and that for just a few days, while I look about myself and decide what's for the best.' She was breathing rather hard, she'd never before been inside a working man's house. Swarming indiscriminately to and from their work, gaudy at their leisure, Rose was a little afraid of the working classes.

'I can pay in advance,' she added, wondering whether this might be the form.

A couple of little children came in from the damp back yard carrying a tin peggytub between them. Mrs Jannock took the washtub from them and hoisted it to hang from a nail on the wall. The two girls stood and looked at Rose with saucer eyes. She felt in her bag for a mint humbug (old habits died hard with Joan) and proffered one to each as though she, a cornered gazelle, might placate the lion cubs that had turned their interested gaze upon her.

'Say thank you ter lady,' supplied their mother as they sidled close enough to grab.

'Than' kew,' they chorused.

'Your cousin sent these for you,' Rose said, digging deeper and bringing out the whole bag of sweets for the children.

And then, all of a sudden, it seemed to be decided. Apparently no further information was necessary apart from whether the lodger would be taking her meals with the family or brought in. For, whether decent or not in herself, the lady's finery suggested that a decent rent might be asked and, besides, she'd offered a guinea straight – off, dabs down. Mrs Jannock concluded that though Joan's stray might be gawby, she had no real harm in her.

Rose was consigned to the company of the hugely respectable bed that occupied the greater part of the back bedroom, a chest of drawers and a poker-work text that informed her from the wall, 'Tis here we pledge perpetual hate, to all that can intoxicate'. So much for her father's opinion that the working classes squandered their pay on alcohol and showy knick-knacks. She dared not venture downstairs again but repaired to the seclusion of bed while it was yet light, and tried not to think back to the dangling difficulty of Harold and her parents or ahead to the problem of how she was to get by on her own.

Since Rose did not have the courage to appear for early breakfast, she did not meet Mr Jannock and his son Tommy. By the time she made her way downstairs, both had left for work two hours previously, the senior Jannock as an overseer and the junior as apprentice – two units of the thousand employed by Walker and Hall's Electro Works (manufacturers of silver and electro-plate). She knew the name of Walker and Hall from the fabled fifty percent discount offered to those favoured customers who, like her own mother, had been 'introduced'. At breakfast, which she ate self-consciously while her landlady folded sheets (that lady was never at rest), she learned that when Mrs Jannock had been Miss Washbourne, she'd been employed as a burnisher in the same Electro Works on Howard Street.

'That's skilled work,' her landlady baldly informed her.

'Is it, Mrs Jannock?' replied meek Rose. Then, trying to show an interest in others' concerns, as she'd been taught, 'I believe my mother has an electro-plated crumb collector and a celery stand from Walker and Hall, perhaps you burnished them?'

''Appen, for I was one of the best at my job, young woman, and well paid wi' it.' Since she'd stopped what she was doing to talk Rose noticed that Mrs Jannock's hands, so accustomed to the work she was describing, had involuntarily begun to drag back and forth across the table top as though to polish it to a silvery sheen.

'Aye,' she went on, 'when Mr Jannock an' me started courtin' I could tek 'ome more than 'im.'

'But you left off working when you were married?'

'Mr Jannock is a proud man.'

'Wasn't he proud that you should be earning such a good wage, even more than him?'

'Let a man ask a woman's wages an' that's not the answer 'e wants t'ear, young woman. No, Mr Jannock is a man who prides 'imself in providin' an' yours truly mun shift to make two ends meet in th'ome.'

Between the two little girls, Dora and Florence (who were known collectively as Dor and Flor), and fifteen-year-old Tommy, there loomed a large gap of eight years which Rose learned, as the morning progressed and folding gave way to ironing, had been filled by erstwhile Jannock infants, poor innocents who, having been born 'too good for this world', had taken one look, agreed, and swiftly departed it.

In the afternoon, Rose went to the corner shop for her landlady to buy potatoes and was surprised that very few coppers bought so very many. Then she volunteered to peel them for Mrs Jannock and they had, unaccountably, got even more numerous.

At that day's 'losing' time, Rose was introduced, by degrees, to the other inhabitants who overcrowded 16 Raglan Street as they returned from school or factory. All except the family's other lodger, Mr Samuel, who shared a room with Tommy when he was in Sheffield. Mr Samuel, being a travelling representative for the same Walker and Hall, was very often away from home and thus a most perfect lodger for busy Mrs Jannock.

Mr Jannock was likewise not much in evidence. Like the good husband he was, he could be relied upon to orbit the warm female centre of home without interfering much in its diurnal course. He existed in those compartments labelled ''is work' ''is works' meeting', 'at chapel', or simply 'not to be disturbed'. This last found him asleep, fully buttoned but unbooted, on the matrimonial bed, or reading the paper in front of the back kitchen range. He was given his due respect as the breadwinner but how his wage was spent was, very properly, left to his wife.

For all his pugnacity, however, Mrs Jannock managed him very well without recourse to any of these womanish persuasives. Had they been asked who was the head of the family, Rose doubted whether the notion of Mr J. being equal in rank and authority to Mrs J. ever entered the heads of the inmates of 16 Raglan Street.

At the end of the first week Joan managed to slip away on her half-day to visit her aunt and bring news of home to Rose. The two girls sat on the bed, under the tract, as Joan sorted the truntlements she'd managed to smuggle from home.

'I brought two or three things o' yours as shan't be missed,' Joan said, emptying some valueless baubles onto Rose's lap. She seemed hangdog and irritable after the excitement of orchestrating the flit.

'Have I been very cruel, Joan?' asked Rose.

'Aye, well, as to my mistress, I should say it's seized 'er heart sadly.'

It occurred to Rose that Joan was out of sorts because she'd been found out in the plot.

'Do they suspect you, Joan?'

'I was sent for, miss, and I were that flaid. I thought to missen, oh 'eck, lass, there's goin' to be trouble now. But I never told on you, just played 'arf-baked like. Then master got 'is dander up over that Mr McKinley again and mistress took to blutherin' fit to bust so they soon forgot us.'

'I suppose my father has been very angry,' said Rose, trying to forestall more information about her mother's pain.

'Well, I wouldn't say *angray*. 'E keeps t'is room and 'e's ever so short with that Mr 'Arold Webb. I 'eard a terrible to-do the day you bobbed. Yellin' blue murder, they were.'

Joan had roused herself in the re-telling of this high drama but was soon subdued and fretful again. Rose wondered whether there was some other cause for her distractedness but that night she cried only for her own distress. She could never return home again now. She had travelled too far from it.

In her second week as lodger Rose began to appreciate the rhythms of the working-class household. Here, at the very impacted heart of the beehive, the bees did not buzz in aggressive anarchy but lived lives as trammelled by routine and rectitude as did her own tribe. Indeed they put more real, everyday effort into keeping clean, pious and solvent. Rose wondered whether even her own mother would have insisted on changing her linen every day if she'd personally had to wash, starch, air and iron it, or whether her father would have walked two miles to his worship, and back, at the end of six days of hard labour.

Two weeks showed her that toil, contrivance and cups of tea were what kept respectable, working-class heads just above water. Close proximity taught her that their actions and affections were as explicable as those of her own family. But two weeks did not find her any more inclined, or equipped, to cope as an untrained woman of no means. And if Rose now left off privately characterising them as *types* the Jannocks were not so lax about labelling her. She was an oddity, and that label stuck. For though she was a great, grown girl, it did not once occur to her (after her experience with the multiplying potatoes) to offer help with the housework. Mrs Jannock wondered at the quantities of lace on every item of clothing she casually put in the wash. She had not the wrists of a burnisher. She had not the wit for a proper wife.

Miss Rose Seaton was neither use nor ornament. Indeed she habitually sat about in the middle of the day book-reading as though this were a perfectly seemly employment. The only contribution to the household she could offer was money for bed and board. Rose knew this was unsustainable. But when the hot anxiety over dwindling funds crept over her in bed at night, she'd reason them away. After all, Raglan Street was just a staging post for her next move, a place to look about herself before she leapt into the unknown. Very soon she'd be gone.

It was on a Wednesday afternoon of the third week, while Mrs Jannock was away from the house and Rose was re-reading *Sense and Sensibility* in the front parlour, that a cab drew up at the door. A cab was enough of a novelty in Raglan Street to bring women out onto their doorsteps. Rose, too, watched and saw the cab driver come round to help the occupant out onto the pavement. It was Marion. She approached number sixteen, scuffing Mrs Jannock's whitened step, and knocked immoderately at her well polished knocker. Rose flew to the door to meet her. It was bad enough arriving by cab; must she draw even more curiosity with her public knocking? Raglan Street Rose had learned that the front door was for show, not use.

'How did you know?' she demanded.

'Oh, my dear, I had to find you to be sure that you were well. Mayn't I come in?' Marion asked. 'You know I can't stand for long.'

Rose could do no other than take Marion's arm and support her to the front parlour. She knew that it must have been hugely difficult for her friend to attempt this journey.

'It was Joan who betrayed me, wasn't it?'

'Please, Joan doesn't deserve blame. I put her under moral obligation to tell me. Poor girl, she was very unwilling to, only, knowing that you needed a friend, she gave way at last. And I am a friend, Rose. You do believe I'm a friend?'

'But you are a sister first – his, not mine.'

The two sat in silence until Marion went on, 'True. And I love my brother – both my brothers and my little sisters – and I wouldn't have them hurt for the world. But sometimes one must acknowledge that even a loved one may do harm. Harm out of a mistaken apprehension. Though it does hurt me when I consider that he really does love you, Rose. You can't blame him for loving you.'

Rose began to cry. 'I don't blame him. I don't blame any of you, but I will not have love imposed on me, Marion. A heart must be freely given.'

Marion sighed and the two girls sat closer on the sofa.

'I have not come here to talk you into coming home, either to your parents or to Harold. I will not betray you to either. I come only to offer my friendship and any practical help I can give. But what is it you intend to do?'

'I don't rightly know.' She really didn't. And the prospect of that lonely road which led she knew not where made Rose want to sob on kind Marion's bosom.

'I have a little nest egg—'

'Oh, Marion, don't. I'm not a child – I must take responsibility for my own future.'

'Then may I ask one thing of you? Don't leave here without sending me word. I would hate you just to disappear.'

Rose could only acquiesce.

Later that day Rose was introduced to her fellow lodger, Mr Samuel, home from his travels to Leeds and beyond. He'd be stopping with them for a fortnight, doing his travelling locally by foot, tram or trap. Rather squat with yellow side whiskers, cultivated to convey maturity, Mr Samuel was a young man who reaped affection wherever he broadcast his good-natured smile. Dor and Flor were promiscuous with theirs, frisking him for the sweets he'd hidden in every pocket and demanding he heft them up the stairs. They each clung to a leg, crying, 'Fooit walkers! Do fooit walkers, our Sam.'

He was referred to as 'Sam' by everyone, so that Rose thought he'd been christened Samuel Samuel until she learned his given name was a cause of embarrassment to him and thus never invoked.

The family, plus lodgers, had a beano that evening, Mrs Jannock providing them with as nice a piece of haslet as the recent upturn in the family economy could afford, and they were very merry upon sarsaparilla and 'corporation pop', as Sam Samuel called tap water. Rose had not expected to feel so happy.

The whole household was enlivened by Mr Samuel for he had that talent of making a noisy party out of any little gathering. A cup of tea and a slice of buttered bread were sufficient cause for Sam to play a mouth organ or fold newspaper hats. And he was just as happy to discuss politics with Mr Jannock as he was novels with Rose. For Sam improved himself by reading, reading anything that came into his hands, and talking, talking to anyone he met upon the road, whether a tramp in a ditch or a socialist on a soap box. And so extensive was his reading and his talking that he couldn't be beaten for general knowledge or surprising opinions. Indeed, some of his opinions were so surprising that if dogmatic Mr Jannock hadn't liked him so well, he might have been inclined to turf his occasional lodger into the street.

At the conclusion of one particular debate with his landlord, provoked by an article on the front page of the illustrated newspaper concerning the famine in India, Rose feared the only resolution could be a bloodied nose. Mr Jannock was maddened by Sam's dialectic upon the exploitation of the native cooly who was, after all, a brother working man, whatever the colour of his skin. 'None o' tha buck, lad!' warned Mr Jannock. 'You know they're nothing but the white man's burden!' She expected fisticuffs when Sam Samuel cheerfully replied, 'I don't make this stuff oop, tha knows. I had it from an Indian chappie, a lawyer if tha please, I met i' Manchester.' But Mr Jannock laughed at that, saying, 'A course tha did, lad!' Evidently he'd enjoyed the ding dong.

Sam Samuel certainly had a way of overwhelming one with quotes and anecdotes. Mr Jannock found it quite a trial to keep his head clear of them so that he could point out the errors in his lodger's thinking. But when all was said and done, Sam's chief fault was an over-supply of disinterested compassion.

Rose liked him; she liked him for his lively, inquiring mind and his kind heart. She was sad when the time came for him once more to leave them for the road and the chance encounters he would make upon it. It did not occur to her that his return might find her still keeping company with bed, chest and tract.

# Chapter 25

Lacking the get up and go to get up and be gone along the tricky high road of life, Rose continued drearily on at Raglan Street. One weekend, after Sunday chapel, school and dinner were done with, Rose, curbed indoors and desperate to escape the stultifying effect of the warmth and the boiled-cabbage odour of enforced sanctity, proposed that she and the girls, Dor and Flor, go on an outing to the fields. The open countryside lay just half a mile from Raglan Street, where the houses ended abruptly in a hawthorn copse and farmed land began. Strange to be walking down these lanes fresh with flowers and darted through by birds when back-to-backs and the urban horror of the shared midden were just behind, as though one stepped backwards from the industrial age directly into the agricultural. From now – to then. Here, in the rural past, lay the old ways, the old words, the old trades. There, on the road to the future, was perpetual flux. Here a skill, or a word, or a tool was passed down for generations; there, advertisement hoardings told one the latest way to use soap. Yet despite the hurry, it occurred to her that the modern life of the town was strangely timeless, the year's passage told only by weather being 'too 'ot' or 'fair t' middling' or 'nesh', and counted out by clock and calendar. In this country lane she experienced again the pulse of her own rural childhood, the mechanism of deep time that drove the cyclical year, in the seasons of plants and animals and men.

She looked about her and wondered, had she really missed the ceremonial of the sheep shearing? For the flocks ranged pinkly undressed across the hills. Had she lingered so long in the town that the wild bees had swarmed already and been tempted into these field-edge hives with honey and herbs? And it broke upon her that this was July. Dor and Flor romped after butterflies while Rose lay on her back and watched the larks idling deep at the bottom of a dark blue sky and listened to the grasshoppers that sang in her ears. The standing grass in the field on the headland was consumed by the slow scythe and Rose saw that time went on unchecked. The future tugged at her, impatient to be lived.

All the next week Rose stalled, though she had seen that summer's zenith was already past and the shortening days called for her to frame herself and be gone. Inclined to mope indoors, she was no longer such an eager companion to Dor and Flor, preferring the quiet company of Marion who contrived to come every other day in her mother's trap on the pretext of visiting a poor family. Mrs Webb was glad that her daughter should be showing an interest outside the home but Marion was so nervous of being found out that she elaborated the woes of her imaginary family to the extent that her kind-hearted mother determined to come herself and have words with the wastrel who denied his own bairns. Marion was fortunately able to persuade her that provisions from the farm would be sufficient to prevent them all from starving to death. Thus Mrs Jannock was always very happy to see the lame lass and her full basket. But, gladdened as she was to have a friend to talk to, Rose was aware of Marion's agenda that she brought nestled among her tomatoes and broad beans.

At that week's end the two young ladies sat with the teapot and a spice loaf in the front parlour, whose use had been given up to Miss Seaton by her landlady in consideration of her breeding and her half-crown supplement.

'I'm worried over Harold,' Marion remarked. 'He's that much in his books, does naught but pine away indoors until he's quite grey with lack of sunlight.' She looked at Rose to gauge her reaction.

Rose was rescued from having to make a reply by Sam who came upon them full of beams. He'd returned that morning from his travels, like a more regular Father Christmas, to distribute spice, as he called sweeties, and dislocate his knees playing 'fooit walkers'.

'Oh, I do beg pardon,' said he, looking at Marion. 'I came in search o' my pipe. The little girls are always takin' it – dressin' it up in 'andkerchiefs an' lakin' wi't like it were a proper dolly, if you can imagine!'

'Won't you have a cup of tea with us, Sam?' asked Rose, glad of the diversion as well as keen to show off the self-educated phenomenon.

'I will,' said he, looking again at Marion.

'Miss Marion Webb,' said Rose formally, 'may I introduce my fellow lodger and friend, Mr Samuel.' Rose realised she still had no idea of his given forename and looked at him inquiringly.

He said only, 'Sam. I get Sam.'

He beamed at Marion and she blossomed. Rose wondered whether he had noticed that she had a withered leg. Then she thought how nice it was that her friend should have this opportunity to extend her very limited circle of friends to include Sam Samuel, who was so gentle and kind and, apparently, so unjudgemental. The three talked on and Sam told them stories of the people he had collected upon the way.

'It near made me weep to see it. The father 'ad supped 'is pint afore 'e admitted 'e'd no money to pay for it. 'E ran from landlord calling that 'e'd leave little lad behind 'im as guarantee. Said 'e'd be back with money directly.'

'But he never returned?' asked Marion.

'That were two year back,' confirmed Sam. 'Two year an' the little blighter's still got up in the gear he was wearin' then, so ragged and tight. 'E wanders about the place beggin' for coins an' scraps and 'e sleeps there, under the counter the night, like a stray dog.'

'Does no one care for him?'

'Aye, well, landlord's not cruel to 'im, but then again 'e's not over-kind neither. I'd say 'e's 'oldin' out still for the price o' that pint.'

'Do you think the father will ever call back to reclaim the little lad?'

'I reckon 'e thought it a fair swap, a pint for a brat. But smally lad waits on. It broke me 'eart to see pathetic chap follow after folk and ax, "Father, faither, 'ast tha cum fer me?"'

Marion looked stricken. 'What's to be done for him?'

'I put an 'alf-crown in 'is 'and and indicated 'e mun 'ide it away but little lad seemed touched in th'ead or summit, jus' stood there like a barmpot. Someone will relieve 'im of it soon enough.'

'Just because the poor little lad is backward and unclaimed! Why is it, Sam, that weakness brings out the very worst in people?' exclaimed Marion passionately.

'I see all manner of injustice an' plain cruelty on my travels, lass, and seems to me that's the way of the world: to those that have shall be given, in spades, and those that have not deserve everything they get in the way of knocks – with knobs on!'

They laughed at that but, as one of the privileged, Rose felt censured. 'Oh Sam, some of the rich work hard for their wealth. My father spends hours and hours every day in his office wearing himself down and, besides, he helps to make the whole nation prosper and gives dozens of people employment by it.'

Marion seeing that Rose might have felt insulted, was quick to add, 'Mr Seaton is not one of those as just sits upon his land, growing fat on investments.'

'And who's to say that he mustn't be well rewarded for his brain work and his enterprise?' Sam smiled at both of them. 'But

I say, come the day when the rich and powerful in the richest and most powerful nation on earth decide we can afford a little kindness for all, even the poor an' weak!'

Rose saw that the look the two exchanged over the teapot was fired by fellow feeling. They seemed to claim each other in their compassion for the dispossessed and she felt excluded. To be honest, she had expected that if Sam must fall in love with someone, then it would be with herself. She'd learned to think of love as her due, or her fate; in her limited experience this was how men behaved towards her. She would not have welcomed his devotion, of course, would have been gracious in her refusal, but it might have been a pick-me-up. Not used to being considered second-best, Rose even grudged Marion her saintliness that it should make her shine the brighter in Sam's eyes. And though she knew that she did herself no credit by this pique, she wondered at Marion's inconstancy in the matter of suitors and crossly speculated what Sam, professed teetotaller, had been doing in a pub.

The following week Marion contrived to call every evening that Sam was at Raglan Street. Of course this shift in their relationship was not acknowledged between them, and Marion could not have been accused of 'encouraging' him – one does not wheedle the sun into being sunny – and he certainly did not deploy silly compliments; what need for these, when she was impassioned by conscience? A strange courtship, this, centred upon the excitement of reform. Rose felt as though she was present at a public meeting, though she acknowledged that this was livelier to listen to, and all three of them were soon hotly absorbed in the politics of *what is to be done?* Rose reflected that she should at least be grateful that while Sam wooed Marion with socialist utopias, she seemed to forget her ulterior motive of luring her back to Harold. By the third evening they were discussing Sam's latest enthusiasm, for building societies, that he'd brought back with him from Halifax.

As they ran on and on, constructing working men's castles in the air, Rose thought of the countryside eaten up, trampled underfoot, by uniform rows of democratic housing and privies and washing lines.

'Why does social justice have to be so ugly and so cramped?' Rose interrupted without meaning to. 'And why must it always come in red brick or grey?'

'While majority live like badly lodged animals, beauty mun wait its turn,' Sam responded.

'But don't you think that the human soul needs to be exalted at the same time as his body is housed and clothed and fed?'

'Aye, lass, men deserve beauty and all the other refinements. But bricks 'n' mortar and bread come first,' replied the pragmatist.

'Bricks and bread *and* flowers,' corrected Rose. 'I know they serve no purpose, I mean you can't eat flowers, but isn't there escape and consolation for everyone in natural beauty?'

'Bricks and bread and flowers,' he repeated, smiling. He put an arm round each pair of shoulders. 'Eh, talkin' wi' you lasses inspires me!'

Marion smiled at him and said, without thinking twice, 'Oh, how I'd love to bring my brother Harold here to meet you, Sam, to share in our debates.'

A chill passed through Rose, as though Harold was indeed in the room. For as Marion and Sam's attachment deepened, she saw that Raglan Street could not much longer remain her secret sanctuary. She *must* be gone.

Rose's only other caller was Joan, whose visits were more infrequent. Yet every half-day holiday she loyally took the tram to visit her aunt in Raglan Street, bringing news of home that Rose was half eager, half unwilling to hear. At that week's end she waited in trepidation for the latest instalment as though for the next chapter in a serialised novel, and almost felt that it was Joan who kept her tied to Raglan Street.

Joan had just told her the latest about Mona's scalded hand when she suddenly said, 'You're not thinking of leaving 'ere, miss?'

Rose, taken aback, said sharply, 'Did you think I'd stop on forever?'

Joan looked down-at-mouth. 'You'll not leave me behind, though. You'll promise to tek me with you when you go?'

'How can I promise you that, Joan, when I have no means of looking after myself?'

The two girls lay back on the hard, high bedstead and gazed up at the ceiling. Rose thought Joan looked puffy and stout.

'You are getting fat,' she said, by way of changing the subject. Joan did not reply. 'There isn't enough work for you to do since I've been gone,' she went on, trying to pinch Joan's waist. Joan slapped away her hand.

'There's quite enough, thank you. My mistress 'as set me to unpicking all those dratted pillow cases as you embroidered.' She held up her fingers for Rose to examine for puncture holes. 'It's been a business, I can tell tha, pullin' out all of them tight stitches – eh, but you're a poor sewer, miss.'

'Unhappy Joan.' Rose kissed her fingertips and the girl pulled herself over onto her side to look directly down into Rose's face. A fat tear landed on Rose's chin.

'I'll 'ave nowhere to go,' sobbed Joan. 'Oh miss, whatever am I to do?'

'Are you suspected?' Rose was suddenly on the alert to that danger. She sat up and asked accusingly, 'Joan, now tell me, you haven't let it out, have you?'

'No, miss. But it can't be long now,' she wailed in reply.

'Swear to me that you'll never tell,' insisted Rose fiercely, and then, remembering her lapse over Marion, 'I mean, swear to tell absolutely no one else!'

Joan shivered. 'You can be sure I'll not tell a livin' soul voluntary. 'Owever,' she swallowed her tears, 'I don't know 'ow long it'll be before 'tis plain enough for all to see.'

Then Rose herself saw.

'You're to have a baby,' she stated and Joan nodded in miserable agreement.

'I am.'

'It's John's, is it?' And then, feeling very modern, 'But it can't be. Wasn't it the autumn of last year that you two fell out?'

Joan, looking more crushed, replied, ''Tis 'is though, miss. 'E tempted me back into going with 'im again i' the spring.'

'Silly girl,' Rose said, stroking her cheek.

Joan cried harder, saying between her loud sobs, 'It were only ever outside, miss – didn't feel like it could count, an' I swear it weren't no more'n a couple of times . . .'

'And he has abandoned you?'

Joan did not answer, only nodded her head.

'He shall be made to acknowledge the baby and do the right thing by you,' Rose said with a confidence she didn't feel.

''E took off a month back, no one knows where,' answered Joan flatly. 'Oh, whatever shall I do, dismissed wi'out a character and no one to turn to?'

The two lay in silence. Their extensive study of the ruined and deserted serving girl in books informed them that, after her master's door had slammed irrevocably behind her and she found herself standing alone in the snow, self-murder (usually by river) or the workhouse were the inevitable outcome. What were the other, practical, everyday alternatives?

'Can't you come here, to your aunt?' asked Rose.

Joan sobbed harder. 'They're Wesleyan!' was her woeful response.

'I see,' said Rose calmly, her mind in a whirl. 'But Joan dear, you can't come with me. I don't know how I shall provide for myself, let alone you and a baby!'

The two girls sobbed and hugged.

When it was time for Joan to leave, Rose said to her, 'Don't worry, we'll think of something, Joan pet. And I promise I won't leave you behind without telling you, and I'll be sure to send for you if I can.'

She said it to comfort Joan but how hollow those words sounded, for she still had not the vaguest idea when that would be or where she would go.

The next day the Jannock household was all at sixes and sevens. Flor had attempted to rid the cat of fleas by bathing it in Jeyes fluid, which had caused it to stagger around the house, vomiting, and left it at last expiring upon the kitchen mat. The little girls cried, Mrs Jannock scolded and Rose attempted to feed Tricks some milk to neutralise the effects of household disinfectant upon its poor little inside.

Sam Samuel still stopped on at Raglan Street and Marion had sent a card to say that she would call. So the knock at the door sent Rose galloping away to receive her friend, her sleeves rolled to the elbows and one of Mrs Jannock's aprons wrapped round her. There stood her cousin Guy.

'Rose.' He held out his hat and gloves for her to take, as though she were the maid of all work. 'I didn't guess it had come to this.'

Rose attempted to slam the door in his face but he put his foot in the way.

'You know Cousin Guy, I was only joshing. Won't you let a fellow in?'

Just then Sam Samuel appeared in a rush. He'd evidently seen the altercation upon the doorstep and taken Guy for a brute – perhaps the very brute who'd been at the bottom of beautiful Miss Rose's tragedy (some species of tragedy was his only explanation for her incongruous presence in Raglan Street). He was not one to pass by on the other side when he saw a bully at work.

'What's goin' off 'ere?' he called loudly. 'I say, 'ands off, Nimrod!'

By this time he was shrugging off his coat and squaring up to the stout, stooping figure of Guy, who ignored him. He turned to Rose. 'I can't bear scenes in the street, so plebbish. Won't you let me in?'

'None of your nonsense, mister,' said Sam, then to Rose; 'Should I cave 'is flippin' 'ead in for 'im, miss?'

'No, Sam. This gentleman is my cousin, Mr Guy Seaton. He was not expected and his call isn't welcome.' She looked hard at Guy. 'But I suppose I must be polite and invite him in.'

The two went to the parlour while the rest of the household conducted itself on tiptoe and in whispers so that they might know what passed between them. Sam was still sure that this gentleman caller was implicated in the mysterious dilemma of his high-born fellow lodger and he was roused to protectiveness. Mrs Jannock hoped for aristocratic romance: reconciliation with the dashing lover (she *was* Joan's relation). Of course she had not seen the popping eyes or soft hips of the suitor at the door.

'Who's the game cock?' asked Guy.

'A friend,' Rose replied, still bridling.

He let that pass and looked slowly around the cramped and shabby room. 'Rose, you must come home. Come back to your own people and to the place where you belong.'

He spoke with such a depth of sympathy that she looked at him and waited for more.

'You can't know what misery you left behind you or you surely wouldn't be able to sit here in this grubby little room with such a look of pettish superiority on your pretty face,' he said, risking a little more warmth now that he had her, as he thought. Too much and too soon, for she rose as though to exit the room.

'Put t'wood int' 'oil when you leave,' she said simply.

'Now, Rose, stop. Blast it! Is there no reasoning with you?'

She paused at the door. 'Who sent you? Was it my father after his absconding bondswoman?'

'Neither your father nor your mother knows where you are. I had it from your maid, what's-her-name . . .'

'Joan,' supplied Rose. 'That girl is like a leaking bucket.'

'Joan,' he confirmed. 'You mustn't blame her, quite some pressure had to be applied to get it out of her. And,' he looked down as though weighing his words with care, 'I had an additional motive in finding you out – I mean additional to restoring you to the familial hearth . . .'

They looked at one another for a while, then Guy continued, 'I know that the old man has been pretty intolerable, but still, an unprotected maiden belongs at home and in the care of her people and all that . . .'

'And the other motive for finding me, Guy?' she asked.

He could not meet her eyes. 'You won't countenance returning to the parental nest under any circumstances?'

'Under no circumstances.' She thought of Harold, imagined him in a rage, and then remembered his tears in the wood, and knew that she could never go back.

'Well then, now then! Here's a jolly turn-up, the thing is I've taken a little house, a cottage really, in the West Country and I'm just on my way there now . . .'

'Guy, are you inviting me to stay? How awfully kind,' she said, jumping up. He paused and gave a rueful giggle.

'I appreciate it's awfully short warning. Will there be time to give your notice here and pack and so on? As I say, I only dropped in here on the off chance.'

'You mean we're leaving right now?'

'The carriage awaits, so to speak.'

She abandoned Raglan Street without a thought for Marion or a word for Joan. Indeed, she felt as though Joan deserved a little punishment for having broken, yet again, her promise to keep a secret.

# Chapter 26

As Rose unpacked her suitcase in the dirty bedroom of the hotel where Guy had brought her, she heard the sound of someone moving about in the room next door, perhaps unpacking too. She stopped what she was doing, suddenly bashful, for it felt an impropriety to betray awareness of a stranger lost in their own intimate sense of privacy.

'She'll be coming round the mountain when she comes, she'll be coming round the mountain when she comes. She'll be coming round the mountain, coming round the mountain, coming round the mountain when she comes!' He sang lustily, evidently uninhibited by the possibility that he was overheard.

Rose went on with her unpacking. She'd had to leave her best blouse at Raglan Street as its lace trim had been unpicked, washed and starched and awaited Mrs Jannock's goffering iron before re-attachment. She hoped that Mrs Jannock would be able to get something for it as she'd had no money to leave as a tip. But then, was a tip appropriate, as would be expected by the ladies' maid of a house where one was a weekend guest? Perhaps not.

She'd miss Dor and Flor. She'd miss Marion and Sam but she doubted they'd miss her, so locked up were they in the present moment of their love for each other and their mission to end injustice in all its forms. Thank God for Guy, then. He'd turned up in the nick of time. Now she was free of the problem of where to go and what to do after Raglan Street. The darling little West Country cottage would provide the breathing space she needed. There she'd have time to sleep safe in the arms of Guy, as it were. Let the future hang, it was too tiring to think right now. Once she'd eaten and so on, then she'd think. Perhaps she would even be able to send for sad, deserted Joan.

At dinner she sat opposite Guy and knew what it was, for the first time in her life, to appear shabby and ill-at-ease among people who could barely claim respectability themselves. She hadn't noticed, until now, how dingy her few clothes had grown and how dull and flat her hair without Joan to brush and dress it three times a day. She must look like Guy's floozy. She laughed to think it.

'Oh, Guy, lemon sole. You do spoil me!' she shrieked, a little hysterical with her wary relief and the pretence that she was a shop girl gone to the bad. Perhaps the wine had made her tipsy. Guy looked mildly surprised at her.

'Aren't you curious to know where I'm taking you?'

She deflated before his eyes. 'D'you know, I'm really not. I'm just too, too tired to care any more. I've lived too long and I've seen too much and I just don't care. You could sell me into the white slave trade and I wouldn't be a bit surprised.'

'Now then,' said Guy equably. 'No need for that. You shan't know a thing if you don't want to. Leave it all up to Cousin Guy.'

'This isn't all a trick to get me back to my parents?' she said, suddenly suspicious.

He looked baffled. 'I should think not, not at all. In fact I'd say we've all put ourselves well and truly beyond the pale now.'

'Good old Guy. Good, good, good old Guy.'

And she was so tired and tipsy that she didn't even try to find out what he meant by this ambiguous remark. She just loved him so. She loved him for giving her this feeling. of floating free, not having to worry about money, or where she was going, or anything. Maybe she had had too much wine.

Later, in the cold and clammy bed she heard again movements from the neighbouring room and hoped that he had not been aware of the sound of her gargling lavishly and spitting into the bowl on her night stand. She thought how rude it was to hear the creak of his bedsprings next door and curled up tight, giggling to herself under her covers. Perhaps she would hear another come into the room and climb into the squeaking bed with him. Perhaps it was Guy! She giggled even more hysterically, little snorts escaping. She could not imagine Guy in bed with anyone. She pictured him sleeping majestic in his moustache guard and hair net. How curious that she couldn't imagine Guy with any species of person in a bed in that way. Poor Guy.

She was only aware that she had fallen asleep because she was now awake. Perhaps the man next door had snored or used his chamber pot? Rose lay very still and listened in the darkness of her unfamiliar room. This room felt large and over-stuffed after the austerity of Raglan Street; the bulky silhouettes of the furniture were not known to her, or the location of the door or the lamp. Then she saw a shape move before the thin curtain that covered the dim window.

'She'll be coming round the mountain when she comes . . .'

He came over to the bed and put out his hand, blindly, to explore for her on it.

'She'll be coming round the mountain when she comes . . .'

Rose gave a repressed gasp as she felt him touch her forehead and he stopped singing and said, sounding surprised, 'You're awake?'

# *Chapter 27*

The next morning Guy ate his kipper, read his paper and bit his nails down with exasperation and still there was no sign of Rose. Should he telegraph to Edy to let her know that at this rate they wouldn't be down in Cornwall until the weekend? He wished that this part of the plan hadn't been left up to him, he had never been one for subterfuges. Still, when he'd seen sweet little Rose dressed in that ghastly apron with her sleeves rolled up to her elbows, it had given him the courage to pull it off; it had been the right thing. Hadn't it?

At last he sent a passing hotel drudge to inquire at the door of the young lady and was surprised by her knowing reply that the lady *and* gentleman would be down directly. What in the blazes?

'So sorry, Guy. You know I'm a terrible one for stage-management. I *do* love to orchestrate an entrance,' said Patrick with that casual assumption that not only would he be forgiven his trespasses, he'd be loved for them.

'This is très rum. I thought the whole point was to meet us on the train,'

'Oh, I've already done that one,' said the impresario, giving Rose a squeeze. 'I must be original. And don't we all love surprises?'

'Well, I don't know, I don't know about this at all. I must say,

I don't like to be made to feel the pander,' Guy replied huffily.

'The thing is, old man, Rose and I had a lot of talking to do to put all right between us. And a rattling train carriage, full of ladies listening in from behind their knitting, wouldn't have been the place.'

But bed had been, thought Rose. If he had been less of a stage manager, would he have been able to woo her back?

'She'll be riding six white horses, riding six white horses, riding six white horses when she comes . . .' And he'd slipped into bed and whispered in her ear, 'Are you wearing red pyjamas? It's too dark to see.'

She'd known him, even in the dark and even with the bushy beard that now tickled her neck.

He'd settled himself, getting comfortable next to her.

'Why do you come now?' she asked. 'You're too late.' A year of weeping and regret, a year of Harold Webb, the Jannocks, Sam Samuel, Marion, Joan's baby, stood between then and now. All these were not a sideshow, they were the real life that she had struggled through to be free of him.

He rocked the bed as he put his arms behind his head and she wondered that, even now, he should be so insouciant.

'I didn't catch up with you that day in Paris. And I should have done. And I didn't pursue you back across the Channel, and I should have done. I hate to think what you must have called me.' He went silent again. And she realised that all that time she'd neither hated nor blamed him even though he'd made her more unhappy than she'd known it was possible to be and still live. Yet, somehow, now that she had the opportunity to take it out on him, she was letting the chance slip. He was so quiet that she wondered whether he dozed, damn him. But he had not fallen asleep for he spoke again in a voice now thick with emotion.

'You probably supposed that I went back to Veronique. And you would have been right to think it.' He paused as though to give her the opportunity to respond but she remained quiet, numbed in her agony.

'Well then.' He swallowed and went on, 'Here's what happened that day, the day you left me. Here's what happened. I was leaving the atelier to come after you when a friend brought me a note from her—'

'And you went running straight off there!' Rose interrupted scornfully.

'It was a suicide note,' he replied simply.

They lay in silence again.

'Did she die?' asked Rose at last, giving him her full cold fury.

'Yes, she did,' he answered. 'Slowly. She'd taken some caustic cleaning fluid which burned her inside but didn't kill her outright.'

Rose had a sudden image of poor Tricks, Flor's kitlin, coughing up blood-flecked froth on the mat.

'I was maddened, trying to find a doctor to help her, first to give her something to stop the action of the poison, at last to take away the terrible pains.' He stopped again and Rose realised that he did not languish but was rigid with the re-telling.

'I wrote a note to you for faithful Gaspard to deliver.' He paused and she heard his release of breath at the irony of that. 'True to form he did not find you.'

'Edy and I left the hotel early that same evening. I never wanted to see you again.'

'Nevertheless it was sent. I couldn't bear the thought of you waiting there, not knowing what had happened, thinking – the worst. I wanted to come myself but I just couldn't leave her to die alone in that squalor and in so much agony. Rose, you yourself couldn't have left her.'

'How long did it take?'

'I don't know. It was dark. And then there were so many papers to fill in and questions to answer. I was arrested and spent the night at the gendarmerie. By the time I was free again and came to look for you, you'd cleared out.'

'You must have known where I went. If you were so concerned, you could have followed me.'

'I know, I know. But somehow I couldn't get that last picture of Veronique out of my head.' He paused and swallowed. 'I tried to drink it away – fell in with some of my old cronies from the debauching days, went on a bender and chased the green fairy into the gutter with them until I was disgusted with myself and with life. And then, when I sobered up, it was too late, much too late. I thought that you'd be better off without me, a bad influence.' He gave a little self-deprecating laugh and she felt her anger bubble in her throat.

'Too late? Certainly it was too late for me. Did you think I could go quietly home and just pick up my old life again, with no consequences?'

No reply.

She went on, 'You can't imagine, can you? To you "consequences" mean a sore head and after a clean slate—'

'No, Rose! I heard from Guy that you were back at home, reconciled with your people, and thought that was probably for the best. Although I longed to go to you . . .'

'But you resisted.'

'And there *were* consequences for me. I took myself off to America, far enough away so you would be safe, out of my reach.'

'You became a remittance man, I suppose.'

He did not like that, but answered, 'Yes, as you guess, Mrs Van der Decken contributed some dollars towards my passage.'

'But you were free to go, free to begin your life again as you chose.'

'Rose, I think I went there to die.' He was quiet again, perhaps to let what he'd said take its effect on her. 'I didn't have the courage to take my own life, like Veronique, so I put myself in the way of fate so that it might be taken from me. I worked my way across country, sometimes as a day labourer, sometimes as a plain hobo, I mean a sort of American tramp, and never was ill or injured or abused or robbed the whole way across to the territory they mistakenly call the Wild West.' He gave a bitter laugh. 'The time was not yet come for my tragic early demise.'

He stopped and sighed and Rose imagined Patrick, a tiny figure plodding across that vast wilderness with the vivid blue of heaven arcing above while she sat in her reverie, enclosed in narrow South Yorkshire. She considered how his story eclipsed her own.

'After six months as a hired hand on a farm in North Dakota I found that I was still, miraculously, alive. And I understood that to be alive mattered.'

'And you decided to come back to England?' Rose was moved, despite herself. Perhaps he sensed it, for he turned to face her.

'Yes. I came back. Strange, that overcrowded, overworked England seemed less of a wasteland, less cruel to me after the Dakotas. If nothing else, this last year taught me that the connection between human beings is the only significance in this lonely world.'

She wondered whether he thought of dead Veronique.

He gently stroked her hair, saying, 'And I realised that if I was meant to live, then my life's purpose must be to cleave to you and to love you forever. My salvation.'

Her heart leapt with unwilling glee. 'But how did you know I'd be here, at this hotel?'

He was taken aback at that for a while. Then he replied, hasty in his relief, now that he thought he might have a chance with her. 'I haven't just arrived home, Rose. It was I who sent Guy to get you. I have to admit he didn't exactly understand the plan. But he was in on it from the beginning, in a manner of speaking. When he told me you'd run away, I knew that you hadn't really settled for the old life and there might be a chance for me, if only I could grab it. You know how I love to follow my instinct.'

'When *did* you get back from America?' she asked suspiciously.

'Six weeks ago.' He hurried on before she had the chance to

flare up again. 'It's taken me that time to track you down. I couldn't approach your old man directly – thought he'd probably give me a horsewhipping – and Guy was pretty hopeless at working out where you'd gone when you skipped the twig.' He squeezed her to his side. 'It crossed my mind that you'd run off with that black-browed farming friend of yours.'

Harold Webb among the bluebells with tears running down his cheeks flashed again before Rose and she was glad that they were in darkness. She spoke up, to forestall further speculation about Harold. 'But you found me out from Joan in the end, didn't you?'

'I found you because dear, romantic Joan was eager to play her part in a happy ending,' he confirmed. 'And then I went about setting up new lives for us to go to.' He was holding her tight in his arms, so close that he could whisper into her ear, 'Let us two try again, Rose, let our lives be only ours from the very beginning, with no ghosts to haunt us this time. I will bring nothing and you will bring nothing, we'll get by living a life of excessive moderation, happy only to be together. For I know that once I've made sense of this life of mine I shall be happy.'

The disappointment of Paris, those dark, penitential Yorkshire months, the sentimental convalescence, drab, pointless – all were forgotten in the febrile excitement of being with him again. Being part of his adventure.

'Rose, I know I'm too hasty and you deserve a more protracted wooing from me. It's every woman's due to have a comfortable seven years in which to consider her answer: a couple to yield, several more to doubt, a month or two for falling out and weeping, then another couple to reconcile and consult the dressmaker . . .' Patrick held her chin and tilted her face though he cannot have read her expression in the dark. Would she soften? Would she kick over the traces?

A door had opened before her; she stepped through it and now all she wanted was to go on and on and never look back.

They held each other and wept together until they fell asleep in each other's arms, innocent as the babes in the wood under their covering of leaves.

So, here she was, starting off again upon the road of Patrick's quest: in pursuit of meaning, happiness, love – what else? He loved her, she loved him; what was she to do but hitch her wagon to his, shake loose and be on the move again? What lay ahead they could not guess, but what lay behind were surely two exhausted lives.

They rendezvoused with Patrick and Guy's luggage at the railway station and set off for the furthest extremity of east Cornwall and the coastal village where a pair of old fishermen's cottages were engaged for the summer. It had been Patrick's idea that they should join the artistic colony that had grown up in this far-flung part of Cornwall, to live and to work.

Rose, jogged by the motion of the train, looked at Patrick, long and elegantly lean, reposing on the carriage seat. He suited his new beard which was of a redder hue than his long curls. She thought how well made he was, although he had always a look of tension in his upper chest, causing him to hold his shoulders a little high and stiff. Still he was a beautiful man. Then she looked at Patrick's worn shoes which he'd put up on the seat next to her. What had appeared to be thin dirty socks she realised was his own grey, unwashed skin. He saw her looking and leaned forward.

'Somehow I know that in Cornwall we can invent a new, simple way of living,' he said eagerly, 'far away from everything that's corrupt and showy. We'll be in a community of like-minded souls who do not consume or strive like the ants in the ant heap, and I'll really begin to work properly at last, you'll see!'

As Patrick talked on about the philosophy which would shape their new lives together, Rose could not stop herself from wondering where the money would come from to pay for it.

They reached London where they changed onto the Great

Western Railway, and still Patrick talked and sang. On and on he talked, and with such manic enthusiasm that Guy and Rose's only recourse was to doze through it. As they travelled south-west, the train skirted the coast and they looked out at the bright sea and Rose felt her stomach leap with joy, even as Patrick pointed out the quality of the rocks and the light and the sky.

At Penzance station, Guy, Patrick and Rose took a fly. On being given directions to the out-of-the-way cottages, the driver drily remarked, 'You be artists, then?'

And from that moment Patrick seemed to have nothing left to say. So they drove in grateful silence through the dusk, down deep-sunk lanes, past windswept trees that grew up bent and then across a field at the edge of the world where the cottages stood, shoulder to shoulder, looking blankly out towards the sea across which the last owners had set out to find their fortunes.

Rose was glad to see that a light burned dimly in one window – perhaps they would be met by a cooked meal and made up beds.

She was handed down from the carriage into cold drizzle and the men unloaded their luggage. The low front door of the occupied cottage opened to show the silhouetted shape of Edy who seemed to be dressed in a brown shepherd's smock with an indigo tablecloth wrapped round her head.

'Welcome to Mount Cottage, welcome to Marazion, welcome to Cornwall,' she said as though it was, all of it, hers to bestow, and she gave unwilling Rose a kiss on both cheeks. Pulling at unresponsive Patrick's beard, she remarked, 'You'll understand if I don't kiss the face fungus – God knows what livestock you're breeding in there.'

They entered the lighted cottage which, with its little windows and smoking lamp, was close and dark. On the kitchen table the remains of a meal had been pushed aside to make way for parchment and watercolour paints and a jug of moon daisies. They had evidently surprised Edy in the middle of a creative act.

'Unimproved enough for you, old chap?' asked Guy, who

stooped to fit beneath ceiling beams low enough to ensure either a humbled attitude or a cracked skull.

Patrick replied only, 'Have you the key to next door?'

After travelling expectantly he now seemed thoroughly deflated to have arrived.

'Well, I like that. One might expect a chap to show a bit more gratitude. I can tell you, I had to fight off some pretty serious London offers to get it,' said Edy crossly.

Patrick wearily replied, 'It's divine, Edy. All of it. Now I must go to bed.'

They lit themselves to the next-door cottage with a candle and shoved open the door.

Evidently kind-hearted Edy had gone to no effort at all to make the place habitable for them. There was a smell of damp and mice, the oil lamp held no oil and the bed no sheets or blankets and the window stood ajar, letting in the cold, Cornish night. Rose sat down on a kitchen chair and began to cry. Raglan Street seemed a civilised ideal of welcoming warmth and comfort.

'Sorry about Edy,' said Patrick, draping his arm over her. 'When you wake up, the sun will be shining and we'll get this place straight and see about us.'

'Why did she have to be here?'

'Did you think I could uproot Guy without Edy catching on and hitching a lift?'

'And my aunt and uncle – do they know?'

'No. Keeping them in ignorance was Edy's leverage in being allowed to come too. She really is like an unpopular little girl who blackmails the others to let her play, isn't she?'

# Chapter 28

As Rose's enthusiasm for this second elopement shrivelled, so his revived. While she sat dully on the edge of the bed frame in the sloping upstairs bedroom, he rummaged in kitchen cupboards and blanket boxes.

'Just what we need!' he called up to her with childlike excitement. 'A cache of candles. Who would have thought the last tenants would have left these behind, and, by jingo, some wine!'

He set about placing the candles on the window sill, cementing them with their own melted wax along the top of the bedhead and standing them in saucers on the floor so that, when they were all lit from his tinder box, the place glowed with the illusion of warmth. Then Patrick opened his pack and he fed her on the last of his chocolate. Sitting side by side they alternated gulps from the bottle of wine until she really felt warmer, or at least her face was fiery with the wine and the cool, damp air.

Rose stirred then, as though she woke, and turned towards Patrick. His eyes reflected candlelight and she seemed to see lodged there the comfort and joy of a homecoming. She jumped up and stamped her chilled feet which ached as though they were iron-shod and clapped her hands until she laughed with the pain. Between them they shook out the eiderdown heavy with damp sea air and laid themselves under it, side by side on the hard, chill mattress, and saw their breath rise, like incense, above their pale faces. Unmoving they watched shadows flicker on the walls and Rose lay in Patrick's lean arms in the brass bed, in the cottage, on the edge of the dark and fathomless sea at midnight and felt cocooned.

'This is your honeymoon night, darling Rose,' said Patrick, holding her hand under the heavy cover.

'I don't think it can be if I am not married,' she answered quietly so as not to disturb the suspended moment.

'I have a ring . . .'

Moving cautiously under the eiderdown so as not to disturb it and let in the colder outside air, he reached into his pocket to feel around for something.

'Give me your left hand, Rose.'

He found her hand and pushed something onto the tip of her ring finger. They awkwardly turned to each other so that they lay face to face, eyes full of candlelight, and he said, 'Rose Seaton, spinster far from this parish and virgin, will you marry me, Patrick Michael McKinley, nominal bachelor and reformed rake?'

They breathed softly into each other's faces while he waited for her reply.

'I will,' she said.

He nodded and continued, 'And do you promise to enjoy his body as he intends to enjoy yours . . . I mean to worship yours?' He gave the devilish smile of a reformed rake and squeezed her hand under the bedclothes.

'Yes. I, Rose McKinley neé Seaton, promise to love, honour and obey . . . but, can I add something of my own?'

He nodded and, unseen, stopped the ring before it had seated itself at the root of her finger.

'Do you then, Patrick McKinley . . .' she faltered, 'Do you Patrick Michael McKinley promise never to be bored by me, or disgusted by me or to forsake me for another even if you're tired of me, tired of looking at my face,' she concluded with a rush, embarrassed by the naked need.

'Yes, yes to all that!' Patrick replied and, kissing her tenderly, pushed the ring home.

He undressed her and himself under the muffling eiderdown. As each piece of clothing was removed, they tossed it to the corners of the room or trampled it down to the end of the bed with their feet. Their two naked bodies came together at last, blindly, in that warm damp dark space. He felt alien to her at first: his hairy chest, his long, lean legs with hard kneecaps and his sharp elbows and jutting chin. But when he folded her close and held her tightly to him, she felt what he felt, the soft roundness of her own body. He ran his hands up and down her sides until she shivered and then he lay over her. She had a sudden memory of the bluebell wood and half instinctively pushed him away. Cautious but brooking no resistance, he covered her with his body again.

Afterwards they passed the night in sleeping and watching. Sometimes they slept together, sometimes one would wake and look at the tranquil face of the other, blue in the moonlight. One by one the candles, reminders of the night, guttered and drowned themselves in wax until only the two biggest burned on, pallid in the early sunshine, and Rose dreamed she was in a beautiful garden.

On starting awake, she realised that Patrick was no longer by her side. She looked at her finger and was perplexed to find there her own gold ring, a present from her mother on her sixteenth birthday. Then she remembered that the last time she'd seen it was when Veronique had flung it aside in that tawdry Parisian attic. So it had come back to her. But was it bad luck to have used one's own ring? Rose felt obscurely that she'd married herself.

She found her shawl at the end of the bed and wrapped it round herself to look out of the bedroom window for Patrick. What appeared to be a mist-wreathed fairy castle floated just offshore, like the mysterious flying island of Laputa, in *Gulliver's Travels*, that trailed roots and ladders by which the inhabitants climbed up or down. Then she saw Patrick, standing on the beach, looking out towards the island as though he was considering whether to go to it and stow away. As she looked at Patrick standing upon the brink Edy, wrapped in a blanket, approached him like a crab scuttling across the sand. Little sneak, thought Rose, although it made her glad to know that however Edy tried to ingratiate herself, Patrick did not want her. Patrick loved only her. She turned the ring on her finger and smiled.

When they joined Edy and Guy for breakfast, they found a local fisherman's wife, Mrs Black, cooking eggs and bacon. She'd been engaged to do for both cottages and would shop and cook and char for the rest of the summer.

Patrick ate ravenously, and looked only at Rose.

Mrs Black evidently did not approve of 'artists'; they, however, being unused to considering that servants might have opinions, ignored her clashing frying pan and remarks about blankets being for inside use only.

'A shame you missed the cricket match,' Edy said, shovelling eggs. 'We had such fun on the beach. I must introduce you to the gang. Stanhope Forbes himself and Elizabeth F. are adorable both. But I have my own particular *friend*, she's a wild colonial, would you believe! Terribly talented, shockingly *nouveau*. You must meet her.'

Patrick winked at Rose and said nothing.

Guy said, 'Never mind the artistic bohemians, have you sent your card to the St Aubyns over there on the island?'

'No, I have not! We're here for plain livin' and high thinkin', not to pursue social connections, aren't we, Pat?'

But Patrick still did not answer; he was too busy stroking Rose's leg under cover of the table.

'Is that who lives in the fairy castle, the St Aubyns?' Rose asked, feigning interest. She didn't want to hurt Guy's feelings.

'You mean St Michael's Mount – yes, I believe they've been living there for a couple of hundred years, moved in after Jack rid the place of the resident giant. But it's not a real island, you know. When the tide is low there's a causeway one can walk across so it's not completely isolated in its enchantment.'

'I will have to see about getting materials.' Patrick spoke at last.

'No problem there, you must walk round the bay to Penzance or take a cab to Newlyn or St Ives. Everything you could need is available,' said proprietorial Edy. 'In this neck of the woods, Art is the coming industry, soon to outstrip salt pilchard production, I'm told.'

A wire of anxiety tightened in Rose's chest. Did he want to leave her alone so soon? But he looked at her and said, 'I came with nothing, darling. I haven't put a brush to canvas since . . . in nearly a year and I would surely die of despair to be here, looking at your beautiful face, with no means of immortalising it.'

So Patrick walked off to Newlyn, Guy engaged Mrs Black in the niceties of how his shirts must be boiled, and Rose and Edy were left alone together, for the first time since Rose had fled to Raglan Street.

'I suppose that at least your parents are now correct in their assumption that the fiendish Patrick McKinley abducted you – there might be some satisfaction in that, however metaphysical.'

'Is that what they thought had happened to me?'

'Of course, what else? Wasn't it as plain as sin? At least you proved them right in the end!'

'I wish I hadn't made them unhappy. I suppose they will never accept Patrick now.'

'I should rather think not!' snorted Edy. 'Anyway, here you are, and here we all are.' She looked speculatively at Rose. 'I'd strongly advise you to find something to do with yourself. Take up potting or some such. You really won't fit in here one little bit if you don't *create*.'

Rose escaped her cousin and walked down to the curving sands of Mount's Bay. In the midst of a vast solitude, terns and the constantly bobbing dippers were the only living things in sight. The sea seemed to suck up into itself her tiny, irrelevant life. The salty wind blew her head empty. She was like one of the little birds that ran in and out at the margin of the sea, leaving the chain stitch of their footprints for the waves to wipe clean, and wipe clean again. And she felt happy in her pointlessness. No need to struggle, just be – part of the indifferent, natural world that carelessly, ceaselessly renewed itself. The only thing of significance was that here she loved and was loved. And here there was nothing to remind her of Sheffield: no distant prospect of chimneys, no smell of smoke carried on the wind, just the endless sea and sand and sky. She took off her shoes and stockings and walked and walked along the sand, round the curve of the bay until she reached the castle on its mount. The causeway that linked the island with the little town was now exposed by the retreating tide. How like a fairytale, this intermittent link between the real and the magical worlds. The prince can break in and carry off his princess to begin her happy ending, she thought, but only if he's decisive and quick. She hugged herself tight and whirled around on the flat sand.

As she wandered back to the pair of cottages, she saw that Edy, now wearing a scarlet smock and green button boots (*haute couture* did not suit in arty Cornwall), was sitting in a deckchair in the garden of her cottage with another woman. Rose toiled up the sandy bank to them, her feet gritty and dirty. A little, hairy, irritable black dog which was tied to the strange lady's chair yipped at her. Approaching from below, grabbing coarse grass to help her climb, Rose felt at a disadvantage. She saw that the other woman was as small as Edy but doll-like rather than runtish and with a pixie perfect face framed by very thick black hair which was cut in a heavy fringe.

'Hulloo there,' called Edy as though she were hailing a passing boat. 'Come and meet Keziah Trewren, my traveller from New Zealand.'

'Don't listen to her,' said the pixie, ignoring the paroxysms of her dog. 'I might come from New Zealand but I'm Cornish in my principal parts, except for my murderer's thumbs and those I get from a Danish great-grandmother.' She showed her strange, strong thumbs which were at odds with her graceful limbs and small features.

'Keziah, this is my disconcertingly pretty cousin, Rose Seaton,' said Edy.

'Tena koe?' Keziah Trewren held out her ill-made hand to shake Rose's.

'Is that "how do you do?"'

Keziah smiled in reply.

'Very well, thank you, then,' said Rose, and let the dog smell her fingers until he shut up, before continuing, 'Who did the great-grandmother murder?'

'Perhaps the great-grandfather, he certainly deserved it. But don't worry, nurture triumphed over nature in the succeeding generations and I am personally inclined to murdering hardly at all. Although I'd probably best steer clear of marrying black-tempered Cornishmen.'

Rose fetched herself a kitchen chair and set it down beside Keziah Trewren, and they all three looked out long-sighted over the bay.

'Do you paint?' asked Keziah.

Before Rose could answer, Edy said, 'No, she does not. Her artistic impulse finds its expression in fleeing. My cousin Rose is a phenomenal absconder.'

Rose could have murdered Edy, thumbs or no, but Keziah leapt with enthusiasm.

'I knew we'd have something in common the moment I saw you coming up the beach. And my Impy was clearly beside himself with glee,' she said, by way of introducing the dog. 'I



LIMERICK
COUNTY LIBRARY

come from a whole continent of absconders and am descended from a long line of the breed myself. The Trewrens gave the go to mother England and scampered right across to the South Pacific, only for me to bolt all the way back again—'

'To the very cottage that her forefathers once inhabited,' Edy interrupted.

'Oh, Edy, don't make it sound as though I'm a sentimental idiot set on lyricising the old country and hanging on the words of adorably gnarled fishermen. You and I,' she said to Rose, ignoring Edy, 'must talk about wandering. I think restlessness is a perfectly acceptable pursuit, for how is one to learn if one stands still and never meets anyone new? And all the best stories in literature are about itchy feet – look at Ulysses.'

'Ulysses was travelling home, not running away from it,' commented Edy sourly. 'Better to quote the tale of Karen and her red shoes,' she went on, reciting in a witchy voice, '"Dance you shall, dance. And she danced and was obliged to go on dancing over field and fell, by night and by day – but by night it was most *horrible*!"'

'Edy, dear, you know that is a nasty, cautionary tale invented by the clergy and school masters to keep us girls tame and plain. I'm all for red satin shoes and dancing.' Keziah stood and, taking Rose by the hands, danced with her around the sandy garden, pursued by the dog and singing, 'See me dance the polka!' until all three were panting. Rose liked Keziah. Even if Keziah hadn't had the added appeal of being effortlessly dismissive of Edy, Rose would have liked her. She was perhaps only the second person in Rose's life for whom she'd felt this instant attraction. Perhaps it was because of what Keziah Trewren dared.

That evening, while the last of the sun still warmed the land, Rose and Patrick lay in bed without the cover, wrapped only in each other's arms and legs. She told him about the beach, about Keziah Trewren and her nasty little dog and her murderer's thumbs. He enthused about the Newlyn artists and their plans for an out-of-doors painting expedition tomorrow. It was comfortable lying close in bed, discussing the past day and sharing plans for the next: easy to have been apart, content to have come together again.

'We shall be happy here, shan't we, Rose? I feel that we shall.'

He kissed her and she kissed him back and thought that, yes, they should.

# Chapter 29

Rose and Keziah had arranged to meet the next morning to go for a walk along the curve of the bay, after breakfast. As they left the windswept gardens of the twin cottages, the dark and the blonde head were angled together as though they shared a secret. Impy spurted away in advance of them, a single spy, sent to explore and then back to report on what he'd found.

'Isn't your Mrs Black a caution? I swear that woman can disapprove with the back of her neck,' said Keziah.

'It's mostly me and Edy she doesn't like. She can't get the measure of Patrick, that's his technique. And, despite herself, she's impressed that Guy knows how to get grease spots out of silk.'

'Your husband *is* intriguing. Possibly the most intriguing man in the whole of the east Cornish peninsula.'

Rose was pleased with that: her husband was admired.

They walked on along the tidal margin where the dry sand softly slipped or, sea-soaked, sucked at their feet. They halted, a little out of breath, and looked to the horizon.

'It's a funny thing how these Cornwallers feel invaded by us artistic incomers, isn't it?' Keziah remarked. 'I don't know why they can't just imagine us all as divine shipwrecked sailors.'

'Perhaps because we come and go by the Great Western Railway?' Rose teased.

'Well, I at least bothered to cross the sea,' she replied.

'But why did you wash up here, Keziah, if it wasn't for the gnarled fishermen?'

'My dear, if you could only know how very little, dull and far away New Zealand is.' She flung a stick for Impy who sped away, yodelling. 'Not unlike living in Surrey, if Surrey were relocated on the moon. Anybody who wants a life of the mind has to get out.'

'So you escaped?'

'Ran for my life!' Keziah corrected her. She pulled the stick from the jaws of dancing Impy and threw it again, shading her eyes against the sun. 'Don't misunderstand me, it was a blissful childhood – scones and jam for tea, and after games of canasta.' She looked obliquely at Rose. 'But always the feeling that there was something nasty stalking one in the southern twilight.'

'My goodness,' said Rose, 'you make it sound so exciting!'

'Darling, it's not. New Zealand is a lovely place to live for the pre-pubescent, the senile and their dogs. It just wouldn't do for me – turned me vicious.'

They went on again until they reached St Michael's Mount. The causeway was being nibbled away by waves.

'If you were trying to avoid the strange and mysterious then wasn't Cornwall the very worst place to come – all those mischievous Browneys and Boggarts and Knockers, and the bells of the lost land of Lyonesse ringing out under the sea?'

'But, darling, it's so benign! Just think of King Arthur. His name is taken in vain above every teashop door. In New Zealand it's all the other way about, nothing spoken, everything going on beneath the surface.' She paused to consider. 'It's like a very, very boring dance with a murdered body lying below one's feet in the cellar, which everyone knows is there but is too polite to mention.'

'And that's what drove you halfway around the world?'

Keziah laughed. 'Dear heart, no. In the end it was the doilies on plates, the quilting bees and the bully amateur theatricals that did for me'

'We have all those here,' Rose laughed back.

'Well, I must admit, there was the tiniest bit of a scandal too to send me on my way.'

They stopped again and Rose looked closely at her friend, who turned away from the unspoken inquiry. To bridge the moment, Keziah picked up Impy and nuzzled him hard until he yelped and then she said, 'That is a story that must wait for another day. However, it *was* the most exciting thing to happen on North Island since seventeen ninety-two.'

The two girls and the dog turned back the way they'd come, stepping in their back-to-front footprints as they went.

The late summer days passed and the little colony of artists who lived in and about Newlyn and St Ives visited and re-visited. Patrick would bring back a Frank or a Fred or a Walter to argue about what would be a truly English palette and a truly English subject, uncontaminated by the light or the vitiated romanticism of France. They set up easels on the beach, they used cool tones and painted ugly fish factory girls with big, chapped arms, looking out to sea; they painted china clay pits and abandoned tin mines. They turned from serried canal-side poplars and sought out the sloped, wind-blown trees of the Cornish coast. The two cottages on Mount's Bay were integrated into the loose network of artists. At any time there might be three or more sharing the spare bedroom. The greater the crowd and the more the chaos, the more Patrick loved the merry company they kept. He issued casual invitations to come and share a pickle with anyone he picked up. He got up treasure hunts and marathon sing-songs and games on the beach. And at the end of long summer days of painting they'd drag the easy chairs out into the garden to sit outside and drink and argue by the light of the moon. An Arthur would play his banjo, an Alfred expatiate upon the need for honesty in art before he passed out with too much brandy. All were like happy children who leave their suppers and leave their sleep to join their fellows in anarchic play on the beach. Rose was nearly as thrilled as Patrick by this carefree existence. They were like the benignly smiling parents of this raggle-taggle gang of lost boys. Her one tiny grudge was that the only proper, exclusive intimacy she had with him was in their bed – but then, she explained to herself, Patrick was such a beacon for others that she knew she could not keep him hidden under a bushel, or a bedspread.

A tradition grew up that anyone who visited the Mount's Bay cottages must leave their mark: paint a mural on the wall or decorate an item of furniture or even a pot. Keziah contributed a dado line of long-legged running birds round Rose and Patrick's bedroom walls and then added monkeys hanging by their tails from the cornice. These days Mrs Black flinched each time she entered the cottage. She spent a whole afternoon scraping off the flowers that someone had painted in enamels on the stove and threatened to report them to the authorities. Patrick commented that Mrs Black evidently had a high-up connection at the Royal Academy.

Mrs Black had another reason to find these summer visitors wanting: they stretched the housekeeping. As far as she was concerned, it was to the small blonde lady, and to her alone, that she'd answer. And if this lady didn't give her sufficient money or menus for meals to feed an army, then the hangers-on could lump it.

Rose began to appreciate what it was to be poor, as poor perhaps as Veronique's parents even, but she hadn't a notion how to scrimp and screw and make do. Since they never ate alone, they never had enough and that was an end to it. All her daydreams were of food, but Patrick was never bothered by hunger or dread of future want; he thrived on inadequate nutrition and uncertain prospects, seemingly nurtured solely by love and turpentine and present company.

A month after their arrival in Cornwall, as they lay in their salt-blebbed brass bed, Rose said, 'What I wouldn't give for a really lovely cutlet!'

Patrick squeezed her to his side. 'Is that the highest you can wish for, a lovely cutlet? If you are going to wish for something, shouldn't you at least ask for the stars?' He waved a hand at the window against which bulged the night sky.

'Well, I'd settle for having lots of money, then I could have all the cutlets I could eat and everything else I wanted as well.'

'And the stars?' he mournfully asked.

'Well, I can have the stars whenever I look up. They'll continue to be there forever and ever, not caring for me, here on earth, starving for a good meal.'

'I'd rather have the stars,' he said, and disengaged his arm. 'I don't yearn after *things*. I'm really not a very satisfactory product of the times. I don't belong to my day at all, Rose. Everything this banal century celebrates about itself, I hate. I hate the machine-made ideas and the mob emotion, the keeping up with the Joneses, the shop-bought dinners and John Bull and factory girls out on a Saturday night and "made in Sheffield".'

Rose was shocked by his vehemence. 'Of course it's all second-rate and ugly,' she forbore to challenge the inclusion of Sheffield, 'but you can't blame people for liking to buy their dinners, or for wasting their wages on a spree or on ugly ornaments, or for jingoism or Empire or the Queen or any of it.' She hadn't lived three long months in Raglan Street without appreciating that it was just these cheap little pleasures that sustained life when there was so little hope of better. 'Anyway, we aren't like that.'

'But I think we are. Our class strives for things and money, it's just that educated tastes aspire to a cutlet rather than boiled beef and carrots and we prefer swanky seats at the opera to stalls at the Alhambra, but it all ends up in the same fatty degeneration of the soul. The artist, if he wants to create something that is not merely there to serve the industrial beast or the degraded tastes of the common man, or the pretensions of the fashionable one, must be free of it. Art allows one to endure one's existence and poverty sets one free.'

'What possible freedom is there in having no money and no possessions?' she said, stung by his dragging her innocent cutlet into it.

'I do not claim it is an easy life but once you've got beyond the modern creed that owning things and having financial security equals happiness, it may be a more beautiful one.'

'But Patrick, owning nothing, having nothing, means scavenging after coins for the gas meter and it means bed bugs and bad teeth, and I don't suppose you find those beautiful or inspiring!'

'Indeed not but I think it is possible to rise above petty discomforts and live the larger life. I prefer the gypsy idea of living outside society and only for the present. For them it is unmanly to save and plan for the future, honourable to spend every coin and beyond on today alone and as splendidly as possible.'

'It's all very well to be cavalier about money but I don't think you're being very honest. You had no scruple about taking Edy's and your mother's contaminated money. And you can't deny you'd happily accept an allowance from your father, got from a fortune that was made by real chained slaves!'

He turned from her on the narrow bed.

Really angry, she added, 'Patrick, have you forgotten how you spent all of last summer contriving over it, chasing after it?' She looked at his hard, inexpressive back. 'Admit it,' she sobbed in her frustration. 'Freedom comes from wallets!'

He withdrew further from her so that their bodies no longer touched, and she turned her own back on him to cry herself into troubled dreams full of menu cards.

It was the first time they had gone to sleep together in their Cornish bed without having first made love.

# Chapter 30

The fine late-summer weather held and Patrick remained happily in the thick of the talk and the work and Rose was glad of it. She herself tried to be only happy, tried not to worry where this rootless life would lead them. After all, she was loved by the most glamorous and the most handsome and passionate of all the bearded artists; certainly the most intriguing man in the whole of the east Cornish peninsula. And she loved him. But she felt most comfortable in the slow and peaceful company of Cousin Guy. He was like a rather splendidly attired and ponderous bird that had somehow found itself living amongst flashy, quarrelling jackdaws. He was a bird that preferred to keep to its cage, so inured to captivity that he considered those common birds that flew about outside rather cheap. He had no shoes suited to beach walks, he was too vain to show his figure in a bathing suit and his nose burned in the sun. And although he was ridiculous in his spats, still she was glad of him.

Patrick was happy because he was completely absorbed in his painting, wrapped up in perfecting 'style Newlyn', whereas Guy was not bothered in the least about 'art'. He might possess the three prerequisites of the creative life, time, money and idleness, but he was not impelled to dabble as was his sister – perhaps because, unlike her, he possessed that fourth virtue, judgement.

Like underemployed English gentlemen the world over, upon whom the sense of the length of hours weighs heavy, he held off the tedium of life by inventing rituals to succeed rituals. Having manned himself each morning with as thorough a toilette as could be contrived in the primitive cottage, he followed this with a brisk constitutional walk to buy his paper, *The Field* (specially ordered from London) which he then looked into for the rest of the morning. However, it had to be said, that the marker of luncheon was sometimes still only a far-off glimmer of hope by the time he'd done with it, but nevertheless the day's mid-point always found him cheerful, for it brought together the two households. In particular it tempted Patrick indoors to eat what scraps were left him by his hungry friends. Then there was the prospect of the afternoon and how that was to be got through without discernible employment. Having no colonial district to administer, no war to direct, no club to attend, Guy resorted to those useful time-wasters, tobacco, literature and napping. He practised all three with a commendable diligence. Rose found him very calming to sit with but she did wonder what it was that had brought him here to deepest Cornwall, and what kept him there, when he might have dozed in his own comfortable library.

In and out of the days wove Keziah, a lively counterpoint to amiable Guy. Almost every morning she came traipsing along Mount's Bay, wearing a heavy Chinese silk dressing gown over her bathing dress, a long rope of amber beads the size of duck eggs round her neck and a green parasol held over her dark head. As she came she could be heard calling like a parakeet for Impy to '*Leeave* it!' or 'Heel, dratted beast!' For Rose there seemed to exist a perfect understanding between them, the confiding friendship she'd longed for. She told Kezzie everything, including her most secret doubts about Patrick and his black crow. Only once had she caught a glimpse of the viciousness that Kezzie claimed New Zealand had bred in her, but it had tainted that trust.

Rose had been sitting for Patrick on the beach on a beautiful morning, the sea as clear and blue as the sky, both content to be thus companionably employed. He'd dressed her in a chequered blue and white skirt with a yellow bodice, letting her hair blow loose, and told her he wanted to capture a look of longing as she scanned the horizon, perhaps for a lost fishing boat. But, looking out over endless waves, Rose had imagined herself a mermaid who'd given up the sea for her land-dwelling lover. Seated on her rocky promontory, she'd truly seemed to feel regret for her old life beneath the waves that was willingly, thoughtlessly shed for the hard road of love.

Patrick had been preoccupied with fixing her elusive expression of remorse and resolve; even when the tide began to change he couldn't stop, and Rose, too, was lost in it. It was a connection with him that she'd never before experienced. She thought, this is what he feels when he paints. And when his painting goes well, it is transcendent!

So when Kezzie had come for her, Impy following behind dragging a length of seaweed, without thinking anything of it she'd dismissed her friend. The insouciant Keziah had transformed into a stamping spitfire and stormed off back to her lodgings.

'She's only jealous,' observed Patrick, putting down his paintbrush. And the spell was broken.

By the next day, they were friends again, although Rose remained a little wary. The two of them lay side by side on the beach on the bedspread Rose had brought from their cottage. Now it was September the days were perceptibly cooling and it was not quite comfortable to lie out all morning on the bare sand. The chill made Rose consider summer's end and how they might live once the days could no longer be spent idling out of doors.

'What is it like here in the winter? I mean, what do all the artists do when it's too cold to work *en plein air*?' she asked Kezzie.

'Some of 'em go home.'

'I thought they lived here.'

'Not all. The dilettante tendency fly back to their Chelsea

studios and the rest throw on more woollens and blow on their fingernails.'

'And which are you?'

'Well, most would group me with the dilettantes – allowance from wealthy Papa, rather too interested in larks,' she said languorously and then paused for a moment. She was lying flat on her back in the inky puddle of her own thick hair, Impy asleep on her chest, so that Rose could see her perfect profile. Ah, thought Rose, the private income.

With sudden intensity, Keziah said, 'But don't think that I'm not deadly serious about my work, Rose. Women must be, if we're not to end up sidelined as wives and mothers. I intend to wring out every last drop of experience on my own terms!' She turned on her side, letting disgruntled Impy spill onto the sand, and hoisted herself onto her elbow to look Rose full in the face. 'Rose, whatever you do, don't just slip into becoming the wife of the artist.'

Rose, taken aback, answered defensively, 'Well, I'm not a real wife. This ring doesn't mean anything in law.'

Rather sharply, Keziah answered her, 'You don't have to be married to be one. Anyway, what I'm talking about is a state of mind.'

'I certainly don't make a very good wife, if that makes you feel any better. I don't cook or clean or any of it,' she replied, a little bemused that Kezzie should be so down on the very idea.

'Rose, spinster scullery maids do housework,' Keziah corrected her. 'What I mean is, beware of giving over your whole life to him.'

'But I haven't . . . I do have my own life,' she protested. 'I'm quite free to make my own friendships, I come and go as I please, I read . . .' Then, because she'd run out of examples of how she was emancipated, she challenged Keziah, 'Anyway, how is your life so very different?'

'As I say, I'm an artist to my very tips, darling! Every bit as dedicated as your Patrick.'

She sounded so fierce, Rose began to suspect that Kezzie had probably terrified her parents into that monthly remittance.

'If, as you point out, I'm not an artist myself, I can still have the satisfaction of inspiring him to make his best work.' Rose did not like to feel herself lectured to by this girl who was probably only a year or two older than herself.

'Ah, the lure of immortality – so hard to argue against!'

Wondering whether Kezzie's nastiness could perhaps be put down to not having a brilliant artist lover of her own, Rose objected, 'Well, being so close to Patrick, I understand what it is to be an artist. I'm part of his world.'

'But perhaps you don't understand how selfish he is, how artists only value what they can take and use.' Keziah looked at her intently. 'It seems to me that your greatest asset is beauty . . .'

Rose spluttered into the sand.

'And there is a lot to be said for being beautiful. It is a useful tool; I certainly make the most of it. But beauty is also weakness, it makes women go to sleep, because they think they are loved solely for who they are and that they will be loved for always. They don't understand that they are loved for the only thing about them that must be lost. Beauty stops them from growing up. It stops them from striving to become themselves so that there will be something left when beauty is gone.' Keziah, perhaps realising she'd gone too far, said more gently, 'All I'm saying is, Rose, don't be content just to cast yourself as his little helpmeet, thinking that's enough to keep him loving and wanting you, or that muse is a job for life.'

Rose had a sudden insight into what might have made Keziah so averse to the idea of marriage.

'Did you run away from a husband in New Zealand?' she asked, stopping Keziah in her tracks.

'Not just a husband.'

'What exactly drove you out of New Zealand?'

'You mean apart from the doilies?' answered Keziah, trying to sound flippant.

Rose was silent.

'I ran away from Mr Higgs.'

'Who?'

'Mr Higgs, my necessary nuisance, my husband,' Keziah supplied grimly. 'He was a little, little man who wore an expression of greedy glee every time he looked at his wifey. Made me want to kick him in his self-satisfied teeth. Home from the office came the hunter, as pleased with himself as a boy with the complete set of tin soldiers to line up: his wife-pal, his tip-top house, those splendid fellows his friends. All absolutely ripping. Utterly *kapai*!' Keziah spat out the words.

'And then he'd drag around my neck, begging for reassurance and for me to listen to his story. What a day he'd had of it! Did I think he was getting a tummy? Would Duggan invite him to sail again this summer? He needed me, his darling little pet: crying into my hair. On and on he fretted and demanded, never let me rest, never let me be!'

Rose was rather startled. Is that what Keziah thought she did to Patrick?

'Patrick and I don't have that kind of a relationship!'

'I don't say that at all, Rose darling, I only try to warn you off tying yourself to him as I did to my Mr Higgs. Don't make your life little and small just to fit.'

Rose stood up and tugged at the bedspread, but Keziah was still lying on part of it. She had to pull it out from under her to free it. Keziah jumped up and tried to put her arm round her friend, saying, 'Don't be angry with me for saying it. I only do so from love.'

Rose made no reply as she carried the bedspread back indoors with her.

# Chapter 31

Keziah and Rose didn't see so much of each other over the next week. Both had been bruised by that last encounter on the beach. Rose was preoccupied with the notion of herself as a wife, however unmarried and what that might mean. Was it necessarily a condition to be avoided? Her parents had thought it the only cure for her shameful condition – at any price! But Keziah considered the title damaging enough to have travelled halfway round the world to shake free of it. What was a wife? Mapus, Mrs Jannock, Mrs Van der Decken, Mrs Black? God forbid! She did not feel an affinity with any of them. When she tried to imagine a proper wife, she saw a little clockwork mouse – wind it up and it rushes around tutting and performing its little mechanical tasks over and over. She was not that mouse.

And wives seemed always to wear an expression of disapproval, as though their wifely duty was to note their husband's every shortcoming. But she did not nag or disapprove. To be honest, she did not nag Patrick because she really felt no need to: she was as likely as he to be late for the dinner that Mrs Black cooked; she didn't care about sand in the bed because she didn't make it up or wash the sheets. In fact she only knew how to be as childlike and irresponsible as he. She liberally admitted to herself that sometimes she was lonely and that she could do with an occupation – something for herself alone – other than reading or sitting interminably for her portrait, or lying on the beach. But she had not drawn a line under her life, really she had not. Patrick was wonderful and she was wonderfully happy and a future together with him was certain. Rose thought, we are like two friendly children allowed to play without ever being told to wash hands and faces or eat up our crusts by an adult. It was freedom, it made them happy. But she could not avoid the knowledge that, at last, night must fall and then what would the children do? So Rose sat with Guy while he rattled his paper, feeling vindicated and unwifely and waited for the moment when Patrick would come back and set all their lives spinning again.

Then Kezzie was made homeless: the room she'd taken in the house of a London painter was needed for her visiting brother. It seemed only appropriate that she should lodge with them, sharing the second bedroom with Impy in what was, after all, her ancestral home. In the event, though Rose had worried that Keziah and Patrick might not be friends, she was glad to have Kezzie under her roof, where she'd be able to show off at close quarters just how happily unmarried they were, and the rent she paid would help to placate Mrs Black, who'd begun to grumble that she would take herself off and leave them all to it if they didn't find more housekeeping.

They all three carried on together amicably enough in the cottage on Mount's Bay and a week's proximity returned the girls to almost the same point of sisterly companionship that they'd felt for each other in the early days. Rose's only remaining concern was that her husband and her friend were indeed not quite easy with each other. But though they hardly exchanged a word, let alone a look, Patrick and Keziah had taken to working together, setting up easels next to each other and criticising each other's efforts. They fought a sort of portraitists' duel. He painted her lying on the beach with her green umbrella shielding her head from the sunlight, so that her legs were as white as a fish's belly and her face all lost in black hair and shade. And she painted him, in profile, lying in the front garden, reading a book that was propped on his chest. Rose thought Keziah's portrait rather childish and unfinished looking although it was most definitely Patrick. Then they turned on Rose, painting compulsively, competitively, side by side, barking out instructions so that she felt less muse than performing bear. As they argued about the colour of sunlight, Rose began to think that they might even grow to like each other. Patrick had worked his usual magic of making himself loved.

Patrick, having gone off one evening, went to visit his friend Fred, to discuss the death of romanticism. Keziah and Rose finished the fish pie that Mrs Black had left in the range for them (without saving any for Guy or Edy), and now sat, with their feet up on chairs, while Impy stood on the table and licked the pan.

'Isn't Edy a cure? Going about like a ship all rigged in multicoloured bunting, a-fluttering in the breeze.'

'My cousin likes to think she's a walking example of the avant garde,' replied Rose. It was a game these two played, slandering Edy. Sometimes it made Rose feel guilty that she colluded so willingly in Keziah's spite. After all, Edy was her cousin and she had, perhaps inadvertently, rescued her from Raglan Street. Besides, it was she who paid for everything: the lady patroness of the Mount's Bay artistic community. Rose understood why Edy was cross with them, friends and co-conspirators, but not why Keziah hated her so much in return.

Keziah lifted the dog off the table and onto her lap, saying to it in a baby voice, 'Did my precious pup enjoy his *kai kai* den?' and Rose privately excused her lapse into mawkishness.

Then Keziah asked, in quite a different voice, 'Shall I tell you about the painting I'm conceiving at the moment?'

Rose nodded pleasantly and her friend went on, 'It's from a Cornish story called "The Spriggan's Child" – you've probably heard it. A wife is away from her cottage, working in the fields. She's left her baby asleep, having been careful to bank up the fire and brush away any ashes from the hearth. When she returns that evening she finds the cradle overturned and, though she searches the place thoroughly, there is no sign of the baby. At last she lights the fire and as she throws a faggot into the flames she hears a baby's cry. And there, lying naked as the day he was born, is her boy. Now, here's the queer part. From that day on the baby pines and cries and, stranger still, it never seems to need sleep. And he has,' she searched for the right word, 'an *unlovable* look to him, with a large, lolling head and spindly limbs. The mother takes against it and beats the brat when it whines, but it just blinks back at her and whines again. She wishes the child would die but it clings on, getting sustenance from what food she allows it and always fretting and bawling until she thinks she'll die with tiredness. She knows it for a changeling child and so resolves to work a spell, or holy charm, to restore her own, stolen, baby. The cure is to take it on the first three Wednesdays of May at dawn to the chapel well and plunge it deep into the bone-chill water. Then, however the thing might roar with fury, she must carry it round the well three times.

'On the third and last long walk, through the rain and cold to the chapel, she seems to hear a strange shrill voice in her head that she thinks comes from the cursed baby weighing heavy in her arms. The baby says in an old man's voice: "Give me milk, bear me on your back, while I have my woman slave I'll not lack." She drops the wicked thing on the ground where it screams blue murder as though it would die. She grabs it up and, flinging it over her shoulder, runs back home where she decides that she must punish the little parasite. To do the job properly she must make herself strong and beat the little devil black and blue. Bruise it with the heel of her shoe until the shoe flies out from her hand, break the broom handle on its back and keep away from the sight and hearing of her neighbours while the job is done. And doesn't that brat roar and protest! Then it goes all quiet, and quite soft. It seems then to the wife that it smiles and at last it shut its eyes and sleeps. But the wife is not to be fooled. She knows not to turn her back on it until the end of night.

'When morning comes she sees that the foul imposter has gone, leaving only the mark in the bed of ashes where she'd thrown him and, miracles, lying in his own cradle by the fire is her own sweet babe. And, though it looked quite wild, and as though it had lost its wits, she knew it for her own child.'

'It's a very cruel story,' said Rose, shocked at Keziah's relish in the telling.

'Aren't all folk tales, with their wicked stepmothers and hungry witches? Anyway, this one's enough of a standard for there to be variations on the theme. Apparently one can also prove a changeling by standing it on hot coals or smoking it out with green ferns on the hearth.'

'Which part will you illustrate?'

'It will be a series of paintings. The last scene, when the baby is lying in the ashes, will be the one I start with.'

Rose shivered.

Over the next two weeks Keziah worked and re-worked her picture of the baby in the ashes until the paint appeared to coagulate on the canvas. And day by day it seemed to Rose that she showed a different outcome. When the Spriggan's child was black and blue and most distinctly dead, she'd over-paint its flesh with the tint of life and then restore the human baby once more to life.

At the end of the second week Rose found her standing before the lurid picture in tears. She put her arms round her to comfort her and Keziah sobbed, 'Don't look at it, it's *pukaroo* – a stupid muddy mess! Oh Rose, what am I to do?'

If Keziah and Rose cut Edy, Edy did not lightly accept being cut by them, though whether she was more furious at having to share Keziah with Rose or Rose with Keziah was difficult to tell. She seemed to resolve this conundrum by being equally vile to both. Her revenge came in gathering to herself a band of tentative female flower and fairy artists. Judging by the way Edy stabbed the portraits of flowers onto canvas, Rose thought her cousin was more suited to vinegar than violets; her pictures made the most inoffensive poppy look full of bloody intent. Rose guessed that Edy would eventually shake off the whimsical followers and graduate to illustrating Shakespeare for children with the kind of picture plates that gave sleepless nights: Gloucester having his eyes popped out or Cleopatra nursing the asp.

Today Edy abandoned her nine muses and at the sniff of discord, sidled into the kitchen of the twin cottage next door. Keziah and Patrick were off on a painting expedition and Rose was sitting, still in her nightdress, eating toast.

'So, the wild colonial girl's tired of chats on the beach?'

'Not at all, Kezzie and I plan to spend the afternoon together.' She might have said more but Edy was apparently her enemy now so she thought it safer to deflect her cousin's curiosity. Rose certainly felt the want of someone with whom to share her secret, but it could not be Edy. She'd first suspected she was pregnant at the end of August, and had decided to wait to be sure before confiding in her dear friend Keziah and telling Patrick he was to be a father. But as the month passed she'd held back. Seeing how happy Patrick was since they'd come to Cornwall, she worried he might regard the acquisition of a baby as an impediment to their carefree, possession-free life. She felt less and less sure how he would react. And recently she'd decided that she could no longer quite trust Keziah. So she'd told no one. Could tell no one.

Edy snooped about the kitchen. She picked up Keziah's picture of the Spriggan's child, which was turned face to the wall, took a long look, and sucked her teeth.

'Rose, I hate to have to tell you this, but I think I really ought. I happened upon some information . . .' She put her hand on Rose's shoulder as though to brace her. Pure malevolence lit her triangular face. 'Apparently Keziah had another reason for leaving New Zealand, I mean apart from the desire to travel and paint.'

'If you mean she left Mr Higgs, her husband, I already know that,' broke in Rose.

Edy snorted. 'If that were all!'

Rose stood up, trying to make Edy leave, and said, 'I don't care to gossip.'

'Rose, this isn't gossip, this is full-blown scandal!'

'Well then, I don't care to scandalise.'

'But that's just it, I wouldn't be able to live with myself if I thought I'd left you here with her, without you knowing the full story. Rose, you must listen to me, for the sake of your baby.'

That stilled Rose. 'How did you know?'

'Well, I know now, don't I?' Edy had Rose's ear now and hurried to drip the poison in, so that she might watch it take effect. 'Anyway, Keziah Trewren, I mean Mrs Higgs, left Auckland because her own baby was murdered.' She judged that she could safely pause for dramatic effect now.

'There was something wrong with it, apparently – one of those vacant, big-headed imbeciles that get put away in private hospitals. But Keziah wouldn't let anyone near the thing, insisted on doing everything for it. Then it disappeared from its cradle and a huge manhunt was raised. They found it, battered to death, under a hedge at the end of the garden.'

'How did she escape the police? Have they chased her here?'

Gratified that she had had the intended effect, Edy said disingenuously, 'I do not believe an absconding wife merits the attention of the police, although her husband, Mr Higgs, is certainly anxious to trace her. A native kitchen maid was accused of the abduction and murder. Apparently her own child had died at birth and she'd been driven mad. There is no explanation for why she might have killed the thing she coveted, apart from innate savagery.'

'And Mr Higgs?'

'Bereft.'

Rose could not stop herself from glancing over at Keziah's canvas in which the imposter baby was stilled among the ashes.

'I just thought you'd better know. Always best to get to the truth of the matter, however painful, isn't it?' Edy, satisfied, scampered back to her lady acolytes.

Rose hugged herself protectively and, for the first time since she'd left Raglan Street, considered Joan and felt a pang of regret and guilt. The poor abandoned girl, what had become of her? Rose felt that she now properly understood the panic of having responsibility for another when there was no one to turn to, nowhere to run.

# Chapter 32

That evening the three women and Patrick and Guy sat outside, wrapped in blankets against the chill and smoking nasty green cigars against the gnats. For once there was no one else there to rouse Patrick to anecdote or theory. A dullness had fallen over them, but Patrick could not be dull. He stood up, saying, 'Who's for a bathe?' and started down to the beach.

'Oh, must we?' Guy groaned but he nevertheless stood and looked after Patrick, leaping towards the milky sea, pulling off his clothes as he went. Edy was not loath – Rose was surprised to see that she had already cast off her gown and was struggling free of her duds. Keziah noticed too. She gripped Rose by the hand and muttered in her ear, 'I'll be damned if the hellcat gets there first!' Rose and Keziah ran in long strides after Patrick. By the time they reached him he was already standing, shivering, on the shoreline, naked, glaucous in the light of the moon. He turned to them. 'Come on then.' He started to splash into the foam, legs pumping with the high-stepping motion of chopping through the waves. He turned to them again. ''Urry oop an' ge' tin, watter's be-ootiful!' he said, putting on the Yarkshire. He was chest high in heavy waves by the time that Edy, who'd caught them up, plunged unhesitating after, squeaking with the cold.

Then, because she could not pursue fast enough on her legs, she launched herself headlong to swim, quick as a rat with her thin hair slick to her little skull.

'Damn her!' said Keziah, and started to roll her stockings down her slim legs. Rose followed suit and they were both soon naked, standing in their puddled clothes. Keziah ran strongly through the breakers looking like a lithe Greek goddess of the hunt and Rose splashed behind. Soon all three huntresses had brought their spoil to ground. They sported around him and he looked on complacently, Hylas among the water nymphs. Impy, left on the beach, danced wildly and let off warning volleys: come back, come back, you'll all be drowned!

Rose, looking back to land, saw that Guy had lumbered to the sea's brink and was clumsily stepping out of his clothes. He neatly folded them and placed them in a pile on the beach.

'Look!' she called, pointing, 'An elephant's coming down for its bath!'

Guy, ungainly as he balanced on one tree-trunk leg to pull off his trousers, looked so like a kindly pachyderm doing a trick that they all laughed.

'What's the joke?' he called, approaching the sea's edge in his saggy, woollen combinations. And they whooped.

Guy started to lumber towards them through the shallows, planting each thick, veiny foot with care as though he observed their progress from such a great height that he could not spot potential elephant traps. Battered by larger waves, he tripped and collapsed up to his chest in the cold water, his undergarment billowing around him. Rose, feeling guilty for the laughter she'd provoked, swam back to him.

'You see, I've never been happy in water,' he stuttered through mauve lips.

'It's not too deep. If you just swim a little way there's a nice, hard bank of sand to stand on,' she said and led the gentle beast out to where the seal-dark heads of Keziah, Patrick and Edy bobbed.

Rose could feel Guy's hand trembling in her own. He clung tightly to her.

'Poor old Guy, not celebrated as a wet-bob at school,' he called, trying to sound jovial. Then he whispered to her, 'I say, keep a hold, won't you. I'm not good out of my depth.'

She squeezed his hand in reassurance. 'I don't think you will be – you're so tall you should be able to make it without swimming.'

Just as they reached the hard shelf of sand, the other three turned and dived away like teasing mermaids and Guy groaned. 'I really don't think I can do this,' he said, and yet he struggled to walk through the sea after the flashing white bodies. He looked and spoke with such wistfulness that she realised that it was all for Patrick. He would risk even this ignominy and fear to follow him. And it occurred to Rose that she was her cousin's stalking horse for getting close to Patrick. The shock of the thought made her plunge away from Guy, leaving him behind, stranded on his bank.

She soon reached the other three who had swum to an outcrop of rocks. They scrambled onto it, to sit, panting in the moonlight. She pulled herself up beside Patrick and he put his narrow, cold arm round her. Rose felt very cold and hard. She and Patrick and Keziah were kin in their beautiful nakedness. Their skin fitted so nicely it was as though they were splendidly dressed. Strange to see Edy's imperfect little body without its lurid coverings, for nakedness is the truest, the cruellest leveller. Strip away the trappings that money buys and what is left to be judged but the bare, forked creature? From some devilment, or perhaps to punish her for this morning, Rose started to sing, to the tune of the music hall song:

'After the ball was over, she took out her glass eye,
Put her false teeth in the water, hung up her wig to dry;
Placed her false arm on the table, laid her false leg on the chair;
After the party was over, she was only half there!'

The others looked at her, uncomprehending. Rose laughed and laughed. Perhaps it was the cold that made her cruel, perhaps it was this new need to protect herself, from all of them.

Rose splashed Edy. 'Look at me,' she said and stood, magnificently self-conscious and poised. Then she dived perfectly off the rock into the biting water. When she came up for air, the taste of the sea in her nose, Keziah and Patrick were standing side by side on the rock, ready to dive after – Keziah, small, dark and compact, in counterpoint to Patrick, long and pale gold. With a flash of his legs, Patrick launched himself, but not far enough out, for he cracked his head on a hidden rock. Keziah jumped in and she and Rose hauled the stunned Patrick back onto their perching place where his head oozed blood. Chastened, the three women dragged him back to the shore where Guy was putting on his clothes. Somehow they managed to haul him back to the cottage. By this time they were all shivering violently and Patrick was green with shock.

Inside the cottage, under the light of the oil lamp, they felt shamed in their nakedness and rushed to cover up, quickly dragging on damp, salt-sticky clothes. Having helped Keziah and Rose to get Patrick, trembling and moaning, into his bed, Guy and Edy went home to their own cottage.

'I can't s-s-seem to get warm.' Patrick chattered and trembled compulsively. Keziah went to her room and came back dragging her eiderdown which was still full of sand from the beach. She dumped it on top of Patrick but it was clammy and brought no comfort.

'What are we to do? Oh, what are we to do?' wailed Rose.

'We must use our own body heat,' her friend ordered.

Rose climbed in on one side of the bed and Keziah in on the other. It seemed the most natural thing to do and both wrapped their arms and legs round him as though to anchor him and subdue his violently shaking body. They all went to sleep at last between damp, sea-smelling sheets. Several times that night Rose dreamed that she was lying in her bed at home in Sheffield and seemed to hear the sound of waves breaking against its cast-iron walls.

When she woke in the early morning, the wan sun shone blearily through the panes of the little window that looked out over the bay. Rose lay gritty and grimy but snug, tucked under Patrick's right arm. Under his left, she knew, nestled Keziah. She tried to look at Patrick's head to check the condition of his wound without disturbing him. He was snoring asleep.

Keziah's black head bobbed up into view and she commented brightly, 'He is not a corpse. He lives!'

'Yes,' answered Rose. 'But I don't know that I do. I smell like a dead crab and I don't know when I ever felt more in need of a hot bath. I haven't had a proper wash since we came here – Guy and Edy requisitioned the bathtub.'

Keziah giggled, careful not to wake Patrick. 'Let's go next door and steal it back. I've got a cake of the most divinely decadent French lavender soap we can squander.'

The two slipped out from either side of the bed and scampered downstairs and through the front garden to their neighbours' door, pausing to tip the chamber pot over the garden fence. Rose quietly lifted the latch and they crept inside and took the enamelled bathtub from its place on the wall. One of Edy's flower paintings was propped up on the kitchen table with her brushes and paints untidily around it. Keziah took up a brush, loaded it with vermilion and, with a couple of strokes, painted a distinct female sexual organ right in the middle.

Rose spluttered, 'You shouldn't have done that! She's bound to guess who it was.'

'Let her. I don't care.'

They carried the bath back between them to their own kitchen and took it in turns to wash luxuriously in gallons of water heated on the old range. Last, they washed Patrick, although he objected, then bandaged his wound and trimmed his beard. Then all three sat at the kitchen as clean and good and innocent as children and watched the mice playing on the table while they waited for Mrs Black to come and cook them their breakfasts.

# Chapter 33

The day proceeded blue and calm, there was no sign of the next-door neighbours. Rose felt a little flat after the excitements of the previous evening; perhaps she'd looked forward to a spat with Edy. She also noticed with disappointment that now that Patrick was up and about, relations between him and Kezzie seemed to have cooled even further. Perhaps they were embarrassed to have shared the marital bed. They only addressed themselves to her and seemed to ignore each other completely, to the point of avoidance. By mid-morning taciturn Patrick had unwound his bandage and set off down the beach to visit his friend Harris. Rose, Kezzie and Impy were left alone.

'I've changed my mind about your husband,' Keziah said in a measured voice.

'Oh?' responded Rose, trying not to betray her disappointment that perhaps Kezzie no longer considered Patrick fascinating.

'It's just no good for you. It's all wrong.'

'What do you mean?'

'I mean you've fallen in love with someone you really oughtn't. Don't misunderstand me, Rose, I speak only for your own good.'

'Oh, I know he's preoccupied sometimes and he's not bothered by washing but really I've never been happier, or more settled, now that we've found a community of like-minded people to live amongst.' She almost felt she had to reassure her friend.

'But you know that he can't stay happy, Rose, don't you? He'll never be satisfied, never be still, and he'll weigh you down with, what did you call it, his black crow?'

'I shall cope,' she replied, imitating cheerful resilience. She didn't point out that Patrick, too, had never been happier since he'd been with her in Cornwall.

'Of course he's made the very same mistake. I mean he's fallen in love with someone he oughtn't.'

Rose was horrified. 'How can you possibly think that?'

'I know it, Rose,' replied Keziah in the pompous, arty voice that Rose had come to mistrust. 'Because I, too, know what it is to be an artist; but you, dear child, you can never know, should never know. You were not made to stand it.'

Rose was furious now. 'First you tell me not to give my life over to him because he's not worth the sacrifice and now you tell me I've made a mistake and have aimed too high!'

'Dearest Rosebud, I never once said he was unworthy. He is, or he could be, great. It's just that he needs more than you can offer and stay intact. And you demand things of him he cannot give. In the end, Patrick will bring you down, burn you up, and that, in turn, may destroy his talent.'

'But you are uniquely equipped to withstand his genius, I suppose,' Rose said coldly, sharp with fear that this was exactly what Keziah Trewren intended, for wasn't she indeed more suited to being Patrick's lover, even down to Daddy's monthly allowance?

'Darling, what you two need is to be kept safe from each other. You need someone to stand between and bear the brunt. You both need me.'

'We neither of us need you; we have plenty of other people!'

'Do you, Rose?' Keziah laughed nastily. 'Guy the gussie and his droopy drawers and that little parasite Edy?'

Rose felt suddenly protective. 'They are my family.'

'Don't you see, Rose, I shook us free of them so it would be just us, our own little family, in marvellous counterpoint?'

Rose was chilled now. 'And will the next job be to rid him of the little wifey who drags him down, smothers him, and replace her with a proper consort, one who can stride alongside the great artist?' She looked into Keziah's dark eyes and saw a strange, hungry excitement.

Rose grabbed up her shawl and ran from the cottage, down the incline to the beach and along the bay away from Keziah whose following call was ripped into shreds by the wind.

As she hurried along the beach, the tears pouring down her face, she saw a familiar figure ahead shambling through the sand like a bear with a walking stick. It was Guy, the only person left in the world she could trust!

She ran up behind him. 'What are you doing here?'

'Rose!' He was panting with the effort of plodding. 'Blasted Pat asked me to meet him on the beach to help carry a canvas back to the cottage.'

'When was he supposed to meet you here?' Rose looked out eagerly. She so wanted Patrick now, to hug him and hear his reassurances.

'An hour ago,' Guy replied bluffly. 'You know Pat – dependable in his undependability!'

Yes, she did. The two sat on a grassy tussock at the back of the beach and waited for Patrick to appear.

'Do you think that I smother Patrick?' she asked meekly. 'Am I too demanding of him?'

He looked at her fondly. 'I rather think it's the other way around, my dear. Patrick is someone who needs his *housekeepers*. I think of us all, you, Edy, me, as housekeepers to Patrick. He's trained us all to be good at anticipating his needs and answering them, all to give him a more comfortable life. He's like a queen bee with all the worker bees milling around, stroking him and feeding him jelly.'

They both laughed and then were silent while the wind whipped sand around their heads and into their eyes and mouths.

He was right, Rose thought. Patrick was one of the clever ones who worked that trick of making others gladly volunteer to provide for and provision them.

'Only trouble is,' Guy said sadly to himself, 'housekeeping does not make one attractive in one's self.'

He gestured that they should walk off the beach and find some shelter, which they did among some stunted bushes. He pulled out his handkerchief for her to sit on and they smiled at each other. She could trust him, always ready with a clean linen handkerchief; good old Guy.

'I think Keziah Trewren is crushed on Patrick,' Rose said, as lightly as she could manage.

'Is she?' he replied neutrally.

'She thinks I am not suited to being the wife of a great artist but that she is.'

'Balderdash!'

'It is, isn't it, Guy?'

Guy responded to her hurt. 'She's a little pest!' And he put his arm comfortingly around her. 'After putting her up for weeks and feeding her and her blasted mutt, that really takes the Huntley and Palmer!' He squeezed her to him and they sat in silence for a moment until Guy added, conclusively, 'You know Edy never liked her and Edy, whatever her faults, has always been a fine judge of character.'

Rose laughed at that.

He put his hand on her knee and went on earnestly, 'But you mustn't worry about Pat – I mean if you were. Whatever else he is, Pat hasn't an atom in him that's not honourable!'

Rose was not so certain.

After they'd sat in companionable silence for another twenty minutes they decided that they'd probably missed Patrick, or that he'd changed his mind and wasn't coming, and they set off home. She leaned on Guy, though he seemed to need more support from her as they staggered through the wind, half blinded by flying sand. As they approached the two crouched cottages, Rose said, 'Guy, come with me, won't you? I'm frightened of what that woman might do.'

They neared her cottage and Rose listened out for Impy's bark but heard nothing over the wail of the wind. Passing into the garden, Rose experienced what felt like a blow to her chest as she looked through the kitchen window and saw Patrick sitting at the table opposite Keziah. She turned to run but Guy held her arm more tightly and guided her to the door. 'Better to face the music,' he said and pushed her through it.

The couple at the table turned whitened faces towards them. Keziah stood and said in a distinct and artificial voice, 'You know, Patrick, you have disappointingly little imagination. I took you for a risk-taker but now I see you'll most probably end your days an RA.' She turned on her heel, pulling the whining Impy behind her. '*Tua rika rika*,' she muttered under her breath as she opened the door and stepped out to disappear almost immediately into the swirling sand.

'And a plaque on your house too,' Patrick tossed after her.

'A near escape,' commented Guy. 'D'you think calling you a toe-rigger or whatever it was, has put a dreadful Maori curse on you?'

'I should think Antipodean curses don't travel – they come out upside down, and so can only do one good,' replied Patrick.

They were sitting before the roaring range, giggly with the relief of having survived the whirlwind departure of Mrs Higgs and her familiar,

'Makes me feel like a sailor plucked from the arms of one of those naughty women who sit on rocks and lure men to their peril,' Patrick said.

'Where do you think she'll go?' Rose was still a little worried that Keziah would be back, if for no other reason than to collect her painting of the Spriggan's child which was still leaning against the wall.

'She won't be back here,' replied Patrick. 'I gave that cur of hers such a kick in his backside, he'll drag her to Land's End and beyond.'

Rose laughed and mimicked Keziah. 'Impy wimpy, let me kiss my precious pup where he hurts.'

That night, sandwiched between clammy sheets, she asked in a small voice, 'Why did she get so angry with you?'

'I turned her down,' he replied easily.

Rose smiled a grim smile. So much for Mrs Higgs' assumption that all she needed to do to win him away was to declare an interest. Nevertheless, perhaps to wring a little more triumph for herself, she pursued the point, 'Weren't you at all tempted?' As soon as she'd asked it she wished the question unsaid, for she knew that Patrick would not dissemble to save her feelings. To him, the invitation to honesty was like a challenge.

'To be honest,' he said, and she bit her lips, 'I thought she'd probably run away with you. So it came as something of a surprise.'

'With me?'

'Didn't you notice, really?' he asked indifferently.

Rose was speechless.

'Then I saw that what she really wanted was to add me to the ménage. In the end it was a case of divide and rule, you know – the very special friend of each of us, worming her way between. I couldn't be doing with that. So I said that I thought she'd made a mess of her painting, and that was enough. You know the rest.' He turned over and went to sleep.

Rose lay marooned on the life-raft bed wondering whether, if he'd thought Keziah genuinely talented, there would have been a different outcome.

# Chapter 34

Summer dissolved into wet and, just as Keziah had said they would, the majority of the artistic community began to drift away or kept to the warmth of their own firesides. Edy tried to sell her flower paintings in Newlyn and Penzance, without success, and was talking about showing them to a London dealer or of writing some accompanying text and offering them for publication as children's anthologies of wild flowers of the West Country. Guy read his paper and complained of rheumatism.

The isolated cottages on the bay grew lonelier, the sea turned to slate and the sky to lead and Rose saw a far-away look in Patrick's eye, as though he gazed across deserts to rose-pink horizons. She remembered their first morning and how she'd thought that he was Gulliver, looking out to sea, always impatient to discover and explore new peoples and lands, always disappointed.

One mid-November morning Edy marched into the cottage determined to punish Rose a little more for her alliance with Keziah.

'You know that the rental on the cottages runs out in a fortnight, I suppose,' she said with relish.

'Oh yes?' replied Rose vaguely, trying not to give her cousin the sniff of fear.

'It's always best to confront rather than evade, don't

you agree?' Edy challenged. 'I expect you also know that I am the guarantor of the lease. It's my job to make sure that both cottages are vacated at the end of the month, this month, in the condition in which we took them on. I mean to say,' she said, 'all this decorative stuff will have to be got rid of.' Edy looked pointedly at the floorboards, painted in alternating stripes of blue, white and green, at the mermaids either side of the door and the boggarts' faces peeping from every pot and pan.

'Oh yes,' said Rose, keeping her eyes trained on Edy, to stop them from darting nervously about the room, cataloguing the damage.

'I've arranged for good Mrs Black to clean up our cottage after we've gone – I can tell you, that woman is one for naming a price! Guy and I will be travelling back to Yorkshire the day after tomorrow. Have you plans? Only I should hate to think we'd left you in the lurch.'

'Oh yes,' was Rose's bland reply. She could see that Edy hated that. Edy wanted to know their plans – so that she could decide whether to come too. Rose made a show of going back to brushing her hair.

Seeing that she would not be intimidated, Edy tried another tack. 'I presume you've yet to tell Patrick about the infant?'

Rose could not stop herself from saying, 'You won't tell him, Edy, will you?'

'Your secret's safe with me. However, as I say, the future must be faced.'

'You're right, of course, Edy, and I will tell him.'

'Anyway, must pop back next door – so much to arrange before the off.' Cheerful now that she'd spread a little discord, Edy got to the door before she paused and repeated in a tone of light malice, 'And Rose, don't forget, all this must be left just as you found it.'

Cold and smelly and damp, thought Rose.

How she longed to be free of Edy and Guy, of all of them, so she could have a private life with Patrick but she knew that come summer's end, hard realities must indeed be faced.

All that day, just as Edy might have guessed, Rose worried. She dared not bother Patrick with the imminent problem of their eviction – Gulliver was so intent on that distant horizon that she knew he could not focus on the here and now. But that evening he brought the matter up himself.

'I'm sorry, Rose, I can't bear this wind. They say winds drive people mad, don't they?'

She did not reply and he continued, 'You know me, can't stay happy for long, must be on the move.' He looked out to that distant, rose-pink prospect. 'It's a beautiful place. And I think we've spent a happy summer here, haven't we? But I think it's wrong. I think Cornwall's time has come and gone. Don't you? I should have been here fifteen years ago, before it became like a resort for weekend painters. Do you remember what that cab driver said? "You be artists, then?"'

'That was months ago, the day we arrived!'

'The problem is I can see just what it will be like ten or fifteen or fifty years in the future: little pastel painted villas built right down to the sea. Everywhere roads and shops and pubs and chariots bringing bank holidayites on the razzle dazzle. The island turned into a fancy hotel for rich weekenders and boarding houses along the prom for every 'Arry and 'is 'Arriet.'

'But it's so remote and wild.'

'Not while the railway can have one back in London in half a day and models brought up for the weekend. It will all be spoiled. Everything is spoiled in the end.'

# Chapter 35

After Guy and Edy left, it felt as though the whole world was shutting up shop, battening down the hatches. But, having declared that the time had come for them to depart, Patrick did not discuss how or where. So they squatted on in their cottage, promising the next quarter's rent and making no plans.

Since good Mrs Black no longer received money from Edy to cook and clean for them all, there had been no cooking or cleaning. Rose woke one morning and, going downstairs to light the little range, looked at the debris and devastation of the night, of the week, of the month before and was ashamed. Everywhere dirty pots and pans, dishes and cups. She tied her hair in a duster and set about cleaning, full of a furious energy that she did not know was the animal instinct to prepare her nest. As she scoured and scalded, Patrick, woken by the sound of plates cracking into the sink, came down and smiled at her in her turban.

'I shall have to paint you just like that. I'll call it "Muse in a duster".'

She banged open the cupboard and looked into it, saying, 'Be serious, Patrick. We've nothing at all in the house to eat!' and sat down on the kitchen chair and began to cry.

'Don't worry, darling child. It's only food,' he said, sitting her on his bony knee. It was only food, but they could not very well go on forever without it. She decided that she *would* worry, if not for herself then for her baby. But though she searched the cottage she turned up only ninepence in coppers. The only thing of convertible value she could find was the string of amber beads that Keziah had left slung over her bedpost. Rose walked to Marazion with them weighing heavy round her neck, uncomfortable memento of Mrs Higgs. Finding nowhere in the village to either sell or pawn them she resolved to try her luck in Newlyn. But once there she lost her nerve, and instead went into the post office to idly ask if she had any post. Surprised to find that there was a letter being held for her, she accepted the envelope as though it were an unexploded bomb, only to recognise, with relief, Guy's handwriting:

> Dears – Bad news, I'm afraid. Rose, your father is failing – literally being consumed by a cancer. Poor mama fears that he will not last and is anxious for rapprochement. His only child, etc., etc. Darling, please be generous – as I know you are – and hurry home to see the much reduced, sad old man. Kisses to both, Guy.
>
> PS: I have it on best authority – fling yourself upon the parental bosom and all must be forgiven.

Rose walked the long walk back to the cottage, pushing against the howling, weeping wind. But even though she was over-brimming with the news, she would not let it spill.

That night she lay, a lone watcher, on their storm-tossed bed and knew that the night was not a reposeful place to brood. There were the secret sounds of the house itself to listen for: the creaks and shifts of old timber, tortured like a ship running under stress; the interminable east wind soughing through rigging trees and slapping the hull; and right at her back her husband's snores, rhythmic as the stroke of oars pulling easily away from her. She did not want to be left alone in this unquiet night.

She tried to comfort herself by attending to those small noises that ebb and flow within a house. She listened for the domestic burps and gurgles of digestion, the creak of joints rubbing, the gasp of inhalation, the sigh of exhalation. Now that she had turned her ear from the wind that raged outside to this interior space, the tiny patter of a mouse crossing the floor was plain. Trapped, the mouse grew bolder and its footsteps louder. It seemed to run round and round the room, trying to find a way out. It wasn't until the drumming of unseen feet became too loud for her to bear that Rose called out to Patrick in the dark, 'I must get out of here. I must get back to Yorkshire!'

It was the push that Patrick needed to finally let the wind carry him away, blow him clean out of Cornwall. The very next morning they would cadge a couple of seats in the rail compartment that Patrick's wealthy friend Morris had reserved for his own removal – for Patrick was ever resourceful when he'd settled upon a course – and travel back to the place where lived her shame and Harold Webb. She must get far away from the murdered Spriggan's child that had got in under the bedroom door.

Because they owed Mrs Black a fortnight's back wages and the promised rental, Rose left her the guilt beads with a note saying, 'Dear Mrs Black, Sorry. You may sell these.' Then, as an afterthought, for she imagined a vivid tableau of Mrs Black turning the dressing-up beads over in her hands and then slinging them away, 'PS: They are valuable.' Then they bundled up Patrick's canvases and crept away like thieves, leaving the cottage door open so that the sand blew in and the wet, salt air dulled the painted boards and spoiled the mermaids by the door. The thick eiderdown they'd left slumped like a dead animal across the empty bed, blotted up the damp once more and lay rotting. The little low bedroom window was soon fogged with salt spray. Even the mice could no longer make a home here. They, too, ran away, abandoning the cottage to the old and everlasting rule of the elements.

So they left wind-worried Marazion for Sheffield, settled on its seven hills, and found that autumn in all its melancholy beauty had got there first. The alders were toasted to a nut brown and the horse chestnuts lapped by their own spilt gold and from the train window she smelled bonfires, for now was the time for the burning of leaves. At Sheffield station a different reek greeted her, not the soporific of wood smoke that bemuses the dying, autumn bees but industrial vapours to sour the nose and skin the throat. It was not a glad homecoming. Knowing that she could not take Patrick directly to her parental home, Rose led him to the only place of sanctuary available.

The door of 16 Raglan Street opened, as it had all those months before, to reveal Mrs Jannock polishing a plate.

'You've come back then,' acknowledged that lady, looking Patrick up and down. So, trouble had tipped up again like a bad penny. Only, by the look of her, and the rapscalliony fellow alongside of her, the penny had swelled to a bob.

'Mrs Jannock, how have you been keeping?' Rose ventured.

'Middlin',' came the terse response. And still she stood and polished.

Rose continued brightly, 'This is my husband, Mr Patrick McKinley.'

'You've wed, 'ave yer?'

'Oh yes,' gabbled Rose, holding out her left hand to show the legitimising ring she wore there. 'We've been passing our honeymoon in the West Country but have returned home because my father is ill . . .' Rose ran out of words and since Mrs Jannock forbore to inquire why they did not proceed thither but scrutinised the nomads on her doorstep, it was left to Patrick to take the next turn at conversation.

'How nice to meet you, Mrs Jannock,' he said, shaking her by the hand that held the dish cloth. 'I'd be most grateful if you could let us have Rose's old lodgings for a day or so. We left in a hurry, without making forward arrangements – there was no time to write a letter in advance of our arrival to beg your hospitality.'

Mrs Jannock shifted her weight and Patrick, taking this for a softening, persevered. 'I left some luggage at the railway station. Perhaps your lad would be so generous as to help me with it. He'll have a sixpence for his trouble.'

Mrs Jannock shifted again.

'I mean a shilling.' He plucked the coin from his pocket (Rose wondered where he had been hiding it) and held it up for her to see, before palming it. He really was a charming con man.

'You'll be wanting that blouse you left behind,' remarked Mrs Jannock to Rose and then, miraculously, she stood aside so they might enter that familiar hallway and deposit their traps in the back bedroom where bed, chest and text awaited.

Downstairs again, Patrick was kidnapped by Dor and Flor, who were shockingly impressed that he wore shoes without stockings and grew his hair and fingernails long. They carried him off to meet their guinea pigs, Gertie and Buttercup. Rose ventured to the scullery to further placate Mrs Jannock.

On entering the kitchen she knew by the smell of baking that this was Friday, by the absence of Mr Jannock's cap from the peg that the clock had not yet struck six, and by the cutlery arranged on the table that Sam was not in residence. So, things went on much the same. But no, for there had been revolutions in Raglan Street!

Noticing that she looked around the room, Mrs Jannock said with significance, 'No use lating 'ere for our Sam.' She poured out a second cup of tea, as though for an intimate, and Rose realised that she'd been promoted to supping on equal terms with the matron. Apparently a married lady, Rose was now a suitable recipient for proper women's talk. And Mrs Jannock was keen to unburden.

'You'd 'ave more luck down at that Webb's Farm since 'e copped on with that lass with a gammy leg. 'Igh an' mighty Miss Marion Webb never calls 'ere nowadays. It's 'im as does all the runnin'. An' 'e treats us as a common lodgin' 'ouse, you might say.'

Rose nearly choked on her tea at that conundrum.

'And 'er lame,' went on Mrs Jannock disparagingly as she sucked up her tea.

'How long has he been calling on her at her own home?' Rose was incredulous.

'You may well ask. All I know is,' here she paused for emphasis, 'this backend she's bin flashin' a right dazzler of a diamond on 'er finger.'

'They are engaged to be married?'

Mrs Jannock nodded significantly. 'And 'im a fine, well set up young man.'

Rose didn't comment upon this judgement; she remembered Sam as rather stunted.

'Who'd a thought a cripple could act so crafty?'

'Oh, I wish I could see Marion again,' sighed Rose.

'Well, you may, lass. There's tram at end of road will take you.' She looked speculatively at her young visitor. She'd been through the mill, and no mistake. It was certain sure she was expecting and that husband of hers wasn't much cop. She'd live to rue it, concluded Mrs Jannock.

When Tommy returned home he was put to work helping Patrick with their necessary luggage (Patrick's paintings were stored securely at the railway station, as though to be in easy proximity of the means of onward travel, if the fancy overtook him).

That evening he and Rose sat by the fire in imitation of domestic well-being. Rose could not concentrate on anything but watched as he whittled away at the heft of wood he held. It was a habit he'd cultivated in the Cornish cottage. Every evening, when it was too dark to paint, he'd taken up his whittling and worked on it while he sang or whistled through his teeth. And, in all that time, he very rarely ended the evening with more to show for his work than a pile of chips at his feet.

He glanced up at her and said pleasantly, 'Bert and Fred are thinking of holing up on a London barge they've discovered beached on the Medway to live off whelks. If we're quick we can join them and have the place habitable for winter. What d'you say, we all paup along together? Or perhaps we'd be better off further afield . . .'

'But Patrick, don't you see I must go to my father? He as good as sent for me.' Anxiety clenched within her that she would be compelled to set off again running along behind the leading red-gold beard to live among Galician fishermen or Scottish crofters, or wherever that elusive locus of the fulfilled creative life lay. For, though his was a vague and unpunctual star, nevertheless she knew that his was the star she must follow, baby or not.

The next morning, before Patrick might have the time to send to Bert and Fred in Chatham, Rose dressed herself as tidily as she was able and set off, unannounced, to the iron-girt home of her girlhood. She was so nervous as she approached that she almost turned back, but the thought that this was possibly the last opportunity she'd have to steer the course of her own life kept her walking.

She was greeted at the door before she'd had a chance to knock. Evidently she'd been spotted coming up the drive from the same window where once she'd kept vigil, waiting for life to surprise her.

'Joan!'

For there she stood, in all her glory.

'Eh, miss, tha've come home to us.'

# Chapter 36

Four months she'd kept away from them. Four months without word. He'd spent himself in loud anger and accusations for the first two: a big, public bonfire that burned itself up to no purpose. But all the while, deep inside, where it could not be seen, self-reproach had burned steadily with a more intense, a deadlier, heat. He could not find it in himself to turn his anger on Webb, seeing as the lad himself smarted, and he could not hate his daughter. And so the secret, corrosive rage smouldered. His wife had carried on through the months of Rose's absence living an outward version of the ordinary and everyday. She'd continued to order luncheon and dinner, had taken regular constitutional drives with Cousin Albert's wife, had shopped for new hats. He wondered at it. And it was she who had discovered that Mary Ibbotson's girl Joan had got herself into trouble. How she'd squawked, worse than Rose when she'd come back to them from Paris!

He thought back to the very day, Saturday, 12 March 1864, when he'd taken little Mary under his wing and made himself responsible for another's life and with it, it seemed, all her descendants. Just past that notorious midnight six hundred and fifty million gallons of pent water had sprung from the breached embankment of the newly completed Dale Dyke Dam with the noise of a hundred engines letting off steam. Unleashed, the unstoppable waters fell upon the Loxley valley and forced their eight-mile wrecking route down valleys and waterways towards sleeping Sheffield. Two miles to the east, they'd have known nothing of this disaster had not one of his father's men ridden over in the early hours to raise the alarm. He told them that already Hartford Steelworks were inundated, their melting pots likely destroyed in an explosion of steam when water had met hot metal, and that the entire stock of grain and flour that was in the corn mill on Nursery Street had been seriously injured or washed away. Robert had volunteered to ride to Sheffield with the man to check on the safety of their own works. A young man of just twenty, he'd relished the excitement of that ride through the freezing rain. Having seen for himself that the factory was safe, he turned his horse in the direction of Bradfield and the mouth of that mighty spillage to judge for himself the extent of the catastrophe. As he trotted along the wide path that the flood had carved for itself, it was just beginning to be light – he remembered a bitter, mean morning, sullen and still after the bravura of the night's works. Looking to left and right, he wondered that there had been enough water in the whole of Yorkshire, let alone in the reservoir to produce this quantity of mud; it blanketed everything and smelled to him rank as newly opened graves.

He came upon a row of cottages that had once stood beside the river but was now marooned on an undercut cliff made of mud. In this forsaken hamlet people seemed to sleepwalk in their filthy, wet nightclothes. That was where he'd found Mary Ibbotson, wandering abandoned in the mud, holding a chipped cup as though it were the most precious thing in the world.

'Where's Dada and Mamma?' she asked, bewildered.

Poor little mite, her parents had been swept away. He picked her up, put her on the front of his horse and rode home with her.

In the next days he'd busied himself on her behalf. He

sponsored her with his own money at the Orphans' House until she was old enough to take up employment.

When she married he'd been the one to give her away and he'd paid the rent on the couple's first home. So Mary had grown up and lived a life that, without him, would have been stolen from her. When she died of typhoid fever, what must he do but take in her child, Joan. For, having saved a life, it seemed he could not shrug off the unfolding responsibility of that act. And now, though no doubt he should have cast Joan from him in her shame and sent her packing, he could not. She was Mary's girl, the living link with that time when he'd not been just an old, disappointed man, and he'd always do his best by her, just as though she was his own little girl. And, even deeper than this, he did it for Rose, who was somewhere in the world and perhaps needed someone to be kind to her. So Joan was allowed to stay on. She'd knelt at his foot and tried to kiss his hand, swore that she'd name the child Robert. And that evening he'd sat in his study with the decanter of whisky and cried with a kind of bitter joy.

His wife had come upon him, Mary's chipped cup in his hand, looking vacantly ahead.

'Elizabeth-Jane, I doubt myself. I have always doubted myself.'

This was all he said and it had chilled her to the bone.

'My dear man!' She took his big, dear, heavy head in her arms and laid it upon her bosom so that he could weep there. But he got no comfort from it; if anything, he felt emptier still. Elizabeth-Jane looked at her man of substance and saw that he subsided before her eyes. The core of his self-belief was quite burned away now; truly, he was a hollow man.

He sat in his leather chair, behind his desk with its mess of papers, and commenced his long, slow collapse. Every Wednesday and Saturday Harold Webb came to him with documents to sign and reports to read. Harold, taciturn, black-browed, deferential, had become his most welcome visitor. Robert clung to him, solid and real, as though he were a beam that had bobbed up in front of the drowning man.

Now it was November and he was confined to his bed. The prospect of winter stole even the pleasure he had in the prospect of a young Robert. He seemed to remember that it was perpetual June when he'd been a young man. In those days the very earth had been in its pomp of spring. November was an old man's month, it heralded December when the year reached its exhausted end at last and presaged death. This November matched the cruelty of the times, he thought; it betokened a bleak and bitter future for the world. For it seemed to him the great old days were gone and passed into night, the works of giants must crumble and all the wealth of earth stand desolate. If once he'd considered the rescue of Mary Ibbotson to have been the sole act that gave his long life its proper meaning, thirty years on he saw that it was perhaps the moment he'd become stuck in the mud of the past, unable to forge ahead on his own account, to grow as old and used-up as was the exhausted world. Now only loneliness and diminution lay ahead, an inevitable falling off towards ugliness and destruction. He did not want to live to see it.

When Elizabeth-Jane came to him, smiling with happy news, he could not tell what time of day or night it was; he already heard the coming roar of the waters.

'Rose is found! She's come home to us!'

He gave a great sob that sounded like a terminal crack and the last retaining part of the structure that had supported iron Robert fell in.

Rose looked at her father, raised up upon his great cast-iron bed, only his nose standing proud of the heap of his bedclothes that seemed to weight skin and bone to the mattress. She wondered at that nose which had emerged as the flesh of his jowls had receded, like exposed prow left behind in the shipwreck of his face. She felt sorry for this poor old man. Why had she feared him? She leaned over to kiss him and her mother whispered, reassuring herself, 'You'll find him not too clever just at present, but Papus will surely rally now you've come home to us.' She patted Rose's hand. 'Just in the nick of time, eh, my pet.'

But it was too late. Robert had turned his head to the wall and the last good act that he had meant to do to put right an injustice before he went remained undone. He had intended to send for Harold and his half-made will but now he could not seem to speak it out loud. So the two women who watched at the side of the bed had never a sign that he could forgive, that he had long ago forgiven, that he had loved his darling always as the best part of himself, his treasure on earth. At the close of the second day, Robert Seaton surrendered to the inexorable waters and was gone, swept away.

# Chapter 37

Since Joan was now too bulky to be seen by her sharp-eyed aunt, Rose sent in her place another from among the household servants to bring Patrick to her from Raglan Street. This lass returned with his message that, since she was occupied with family matters, he had thought it best to take himself off to Chatham, down to the estuarine mud and the sea.

The next day she received a letter from him. He wrote, breezily, that since, as she knew, he could sleep comfortably on a clothes line, he would be able to lodge with Bert and Fred for pennies and that they were living like three boys on a spree. He sent her a little sketch of the three of them, all with belligerent beards and jutting pipes, poised on the tilting bow of the barge, each with paintbrush rampant before a canvas. He signed the jolly note with his thumbprint in Medway mud.

In the days that followed her husband's death, Elizabeth-Jane, always occupied with the little tasks of the household, busy as a tugboat, now drifted, rudderless. Rose would find her marooned in odd corners as though the tide of her grief had washed her up and then left her stranded. Rose, who had formerly entertained herself with the image of her own untimely death and her parents' chastened sorrow over it, was punished for that caprice. Death's retaliatory sting is sweet only in the imaginations of the living and then only when it is invoked in vain.

Now that she must take a firm hold on life, the rigours of organising the funeral show fell to Rose. She found that life with Patrick had made her capable – if not a housewife then at least a manager. She ordered suits of domestic mourning to be made for the servants and suitable weeds for herself and Mapus. These banners of woe were the first new clothes and jewellery she'd had in months (she would grow to hate the smell of crepe). Such were the stringent rules and regulations of death's etiquette – proper gloves of dull black kid, black-edged handkerchiefs, funeral cards illustrated by a broken column and relevant dates – that the immediate pain of personal loss was dulled by pressure not to skimp on ritual.

The ceremonial carried mother and daughter through the announcement of the death and the funeral procession and service without collapse. As they followed the featherman carrying his tray of black ostrich plumes and the child mutes, Rose knew, with some satisfaction, that Papus, too, was equipped as finely as society might demand. She knew that within the one-and-a-half-inch oak case of his coffin (with best brass nails and four best brass handles and grips), he reposed on a superfine cambric tufted mattress and pillow and was wrapped in a glazed winding sheet. And, even though he was not interred in cast iron as he might have wished, nevertheless the splendidly accoutred coffin was heavy enough to nearly kill the bearers who staggered under it. Yet it was impossible to comprehend that this was her own dear Papus, bare of all his worldly dignity and goods, laid in elemental clay. Impossible to comprehend that someone as substantial as Papus was now only measured in the huge gap he'd left behind in her and her mother's world.

Afterwards there was a very proper tea of crab sandwiches, a ham and white cake which remained upon the sideboard, untempting to palates diluted by tears as salt and ashes. Elizabeth-Jane sat in a corner chair and retreated under her enveloping widow's veil which she let down like a curtain over her grief, leaving Rose to preside over the teapot as death's hostess until the last guest had left the old, cold, masterless mansion. It fell to the servants to finish up the funeral feast.

In the days after the funeral Rose was occupied not only with the business of mourning but of running the household. For it seemed that Elizabeth-Jane had forgotten how. Arrangements had also to be made for the reading of the will, for which a small gathering was expected at the mansion, including the principal limb of the Seaton family tree.

The day of the will-reading was wild enough to make those who'd assembled for this dour ceremonial converse in high and excited voices about the travails they'd gone through in getting there at all. They stood damply about exclaiming upon the weather and eyeing up the ornaments until Rose had to run away upstairs to breathe. She came upon Edy, dressed in purple, edged with inappropriate yellow, snooping along a corridor and smoking a cigarette in a jade holder.

'Awful crowd, ain't it?' she commented blithely. 'Must have come from miles around, struggling through the storm. Still, like they say, where there's a will there's a relative!' Edy rasped a little smoky laugh and Rose walked away from her, without reply.

She found Guy leading her mother into the library where the family solicitor was already ensconced. The large mahogany table seated the immediate family; others who thought they might have an interest sat just outside the inner circle, and the servants stood behind them. Rose did not notice that Harold Webb was one of the last to enter the room. He joined the standing servants, discreetly shaking the rain from his trouser legs, careful not to disturb the proceedings.

Everyone settled in for the entertainment, suiting their expressions to sombre complaisance. The room was cold, the rain slashed the windowpanes hard enough to make them rattle, and several gentlemen's thoughts turned to the whisky decanter that awaited in the drawing room and several ladies to the fire that burned, uselessly, there and not here. Still, expectation went a little way to pinking their cheeks and noses for them.

Mr Mayhew, the solicitor, cast his yellow eye over the assembly and began to read. And as the material property was steadily distributed – trinkets handed out to left and to right, livings to the loyal, bequests to the deserving – there was a discernible relaxation in the room; it was apparent that the old tyke had made a *good* will. The meat of the matter, the disbursement of real property, was still to come and now Mr Mayhew took the opportunity to pause and look again at the company as though he sought out one in particular. Most of the assemblage turned its eyes upon Rose, feme sole and putative heir to mansion, lands and half share in the Seaton and Gast foundry. It certainly would be a thumping sum for a girl not yet turned twenty-one – a temptation to marry that would overturn objections to even her rackety history.

But Mr Mayhew did not seek out Rose; he looked for the young man who stood modestly at the back of the room, though he might properly have occupied the head of that baronial board. For Robert Seaton's last will and testament, rough drafted not a month previously but nevertheless properly signed and witnessed, recognised only his old and new business partners. Mr Walter Gast junior was to receive one-quarter share of the deceased's holdings in the company, with another quarter to be settled on Mrs Elizabeth-Jane Seaton, the interest and profits accruing from which were to be totally under her discretion. As to the remaining half of Robert Seaton's interest in the firm, that was to be settled on Mr Harold Webb who, having devoted himself to the expansion of the company, had proved himself such a forward-looking man of business that he might be depended upon to keep Mrs Seaton's dividends healthy. At this point Mr Mayhew read out the codicil that had been included in this revision: that Robert Seaton hoped by this generosity to give the young man, above named, a chance to prove his benefactor wrong with his new lines and new designs and the exploitation of new markets. Further provision was made for Elizabeth-Jane, although not sufficient for her to stay on in the old style and in the old house. The house itself and its grounds would go to Cousin Albert Seaton to be re-amalgamated into the ancient family estates, and thereafter passed down the female line. Of the deceased's daughter, Rose, there was no mention.

Unable to escape through the ranks of chairs and beneficiaries, Rose was obliged to hear out her sentence. Her father had cut her off without even the proverbial shilling – she could hardly take it in, dared not consider the implications. She would keep her dignity, she would not be humbled in this public place. Head high, she looked around the room, and caught the eye of her nemesis, Harold Webb, and shamed him to a blush.

When the company was released to the warming effects of whisky and fire, Rose withdrew to her father's study. She hoped that loathsome Edy would not find her out there. Sitting at the desk, she sifted idly through the documents that lay upon it and wondered at this monstrous reversal of the course of nature that severed the father from the child. Flesh from flesh. For nineteen years she'd been his daughter but, as though she too had been swallowed up by the earth, he'd casually replaced her with a son.

The study door opened and Harold Webb came cautiously in.

Rose stood to fly but he held her by the wrists, saying urgently, 'I did not contrive it! I did not even know that he'd done it! I'm sure his decline was too quick to find out your new circumstances.'

She said nothing, but struggled to free herself.

'I don't want it. If I could undo the blasted thing, I would. Rose, don't hate me!'

'How can you ask that? You, who have taken everything from me.'

'I'll hold it in trust for you. I'll work even harder and make money for you and, apart from paying myself a wage, I won't touch a penny of it. I swear!'

She still struggled to free her wrists and finally he let her go, saying, 'Nor will I ask anything of you in return.'

'You stole him from me!'

'What I did, I did for your sake alone, Rose.'

Rose slapped his face and, while he stood stupid as a poleaxed ox, ran from him, escaping up the stairs to her bedroom.

Later that evening, when all the guests at the will-reading had been sent back into the storm, the two women sat together by the fire.

'Eh, but I'd never have thought your Papus could have put me in the way of moving homes. Not at my age. Really I didn't. That he should have left me so unprovided for, to shift for myself,' wondered Elizabeth-Jane, accustomed as she was by long habit to her pleasantly uneventful life. She knew better than to comment on the preferment of Harold Webb although it did baffle her.

Pregnant, unmarried and dispossessed, Rose tried to comfort her mother, patted her cheek, rearranged a shawl, and bit her tongue.

'I don't know what I might have done without you, my love,' Elizabeth-Jane went on, that impulse of affection perhaps a cover for the thought that, obscurely, Rose's errant behaviour had killed her father and impoverished her mother. 'It's my only comfort that I shall have my child by my side to share my grief and ease my last, lonely days. For you shall always have a home here, my pet.' This made her cry in self-pity and Rose resolved that she would be that good daughter, would devote herself to poor Mapus, so stalled and lost without her man.

Contrition also decided Rose to be a better friend to deserted Joan, now in the last weeks of her confinement. With stoic devotion she would mend the hurt she'd caused others by her selfishness. However, to be forgiven by Joan seemed to mean she must swap roles with her grumpy maid, spending hours on combing out her hair, rubbing her sore back and massaging her cramped feet. And, of course, she must read to her. Joan, in her splendour, was as imperious a mistress as she was now unmissable, for an eight-month belly was not as easily disguised as was her own four-month bump, concealed under generously cut mourning clothes and a shawl. It did make Rose wonder how, now that the upheaval of the funeral and the will-reading was done, Joan continued on in the household, un-shunned. She would like to get to the bottom of what caused Mapus to turn this resolute blind eye.

'I would have sent for you, Joan dear,' Rose said, as she served tea, 'though it seems there was no need in the end.' She let the delicate implication of this incongruity hang.

'There's no call for apologies, miss,' Joan replied, struggling to find a more comfortable sitting position. 'I'm surely better off 'ere than gallivanting after you the Lord knows where.'

'My mother was happy for you to stay? I mean . . .'

'It were your own sainted father as said I could stop on 'ere,' Joan stated, easing a burp.

Rose was flabbergasted. 'My father knew?'

'Aye.'

Rose looked at her maid, searching for the sense behind this revelation.

'I'll swear Mister Robert Seaton were the most kindliest, the most forgivingest man as ever walked upon the earth,' Joan averred.

'He knew and he forgave?' asked Rose stupidly.

''E did. An' 'e said I weren't to fret no more, there'd allus be a home 'ere for me an' my baby so long as it were needed.'

Had she ever known her father? Had the man who'd raged himself into apoplexies over her harmless Paris flit softened to magnanimity before the shameful spectacle of a sinning maid? Rose felt tears pricking behind her eyes. Did this confirm that he'd never wanted her, loved her?

Joan, perhaps guessing her train of thought, said forcefully, 'I know 'e 'ad you in mind, miss. I know 'e did!' She took Rose's hand and patted it. 'Perhaps some'ow 'e knew, or guessed, an' wanted to show 'e forgave you an' all.'

Rose could not understand what Joan was saying. 'He couldn't find it in himself to forgive me for running after Patrick the first time so I don't imagine he'd have let me off this latest exploit.'

'Not that, not 'im,' Joan said dismissively. 'I mean to say, *your* baby.' Then she added, a little awestruck, ''E sent you 'is gracious pardon from beyond the grave, like.'

'My baby?' Rose repeated stupidly, as though the idea had never occurred to her.

'A course,' said Joan, reaching to touch her through the crepe, 'did you 'onestly think *I* wouldn't guess? I don't need telling, tha knows, I'm not as green as I'm cabbage looking!'

They both laughed and hugged, bumped bellies, and laughed again.

'But you'll keep my secret a little while longer, won't you Joan. I'd rather not upset mother at present,' Rose asked, looking at Joan with pretend severity, 'at least try to this time.'

Joan looked as though she might flare-up but instead, said, 'Eh, but tha'll never guess what 'e said to me one day, when he still got about the place an' could take an interest. "Joan" 'e said, "I should like to see a granddaughter afore I die." ' Joan wiped a tear away and looked smiling at her mistress. 'Now, what are we readin' today?'

Rose celebrated the sign of her father's forgiveness and love from beyond the grave in the small daily kindnesses she continued to do for Joan. And in his last, generous-hearted act found a kind of peace and reconciliation of her own, to balance the damage caused by that ill-wrought will, until finally she forgave him and wept for him.

So the three women continued in quiet withdrawal from the

world. Though Rose wondered how many more weeks would pass before the unmistakeable thickening of her waist must complicate that simple future. As for Patrick, she'd leave him on his barge in ignorance of the baby. She'd think about him tomorrow. Today, she'd protect Mapus from the truth and hope that procrastination and denial would continue to provide the answer to her own dilemma.

# Chapter 38

Cousin Albert, having no immediate need of Robert's hefty house (his own daughter turned up her nose up at it), benevolently suggested that Elizabeth-Jane might stay on there for as long as she was so inclined. But both she and Rose knew it would be folly to linger. As luck would have it, Albert himself was able to offer a more easily managed alternative: a Georgian *cottage ornée* which had survived the corrective impulse of a sterner age and stood in all its feminine frivolity just the other side of the park. It had been used, until recently, by his own land agent and was now available unfurnished. Elizabeth-Jane and Rose must decide how to compress the contents of a mansion into a cottage. It was a calculation of weight as much as dimension that decided the fate of many items of furniture. The same pruning process among the staff was also necessary. Their home would be offered to rent for the present, although Cousin Albert did not hold out much hope of finding a taker for the ugly, the uncomfortable and the unworkable.

On the morning of their removal from that dark and melancholy mansion, Rose posted a letter, addressed to Mr P. McKinley (artist), London Barge, Medway River, Chatham, KENT. It was a vain hope but a few days later a letter for her was delivered by Tommy from Raglan Street where it had been waiting. Evidently her change of circumstances had not reached him on his lopsided home, for he made no mention of Robert Seaton's death. Inside the envelope was a postcard-sized piece of parchment upon which was illustrated in cross-hatched Indian ink, like a cartoon from *Punch*, the comical exploits of Bert attempting to boil an egg over a candle, in two parts. The first showed his efforts to counteract the tilt of the floor and the next picture the egg cracking open under the mild influence of the candle flame to disclose a newly hatched crocodile. The caption read: 'Damn these Egyptian merchants and their cheap goods!' On the back he'd written simply: 'Darling, don't come. Nothing to eat here that don't come from mud, consume mud or have mud in it! Love PMK.'

Next week another envelope was sent on from Raglan Street. This picture postcard, entitled 'Nilus' mud, continued . . .', showed a sequence of ink illustrations delineating Fred's attempts to wash his socks. He started off cheerful enough hanging them on a line rigged on deck. The next illustration showed him looking for them over the side where they'd been blown. The following few frames depicted Fred acrobatically attempting to extricate them from a bush by the river bank, only to land waist deep in mud himself before finally managing to reunite them with the line. The last showed a mud-shod Fred guarding his socks from gusts. On the back were the words: 'As I always maintained, one keeps one's feet cleaner by leaving off stockings! Dearest R, down to our last jar of jam, claims to be fig and rhubarb but is nearer to fig and string. Fred and Bert send their best. Love PMK.'

In this epistolary conversation Rose was mute, for, though his illustrated cards spoke to her in the authentic tone of playful Patrick, her replies apparently did not reach him. He never referred to the contents of the letters she sent him, never addressed his cards to her new home. So she was obliged to write answering letters that she threw into the void that held Patrick: messages in bottles entrusted to the fickle sea, which might, or might not, wash up in the Medway. Kent seemed such a terribly long distance from Sheffield. Before long his weekly letters became fortnightly, and then they dried up completely. She sat tethered by her window, hour after hour, to monitor the clouds, like boats, that fleeted across the sky and once again found herself buried deep in the Yorkshire winter and regrets.

It seemed to her that in that season, regular as Proserpine, she must descend into this dark and earthy place where the sun may not reach. Yearly, like that doleful Queen of Erebus, she waited for Patrick's return as though she awaited the release of longed-for warmth and life. And this winter, it seemed, her poor mother followed her into that kingdom of the dead.

The women, clothed in black, with black all around, did not celebrate Christmas or the old year's passing or welcome in the next. Nevertheless, just as they are appointed to do, the winter days duly lengthened and lightened. Once more optimistic snowdrops pushed their heads above the crust of snow, the hills were suddenly jubilant with rubber-limbed lambs and Joan's Robert tumbled into his place in this glad new world. Elizabeth-Jane and Rose awoke and struggled free of the tomb, for spring around the corner, and a baby in the house must bring an end to the season of loss and grieving.

Rose, the nursery maid, attended upon the new master of the household and his happy mother and wondered that Joan should so extravagantly adore this by-blow of deceiving John. But it was as if baby Robert had no other progenitor than the man whose fond memory was commemorated in his name. Joan, the student of literary romance, who'd most passionately believed that true love was a couple, composed of man and woman, had revised her opinion. At the centre of the universe, she now plainly saw, were a mother and her child. Rose worried she wouldn't be able to love so freely the baby that she'd kept hidden from her own mother – worse, from its own father. Unacknowledged, it lay heavily upon her womb like a guilty conscience.

Then Rose received a note from Bill Bertram telling her that there was really nothing to worry herself over but that Patrick had been seedy and not up to writing himself this last month or two. However, he concluded encouragingly, 'Pick' was now well on the mend and would send something of his own soon. The very next day a card from Patrick arrived entitled 'Breezy, Sneezy, Freezy'. It showed Patrick himself, with a big red nose, lying in his hammock which stretched across the width of the boat, not unlike a modified clothes line. He was secured at either end, frozen fast by toes and hair. On the back was written only, 'O, for a beaker of the warm South!' She worried.

It was the evocation of the blissful Mediterranean that chilled her, the lure of the siren song of the south. Must she up and run again? She knew Patrick would not wait. Once he'd turned homesick eyes to the horizon and caught again the whiff of mutiny and treasure islands, there'd be no holding him. So she must make her own choice: stay here as a dutiful, penitent daughter or resume the role of Patrick's itinerant wife.

The day that Rose wondered how she might take off across country carrying the unborn, undeclared babe and bags, while encumbered by full mourning, her mother casually brought up the matter of that inexorably enlarging belly. She'd no longer button her lip. Rose had risen, ungainly, to issue orders for luncheon and Mapus remarked, 'When one can no longer bend in the middle it makes it very uncomfortable to leave a chair. Eh, it 'minds me of when I carried you, my love, and your dear Papus used to say, "Send fer 'oist, there's an 'eavy load wants shiftin'!" '

Rose was silent. But there was no need for comment.

Her mother went on fondly, 'Will it be a spring baby, Rose my dear?'

'I calculate late April or early May.'

'Apple blossom time.'

The two sat in silence again before Elizabeth-Jane went on, 'Why do you not send for him, for I know he writes to you?'

'Would he be welcome?'

'A course, lass.' Her mother squeezed her hand. 'It doesn't seem such a terrible thing nowadays, does it?'

Another blessing given to her from beyond the grave, Rose thought, looking into her mother's kind, forgiving face.

'At least he's not run away without a word, like that scoundrel of Joan's. We've only to arrange a small, very private, wedding and set all straight afore springtime. No one shall be the wiser – and if they are we'll face 'em out. It's been done before and, no doubt, can be done again,' continued Elizabeth-Jane comfortably. If he was the one her daughter wanted then she'd sensibly see to it that, long overdue, the right match was made and her damaged family mended.

Rose went to poor, worn Mapus and held her as close as her taut belly would allow.

'This house of women and babies could do with at least one man in it!' said Elizabeth-Jane.

Since she could not fetch him herself, Patrick must be brought here to her, where she could stall him awhile. But whom to trust? It occurred to Rose that the only person who could be depended upon to go to the ends of the earth – or Kent – for Patrick was Guy.

He went of course, as she knew he would. He even managed to get away without spilling the beans to Edy. Then he, like her letters, disappeared into a void.

At last word came. He'd found Patrick abandoned on the sinking barge but he'd found him very ill, his chest weak and much emaciated. 'Our poor lad', he wrote, 'his splendid wings so frayed and soiled and torn.' She cried at that but was glad that he was evidently in no condition to fly.

Dependable Guy moved him at once to a family-run hotel and engaged a woman to nurse him there. There was no possibility of travel until he was restored to strength and so Guy would remain until Patrick was well enough to be removed. And the enforced temperance of that house of mourning and slow maternity, where nobody came and nothing occurred, allowed Rose to rest, at last, and wait for Patrick to be brought back to her. The child inside her waited too, lying like the seeds, cold and low, until it should be quickened by the sun's return.

# Chapter 39

March blew in and with it the news that somebody had been sufficiently seduced by that mode of late nineteenth-century decoration aphorised as the 'gospel of gloom' to take their old, cold home, although Cousin Albert was strangely reticent about who the tenant might be, beyond saying that he was an unmarried man, who lived quietly and never entertained. Guy stayed on in Chatham and wrote in detail minute enough to satisfy even Rose of the patient's slow convalescence. He revealed more of the circumstances he'd found Patrick in: not only ill and alone but suffering nerve shock at the death of his friend, Bert, who'd drowned mysteriously. 'Darling,' he wrote, 'he is so terribly down over that unfortunate accident – blames himself. Please only write of happy things.'

And so she'd sent to him of their lovely future together and promised that soon, very soon, they would depart for the beautiful south. Privately she reasoned that she must only get him back and then they'd see.

He was returned to her at last, delivered in a growler, she felt a little grudgingly, by Guy.

'A business getting him away in the end,' he excused himself later, confidentially. 'Became quite the private hotel *portraitiste:* every one of the use of sitting-room and cruet ladies demanded their heads. You know how the dear boy likes his limelight!'

True to her word, Mapus received him affectionately, privately comforting herself that she offered a roof over the head of a poor invalid rather than succour to a seducer.

But, once the longed-for reunion was come, Rose was shy of him. The evidence of her seven-month secret was now unmissable. She'd never been more aware of the body she occupied, metamorphosed by maternity. She felt as large as a cow. Patrick, too, was changed; if it were possible, he was more aesthetically wasted, more romantically brooding. Rose took cover under the bustle of arrangements to be made for his comfort and care and did not acknowledge that betraying belly. He thinks I'm deceitful or ugly or worse, mused lean Jack Sprat's miserable wife.

In fact, he was fascinated.

'You're so . . . so huge!' he remarked approvingly when she came round his bedroom door, belly in advance, and found him out of his bed smoking a pipe.

'By the time I knew, you were in Kent and I couldn't tell you, not by letter,' she blurted, pulling her shawl round herself defensively and hoping he wouldn't count back.

'So you kept it for a surprise?' Patrick encouragingly slapped his knee. 'Come over here to me, my fine beauty! I think I can bear it,' he added, mock lascivious.

She sat, trying to make herself light on his sharp knees, and he stretched his arms round her. 'So solid! My darling Rose, you were never lovelier.' Under her, he groaned delightedly and laughed in turn.

'You don't mind?'

He looked at her, genuinely puzzled. 'Me mind? Mind what?'

She relaxed her legs, letting him have more of her weight, as though to test for truthfulness, and he groaned again and held on tight to keep her firmly seated. Putting her head on his shoulder, she whispered, 'I thought you'd be cross because you can't stand to be burdened down.'

He laughed. 'Less keen on being crushed to death, to be honest! Though it does have its attractions. What a way to go – flattened by bloomin' motherhood!'

Self-conscious, she slipped off his lap to sit beside him on the bed.

'You mean I'm fat!'

'Never!'

'Do you know what the Spanish call it? *Embarazada*, embarrassed.'

'To the contrary, you should be proud! Here's an expression for you, Rose darling: you are *proud with child*.'

He knelt on the floor and put his cheek close to her belly as though to listen there and felt the occupant rummaging within, joy on his face at the feel of his child.

'Can I have a look?' He seemed to ask the baby direct.

They locked the door and he tentatively unwrapped her, slow and careful as a boy would an unimaginably wonderful birthday present. He would not let her be bashful although she felt like an anatomy displayed upon a table. When she was revealed, he said, his voice thick and reverent, 'What is it they say – the world's a pregnant woman?'

Then he explored his bounty, tracing every silvery rupture or scrawled vein, delicately proving with his fingertips her belly's resistance and leaving a snail's path of kisses. Caressing and adoring, he gave Rose back her beauty.

Every night they secretly met by lamplight, so that he, puffing furiously at his pipe and scribbling on scraps of paper that he stuffed in his dressing-gown pockets, could add to his sketchbook diary of her pregnancy. For, ill as he still was, Rose's splendid new state sparked a febrile excitement in him. He suspended the grandeur and gravity of her body upon a single, eloquent line of charcoal. His smudgy crayons, warm oranges and pinks, showed her (lying incongruously before the bedroom grate, on the carpet) as a lavish, musky fruit that must split apart and spill its glossy seeds. His fingers handled her in oils, slippery as blood.

*Encre de Chine* discovered her among shadows. She had never been looked at with such love and so little passion. And, perversely, the closer he looked, the less she felt she existed. She was 'pregnancy': his subject. But Rose knew that, at least for the moment, it would hold him here, tied to her and Yorkshire.

Weeks passed. It was now Joan's turn to bring the tea and endure fads and short temper. But Joan had the privilege of topping every complaint her mistress suffered with a worse experience of her own.

'Eh, *I* were that pained with me dinner repeating on itself I thought it must eat an 'ole clean through me!'

'Don't be so melodramatic. I'm sure indigestion is much the same for everyone,' replied Rose, irritably pressing her hand to her chest where it burned her.

Joan muttered darkly, ''Owever bad it takes you, that's *nothing* to the pain of childbed!'

'You don't frighten me, Joan. Just because you carried it off with such wonderful fortitude doesn't mean I can't!'

'I'm sorry, Rose my pet, you know I don't mean nothing by it!'

She went and fetched baby Robert and they played with him until they were friends again. As Joan took him away to be fed, a letter addressed to Rose was brought in. All these long, sequestered months she'd had no other correspondence than what Patrick or Guy had sent (and a few calling cards, left on the little silver tray in the hall with a corner folded for condolence, which she'd ignored). Under cover of deep mourning, which conveniently lasted as long as a full-term pregnancy and beyond, she'd received no callers, not even family.

Inside the letter was a stiff card from Mr and Mrs Webb of Webb's Farm upon which was engraved an invitation to the June wedding and wedding breakfast of their eldest daughter Marion and Mr Pentecost Samuel.

Well I never, she said to herself. Pentecost! Won't Mrs Jannock be inconvenienced, and whatever will Dor and Flor do without their *fooit walker*? Then she thought guiltily of how Marion had sought her out and offered her friendship when she was friendless in Raglan Street and how she'd as good as promised her that she'd not leave without saying goodbye, only to run straight out of the door of number sixteen without a backward glance, never mind a parting note. She was about to crumple the envelope when she noticed that there was a letter enclosed.

Dearest Rose, I hope a June wedding gives you and Mrs Seaton sufficient interval since the death of your late, much regretted, father to feel yourselves ready for this return to the world. Though I shall find it hard to wait three long months before I can call myself *Mrs Samuel*! Just think, Rose, me a Mrs!

Rose was a little taken aback by the sudden switch of tone. She was not used to excitability in her invalid friend. But the enthusiasm continued into the next breathless paragraph:

Sam and I have such plans – Rose, we are so fired up to begin our life together and do some good. We had an idea to start a kind of club for youngsters in Sheffield, where lads may come to read or listen to talks. But then we had an even bolder notion – to found a socialist settlement on some rough land of my fathers and bring like-minded working men and their families together to work and live mutually. It shall have pigs and chickens kept in common and perhaps a couple of cows . . .

Ah, the brotherhood of man, Rose thought sourly. Socialist pigs and communal cows. What next, democratic washing lines? She read on:

So you see, we shall all be able to market-garden together, sharing expenses and labour, each according to who is fittest.

And those that aren't inclined to agriculture may continue to find employment in the city but dwell somewhere clean and wholesome, but also beautiful and close to nature.

Rose found Marion's strident cry of 'back to the land', even on paper, hard to bear. It seemed as though the two friends had changed places, Rose now sofa-ridden and Marion running off to live in a model community. She glanced irritably at the letter and the phrase 'Do you forget it was your idea?' jumped out at her. What was? She scanned the end of the letter for explanation. 'You must remember, Rose, in Raglan Street, it was you proposed bricks and mortar *with flowers*.'

Rose was nonplussed. 'I'm sure it never was!' she countered, surprising herself by speaking it out loud. Then she considered that perhaps, after all, it had been her idea. She put the letter and the invitation aside, complacent in the expectation that before those three long months were up, she herself would be a Mrs.

In the event, taking into account the deleterious effects upon him of late nights and artistic agitation, Patrick was insufficiently recovered for their secret *going to church* until well into April, by which time Rose was in no condition to do so. So the thing was put off and even Elizabeth-Jane, that fond and fashionable mother-of-the-bride, approved the delay, if it meant that Rose would have her waist back and be free of her ubiquitous black costumes. It was decided, that the wedding would wait until after the baby was safely born and Rose had stopped expanding. To pass the time until her daughter should have a shape again, Elizabeth-Jane diverted her need to shop into equipping Patrick. And he, of course, without seeming to notice or care, let her. At her own expense she had him remade, in tweed and linen and cotton twill and finest English shoe leather.

Just as the world breathed the first cut grass and apple blossom, just as she'd finished kitting him out to her satisfaction and accepted him into her heart (with the gift of a pair of cast-iron cufflinks that had belonged to her late husband), the baby was born, a bastard. It made Elizabeth-Jane cry to think it, but she, so much wiser as a widow than she had been as a wife, kissed it and blessed it and called it grandchild.

# Chapter 40

Her mother said she was Elizabeth. Patrick wanted Rosebud or, more seriously, Flora, because she'd burst forth in the springtime. But plain Elizabeth she was.

After giving birth, Rose was feverish so her dear, practical Joan took over the baby and fed her with her own. It was nearly a month before Rose could properly hold her child and by then it was too late to feed her herself. At first she was backward with Elizabeth, she did not fall instantly in love with her baby as had Joan with her Robert. She even worried that Joan (overflowing with mother love as well as milk) loved Elizabeth more naturally than she could and that the baby must prefer her in return. But, having recovered her strength, Rose learned to love until it made her cry. Ah, the frailty of joy! She sat and thought that she might have died and left her poor darling motherless, and the tears coursed down her face. Even more absurdly, the certain knowledge that Elizabeth must herself suffer, must, one day, even die, was unutterably poignant to her. This mutable world seemed too cruel and dangerous a place to keep a child in. Impossible to protect innocence from the everyday hurts that slip in under the door, or from those unstoppable catastrophes of history that sweep life cheaply away.

Patrick harboured no such theoretical terrors; he could not be doing with making himself wholly responsible for another's life and happiness. Rose envied him. Easily he welcomed the baby in, loving and accepting her as he did any happy addition to life's raucous conviviality. She imagined him, a satisfied gypsy king overlooking his busy, barefoot brides and his many fat babies as they rolled in the dust.

Now Patrick embarked upon his series *infancy*, natural successor to *pregnancy*. This, apparently, was to be his period of domestic interiors. Elizabeth-Jane thought there must be hope that he might yet earn a living as the painter of babies' portraits – done up in velvet and ringlets, to suggest sentimental days of yore. Even she knew of the perfectly respectable celebrity (and fortune) of that artist/baronet, John Everett Millais.

Patrick duly produced a lovely oil of baby Elizabeth kicking, white and pink, upon a chaise longue, with arms raised to Rose who looked down adoring and dangled a sprig upon which was a rose in full flush, together with its bud. He called it 'Mistress Baby'. But Rose suspected that, apart from the flowers, he'd hidden another joke in the wry renaissance mask of a Madonna that she wore. Mapus, having no artistic education (apart from admiring 'Bubbles' and 'Cherry Ripe'), enshrined the picture over her bed, as though to confirm the charming belief that all daughters manage virgin births and all babies are the very Lamb of God – at least to their grandmothers. A beautiful wooden sculpture of the sleeping Elizabeth, curled and naked, primitive and powerful, like a tribal artefact, did not, however, please Mapus. She preferred her granddaughter to be represented as she was: a Christian deity. But his best work was the simple ink sketches he dashed off, all done in curves, of the baby's profile, so ripe with promise and yet so vulnerable, that Rose could hardly bear to look at them.

All this while, in the cottage tucked away at the edge of the park, they continued to see practically no one and went nowhere. Nevertheless, somewhere, people worked and money was made. Somewhere the ugly necessities of life ground on to provide the bumper dividends from that quarter share in the family business that kept them all comfortably provided for.

June passed and one warm day Rose remembered that by now Marion had surely donned orange blossom and attained the title *Mrs* and, despite herself, it rankled that she had not. She found the wedding invitation where she'd left it, on the dusty mantelshelf, unanswered. She showed it to Patrick who was tickling his baby on the rug.

'Poor Marion, it made her so pleased and proud!'

He, smiling, answered only, 'Matrimony!' as though it was a shared joke, and went back to tickling.

'Still,' Rose said, a lump coming in her throat, 'she believes in it.'

'How does Shelley describe marriage?' He answered himself, speaking the lines with appropriate dolour. '"The code of modern morals, and the beaten road that those poor slaves with weary footsteps tread, who travel to their home among the dead," something else, something, something. Ah, I remember. "With one chained friend, perhaps a jealous foe, the dreariest and the longest journey go."' He grabbed her by the ankle, saying cheerfully, 'Thank the Lord one cannot be chained to a rose!'

She said nothing. The right time would surely come.

July became August, and then September, when the cast-iron portion of mourning might be judged to have eased, but still nobody came to disturb their bliss. Rose guessed that word of the scandalous ménage had finally seeped out and that they had been cut by Yorkshire society. Even Edy and Guy made no effort to call. And Rose was glad.

October and November passed them by with once more the smell of bonfires and decay. With December came the anniversary of Papus's death and the last year of the old Queen's century, and the cottage in the park might have been an ornate island lost in a snowy sea.

This was a bad time for Patrick. The centennial evening of Victoria's long reign may have been a golden one, but what weather the morning would bring was unknowable, terrifying to him and he hid from it under the wing of his black crow. Often his nightmares replayed the horror of Bert's death, when he seemed to see his friend, a baleful spectre, filthy with tidal mud, come to reproach him for continuing on in the world.

'He was a better man than me. A better artist,' he said to Rose as she stripped off his sweat-soaked nightshirt.

She nursed him and navigated him down the dreadful tunnel of January and February, when he was ill with his old lung complaint, and brought him through and out into the relief of spring again. Once more Patrick was happy, he let go the ghost of Bert, and took up his work again. Rose hoped that he'd realised at last that happiness was to be found at home. Her only doubt was that this seclusion could not last. Patrick must have company and new beginnings.

By April her baby had turned into a red-gold girl, the twin of sweet Robert. Somehow the sins of the parents were not visited upon innocent heads, for both these children of shame, whose natural name was foul to the wider world, were only healthy and happy in that enclosure of loving women. Then, around the time of Elizabeth's first birthday, as Rose and Patrick were sitting together over breakfast in the garden, he looked out to all that was springing, green and fresh and wick, and remarked, quite neutrally, 'England's dead. Isn't it?'

Rose, trying to stay calm, replied only, 'You should walk out into the woods. That will cheer you up.'

He went on wearily, 'I close my eyes and dream of Arcady. Open them again and what do I find? Sheffield.'

She laughed. 'It's not all that bad!'

'You don't understand. I can't breathe the air here and I can't seem to see in this northern light. And I'm always aware, nagging away, that just over the hill is the creep of the new.'

Rose felt that she'd swallowed something cold.

He went on gently, reasonably, 'Rose darling, I can't work if I stay in sorry England. I need sunshine and natural beauty. I need something magical and ancient that's bred into the very stones of the place.'

'But Patrick, you've been working so well here. Surely you have enough to interest a dealer or a gallery?'

Patrick's expression hardened. 'That's not the point. I don't paint for my own pleasure, or other people's. I especially don't do it for flashy celebrity.'

'Of course not, my darling,' she mollified, trying to keep her voice light.

Though it was a warm spring morning, he shuddered. 'Rose, I can't seem to shake free of him . . .'

Knowing that he meant Bert, she stroked his hand, for there was nothing to be said that would cleanse him of that clinging mud.

'I feel death all around me.'

'But must we go abroad?' she asked gently.

He stiffened and looked away from her. She took hold of his hand, which lay on the breakfast table, and noticed that it held the letter with a foreign stamp that had come in the morning's post.

The singing of the indifferent birds filled the silence between them.

At last he spoke. 'Yes, I think we must.'

Because she did not respond, he disengaged his hand and opened out the letter. 'As luck would have it, I received this from Mrs Van der Decken – she's come to land in Naples, for the present.' He read:

> I have more rooms here at Villa del Campo than I can possibly count. You and the charming Rose are welcome to join me in Napoli – although the rent I shall charge must be a high one, since you have both been so naughty, running off and leaving me to my own company in Paris. In payment I ask to indulge in a foul temper and condescension. But, as I say, the rooms here are so many that it is quite possible to live together in the

happy knowledge that one might never meet accidentally. You are both quite welcome.

So, the beautiful south had found him out even here, tucked away under the edge of smoky Sheffield. Or he had pursued it – that letter must have come in response to one of his own.

Stung by that understanding, Rose changed tactics. 'I don't understand why, since you profess to hardly know, or even like, your mother, you're always after her for something.'

Patrick's jaw hardened as though she'd hit him on it and he stiffly replied, 'As you say, I don't enjoy Mrs Van der Decken's company. From time to time, however, I choose to accept her patronage, for the sake of my art.'

'Ah, the grave responsibility of your genius,' she said, risking all.

His reply was sternly dignified. 'My work *is* a responsibility.'

'Don't you think it would be more honest to earn your own way in the world? I mean, to make enough money of your own, never to need hers?' How she wished he could be free of his 'housekeepers'.

Because he did not reply she unwisely added, 'Patrick, I'm sure if you set your mind to it, you could make millions!'

'If I was the most respected artist in the land I believe you'd still consider me doubtfully employed because my intention is not solely to make money.'

'Not at all! You know that I don't love money, Patrick. All that I love is here in this house. You said yourself that the connection between us is the only thing that matters in the end.'

He went round the table to hold her in his arms. 'And I haven't stopped believing that.' He stroked her hair, and she was glad that he forgave her, even though she'd called him a genius. 'But I can't just stand still. I need to be off on the high road, so to speak, away from here, away from him.' He broke off to gather himself again before saying, in a livelier tone, 'And Mrs Van der Decken provides the opportunity. But not alone, no longer alone.

Rose darling, I need you, my life's travelling companion.' He kissed the top of her head. 'I want to see my Rose in that golden Italian light – a child in Italy, with a child's perceptions and unforced delight.'

No mention of the child's child.

'When do you plan to leave?' she asked quietly.

'Well, that's just the thing.' Now he was enthusiastic, unstoppable. 'We may easily be packed and ready in a matter of days.'

'Elizabeth—'

'Oh, I don't think we can impose a baby on Grandmama Van der Decken. Can we?' He tried to jolly her. 'Just imagine, the albatross with our chick, she'd probably snap her up as a morsel! Besides, it would be safer for her to stay here, with Joan and your mother and Master Robert, where, you know perfectly well, Rose, she's loved and cared for.'

'Patrick, I can't leave her behind!'

Now he tried to be firm with her, disparaging. 'Don't turn into one of those masochistic women who use their dratted children as an excuse not to lead a life of their own.'

'But, she's so little.'

'That's my point. What possible benefit can a baby gain by travelling into hot and disease-prone lands when the alternative is to stay put at home, safe and loved?'

She only sobbed.

Exasperated, he continued, 'I don't ask you to abandon her, for goodness' sake!'

She sobbed louder and he was gentle again. 'Can't you take this chance while she is hardly old enough to notice whether it's Joan or you who feeds her horrible mashed carrot?'

She turned on him then. 'This is some kind of test of me, isn't it? You want me to give up everything, to prove to you that I'm completely yours! Well, I can't do it. I can't pass this test, it's too much to ask of me!'

'But I don't demand any sacrifice from you, Rose,' he answered, sounding perplexed. 'I never have.'

'You don't understand, do you, how I've risked everything?' she muttered in reply.

'Just because I want more from life than just a home and . . . and . . .' He held out his arms as though to embrace every other comfort the world could offer and let the sentence hang. 'I don't expect that of you, Rose darling. You were always free to accept or decline. You are free to choose for yourself.'

Rose cried out in exasperation, 'But I'm not. Don't you see, I'm not!'

Patrick took up the letter and said matter-of-factly, having made his case, 'You do understand I shall have to reply to her sooner or later. Let me know whether you will come or stay.'

He walked away into the garden and she watched him go. He was so sure.

For hours that evening Rose looked at Elizabeth sleeping, as though to glut herself. There was no choice to be made, her only course was to stay.

'A man's all very well, but in the end it's babies make women happy.' Mapus had crept in and settled comfortably beside Rose. She looked complacently at her daughter as she watched over the child.

Rose said nothing, but a tear slipped down her cheek. How could she tell her dear, silly Mapus?

Her mother patted her hand and whispered, 'Eh, but I don't say that mother love is not double-edged, my pet. The child you love, the very one who brings the greatest happiness in life, has the power to cause the greatest pain.'

'I did not intend to hurt you,' started Rose, mistaking the 'child' as herself.

Elizabeth-Jane, seeing her confusion, was full of compassion and forgiveness for those past crimes. 'I know it, love. A young girl in love's a selfish creature, but she can't be blamed for that. And I have never held it against you.' She reached into the cradle and touched the baby's cheek and then her daughter's. Eyes shining with love, she said, 'When we are mothers ourselves, we gladly learn to put our own wants after those of our child.'

Rose felt cornered by her mother's calm certainty. She looked unhappily down at sleeping Elizabeth. Did her mother guess that only this morning she *had* considered her own, selfish wants, if only for a minute, before those of her child?

'But you'll find motherhood is its own reward, Rose. Especially now, when she needs you so,' Mapus went on complacently.

'Oh, I'm not so sure she distinguishes between us, so long as she's comfortable and her needs answered by someone, she's happy,' Rose said, testing the feel of the argument in her own mouth. Mapus said nothing so Rose continued glibly, though she did not feel it, 'If I wasn't here, Mistress Baby would barely notice or care.' She affected a laugh. 'Hasn't she enough women at her beck and call?'

'Rose.' Alert, Mapus looked at her daughter, who could not hold her eye. 'Tell me you're not thinking of going off with him again?'

Rose was mute.

'Let him go his own way!' she commanded, sharp with shock now. 'Let him be, let him go!'

'But you don't understand, Mapus, I want him!' replied her unhappy child.

Elizabeth-Jane gave her daughter's shoulder a little reproving tap and then let her hand lie heavily there as if to stay her. Rose continued to look down at her sleeping baby. 'He is her father.'

'I know, I know,' soothed Elizabeth-Jane, clumsy hand stroking now.

'Once he's gone, who's to say he'll ever come back to us?'

Putting that fear into words, she seemed to see clearly down the long and lonely, uneventful road that lay ahead and something turned in her. Panicky, she said, 'I shall be left behind here. Left behind with nothing!'

'You will have your child!'

Rose shook off her mother's comforting, restraining hand. Trapped, she thought the terrible thought: choose Patrick and liberty over Elizabeth. And even as she resolved that she must never consent, she knew that she had consented and that she would up and run again wherever he led.

In a hectic rush she justified her decision. 'You've seen how he does not thrive here. He just needs the tonic of mild weather and purer air and me to care for him, to make sure that he eats. Really, he needs me more than she does.'

Her mother turned her pale face away.

But Rose could not stop. 'Mapus, we'd only be away for a month or two, and I promise, this time we'll write . . . you'll know where we have gone . . .' While she spoke, Rose rocked Elizabeth fiercely enough to wake the child into wailing. The little girl reached out in the dark to her mother but Rose had already jumped up, nervous as a cat.

'Rose, stop this now! Go to your room and think on your responsibilities.'

'You can't understand, can you? You never loved my father as I love Patrick . . .' She knew she struck a blow to her mother's heart, and yet it brought bitter relief. 'How can you tell me to give up my life when you've never had one of your own? I've been in the world and I can't settle for just a corner of a room!'

She ran away to tell Patrick that he must quickly write and accept Mrs Van der Decken's invitation for both of them. Once again she would step in behind Patrick and follow the restless path he trod. All in the name of her freedom.

# Chapter 41

The modern nomads travelled by train to London and thence across the Channel to Boulogne. From there they went across country to Paris and onwards to Strasbourg, Basle and then Lausanne – a trip without stops, which was accomplished in just eighteen hours. Their route met the massive barricade that defends Switzerland's southern border, at Goeschenen, where the St Gotthard tunnel, a thirty-one-mile system of viaducts and bridges and tunnels drilled through and gouged out of the mountain, made the perilous adventure of an alpine crossing into a picturesque rattle that brought them out into the geographical feature that was the Italian peninsula. Then on to Como and Turin, then Milan and at last Genoa where they stopped. They broke their journey here for two days then resumed travelling south again, always south, without further rest until their journey's conclusion was reached.

These were the bare bones of their journey, the narrative of the miles as they might have been recorded in a travel journal, evidence for posterity that in 1899 Rose McKinley, née Seaton, had been an independent young woman, companion of a brilliant artist, who'd taken herself off, halfway across Europe, at the drop of a hat. No room, in a bragging roll-call of capitals and first impressions, for the huge untold story of an abandoned baby.

No room in Rose's heart to experience anything else. And all that long way they hardly exchanged a word and Patrick did not sing – not even his habitual railroad song, 'My Girl's A Yorkshire Girl', that he'd told her he'd sung right across America. It was as if he had put himself into this insensate condition so that he could be sure not to experience anything until he was safely delivered to Naples where he could once again allow himself to speak and see. To Rose it felt as though they shared a criminal secret of such enormity that to intrude upon that silence would be to break too terrible a taboo. Lost to herself, she hurried through the unfolding scenery to journey's end. But, for her, Naples was only the turning point on a route that led directly back north to Elizabeth. So she worked her way through methodically, page laid upon page of that never-to-be-written journal, mile succeeding inexorable mile. And as she looked out of the train window, she devised to herself the reassuring rhyme of the telegraph poles that seemed to repeat, 'It will pass, it will pass, all will pass.'

She lost herself first in the flying fields of France, corduroy striped by shooting wheat and oats and barley and then, in an instant, the shaggy vines that told of the south and left no taste behind them. She knew there must have been towns and cities too, but she could not have named them. There was nothing else to France, just the memory of Elizabeth's face, and a goose girl who'd looked up briefly to the train from her flock. They went through Switzerland, operatic in its grandeur, mostly by night, as in a waking dream. The lit lamps in the windows of high chalets appeared to her as winking stars that had slipped a little below the mountain tops. As they exited from the spectacular St Gotthard tunnel into the surprise of sunlight at Airolo in Italy, she looked round to see that the cloistering Alps turned indifferent backs to them and seemed to rear up larger and more forbidding. Switzerland had shrugged them off, slammed its gates, as though to bar the way back.

Italy was colour and light. Not just an accident of history and geography, then. And these, not the *douanier* who stamped your passport, told you that you'd crossed into the magic peninsula. For Italy *was* magic. Italy would not be denied. There Rose awoke and experienced such a rush of accelerated awareness that her feeling heart was squeezed even tighter. Italy demanded she be *here* and *now*, at the bright point where past and future meet and ignite in the moment. She saw in fleeting symbols: bullocks, white as doves, licking their noses, sunk to their knees, in the morning mist; green shutters; black hair; silver olive trees. Cyprus pines cast blue shadows across chalky lanes almost too real to bear. The Italian light mellowed from the green of morning to thick golden afternoon and a boy sold oranges from a pink tin tray in a dusty station as their train panted to take on water. Her first brilliant Italian day closed upon the luxury of twilight and left her, not happy, not forgetful, but somehow elevated.

Arriving was the worst jolt. It was like being born back into the world, into everyday consciousness, into struggle. At Genoa, where they rested for a couple of days, they stayed in a vast hotel that smelled of that city's famous pesto sauce and echoed with the excitement of tourists calling for cocktails and cabs. Venturing out at evening time, they seemed to crawl down crevasses, soon lost among the zigzag alleys that climb and burrow across the sloping face of the city. Though Genoa was a great port, buried in the scrawled map of hidden ways, there was no constant reference point of the sea. The only hint of it were the sailors wearing red sashes and the swaggering fishermen with suntanned legs, who'd pushed past them in the warren, and the sea smell that wound its way to their cavernous bedroom and mingled with the pesto.

Back in the train compartment she was suspended again in the equilibrium of stillness in motion and allowed herself to drift and dream, now almost dreading the end of the line. For the first time Rose wondered what Naples would look like. In this day of photographic panoramas, the only representation she remembered having seen was a lurid watercolour of Vesuvius at the point of eruption, with little Roman stick figures running helter-skelter. It had hung on her uncle's wall, brought back by some eighteenth-century Seaton grand tourist and journal keeper. What a thing: to live under the malevolent volcano, with always the expectation of disaster.

Naples railway station was as full of steam and milling people as the one in London or Paris or Milan. But here the smells of coffee and fried oil and warmed drains told one that this was south.

Outside the station, they'd stepped into air exhausted by the day to be surprised by the many child beggars, wild and half naked, who surged around them. One urchin, his eyes a couple of crusted sores, shuffled along behind the pack with out-stretched palms, weeping, '*Un sord', signori, un sord', signori.*' Patrick threw a handful of small change among the children, and they were beset by a following swarm of porters, hotel touts and guides attracted like flies by their northern pallor and expensive luggage. They had to hurry to keep up with the grinning hirsute man, the first to get his hands on their traps, who led them to a cab. Having handed Rose over-solicitously into the carriage, the ruffian promptly stuck out his brown and wrinkled palm, itchy for money, and demanded, '*Un po' di moneta.*' Rose decided that Naples was possibly as far south as she might bear at present.

Patrick gave the carriage driver the address of Villa dell Campo, and as they trotted off, it seemed that all the bells in Naples began to ring, as though at a signal from the driver's whip, each bell commencing with a heavy clash followed by a series of rapid little stutters which built and combined into a medieval cacophony.

There was no pavement in this part and their little carriage bobbed along in a tide of wheeled and perambulating traffic. Rustic carts loaded with stained wine casks, carriages, handcarts and cabs threatened the lives of barefoot ecclesiastical gentleman and un-shod beggar alike. Herds of goats, each with a little bell round its neck, skipped between, cattle driven along by men with long whips shouldered through, and housewives jostled in and out of the sausage and wine and fruit shops. An *acquaiòlo* guarded his magnificent stall that proclaimed in gilded letters, '*Acqua, gelata e cocco fresco*' from the urchins who would steal a coconut from the display. And the mobile *maccheroni* vendors, stationed behind steaming cauldrons, lifted up their sample strings of pasta by finger and thumb high above their heads to show how uniform, how strong, how delicious. Somewhere out of sight, within the concatenation of the hawkers' shouts of vegetables and fish and the repartee of their customers, the bawling of beggars and braying of donkeys, Rose thought she heard an accordion playing. The smells of the street, too, seemed to baffle her nostrils with waves of the appetising and the malodorous: fresh fish, rotting tomatoes, baked pine cones, lemons, sewers. But, under them all was the fresh, salt note of the sea. For they'd turned down into a broad avenue and suddenly here it was! The glorious Bay of Naples! It was the last hour of sunlight and the foam took its colour from the vivid, burning sky so that it swashed back and forth like flaming lava and between the rosy sky and the wine red sea stood a large violet island. To Rose, it seemed she must stretch her eyes to take in this whole wide prospect of delight. She turned to Patrick, wanting to share what she saw, but he was looking resolutely in the opposite direction back up at the gloomy royal gardens that ran along the other side of the thoroughfare.

'That's the Castl dell'Oro, the last prison of the last Emperor of Rome,' he said, obligingly pointing out the building to her. It was the first thing he'd said to her since they'd left Genoa.

The cab turned up away from the bay and drove between ill-painted wrought-iron gates, behind which stood a dry garden of agaves and palm trees and oleanders, ugly and untended. A circular drive brought them to the front of the rather shabby square-built palazzo, whose faded and patched complexion called to mind a beauty who'd let go. At the level of its garden the Villa dell Campo was already sunk in dusk while its upper floors and roof were warmed still by the sunset. Its doors opened upon a sinister factotum, dressed in the English manner, who bowed them into the cool dark of a lobby. Beyond it Rose caught a glimpse of an inner courtyard garden filled with the last glow of the dying sun.

Mrs Van der Decken's palazzo was a place of light perceived through shadow and gloom behind light, where an echo of footsteps suggested the presence of spacious halls, and half-closed doors the apartments that stood beyond. A place of moods and hours. Rose caught the scent of elegant ennui that so suited Patrick's mother, but no corporeal hostess appeared to greet them. Just as she had promised, the Villa dell Campo was large enough to have swallowed her without trace.

That evening Rose and Patrick dined alone upon *maccheroni* and red wine in the sparsely furnished, high-ceilinged antechamber that opened off their bedroom. As she ate, Rose still felt the motion of the train. She looked to the window, expecting to see rushing landscape. But the only movement came from the white linen curtains, swaying before the night breeze.

They went to bed without exchanging a word and did not comfort each other by making love. Since Elizabeth had been born they had touched each other rarely. She wondered whether the black crow had followed him even here, or whether the spectre of his poor, drowned friend lay between them in their bed. They lay, silent and separate, each lost in their own sick weariness and longing.

# Chapter 42

The next morning, having made their way back to the entrance hall, voices brought them cautiously into the courtyard garden, where the early sun made this outside air milder than the interior of the house. Next to the monumental fountain that oozed from slimed spouts, they discovered that frivolous wicker chairs and a table with a coloured cloth had been set out at which the chatterers, two unexpected young ladies, sat and broke their fast.

'Hello, you must be Mr and Mrs McKinley. I'm Margaret O'Grady and this is my sister, Dolly.' The accent was American. 'I do so hate to have the advantage but we already know you, so to speak.' She jumped up to shake their hands, leading with her prominent teeth. Both women were elegantly dressed and handsome although Miss Margaret O'Grady's pleasantly animated face had something equine in its length.

'You can bet your boots we know all about you two!' said Dolly, the younger and prettier of the two (more of a pony than an out-and-out horse), also shaking hands. 'A London artist and his beautiful bride! Gee, you wouldn't believe how the expectation of your arrival has kept us entertained.'

Margaret O'Grady mildly admonished her sister. 'Oh Dolly, don't play the Yankee, you know it doesn't become you.' She gestured to the chairs that were set for them. 'Won't you seat yourselves?'

Both sat but could not seem to find their tongues, perhaps lost somewhere along the length of that brooding rail route.

Good Margaret, suspecting well-bred English reserve or shyness, covered over the difficulty with more chatter. 'My sister and I and our brother, Charles, are staying as guests of your mother, Mr McKinley.'

A young man, upon whom the family likeness registered better as masculine good looks, sauntered up and addressed the girls, 'Marg, Dolly, turn off the gas!' and then presented himself. 'Mrs McKinley, Mr McKinley, good to meet you. I'm Charles O'Grady, brother of these two, for my sins, and a distant relation, I believe – we're Chicago O'Gradys,' he added as though this would elucidate all. He bowed over Rose's hand. She blushed at the undeserved title but had the wit to leave it uncorrected.

'We share a maternal great-grandmother,' offered Margaret.

Patrick still said nothing but looked stricken by the news.

Charles O'Grady hung about for a minute more, smiling vaguely at these queer coots, before he, being a man of the New World and unencumbered by unnecessary etiquette, declared, 'I'll shout up that ugly mug Gabrielle for more hot coffee and rolls.' He exited purposefully, calling, 'Eh, Gabrielle, *ancora di caffè*, you scoundrel!' and left Rose and Patrick to the girls.

'Now you are finally arrived you're just in time for today's little *escursione*!' exclaimed Dolly, undeterred.

Margaret shot a warning look at her enthusiastic sister. For whatever reason, she sensed these two needed time and peace to recover themselves. Generously she formulated their excuses for them. 'My dears, you must be tired after your journey. I know Dolly and I were fit to drop with bone weariness by the time we reached Napoli—'

'All those train stations, all that blessed culture!' galloped on Dolly, unaware that a get-out was being engineered. 'And they say in the US that one indulges in Continental travel to *rest*! I ask you!'

'Just so, Dolly,' said Margaret warningly.

But her unquellable sister was off again. 'I mean to say, if you're not *too* beat, we've plans to take a carriage to the Museo Archeologico this morning.'

Margaret kept her course. 'Dolly, since I know that our kind hostess won't be joining us and has plans to rest the whole day in her room, Mr and Mrs McKinley too might like the opportunity—'

'To join us, without being thought even a bit rude by dear Mrs Van der D,' interrupted Dolly, taking Rose's hand and pressing it encouragingly. 'After all, we *are* practically cousins.'

Rose smiled and nodded and thought that she would rather be anywhere else.

'See, Marg, they'd positively love to!'

Charles O'Grady returned, leading the servant with an angel's name and the lubricious look of a middle period Caravaggio.

Patrick spoke at last, sounding strained and artificial. 'Miss O'Grady, I beg I may be let off today. I have a prior appointment. However, I would be delighted if you would entertain my wife, I know Rose could do with fresh air and fresh company.' He gave a little, deprecating laugh and Rose nodded and smiled and wished she had the confidence to resist every kindly plan that people would impose upon her.

Back in their bedroom, she turned on him, their long silence broken on the hard edge of her fury. 'What *prior appointment*?'

'There is no appointment, as you guess,' he replied, his voice very flat and dull after so little use. 'I thought that coming to Italy would trigger something in me, the need to live and work again in a new way . . . God help me, I thought I'd just breathe it in. Inspiration!' He laughed shortly. 'But now I see there's nothing here that's not tired or beat as old England.'

'Then why did we come?' she demanded.

When he didn't reply she almost shouted, 'Must you always keep me in the dark? It's as though I was put in a cupboard and you take me out only when it suits you.'

He was shocked by her rage. 'Darling, don't you see, it's me who's shut up and lonely in the dark.'

She turned her back on him, exasperated.

He went on, gentle and sad, 'I expected that my coming here would be enough to rescue me from myself.' He paused. 'But it seems not.' He put his arms round her and pulled her in tight, pressed against her back and resting his chin on her shoulder so that he could talk softly into her ear. 'Rose, just leave me be to turn myself right way up again. All I need is to lie quietly here in the dark awhile, to lick my wounds, and creep my way back towards the light.'

As they stood in silence, she breathed shallow and quick, aware of his body so close to hers. It had been such a long time. She melted with the tears that had long waited to be shed.

'Don't, darling,' he said, turning her round to kiss her wet eyes. 'I really won't be able to bear it if you're unhappy too.'

She tried to stop but all that repressed pain and guilt erupted from her throat. 'Why did we come?' she asked again, but he only held her tighter, so that she sobbed into his chest. They stood like this for some minutes until she was calmer.

'I know that I can't stay happy for long, but you . . .' he paused, 'you, my darling Rose, were not made to suffer.' He stopped again as though to consider and said in a voice thick with meaning, 'Sometimes I wonder whether my best ideas grow in these dark, lonely places. I can't have one without the other.'

They stood in silence again and she thought resentfully of all those jostling friends and hangers-on he'd invited to crowd out their Cornish cottage.

'I thought you loved mobs of other people and larks.'

'Sometimes I do but then sometimes I don't,' he replied, in an effort to throw off the melancholy cloak that hung around him.

Then he added, in a cockney accent, forcing cheerfulness, ''E dunnow where 'e are!'

They disengaged and he held her away from him by the shoulders, to look her full in the face, and said encouragingly, 'Rose, I'll only need a couple of days away from people to regroup. Just for the present, darling, will you draw them from me?'

He kissed her on the forehead when he saw that she would.

'American cousins are too vivid for me to bear at present and I'll need all my strength to take on the albatross.'

Rose shivered, as though the shadow of a wing had passed over her.

'Just leave me to it. Go out into the day, darling, and see Naples. Be happy for me.'

She splashed some water on her face to calm the blotches that had come from crying and left him to the consoling dark.

At ten past ten the expeditionary party that would march upon the museum consisted still of just two. The O'Grady females waited in the marble hall and the *cocchiere* engaged to carry them there waited in the drive. It was not until half past eleven that Rose ran down to join them, wearing her brave face.

'Mr McKinley is definitely decided against coming with us, then?' solicited Margaret, choosing not to mention the wait. Meek Mrs McKinley (who'd obviously been crying) must be treated with delicacy or she might run away back upstairs.

'My husband has a sick headache,' Rose replied, forgetting the excuse that he'd already given.

Dolly covered the lie by shouting out, 'Time to absquatulate, don't you think?' and led the way out to the carriage.

It was only after they were seated and had lurched off that Rose shyly remarked that the party also lacked Mr O'Grady.

'My brother will be joining us at our destination,' Margaret explained. 'He's gone on ahead to collect his fiancée, Miss Minnie Openshawe. Minnie is staying here with her family in a villa on the Chiaia – which is why we were all so grateful to accept your mother-in-law's kind invitation to stay in Naples. Anyway, we shall have the pleasure of Minnie's company and that of her younger brother, Roland, today.'

Dolly swallowed a snort which made her choke until her eyes watered, and Rose summoned herself to make diversionary conversation. 'Have you seen much of Naples, Miss O'Grady?'

'Call me Margaret, please, for I shall call you Rose, even though you are a married lady. To answer your question, yes, my sister and brother and I have seen a great deal of everything, I guess.'

I am a fraud, Rose thought to herself and wondered whether Margaret would have been so girlishly familiar had she known that quite apart from being unmarried she was also a neglectful mother.

'Do you and Mr McKinley expect to do much sightseeing?' well-mannered Margaret inquired.

'You wouldn't believe the hard work it is being an American abroad,' interrupted Dolly. 'Really, it's like some kind of religious devotion one must submit to. We pour into old Europe from Boston and Philadelphia and, I don't know, Idaho, and are set upon this magnificent treadmill for our sins, doing the museums and the galleries and the cathedrals and the *belle viste*. And one has to simply *battle* one's way through the antiquity mongers and the massed Nativity scenes and the photographers selling panoramas just to get at 'em. I can't tell you!'

They fell silent for a moment, distracted by the view of the magnificent bay. Rose tried to imagine what Elizabeth would be doing at home. Right now perhaps she and Robert were playing on a blanket in the garden, or having their lunch. The thought made her smile. I can let myself be quite happy knowing that she's safe and well cared for, she said to herself. But her aching heart told her it was a lie.

Looking up from that inward scene, Rose realised that they seemed to be going westerly, leaving the fashionable Mergellina district and with it the city of Naples. 'Is the museum by the sea?' she asked.

'Oh, we're not going there!' replied Dolly.

'It got rather late and it *is* such a glorious day,' Margaret hurriedly put in. 'You might not believe it, but it has rained every hour since we arrived and, as my sister intimated, we have put in our fair share of observance at the shrines of tourism. But we will most certainly go to study the relics at the museum as a preparation for our planned trip to Pompeii . . .'

'But not today! Today we give self-improvement a miss and drive out to the hill of Posillipo for luncheon,' sallied Dolly. 'There's something so *almighty* about all this classical civilisation that only a nice picnic with cold ham will cure.'

'You do talk flapdoodle!' said her sister and they all looked at each other and laughed.

The two parties rendezvoused in a field which stood at just the right point on the Posillipo peninsula for vistas. The carriage that carried Charles, Miss Minnie and Master Rollo Openshawe also brought the kitchen maid who took charge of the folding chairs and the oil-proof sheet and the rugs and cushions, the windbreaks, the primus, the wine and the water and the cutlery and crockery for their luncheon. It was a wonder that there had been room enough to accommodate the luncheon itself.

Miss Minnie Openshawe, a beautiful blonde young lady who wore a tight yellow dress and a sweet, weak expression, was presented by Charles to Rose. He was solicitous with her as with one who bears a very heavy burden upon heartbreakingly fragile shoulders. Such was the oppressive celebrity of the Openshawe name. Rollo, as far as Rose could judge, was one of the species: medium-sized brown boy. Rose decided that she preferred the harmlessly chattering O'Grady girls.

While La Napolitana arranged their repast, Charles took charge of sightseeing fatigue. He walked them to the tunnel cut in the honey-coloured rock by the ancient Romans, to link

Posillipo with Pozzuoli. Here Miss Minnie conceived an exquisite horror of the dank entrance hole, after Dolly had excitingly described it to her as the 'haunted grotte', and would proceed no further. Accordingly they sauntered to a less controversial stop upon the tourist trail, where Virgil's tomb was to be admired and the finest views over the sparkling bay were to be had – Pozzuoli to the right of them and Naples to the left. Completing the *bella vista* was the volcano, puffing white smoke into the sky as though it was manufacturing clouds.

Contemplating the Bay of Naples, Rose effortlessly experienced the transcendence that religion never could inspire in her. She wished that Patrick might have been there, standing in the sunlight, to see it with her. Surely this natural beauty would have washed through him as it did her and carried away his pain? All was blue. The bowl of the bay, bobbing with ships and islands, matched the arch of cerulean blue above, just as the dashes of bright foam mirrored the white gasps sent from deep within the earth's core up the noble chimney of Vesuvius. She tried to imagine what the landscape might have looked like in Virgil's time, before the sprawl of modern Naples stained the green and the little stick men ran from the spurting fire and brimstone that erupted from that underground foundry. This brought her back to her own home town, where man had made his own fire pits and geysers to spout sulphurous fumes. Naples lived under the volcano and Sheffield sat on top of it and both ignored it as best they could. And while their party stood and breathed and looked and admired and between them could not think of a single sensible comment, Rose smiled to think that she had needed to travel so far to observe this strange congruity between Naples and Sheffield. Gathered for their picnic luncheon, the O'Grady girls began to talk again of the hardships of being American travellers in Europe.

'I think we pay our dues for all this in Yankee enthusiasm,' said Dolly, gesturing inclusively around her.

'I don't see that we owe anyone anything! Just because we

choose to undertake the long journey over here to admire shouldn't mark us out as servile or inferior,' answered her brother.

'Americans have no need to feel inferior to any other race, however old,' Margaret staunchly put in. 'After all, at bottom, we all started out European.'

'I'd say that, in future, Europeans will all be pleased to end up American,' countered Charles. Minnie shifted her tiny parasol a little and chewed a dainty mouthful of her early peach, mindful of juice. He went on forcefully, 'Look how Bell' Italia has already followed the American example – for aren't we both new, young nations, liberated from under the tyrant's heel and bloodily united as brothers?'

Minnie chewed admiringly at her lover.

Rose ventured, 'Doesn't Italy have a king, though?'

'Oh, some anarchist is sure to rid them of Umberto and then they may finish the job and declare themselves a republic,' he replied.

'Poor old Humbert,' remarked Dolly. 'I've always admired him for his rather fantastic side whiskers – but then side whiskers can't be allowed to stand in the way of reform.'

Minnie's jaw ceased its action and she said, with a little frown, 'Isn't it an emperor they have in Italy – or at least in Rome?'

Charles looked at his sweetheart as though she were a child who'd said something precious, and offered her, as reward, some perfect, twinned cherries.

'So, dear,' Margaret addressed herself firmly to her sister, who was beginning to effervesce with mirth, 'they may have the ancient marbles but we have all the coming ideas.' She looked archly at her brother. 'Americans should travel proudly since we come bearing ideological gifts.'

'I didn't mean to suggest that our native enthusiasm is a cringing thing,' Dolly responded, successfully diverted. 'I meant that while everyone else is busy being fashionably bored and saying that the old world civilisations have gone to the dogs, it's dollars to buttons you can count on an American to have the gusto to be thrilled with absolutely everything. I know I am!' With that Dolly ran across the grass, shouting. Rose looked after the dancing girl and considered how many decades separated twenty from virginal seventeen.

On the drive home Rose felt by the warmth of her face that her cheeks were glowing with the sun and the fresh air and the company.

'Oh, I did have a splendid day,' she said without thinking and then felt obscurely sad that she had indeed enjoyed herself.

'Didn't we just!' answered Dolly. She put her arm through Rose's so that she could pull her closer. 'I must say you come across rather quiet at first, but then I believe Marg and I make up for that. Besides, I prefer you to Minnie Openshawe any day.'

'Dolly!' said Margaret warningly, but without any force of conviction.

'Minnie is a very dear girl and we'll love her like our own sister when she is our own sister. However,' she lowered her voice although what she said would be perfectly plain for Margaret to hear, 'she is rather dull.'

'Dolly!' Margaret said again and turned away her head so that she could appear not to be listening.

'Minnie keeps a travel diary. You know the kind of thing – writes it up every night. Only she can never think of a thing of her own to say. She tries, poor girl. She looks deep into her little palpitating heart but she finds no opinions there, no instinctive response toward the beauties she sees about her, no poetry. Rather than condemn her to copying out the guide book, Charles must tutor her so that she will know just when to write "delightful sylvan spot" or "fine middle distant view of the island which floats in the bay like a dumpling in a soup tureen".'

When they returned down serpentine roads to the villa, it was at the same glowing hour that Rose and Patrick had arrived the previous day. Light was fading from the inner courtyard garden and the lamps had not yet been lit so that the house felt very gloomy after the bright day on Posillipo's hill. Rose ran upstairs, pulling off her hat as she went. Suddenly all the air and light had rushed out of her, displaced by that dull familiar weight of longing.

She worried for Patrick, stuck all day in this gloom.

'I'm so glad to be back,' she called through the door that stood open onto the shadowy bedroom, and laid her hat and gloves on a side table in their sitting room. 'It was all so beautiful, but it would have been so much better to have had my first view of the Bay of Naples and Vesuvius and Capri with you.'

He did not reply.

She pushed tentatively at the door and saw that the bed was empty.

# Chapter 43

When the dinner bell was rung later that evening, she thought of sending down that she was sun struck or exhausted but, at last, she steeled herself to join the O'Gradys, and perhaps Mrs Van der Decken, unaccompanied.

Their hostess was not present when Rose reached the room where everyone had gathered before dinner. With relief, she went to Margaret, as though crossing to a safe port, and realised that she had no sensible explanation for Patrick's absence.

'I must apologise for my husband. His head is no better—'

'Rubbish,' interrupted a familiar cracked voice behind her. 'My son has gone to climb Vesuvius. He left this morning and he won't be back before tomorrow.'

Rose turned to her hostess and tried a deep curtsey to cover her confusion. 'Mrs Van der Decken, thank you for inviting me to stay. I hope you are well.'

'I gave up being well in my thirties. I realised I had better and more amusing things to do with my time,' she replied, batting Rose upright with her fan.

They adjourned to the dining room and were seated by two green-coated lackeys (who, despite the identical coats, were not a matched pair – swarthy Caravaggio partnered Botticelli). Charles was placed between his sisters to one side of the long table and the hostess, with Rose, on the other.

A silence ensued in which the first course of *zuppa di cozze* was served. The subsequent absence of conversation was disguised by the justified clicking of soup spoons, for the mussels, creamy and chewy in their broth of tomatoes and peppers, were delicious.

Rose noticed with a start that her spoon bore a Sheffield hallmark.

'Did you enjoy your soup?' Mrs Van der Decken asked Rose, but did not wait for her reply. 'I always make it my business to employ the best of chefs when I travel. Other comforts I can do without but my table must never be skimped.'

Rose blushed and nodded and reached for her water glass to gulp a mouthful – warmed as much by her hostess's pointed attentiveness as by the heat in the soup.

'I made it my business to find a man who's up to the mark on the kind of high-class Frenchified cuisine the old King of Naples would have had at table.'

Just so, for hard on the heels of the soup came a magnificent *timballo di tagliolini*, crowning representative of the pasta race. Mrs Van der D herself uttered a little cry of appreciation as the golden pastry drum was set trembling with promise before her. At her command Gabrielle broached the crust and released the simmering riches, letting spill the shimmering ragu, the peas and pasta that had been layered and baked within. Mrs Van der Decken snuffled among the savoury treats upon her plate, oblivious.

Guests, however (if they wish to continue in that estate), understand that they pay for bed and board with conversation and anecdote. Charles, essaying the job, cleared his throat and began, 'As one of the *prohibited* myself, although far from home . . .' he paused and rubbed his knees, but no laughter answered his witticism, 'may I nevertheless offer any lady some of this excellent wine?'

Mrs Van der Decken cut him dead but accepted the wine with a curt gesture.

At the end of the pasta course Rose wondered whether Mrs Van der D was not a little affected by the many glasses with which she had chased down the *timballo*.

'So, my dear,' she said, leaning conspiratorially close. 'We meet again.'

Rose could not help but jump at the nearness of that rattly whisper.

Mrs Van der Decken laughed in her bubbly chest. 'You must not be afraid of me. I invited you and my son because I wanted to keep company with you. You both amuse me.' She looked rather pointedly at the rest of the company who bowed their heads for shame.

'It was generous of you to invite us.'

'Not at all, I'm always curious to know a tale's ending, all the more if it's a romantic one,' said Mrs Van der D. 'Besides, I like to see a girl show some independence, even if it goes against the best advice, by which I mean my own!' She coughed out another laugh. 'My, but you were eager to dash away after him, it near took my breath away.'

Rose blushed, hoping that the O'Gradys weren't listening too closely.

'It was a bad thing to have done and it caused my parents much pain,' she said, steeling herself not to take the easy option and fall in with Mrs Van der Decken's favouritism.

'I thought to myself, that's the spirit,' persisted the lady. 'Cut loose and fly.' She reached over and placed her veined, knuckly hand over Rose's and squeezed.

Saved from having to respond by the entry of the meat course, Rose flashed a look at the other side of the table to assess whether the O'Gradys had overheard, and knew by their elaborate concentration upon the *capretto al forno* that they had. Mercifully this was a simple dish of kid baked in the oven, served with an accompaniment of *carciofi e patate soffritti*. Rose, defeated by the regal pasta, managed a few mouthfuls of meat and some of the baby potatoes. The stewed artichokes, which she rightly took for thistles, she left on the side of her plate.

The whole company had now begun to glisten with the exertion of consuming heroic quantities of hot food and the stress of its digestion. Mrs Van der D alone remained unperturbed. Workmanlike, she wiped the film of grease from her top lip and downed another glass from the wine carafe that had lodged by her elbow. But when she greeted the entrance of the next steaming platter with, 'Ah, the fish!' a perceptible groan went up in answer. This fish was another triumph of Neapolitan culinary wit – a *buccala*. Not a native to Naples' teeming shores it must be brought, stiff and appetising as a strip of salted sailcloth, from chilly Norway. Even soaked and rinsed and baked with tomato, olives, raisins, pine nuts, capers and garlic, this cod was not a delicacy that Rose could bring herself to look at full in the face.

The O'Gradys, perhaps more familiar with idea of salt cod, rallied and gave a half lively account of it and of their little excursion to the Posillipo promontory. But they were so ill at ease under the hooded gaze of their hostess that Margaret lost her quiet assurance and Dolly managed to construct two sentences without expressing the slightest enthusiasm.

'So my dear, true love continues to triumph?' resumed Mrs Van der D belligerently at the end of the uncomfortable silence that followed this brief attempt at conviviality. 'How determinedly conventional you young women are!'

Rose considered again whether their hostess was not more than a little affected by wine and replied simply, 'We have been happy together ever since,' preferring not to divulge the months when she'd had no idea where he was or the fact that they remained, most unconventionally, unmarried. She also resolved to make no mention of Elizabeth, determined to keep her safe from Mrs Van der Decken's hard, inquisitive beak.

'I myself am one of those women they call *emancipated*,' went on the other, for she hadn't been listening. 'I've never seen it myself – it was just how I was made. My mother was the same.

However, I know that I'm usually accused of it when I'm behaving least like a doormat and so I'll take the title.' She laughed, more extravagantly than was perhaps ladylike, and then looked balefully across the table to where the unfavoured O'Gradys sat contriving amused attentiveness.

Charles, feeling the social spur, started up, 'It is a happy situation when the modern girl—'

He got no further, for their hostess had commanded the *dolce*.

What sweet delicacies were brought: a baba flavoured with limoncello liqueur and one with rum, a festival of such lucent syrops and creamy curd, manna and dates that might have made them stretch their eyes and clap their hands had they been children rewarded after play. But at the end of that long culinary campaign, it was insurmountable. Rose saw even Dolly pale at the challenge. Mrs Van der D's resolute appetite was bested too; having accepted a baba and taken a forkful, she limited herself to the dessert wine.

She once again addressed Rose, a familiar hand on her arm. 'I remember there was a little anxiety over funds,' she said, elaborately sotto voce, and cast a lugubrious eye towards Charles. 'Let's just say help may be at hand.' She lifted a finger conspiratorially to her lips. 'Mama Van der Decken has her plan to help the poor lovebirds help themselves.' Rose noticed that she transferred a crumb of baba from finger to chin and, on seeing that Margaret's face flooded with scarlet, was crushed by embarrassment that all this was unavoidably overheard. In desperation Rose tried to start a diversionary conversation to include the other side of the table.

'When do you expect to visit Pompeii?' she inquired brightly of Margaret.

She was not given the chance to reply. Mrs Van der Decken took Rose by the wrist and leaned in close to fondly slur, 'You'll be glad to know, I already told my son to make the most of connections. I said to him, I said, you'd better look about yourself, that little wife of yours is set on fortunes!'

Since there seemed no way of diverting or disguising the gist of the loudly broadcast hints that she and Patrick had eloped and thereby landed themselves in financial straits, Rose looked in mute and mortified appeal to the O'Gradys to forgive their hostess's indiscretions, since she was now unmistakably tipsy.

As the *dolce* was cleared, Mrs Van der D, perhaps remembering herself, addressed the table more generally. 'A pity my son isn't here to enjoy this splendid food.' She smiled widely. 'He's gone to climb Vesuvius and if I know him he's probably walking up it barefoot!' She turned a bleary eye on Charles saying, by way of explanation, 'He's an artist, you know, couldn't conform if he had a gun to his head, must go his own way.'

They all sat silent, waiting for Mrs Van der Decken to continue but, as the fruit and biscuits were set upon the table, she seemed to have lost the thread and subsided. Again Rose tried to rescue the situation by asking Charles to tell them about Vesuvius. But Mrs Van der D rallied suddenly, announcing, 'As I say, he's an artist. And a damn fine one!' She looked challengingly around the table. No one demurred. 'Has quite a reputation in England, wouldn't you say, Rose?' giving her an encouraging jog. Then Rose understood, with even greater horror, what her mother-in-law was angling for with her knowing and clumsily introduced aphorisms about useful connections and Patrick's talent.

'I say to him, I say, Patrick, you must paint portraits. Portraiture's always a good card to play for honours . . . or cash . . .'

She lapsed again and Rose sat transfixed, her mind racing, trying to think of a way to deflect the next dreadful instalment of the propositioning of the O'Gradys, which duly came.

'Charlie, how's that swell fiancée of yours, wha's her name – the one with the silly laugh? Now, *there's* a subject for a swanky portrait.' She winked heavily at Rose and called for the servant to serve them their *caffè* and *digestivi* in the drawing room.

In agonies, Rose sat and watched until Mrs Van der Decken had drained her last liqueur and, with a satisfied nod of the head, released her house guests from the torture of dining splendidly at the Villa del Campo.

Rose escaped to her dark bedroom where she vomited copiously into the chamber pot all that delicious Italian food in an indiscriminate muddle of bile and frayed meat. Afterwards, relieved of that oppression, she lay with her cheek upon the cool tiles of the floor and slept.

# Chapter 44

The next morning Rose crept down to the inner courtyard. She was relieved to find that only the O'Gradys had gathered there for breakfast. No sign of the dreadful epicure. As she approached, Dolly leapt up and came to her. 'Don't worry,' she said, taking little trouble to lower her voice, 'she only emerges to dine every third day, and never breakfasts.'

They joined Charles and Margaret who was pouring the coffee.

'Dear Rose,' she said with the gentle concern that acknowledged a shared affliction. 'I do hope your husband will be back from his trip to Vesuvius today.'

'I'm sure he must be. I'm quite used to him taking himself off without any notice,' she replied pluckily. Then to head off further kind inquiries, 'But what are your plans for the day? Will it be the famous archaeological museum?'

Margaret smiled. 'Dolly has persuaded me that another day's postponement will only heighten my eventual pleasure in visiting that institution. And, since Charles has charted a little steamer to carry Minnie and her family to Capri—'

'Where we shall visit the Blue Grotto,' he supplied, 'and expect to be away all the day.'

'Dolly and I intend to go for a drive and take the air and maybe do a little shopping.'

'We intend to loaf,' said Dolly. 'And we'd love it if you'd consent to loaf with us.'

The three girls spent a jolly morning driving up and down the new Corso Umberto I, noting the improvements that were being wrought by the process of *lo sventramento*, or disembowelment, which was being inflicted upon the chaotic old city to make it conform to the modern age. To Rose it seemed that the object of this urban rationalisation was to offer uninterrupted sight lines over the ugly and new and block the erstwhile views of the old and picturesque.

At midday they went back to the Villa del Campo and took luncheon in the dining room, mercifully alone.

'How much longer do you plan to remain in Naples?' Rose asked.

'D'you mean how much longer can we bear?' answered indiscreet Dolly.

'That's all down to the whim of the Openshawes,' Margaret explained. 'We are dependent upon Charles and Charles is in thrall to Minnie and Minnie is embedded in the slow machinery that is the Openshawe grand passage, which must grind its way through the capitals of Europe.'

'So, you see, our whole lives are directed by that sentimental hairpin my brother has chosen to fall in love with.'

Margaret ignored her sister and went steadily on, 'I believe that the Openshawe cavalcade will next be marching on Rome. Mrs O has heard that *la febbre* is all that there is to be found further south and she intends to pass the high summer at a less unhealthy resort.'

'And you will go with them?'

'What choice have we in such matters but to pack up our saddlebags when we are bid and follow behind to the next caravanserai?'

Apparently even wealthy American girls could not direct their lives solely to please themselves.

* * *

The afternoon was spent in reading and sketching – pursuits that all three were bred to. It was with guilt that Rose realised she'd passed the whole day without remembering Elizabeth. Perhaps nineteen years, spent in idling, had instilled such a habit of thinking of nothing beyond her book or her paintbox that a bare year of motherhood could not compete. She had an impulse to show kind Margaret the ink sketches of Elizabeth's head, smuggled away in her luggage. Perhaps it would be easier to let the brooding secret out. It would explain her sudden silences and tears. But she resisted, knowing it must be safer, and simpler, to continue to hold it close.

At twilight there was a kerfuffle in the entrance hall. Charles and Patrick had arrived at the same moment. Rose heard her husband's voice from the hall, jaunty and high, although she could not distinguish what he said. As she approached, she saw Charles, noble forehead rosy from his bright sea crossing. He was jovially berating the footsore pilgrim for having left his bride at a loose end. Rose was relieved to see that Patrick seemed to have emerged right way up from inside his dark cupboard. He was once again the charming, convivial Patrick of Cornwall. He even smiled at the teasing of his American cousin.

'I think she will prefer me as she finds me now,' he replied and came over to kiss her.

Rose breathed her relief. She felt like a woman lost overboard for whom the sight of Patrick was like the ship that turned back. Now that he was here she was sure that he wouldn't have just abandoned her to drown in social embarrassment. Yet she also recognised the sensation that she always experienced after his absences – that he came back from unknowable places where, she suspected, she simply slipped his mind.

After Patrick had washed and changed, they met for dinner in the same gloomy dining room, served by the same two-faced green lackeys. Since Dolly's prediction that their hostess would not join them was correct, Rose had only Patrick to worry her.

She so hoped that he'd learn to like the American cousins, as she had, and they him. Ever since the dreadful first dinner, she'd felt a debt of gratitude towards the O'Gradys for their continuing warmth and for never having mentioned his mother's indiscretions.

This evening the chef had reverted to *cucina rustica* and since young people who've tired themselves in outdoor activities and have plenty to report cannot long stay strangers under the emollient influence of simple and delicious food and drink, it seemed the most natural thing in the world for an easy familiarity to grow among the ill-assorted guests happily abandoned by *la padrona*.

Towards the end of the meal Patrick asked for a bottle of the local wine and was brought something labelled 'Lachryma Christi'.

'Since, with these tears of Christ, we are drinking wine grown on the slopes of Vesuvius, I think we might be told the tale of Patrick's barefoot walk up the volcano,' invited Margaret, toasting him.

Looking quizzical, he replied, 'I'd be charmed to, but I hope you won't think the less of me for having worn boots,' and toasted her back.

Dolly took up the theme. 'Such a hazardous expedition! My most loyal correspondents, the Miss Marchards of Chicago, wrote me that when they trod the famous route to the crater they believed that their hair must be fried and their eyeballs boiled by the clouds of steam!'

'Bunkum,' remarked her brother.

They all laughed, pleased with each other.

'I'm afraid that my experience of going up Vesuvius cannot compare to that of those intrepid Marchards,' Patrick replied, looking tolerantly at Dolly. 'All I can offer is some feeble impressions and some doodles that I made as souvenirs of my stroll. And, from what I saw of it, the most hazardous part of the route is right at the beginning when one must hold one's nose and jump willy-nilly into the terrifying traffic of the coastal road.'

Rose was glad to see that Patrick appreciated that Miss Dolly's runaway enthusiasm was endearing rather than artificially vivid.

'Let us take our coffee in the drawing room then, where we can listen to the tale and look at these sketches in greater comfort,' smiled Margaret who had, Rose approved, charmingly assumed Mrs Van der D's neglected mantle.

Patrick went to fetch his sketchbook before continuing with his account. 'So, one comes to Resina, that volcano village which exists solely upon matters volcanic. Here, my dear Dolly, are dangers aplenty. For one is met by an outpouring of guides, overwhelmed by hawkers, and buried beneath an onslaught of unstoppable boys – all anxious to offer their wares and services to the unwary climber. Impossible to walk to the end of the village thoroughfare without finding oneself in possession of a mule, a walking stick, a straw hat and a souvenir cut from lava, and all without noticing that a purchase has been agreed. What's more, one has acquired, somehow, one's own personal tribe of tattered boys to lead one's mount and carry one's stick, souvenirs, hat and coat.'

They examined the first pages of the sketchbook, which showed quick thumbnail sketches and some more finished heads of the guides and boys, then a line of distant donkeys carrying tourists up the slopes.

'I don't believe you, Mr McKinley,' Dolly challenged him. 'You possess too much savoir faire to have fallen for a lava souvenir.'

'Quite wrong,' he replied, reaching into his pocket to bring out an ugly charm made from tufa. He offered Dolly the thing, which she accepted with a blush. Patrick went on, 'Sadly, this is all I retain. The mule bolted, the hat blew off and the stick was dropped. I did manage to hold on to my coat but was relieved of soldi by the boy who'd attached himself to me and later insisted that he'd had the trouble of carrying it the whole way up to the top and back.'

'No savoir faire to speak of,' commented Charles humorously.

'An innocent of the first water,' agreed Patrick. 'However, you will be pleased to hear that I resisted the genuine ancient coins that were dug up, or minted, that day. I did see a nice lady in a pink gown buy a made-to-order Roman antiquity that she was very pleased with. I tried to warn her, since it was a substantial artefact, that she would do better buying it (or its brother) on the home journey but by then she'd acquired a boy or two to take it up to the top and then carry it back down again for her.'

Rose looked at the O'Gradys, faces full of unconscious smiles, and thought that she must share this glittering boy. For while he was happy and enjoying the attention of others, Patrick was the most charming, companionable man in the world. No wonder the O'Gradys fell under the spell.

'So, off one sets, the cavalcade of tattered helpers at one's elbow. Upwards, ever upwards, through the vineyards we march, deploying our sticks and fanning with our straw hats. Yet, it's a curious thing: this first part of the climb is nothing but a disappointingly gentle stroll. Nevertheless, resourceful men, bearing stout ropes, line the route and threaten to tie one on and haul one mightily up the steps.'

'But you were riding on a mule, weren't you?' commented Dolly.

'Not a bit of it. I toiled on foot at the head of my ragged army.'

'The animal bolted, remember,' admonished Margaret. 'Please to continue, Patrick. Yours is a much more entertaining version than that which one reads in the guide books.'

Dolly winked at Rose, who smiled back, saying, 'Good enough to transcribe directly into one's travel journal, don't you think?'

Patrick continued, 'Then one comes to the point where one must face the genuine hazards of volcano trotting, scrambling across the solidified lava stream that writhes still in its liquid agony, and one begins to understand that this is an adventure not just a hot walk. Now the whole aspect is desolate and sterile, the ground all burned black and brown and pierced with little cracks that let off hot air.'

'But not hot enough to fry one's hair,' drolly commented Margaret.

'Indeed. Here the going is like walking upon a pie crust put out to cool some time ago but the contents still hot enough to let off steam when the spoon goes in.'

'And did the lady in pink turn back with her antiquity at this point?' Charles inquired.

'She did not. She passed me, going at a steady clip, trailing her boys behind her. I raised my hat to her,' he mimicked the action and accompanied it with a simper, 'which is when my poor hat was blown away, lost forever. Then, on that lonely road to Emmaus, one comes upon a hermitage, standing on a little spur off to the side of the lava bed which offers a kind of resting point to break bread and drink wine.'

Charles took the opportunity to pass around the liqueur wine and biscuits.

Patrick paused, looking pensive. It worried Rose that within his frivolous account were always the strokes of a darker hue that offset the brilliance in his personality. Perhaps, she thought, it was the shimmer of the bright with the dark that fascinated.

Once they'd all served themselves, Patrick resumed his account. 'After I'd eaten I engaged a room for that night and set off again.'

'Had you shaken off the tatterdemalion army?' asked Margaret.

'No, I had not. I was reunited with all my loyal attendants. Much was the rejoicing,' he went on drily. 'I even found my pink lady again – I passed her when we came to a steeper ascent, at the base of the great crater.'

'The *great crater* – now we're for it!' said Dolly thrillingly.

'Well, it is a truly desolate spot. The landscape is just scorched boulders and sterile ash. A zigzag path has been cut through the lava to enable the last laborious scramble up the final assault to the cone of ashes at the lip of the old crater. So my zanies and I plodded, sunk up to our ankles, through the soft drifts as though we dragged through disconcertingly warm snow.'

'How warm?' inquired Charles.

'Warm enough to keep one forging ahead.' Patrick replied, smiling. 'Here the pie has been more recently brought from the oven and one judges that the contents are still piping hot by the little wisps of steam that escape through the cracks in the crust.'

Everyone sucked their teeth appreciatively at that.

'And the crust feels thinner and more unstable here and, as one goes on, the way slopes more so that one must scramble and slither to make progress. And although this mouth is quiescent, it sends choking clouds of white smoke rolling out night and day as though from a diabolic engine room below.'

'Could you get close enough to the edge to look right down into it?' asked Charles.

'That is just how I lost my stick.' Patrick stood to demonstrate the perilous operation of looking down. 'Several people were shying stones down it and I leaned over to see the effect and dropped my stick into the maw. It rattled down and then disappeared into the vapour, travelling directly towards the centre of the earth. I think it travels still. It makes one understand something about eternity. Or hell.' He turned to Dolly. 'Is that purple enough?'

'Oh yes.'

When Patrick dramatised his life, Rose noticed that somehow he made one's own life seem so much smaller and less significant in comparison.

'But then – miracles – one turns away from the abyss and beholds the most wonderful, wide view that nature ever made on earth: the Bay of Naples!'

It occurred to Rose that she had possibly experienced this same vista at exactly the same moment. She smiled at him, and was about to tell him so but he winked at her, to let him continue with his story.

'At this triumphant moment one is met by quite a new battalion of guides and boys who come at one, rapaciously, from the other side of the old crater to tempt one to another hour's slog to the north side and the *real* summit, site of the most recent activity.'

Dolly was scandalised. 'This isn't the real top of the volcano?'

'No, as the Marchards no doubt know and mourn: this is just the end of the beginning of the volcanic via dolorosa.'

They laughed and he took the opportunity to drink some wine and show them more of his sketchbook – pages and pages of strange, lunar landscapes that Rose guessed were made near the cone of the old crater, and some hellish pictures, gashed with red and black and yellow, of the more active north side, which retained the sniff of sulphur.

'So, now lacking mount, hat, stick, self-respect, I scrambled over ground that is still ragged and raw and full of fissures that roar out powerful blasts to taint one's clothes and hair and scorch one's face. And yes, dear Dolly, it *is* really hot up there. It is elementally hot. I could feel the heat through the soles of my boots as though I walked over the skin of a blast furnace. The boys entertained us by pushing paper tapers deep into the fissures to light our cigars. Then I saw my lady in pink. She was throwing coins for a man who diverted the crowd by cooking eggs upon the ground.'

Involuntarily Margaret fanned herself with her hand.

'Then the most extraordinary thing I ever witnessed happened. I see the moment still.'

He stopped his narrative for emphasis and looked from face to face before continuing.

'My lady must have sensed I looked at her, for she turned to me . . .' He acted surprised delight. 'I called "Hello" and then she must have lost her balance and fallen heavily or a fissure opened beneath her feet, for she disappeared from view. Just plain disappeared.' He snapped his fingers and his audience sat mute, trying to digest the enormity of what they thought they'd just heard.

'Down she went. I ran with several others to look and all we saw was a flash of pink before she was swallowed up, lost in the fathomless bowels of the earth.'

'Did no one attempt rescue?' asked Charles, aghast.

'Oh, several of the stalwart men with ropes came running, but the gap that swallowed her had closed over. It was soon agreed to be a hopeless case. Lost, irretrievably, as was my stick.'

Patrick looked down mournfully and the rest sat in silence for a moment before Dolly cried, 'You are a tease. There never was a lady in pink!'

Patrick laughed. '*Se non è vero è ben trovato* – if not true it is a happy invention. Call her a phantom, a memory of that other bright angel who fell into the pit.'

Dolly punched him appreciatively on the arm.

They called for fresh coffee. Right at the end of the sketch-book, on the last page, was a portrait of a lady who'd turned to look over her shoulder directly out of the picture, with the beginning of a smile of recognition. Rose stared at it. Was she the only one who saw that the edge of the lady's gown showing at her neck was vivid pink?

Again she considered how easily Patrick slipped in and out of her life: his baffling exits followed by his splendid entrances which trailed the hint of adventure. When he is gone, she thought, why do I always suspect that those phantoms who people his hidden existence take my place and somehow make my own life incidental? But then, Rose tried to reassure herself, when he is here, I know I'm at the very centre of his world and he needs only me. Trying to suppress the bat squeak of anxiety that this was also when he could hardly find words to express his misery and confusion, she glanced over at Patrick. He smiled back and beckoned her over to sit next to him. I am his one constant, she said sternly to herself, and that is my strength. Yet somehow the repeated evidence that he returned to her, needed her, did nothing to reassure Rose. She looked at the O'Gradys, passing the sketchbook between them, and saw that now they, too, were charmed; she felt almost sorry for them. She wondered whether they would be left thinking themselves lesser people when, sooner or later, they he let them fall by the wayside.

Charles and his sisters, being Americans, were not shy of passing judgement on Patrick's work. They expressed artistic criticism in the loudly confident voices of those who hold decided opinions, confirming among themselves that his sketches showed talent.

Margaret, holding up the mysterious lady, put her arm affectionately through that of her brother and said, 'You know, Charles, maybe our hostess was right, you really should commission Mr McKinley to paint Minnie's portrait. Now, wouldn't that be a splendid souvenir to remember this wonderful trip?'

Rose was mortified that they obviously had made sense of all their hostess's dreadful hints. Patrick only smiled and inclined his head.

Turning confidingly to Rose, Dolly displayed the ugly lava carving that she held in her palm, whispered, 'I prefer this.'

As she lay next to Patrick that night, Rose ran her fingers through his hair to release the lingering smell of sulphur. How glad she was to have him to herself again, healed by light and beauty. Though it occurred to her it was just this febrile brilliance, which had worked the trick of making him beloved by the O'Gradys, that she alone knew had burned off a protective layer and made him vulnerable to the dark.

'I saw Vesuvius myself today,' she said, her face washed clear of all the worries of the evening by that wide open memory of beauty. 'Maybe it was at the very moment you got to the top of it?'

His reply clouded her expression. 'I can't forget that place – only ruin and desolation. Nothing can grow there.'

'Do you know, I looked at it and thought of Sheffield,' she said, trying to cheer him, 'puffing away like a steel mill chimney!'

'Desolation. Nothing but desolation.'

She pulled off his nightshirt and then her own nightdress and very gently and soothingly made love to him, healed him again, while he wept.

They lay side by side, she watching in the grainy dark, listening to his breathing, until he fell asleep in her arms.

# Chapter 45

In the inner courtyard, the next morning, a perceptible warmth had grown between Mrs Van der Decken's guests, comprised partly of mutual sympathy and partly of shared antipathy. Their pleasure in each other was the keener because of that *padrona* they had in common.

Mrs Van der D did not come down for breakfast but a note was sent requesting Patrick and Rose to wait on her at midday. The escape route into the bright Neapolitan day was cut off. As the O'Gradys sailed off for lunch with the Openshawes, Patrick and Rose walked hand in hand up the gloomy stairwell.

They discovered her among the brown depths of her bedroom. She received them sitting up in her enormous Venetian bed, wearing a heavily embossed and embroidered robe that might have been looted from the wardrobe of a cardinal, a tray of medicine bottles upon her lap.

'I would not like it to be thought that your mother neglects you,' she opened.

'Not at all. We have been keeping company with the cousins you thoughtfully provided for our amusement and profit,' was his glib reply.

'I just knew those O'Gradys would *come in*,' she said with a yawn. 'They needed to do something useful to justify the expense I've been put to in keepin' 'em in style.' Sucking up the last of a sticky green concoction from a short, thick glass, she patted either side of the bed to encourage them to perch there. Taking a hand of each in her grasp, she went on, 'Now, Rose, did you discuss with my son what further use is to be made of the O'Gradys?'

Rose looked at her uncomfortably and Mrs Van der Decken threw her hand from her in exasperation. 'Really, my dear! Didn't I say most distinctly that Charles O'Grady is the portal to the Openshawe millions from which, with your help, my son may benefit?' She turned her attention to Patrick. 'And you, my dear, as I explained in my letter, need make only the smallest of efforts to gather the crumbs that will fall from that hymeneal bunfight that must unite the Openshawe and O'Grady names.'

This revelation came as a shock to Rose.

Mrs Van der D looked critically at Patrick and added, 'You'll appreciate the possibilities, even if you are only half American.'

'What, profit by graft, Mother?' he teased.

'And why not? Patrick, you can charm the very birds from the trees when you set your lazy mind to it. And I'm sure the Openshawes were not so fastidious in coining it or Charles O'Grady shy in putting himself in the way of it.'

'I believe that Charles is genuinely in love with Minnie Openshawe,' put in Rose hotly. She did not like to hear Margaret and Dolly's brother slandered by this sceptic in her ecclesiastical robes. She felt she must resist them both, but they ignored her, locked in their compact.

'And how might you know there are millions?'

'They travel,' she stated.

'The O'Gradys travel,' he countered languidly.

'The O'Gradys are, of course, rich but not what I'd call properly wealthy. They are merely the following gulls.'

'The Openshawes are the fleet?'

'Dear boy, the Openshawes are the ocean liner! They're types who don't just travel for the good of their souls, they travel to spend. And they are the very best kind of parvenu because they don't stint when it comes to buying up culture and taste. I can tell you, a stream of packing cases as wide as the Mississippi will be flowing back across the Atlantic to furnish the Openshawes with a ready-made respectability and a new-minted past for when they get home.'

'I am to fish with the gulls?'

'Perverse boy.' She sounded almost fond. 'As I say, you must paint her portrait – large as you like. The higher the fee, the more they'll appreciate it.'

'You advise I barter my talent?' He toyed with her.

'Talent is not at issue. They might hope for the latest European style in portraiture but what they will be paying for is a *connection*. And connections to the Openshawes are beyond pearls.'

Patrick looked down ironically at his vagabond clothes.

'Never forget that you are also half English, darling son.'

'Does a half count?'

'When the ancestral home is by Adam, I should say it does. Don't doubt that I've put some effort in educating the house guests in the proper trappings of the very best old money.'

Watching from the sidelines of this curious exchange, Rose felt as though a side of Patrick had been revealed that he might prefer to have kept hidden. She'd had a glimpse into the private workings of the curious machinery that effected his passage through life. Patrick might despise money and what it bought but he plainly was a master at putting himself in the way of it. The relish with which it was discussed between mother and son appalled her.

That afternoon Rose and Patrick took a cab to the Sorrento peninsula and walked along the little goat tracks that ran up and down along the coast. They went through scented lemon groves, where blossom and nubby new growth as well as the mature fruit were thick on every bough. Patrick sang a plaintive fragment he'd picked up from the wailing song of their cab driver. He repeated over and over, '*I'te voglio bene assaie, e tu nun pienz' a me!*'

'What does it mean?' Rose asked.

'It's in dialect. But I think it's something along the lines of, I love you too much and you do not think of me.' He smiled at her. 'Typical Neapolitan syrup.'

'Did we come because of the lure of the Openshawe millions?' she asked, trying to sound unjudgemental.

He looked at her quizzically, as though she were a talking parrot. 'We came for this.' He gestured at the magnificent panorama. 'Beauty.'

'You don't play fair by the O'Gradys.'

'I don't care a fig about the O'Gradys.'

Rose could not disguise her shock at his indifference, for, after his display of the previous night, the O'Gradys, poor innocents, were well and truly hooked on him after his display of the previous night.

Seeing that look, he conceded, 'They are pleasant enough, I suppose. He's got something of the unadulterated pioneer to him that I like.'

'Don't hurt them,' she said on impulse.

'Why ever should I do that?'

'I don't know,' she answered miserably. 'It's just how things always seem to end up. People are hurt, or die.'

He strode away angrily. After a while she followed after him and found him leaning against a tree, biting his fingernails. Looking up, he said, 'Rose, Rose, what has happened to us? I've turned into a husband,' he looked very sad, 'and you have become a wife.' He took her hands. 'Let's agree to go back to what we were: two happy children, off on a spree with no squabbles over money or other people.'

She would not let him off the hook so easily. 'But you do think about money. I was there in the room when you two were plotting after it!'

'Oh that,' he said, indifferent. 'That is only a game we play.'

'And is consenting to paint this swanky society portrait only a game?'

'Darling, I haven't consented. I will take a look at the Openshawe girl and, in the unlikely eventuality that she is worth painting – that I can say something I want to say and how I want to say it – then I *may* agree. Rose, there's nothing more Machiavellian to it than that.'

She let her hands lie limp in his and he went on, encouraging, 'Anyway, this commission would be a perfect opportunity to get shot of the witch's dreadful hospitality, wouldn't it?'

As they stood together in the lemon grove, he began to sing again, and suddenly they were surrounded by a band of beautiful urchins, drawn to his mournful refrain. Patrick gestured for them to sit and brought out his sketch pad. Rose, her back against a tree, watched how, effortlessly, he made himself king among these boys. He joked and teased while, with infinite tenderness and love, he sketched their luxurious curls, velvet eyes and the little bellies that protruded through their rags. He is completely honest to his art, she thought to herself. He is true to that, if to nothing else.

Done, Patrick emptied his pockets of every last coin, big and small, and sprinkled the largesse upon the heads of the delighted children. But now that they had found this foreign messiah, they would not let him go. They followed behind impatient Patrick, each trying to keep hold of a piece of his clothing, scrambling and skipping down the coastal track, until their way was blocked by a beautiful shepherdess leading her answering mob of sheep, and they had to stand aside as she passed. Upright and noble, she improved her tramp before her flock by spinning wool upon the distaff she carried. Patrick bounded after her, trailed by boys, and tried to explain that he wanted her to stop awhile for him to draw her. She gravely shook her head and carried on spinning and singing, as she walked on. Patrick turned to Rose, shaking off the jealous boys that clung about him, so that he could put his arm round her shoulders. Eyes shining, looking after the figure that had stepped out of classical antiquity, he said, '*She* is why we came.'

That evening, gathered together for the evening meal, Rose studied more closely how Patrick wooed the O'Gradys. She suspected that he did not himself know that he did it, but nevertheless he made himself beloved here, as he did everywhere. She was quiet and subdued, as she had been for much of their stay at the Villa del Campo, a very dull mate for her sparkling husband. Watching Charles under his charm and Margaret's smile of amusement and Dolly's glow, knowing what she knew, she worried for them.

As they began the jolly meal, it emerged that the Openshawe liner was preparing to slip its berth and set a new course in a northerly direction. Mrs Openshawe was thrilled to have secured the country seat in Tuscany of a real contessa. It was available, furnished, for the summer. Apparently, though Naples was as well supplied with princes as it was with postmen, these were an indifferent species of aristocracy. Rarer and richer were the nobles of the north. In addition, Mrs Openshawe had a horror of the malaria that the unhealthy season just beginning in Naples would bring.

'Mrs Openshawe and Minnie have, very sweetly, invited us to accompany them,' Margaret remarked over-brightly, with down-turned eyes. 'The palazzo is huge and so we may have a wing to ourselves.'

'It really is very kind of them,' added Dolly, defeated. It occurred to Rose that Margaret and Dolly, rich but yet not properly wealthy, were condemned to be always the poor relations reduced to stringing along behind. That thought must be enough to momentarily depress the frothiest New World enthusiasm.

'It will be so much fresher and healthier in the countryside, and the glorious cities of Firenze and Siena are close at hand,' went on good-natured Margaret, making the best.

'As will be Oppenshawe ma and pa, and not forgetting Rollo,' remarked Dolly disagreeably.

Charles looked his disapproval at his younger sister and the older was quick to do her usual diversionary job. 'What a shame that you will not have the chance to meet the Openshawes before we leave,' she said pleasantly to the married couple.

Rose smiled with relief that they might yet slip out from under the plan.

'I hope that they will,' said her brother, unable to hold in his news a moment longer. He addressed himself to Patrick. 'I took up that idea of our hostess's of commissioning a portrait of Minnie in Italy. All I can say is that the Openshawe mama was charmed by it. She suggests you interview her tomorrow and that, if you accept the commission, you should both accompany us into Tuscany to undertake it.' Charles was smiling like a maniac, so pleased with himself for having come up with this marvellous ruse.

Smiling inclusively about him, Patrick said, 'So will this happy band escape malodorous Naples to sit in reposeful gardens, cooled by fountains? I have it! I'll paint us all as fourteenth-century nobles, young gentlemen and ladies out of Boccaccio, removed from the dangers of the city to a place of pastoral retreat to dream of paradise and practise the arts of courtly love.'

Ah, thought Rose, the new Utopia: communal living in bucolic bliss. She could only hope that the fascinated O'Gradys would all emerge from his latest design for living unscathed.

Dolly released a little scream of pure joy. Even sober Margaret looked delighted by the romantic plan, and rational Charles simply beamed.

But has Mrs Openshawe enquired about my credentials for painting her daughter's portrait? A fly in the ointment, perhaps?' Patrick remarked with splendid indifference.

'I told her that, apart from being practically a milord in Yorkshire, you were one of the celebrated Cornwall brotherhood and she was sufficiently impressed by that. Anyway, d'you think

I'd let you paint my sweetheart if I didn't think you'd make a darn good fist of it?'

Patrick replied, 'Very generous of you, Charles, considering the pressure exerted by my over-fond mama.' He winked at Rose, who had to look away.

'Call it a jog in the right direction. I'm sure we would have come up with the same idea, given time, wouldn't we, girls?'

Dolly let off another little scream. 'Do say yes, Patrick! I know we are all hopelessly undisciplined about showing our true feelings and should learn to be more civilised and button up. But don't go all languid and disapproving on us and do just say yes! For I do so want to be done up like one of those medieval ladies!'

Margaret added her plea. 'Having you two along with us would be our selfish pleasure.'

Patrick could not help but smile. But he looked to Rose for consent.

What could she do but let them enjoy their seduction? What could she be but gracious in reply?

'It will be lovely to spend time together in the countryside, and I'm sure Minnie's portrait will be quite wonderful,' she said. And she meant every word.

The whole company seemed to sigh with relief.

Rose added, 'Anyway, I think that I should end up baked in a pie if I stayed here much longer.' They all laughed, rather too uproariously.

He looks, she thought to herself, and they fall. He calls and they come to him. And once they have succumbed, no matter how badly he behaves, they are willingly his for life. Still, she knew he was the most marvellous pied piper while the tune lasted.

The next day, as Patrick and Charles paid their respects to the Openshawes, the girls began preparing for their removal. Rose, having little enough to pack, was in Margaret's room helping her and the maid to fold clothes.

'Today will be the third evening,' Rose blurted, remembering Dolly's warning that Mrs Van der Decken only dined every third day.

Margaret, flustered, said, 'Oh dear! We shall have the opportunity of telling her. Does it seem to you that we are too hasty in dragging you away from Naples? I should hate for Patrick's mother to think us rude.'

Rose replied, 'Don't worry, Margaret, I'm sure it won't be too great a shock for her.'

Margaret, looking doubtful, said, 'I guess you're right,' then paused, adding timidly, 'I hope we shall all be happy there. I mean, I hope you shall be happier.'

Had Margaret guessed about Elizabeth? Before Rose could think of how to reply, Margaret went on, 'Dear, we could not help but notice that you seem often sad. Is there a problem between you and your husband?' Margaret was blushing furiously now. Rose loved her for risking embarrassment because she thought another suffered.

Rose took her hand, saying, 'I am only homesick.'

'Ah, that is it. I hope you do not take offence that I imagined another cause.'

'Not at all, Margaret. Though I know I'll feel better when I've had the chance to send a letter home and receive news from there.'

'But it is too late now, we leave tomorrow,' said Margaret sadly. 'However, as soon as we reach Tuscany I will make it my first job to see about stamps and get one mailed.'

They kissed and Rose left to offer Dolly assistance. She surprised the girl looking at the graven image carved from volcanic rock that Patrick had given her.

'I'm so glad that you will be travelling with us,' she said, running up to Rose and hiding her confusion by burying her face in her friend's neck and planting a betraying kiss there.

'It's not decided yet. Mrs Openshawe might think that my

husband is not a good enough artist to be entrusted with the commission.'

'Not *good enough*? He's the finest artist I ever met,' Dolly protested.

'How many have you met, Dolly dear?'

'None whatever,' she snorted. 'But I just know in my heart that even if I'd been introduced to scads of 'em I'd still prefer Patrick.'

'It's charming that you are so . . . eager, but really, you are still just a very young girl and have had too little experience of life to form sensible judgements about such things.' Rose knew that she was being cruel but she had looked into Dolly's bright little face and seen the guilt there, and her evasive eyes. Poor, self-deceiving Dolly.

Mrs Van der Decken did indeed hold to her established pattern of sociability. Having lurked reptilian in the lethargic cool gloom to digest, she emerged on this third day to gorge again. Dressed in a shiny sheath of green, she was as glistening and dapper as a lizard in its tight new skin, and her little pink tongue went in and out over her hungry teeth to sample the savoury steam that curled off the pasta.

This would be the last supper she'd share with her guests, though she did not yet know it. She sat with Rose and Patrick at either hand and the O'Gradys in their accustomed places opposite. Rose noticed a glance pass between brother and sister and knew that the moment had come. Somehow it appeared that Charles had been elected, or condemned, to go first. At the end of the *primo* he put down his fork and took up the talking stick. 'Dear Mrs Van der Decken, though it is very short notice, my sisters and I have partaken of your matchless hospitality for longer than might be thought polite . . .' Evidently Charles did not care to shilly-shally over elaborate leave-taking. Neither, it seemed, did she.

The blunt jaws left off their muscular champing and snapped, 'So, you're off?'

Rose suspected that, her job done, that profitable introduction effected, she was bored with them all.

Charles bowed slightly in acknowledgement that they were indeed leaving. 'We have received an invitation to accompany the Openshawe family into Tuscany.'

Mrs Van der Decken nodded impatiently. 'I could have guessed that. When do you depart?'

'We are travelling by ship, from Immacolatella, tomorrow morning. We'll steam as far north as Leghorn and from there go across country by carriage.'

Now Margaret stepped up to do her duty. She expanded upon the theme of glad, sad farewell their brother had started, and abandoned, and was still in full flow when Patrick interrupted, hardly bothering to dissemble.

'I think it comes as no surprise that Rose and I leave too, on the morrow, to go into Tuscany at the generous invitation of the family Openshawe.' He, too, seemed wearied of their company, now that the thing was decided.

His mother inclined her head. 'I suppose that I can depend upon you, Patrick, to pop up again in my life's solitary wander when funds are short or unwanted amourettes pinch.' She sank her long claws into the back of his hand and then released. 'It is the mode of our relationship. We each follow our own path through life. I prefer it that way.' The subject of her guest's departure now exhausted, Mrs Van der Decken turned to the more important matter of food. She clapped her hands and the attendants appeared with the *secondo*. As she sat, shovelling in her fish, Rose saw what a very small and lonely creature she was.

# Chapter 46

It was on a fine and blustery day that the O'Grady girls turned their backs upon Parthenope, never once having entered the hallowed portals of the Museo Archeologico.

The sea voyage did not agree with Miss Minnie or her mother, *mal de mer* being another of those mortifications that these cultural pilgrims were made to endure. The Miss O'Gradys and Rose occupied themselves in walking up and down the deck or playing cards in the ladies' saloon. Mr O'Grady, a fine example of a self-made man (and one who quite evidently worshipped his maker), preferred the company of men. So Patrick and Charles were required to smoke and drink their passage, together with Signor Giovanni Barrili, Rollo Openshawe's tutor.

Rose was glad that Dolly should be separated from Patrick for the while. She wanted to study the effect he had had on her at close quarters, away from his unsettling presence. She was almost certain that, when Patrick had broadcast his general charm among the O'Grady clan, Dolly had been more vulnerable than the rest. Rose knew what it was to be a young girl; she did not blame Dolly for it. But she would watch her.

At Livorno they were met by the Contessa's own carriages and steward, sent to carry them to her country estate. A cart was also provided to bring the luggage, of which there was a quantity.

The Openshawe family, together with Charles, took the carriage with the crest, and the O'Grady girls, Rose and Patrick and Signor Barrili the lesser. They were also obliged to accommodate Rollo. Minnie's gown and Mr and Mrs Openshawe's girth had consumed all the available space in their own vehicle. They bumped through countryside that Rose recognised from the train journey, and obscurely her heart lifted. She felt that simply by turning north the eventual journey that would have Elizabeth at the end of it was begun. Now, being actually *in* the landscape, she experienced at first hand the choking dust that spinning wheels whipped up from those pretty white roads and saw the crude roadside shrines that stood at every junction. Rollo entertained the peasants they passed by shooting peas at them. Giovanni Barrili looked glumly out of the opposite window and Rose noticed that, though he was glum, he was a romantically doe-eyed young man. Perhaps a suitable diversion for Dolly, newly awakened as she was to the idea of love?

The Contessa's palazzo was reached down a long avenue of close-growing cypresses which had become so vast in the century since they were planted that they now stood shoulder to shoulder to make a long, dark corridor whose walls were half a hundred feet tall and a mile long. The palazzo was a charming building of faded gold stucco and green shuttered windows, with a sweep of steps rising on either side of the principal entrance. Box hedges, grown in geometrical shapes that each contained a pedestal supporting a bust, made a formal garden at the front. Since the Contessa was not in residence (she, sensible lady, elected to pass the heat-filled weeks of summer at a location even further north), they had all the fun of snooping around the place uninhibited by good manners. All were delighted by the elegant good taste of the interior which the Contessa had directed to be filled with fresh flowers. Patrick and Rose were accommodated in a comfortably shabby room that overlooked the gardens at the back of the house.

After the midday meal Mr and Mrs Openshawe retired to

their siesta but the young people declared themselves lively enough to stroll in the lovely garden and perhaps sit for some preparatory sketches for Patrick's 'Decameron' series. To this end Charles had requested that Giovanni Barrili should be released from his usual duties to read to them from Boccaccio's original stories.

They assembled on the terrace which ran along the back of the palazzo. This aspect of the house was not smoothly stuccoed over as was its façade but revealed evidence of an older, humbler incarnation of higgledy-piggledy windows and arched entrances that appeared, in the patched and repaired brickwork, as ghosts of what had been before. The garden at the back, too, showed a more antique plan than was the mathematical plot at the front. For a while they leaned their arms upon the wide stone parapet and looked down into the beautiful walled bower. Before them lay a lawn of dense short grass sprinkled with small flowers. At its centre a marble fountain spouted and fed the sparkling water channels around the perimeter. Paths running close beside flower beds planted thickly with rosemary and lavender meant that, even at the hottest part of the afternoon, walkers brushing past released their scent. Along the back wall was a long bench seat, over which an arbour supported blue and white wisteria that dangled bunches of flowers, the retreat of bees. Rose smiled to herself. Soon she would write to Mapus and hear news of Elizabeth. For now, cut off from the fretful world, Patrick full of enthusiastic plans, she would endeavour to be happy.

Rugs and cushions were spread out for them upon the grass and Rose made sure that the graceful young gentleman should be seated closest to Dolly. In sonorous voice the troubadour commenced to read, from the beginning of the first of the hundred tales. '*Convenevole cosa è, carissime donne, che ciascheduna cosa la quale l'uomo fa . . .*' Minnie began to snore sweetly. And by the end of the page only Rose was left awake, though she, too, no longer listened to the tale of Ser Cepperello who deceives a holy friar.

A breeze lifted and let fall the floppy tendrils of wisteria. The sight of moving shadows that formed and dissolved upon a sunny wall recalled her earliest memories of dappled afternoons spent looking up into tall trees. Rose was always happy in a garden. She imagined how this sun warmed Elizabeth's face, as she lay in her pram, under those same swaying trees, and felt not quite so far from home. Conscious only of bliss now, too sated to move, she lay, heavy, immobile, incapable and the world stood still and Rose knew that just to be alive was heaven.

That evening at dinner, Patrick and Rose were seated with Signor Barrili, presumably being counted, with him, as superior servants. He wore a frown upon his high, intellectual forehead which was not attributable to Rollo, who'd been sent to bed as punishment for hiding in an empty water barrel and frightening the cook. At last he unburdened himself. 'My dear Sir Patrick' (he was a very proper young man), 'I think you do not understand what these parables of Boccaccio contain . . . They are not polite.' He lowered his voice to elaborate. 'These first stories are concerned only with vice and blasphemy. It cannot be right to speak of such things before ladies.'

'Giovanni, my intention is not to corrupt. You need not be concerned that any in our merry band understands more than a word or two of the original Italian. No, what I intend is only that we sing and dance and tell each other stories like Boccaccio's ladies and gentlemen, so that art and magic may flourish.'

So ended the first day.

Over the next week a daily pattern was contrived: every morning Patrick and Minnie toiled over the portrait, annexing the terrace as a studio, when fine, and an attic room with good light when it was not. Patrick had designed a loosely draping, classical costume for her to wear which was made up in heavy white silk edged with a key pattern in orange. He'd also specified how she should dress her hair and that she was to wear sandals and carry a distaff like the noble Neapolitan shepherdess they'd met spinning and singing on the mountain track. As for the rest of the happy band, they occupied themselves chiefly with lazing and chatting. They were quite often bored.

One sultry afternoon the group gathered in the garden for their siesta. Patrick, who could never rest, was making sketches of them for his Decameron series.

'I simply can't drift off. I do wish someone would tell me a story,' said Minnie fretfully.

'Who should that someone be?' asked Patrick. 'We know that Signor Barrili is too prudish, your lover is snoring and Dolly can't string two sentences together without giggling.'

'Why not you?'

Patrick downed his materials and lay back luxuriously. 'I don't feel like telling a story,' said the arch inventor of happy lies. 'Instead I'll sing you all a song.' He began to sing, with pathos:

'She's only a bird in a gilded cage,
A beautiful sight to see.
You would think she was happy
And free from care.
She's not, though she seems to be.
It's sad when you think of her wasted life,
For Youth cannot mate with Age.
And her beauty was sold
For an old man's gold.
She's a bird in a gilded cage.'

He ended on a melancholy note and they all burst into laughter. Rose noticed that Minnie did not join in, but looked disparagingly across at Charles who'd woken and was lying red and beefy in the sun. He reached over to take her hand, when she ignored him, he lay back with a disgruntled look.

'Which country do you expect to visit next with your family?' Rose asked, taking Margaret's usual role of appeaser.

Minnie replied sulkily, 'Oh, I don't know. Switzerland, I believe. Is Switzerland a country?'

Dolly briefly effervesced.

'I mean to say, is it like one of those duchies or principalities or suchlike?' Minnie said crossly.

'Just so,' stepped in Margaret. 'Like Liechtenstein, or what is that other one?'

Patrick, still lying on his back, spoke into his chest. 'As to whether it's a proper country, it is nowadays so drilled through and gouged about with holes and tunnels and roads and rails in the name of modernity and the convenience of the hoi polloi, I'd say it was more of a honeycomb.'

'Or a Swiss cheese,' put in excitable Dolly.

'I shouldn't wonder that Switzerland's tranquil mountains will soon be overrun by the vulgar at their leisure,' mused Patrick. 'There will be a tea stall on every peak and snow gondolas giving shrieking shop girls rides down every glacier.'

Again, they laughed.

'I see you are no democrat,' remarked Charles.

'Aesthetically speaking, no, Charles. If democracy is the future then I am surely no democrat. It seems to me progress tends to debase high culture and fine art; it's certainly the mechanism by which peace and natural beauty are despoiled for those few who may really appreciate it.'

'The few may become many, given political advance.'

'Charles, my old love, I truly believe that high art and culture are the product of inequality and injustice, not only in the present day but of every age before ours,' said Patrick who still lay easily on his back, head on arms. 'It is the responsibility of the rulers, the people of judgement, sense and taste to keep the commonalty away from them. Democratise and Moritz will become a Margate and it will be off with the head of Michelangelo's David and on with the ass's! I'm for the good old days when the expectations of *the people* were kept reassuringly low.' He laughed, and the others joined in uneasily.

But Rose, though she well knew Patrick's views, somehow could no longer bear to allow him to get away with it. 'Well, I think that everyone can appreciate beauty. And all should have access to it, because beauty in itself is what exalts and humanises all,' she cut in rather hotly. She spoke up for the Jannock girls, playing with butterflies in the fields, and for Sam Samuel with his bricks and flowers, even for Harold working on his shy little portraits of feathers. It was the first time that she had ever spoken out against Patrick, and she thought she must have shocked poor Charles, who had probably never before listened to a word she'd said.

Patrick himself went very stiff and cold. He took up his sketch pad and, turning to Minnie, said in a pleasantly modulated voice, in which they must all have heard the tension, 'Don't move a muscle. I want you just as you are – a metaphor of spring and youth and morning.'

Minnie obediently froze to the spot, a look of vacant self-regard on her pretty face. The O'Grady sisters diverted themselves with the earnest plumping of cushions and Rose bit back her tears, wondering how she'd managed to so utterly spoil the mood.

Charles seemed particularly affected, for he jumped to his feet, saying irritably, 'This playing the muse is all very well for professional models and married ladies.' He tried a gruff laugh and put a placatory hand on his fiancée's shoulder.

'However, it occurs to me this portrait would be more suited to commemorate Minnie in her new estate, I mean as my bride. Mightn't it be put off for a little, old chap?'

Patrick, busily blocking out the portrait, did not respond.

'Just a suggestion,' Charles added. He looked despairingly at Dolly, who did not budge, and marched back to the house.

Then Minnie giggled and pouted and Patrick threw down his sketch pad, saying, 'I can't work with you when you're playing modern American miss.'

He laid his head fretfully on Rose's knee and she gratefully stroked the hair away from his forehead, hoping that she was forgiven and not too much damage had been done. She noticed that Dolly turned her head away to hide a tear and thought, not without sympathy, this is when Dolly's soft little heart is crushed.

They went on in this way through the mounting heat of idle summer; heedless of life's realities the forgetful young lay in the garden to tell stories and squabble and sing songs. But sensuous afternoons were followed by lonely nights full of thoughts of home. For Patrick lay separate and untouchable beside her in their hot bedroom. Not since that night in the Villa del Campo had they made love. Even when she took him in her arms, he did not respond. And, though the air seemed to buzz with the unspent electricity of sexual longing, he never came to her. Sometimes when it was too hot to sleep Rose would take out Elizabeth's portraits and look at them by the light of the moon. Once Patrick woke to find her brooding by the window.

'Now we are somewhere safe and healthy, mightn't we send for her?'

He did not answer at first, but took one of the sketches and studied it in the wan light.

'You know we can't, Rose.'

'Do you ever think of her?'

Again he was silent for a while, before replying carefully, 'Honestly, darling, I don't. I must have a very feeble imagination because things are only real to me when I have them here, in front of my eyes, though when they are before me, they're *so* immediate I can hardly bear it! Just because I'm not always imagining her, running about in Yorkshire, it doesn't mean I don't love her.' He picked up another of the sketches. 'I forget how good these are.' He nodded approvingly. 'To the life.'

'I can't stop myself from imagining her.'

'Poor darling,' he said, kissing her again. 'You'll see, when she is with us again, it will be as though you two were never apart.'

'I only wish I felt that I was doing something better with my life here than I would be there, with her.'

'You are!' he said. 'You're keeping me sane. Rose, I've never before felt so close to knowing what it is I seek. I mean how life should be lived. I know that soon I will be able to settle to my real life's work—'

'And we shall all be together again,' she added hopefully, but he did not reply.

# Chapter 47

In order to make the most of the cool part of the day, Patrick and Rose asked to accompany Giovanni Barrili and Rollo on their morning constitutional which, now that it was August, they were obliged to take just after dawn. They walked down that long file of cypress trees, surprisingly chill in the verdurous gloom. Then, turning out of the palazzo's wide gates, emerged as though from death's dark tunnel into Elysian morning. After strolling for half an hour they came upon a little dell of trees where the sunny air was full of birdsong and the long grass soaked by dew. This sylvan glade lacked only a carefully placed, ornamental shepherd boy, resting beneath a middle-distant tree, to perfect the picture. They flopped down on the grass, their backs against an olive tree, and Rollo ran off to climb and explore.

Patrick sighed. 'Man has not enslaved nature in Italy. Look at this place, its fecundity is indecent. One has only to push one's walking stick into the ground and it will sprout leaves. And they do not rush towards an industrialised future because they have not yet learned to hate the past.'

'You forget Italia is a young country,' remarked Giovanni.

'Yes. But what defines her most profoundly has been the work of its ancestral giants. And, to your credit, you have had the humility and the common sense to recognise that debt. You're not all for ripping down history and replacing it with something shiny and newly manufactured just because it is shiny and new. I believe that people are happier when they live with nature, at nature's pace and in beautiful, harmonious surroundings.'

'But Italia must modernise if she is to be great once more. The *contadini* who farm this beautiful land live upon it as miserable slaves. My friend, you may be sure they prefer the ugliness of the town if they are paid for their work and have some leisure to spend their wages on comforts and manufactured things.'

Rose considered, with surprise, that Giovanni was something of a revolutionary.

'Shoddy things that have no intrinsic worth, things that are made to fall apart so that they must be replaced by another thing that will break.' Patrick clapped him good-naturedly on the back, 'I prefer the honesty of the hand-made or the old and patched.'

'But life is not so simple, I think. Italia has a hidden face, my dear Mr McKinley.' Giovanni laughed grimly. 'If Italia is to be great for all her sons then I think we must tear down all these old things. We must learn to hate all this ancient past and this beautiful nature and love something new, even if it is *bruta*. For me this past belongs to the nobility and the priests and nature to the slave-masters. If she would be free, Italia must cast off these things and learn to make herself in a modern way!'

'In the image of industrial ugliness!' concluded Patrick shortly.

The two men glared at each other, but before either could say more, Rollo, who'd been scaling trees looking for nests to rob, fell at his feet – seeming to have plummeted from the sky like a Daedalus. He moaned that he'd twisted his ankle and couldn't walk home. The two men tried supporting him between them and helped him to hop but it was soon apparent that he could not, or would not, go as far as the palazzo.

'We must take him to the nearest *fattoria* and ask for a cart or something to carry him,' said Giovanni, taking control. He hoped he would not be punished for allowing the boy to injure himself.

They shambled out of the little dell and saw that a collection of farm buildings stood within a short walk. As they approached, the horrible hound that was chained at the entrance to the farmyard began to choke out a warning, but no one came.

Giovanni called out, commandingly, '*C'è qualcuno?*'

No reply.

He led the boy to a low stone water trough and settled him on its edge so that he could find someone to help them. Patrick and Rose wandered, half-heartedly, among the collection of mellow stone buildings grouped around the still yard.

She passed through a low, dark doorway that led into the cattle room. A line of white cows, loosely chained to the sloping manger boards, looked up at her, eyeballs lustrous in the gloom. They shifted uneasily, rustling their ankle-high muck and straw. Overhead swallows skimmed in and out through little high windows to their half-cup nests glued to the ceiling. What a ceiling! Rose looked up into the ample vault of tightly placed thin red bricks. She stood in awe and wondered that poor peasants had made this beautiful intricate ceiling, fit for a church, for cows to stand and look at.

She came out again into the light and crossed to Patrick, saying, 'Only cows.' She kept the wonderful ceiling to herself. Together they went round the back of one of the farm buildings where a kitchen garden of sorts was planted. Fastidious hens picked for snails among the cabbages and the courgette flowers. Though a washing line blew with tattered clothes, and more waited in a basket to be pegged out to dry, there was no sign of human life. They came back into the main yard to see Giovanni going up a steep external staircase. Leaning over the crumbling balustrade, he called to them, 'The kitchen should be up here. If there is anyone, this is where we must find them.'

This farmhouse *cucina* was a cavernous hole, not fit for cows. Its walls were blackened by the soot and smoke and grease that had spilled from the hooded open fireplace, in the depths of which a cauldron hung. The mean fire was the only source of light by which they could make out a table, a dough bin and two chairs. On the floor, scattered with dirty straw and other rubbish, Rose noticed that a broken rush basket had been pushed underneath the table.

They withdrew their heads from the hovel, as though guilty for the intrusion into a private place of shame, and were about to descend the steps when Rose, driven by some prophetic itch, tiptoed back through the door and pulled out the basket to look inside. She dragged it towards the light from the open door and saw that lying inside, still as a corpse, was an unclothed baby. As though in response to the warm touch of sunshine on its shrivelled face, it raised its thin arms and Rose jumped away startled that this little withered thing should have sprung into life. A thin, querulous wail came from its parched lips, the distress call of hunger, and Rose instinctively moved back to answer it. She put her little finger into its mouth to satisfy its need to suck and was about to pick it up the better to comfort it when a woman, carrying a sickly toddler under one arm, rushed at her from the shadowed depths of the room. Yelling like a banshee, she snatched the frail baby away from Rose with her free hand and threw it back into its basket.

All three strangers looked on, shocked by her violence.

In a startled voice, Patrick insisted of Giovanni, 'You must ask her why she treats it so harshly!'

There was an agitated exchange with the woman, at which Giovanni shook his head and frowned. A little girl crept up behind her mother and the scrawny toddler began to cry queasily. The woman was obviously either a fiend or too simple to know how to care properly for her children.

'Is there something the matter with her baby?' prompted Rose.

He would not reply but said. 'We should go from here. It is not healthy for you.'

Rose went closer to the ghastly women, smiling and gesturing that she should take up the hungry baby to nurse it. Giovanni sprang forward to smack her hand away from it, saying, '*Non tocchi!* Don't touch!'

The peasant shook her head vehemently at Rose and mimed the washing of her hands.

Exasperated, Rose turned on Giovanni. 'She will not feed her own baby?'

'It is not her own. It is a *trovato* – an abandoned one that should never have been born. But these seeds that are spilled in sin, they dig in deep and hold tight.'

'But the poor baby must not be punished!' protested Rose.

'You do not understand. The *ignorante* who bore it gave it to the priests and they farmed it here in the healthy countryside. The woman is paid a little for her milk . . .' He stopped short, as though repressing a fierce need to say more. Was it from disgust at the poor little thing's illegitimacy?

'But you can plainly see that she neglects it, Giovanni! You must explain to her that the poor baby is innocent, he must not be punished for his mother's sins.'

That persistent note of distress pulled painfully at Rose's heartstrings until she could bear it no longer. She walked to the door in frustrated agitation.

'Can we send for a doctor? He looks so starved and ill. Something might be done for him,' Patrick said, his face gone white.

'There is nothing. You do not understand, this is not a business for you,' Giovanni replied angrily.

Rose sobbed. How could they leave him, stuck underneath the table, to cry with hunger?

'But it *is* our business,' said Patrick and he stooped to lift the crying baby. 'If she will not look after it properly, then we will find someone who will.'

Giovanni screamed at him, 'You don't understand! Its blood is poisoned – it has taken a disease from its shamed mother.'

'A disease?'

'Yes, something that is passed by the dirty women of the

town.' He continued unwillingly, 'What they call *lue*.'

Patrick drew back from the baby. '*Lue*, what's that?'

'The *sifilide*,' Giovanni whispered. He turned apologetically to Rose, standing by the door. 'You must excuse this word, Mrs McKinley, I do not know how else to say.' He put his hand on the shoulder of the exhausted woman and went on, 'The people who live here took this boy, in good faith, to nurse it for some little money. She says the priests swore to her that it was clean. But now she is infected and her own baby, because her milk is made filthy, and her husband is also sick.'

Giovanni was confounded into silence and all three stood and looked down at the pestilent baby that writhed in its basket and none made a move to comfort it.

'Now she waits for the priest to take it back to the foundling home.'

The woman, having read the effect of Giovanni's explanation on Rose's face, knelt at her feet, pleading, '*Cara donna, me aiuti*.'

Rose flinched away but the woman gabbled on, clawing at her hand and striking her own offending breasts. The little girl and boy joined their cries to the lament. Rose wanted to raise her to her feet, to embrace her, but the woman's need was too great, too ugly.

'What is she saying?'

Giovanni looked blankly at the raving woman, 'She says that this must be a punishment for their sins. She only takes these babies for a little money for her own children and surely they must all die.'

'This is monstrous,' said Patrick quietly.

'It is old Italy . . .' There was that repressed anger again.

'It is the Italy of the priests and ignorance and superstition.'

Then they emptied their pockets of all the money they carried with them, which was little enough, and staggered the long, hot way back to the palazzo with roaring Rollo supported between them. They did not talk of what they had seen.

* * *

That afternoon, when they gathered in the garden, the sullen mood that had overtaken the happy band of hedonists the previous day had not lifted. Perhaps they had caught it from the heavy discontented atmosphere that pressed down on them. For a high-summer storm growled on the horizon and the air was thick with unspent rain. Charles, in particular, was jumpy with dry electricity.

'Come and sit down, old duck.' Patrick called him over to join them on the bench, which was sheltered by the thick wisteria vines, now full of leaf. As they took their seats in expectation of the coming spectacular, lightning overhead cracked its whip again and again to start the show.

'What is the matter, Charles dear?' asked Margaret.

He attempted to sound unconcerned. 'I had an interview with Mr Openshawe this afternoon that has left me out of sorts.'

Minnie looked away.

'I suggested to my fiancée's father that we might set a date for our marriage. Seems it's not to be thought of at present.' Charles was gruff with humiliation.

The whip cracked again and Rose felt the fat thud of the first raindrop.

'Why, that's ridiculous!' huffed Dolly. 'You've been engaged to marry for absolutely ages!'

Charles looked resolutely ahead into the sickly light.

'Minnie,' said Dolly encouragingly, putting her arm through the other girl's, 'surely you can talk him round?'

Minnie said nothing.

Their gloomy silence was drowned by the gathering scherzo of raindrops.

Patrick roused himself. 'Since our fastidious Signor Barrili refuses, I shall tell you a tale from the *Decameron*. One to cheer you up.'

Charles sullenly chewed his moustache ends and Minnie grimaced.

Laughing, Patrick continued, 'Well, if not that, then at least it may help pass this stormy afternoon.'

They all sat in unenthusiastic expectation.

'It's a good example of how guile and cunning help love to run its smooth course to a happy conclusion . . .'

The angry clap of thunder that followed his words seemed to denounce him and they sat in subdued silence but for Minnie, who gave a thin shriek. Patrick looked up at the sky and made the sign of peace.

They smiled a little at that, safe inside the shaggy overhang of tendrils, daring the storm to do its worst.

'Now, in Romagna,' Patrick began, 'there lived a beautiful girl named Caterina. Caterina fell in love with a handsome young man of respectable family whose name was Ricciardo. Miserly Messer Lizio, her father, was having none of it, however; he wanted to keep his daughter's youth and freshness to himself. One day when the two lovers chanced to meet, Ricciardo suggested a merry way of seeing each other privately. Caterina should complain of the oppressive night heat and request that a bed be made up for her on the balcony so that she might repose in the cool outdoors and let the song of the nightingales lull her to sleep.'

The rain fell emphatically now, hurling to earth as though the sky had cracked and could no longer hold back the deluge. And something was released in Patrick too. He grew increasingly loud and excited as he competed with the crump of thunder and the vehemence of the rain. Watching the performance and his spellbinding effect on the party, Rose wondered how she had managed to love and be loved by someone so different from herself.

'The lovers' plan proved successful and bold Ricciardo was able to scale the wall and meet his love on her balcony. Now, as you may imagine, they lay entwined and listened to the song of the nightingales strenuously all night long.'

Minnie sighed.

'By morning, so exhausted were they that, instead of fleeing with the dawn, Ricciardo was still lying in his lover's arms when her father came to wake her. You can imagine his anger . . .'

Again, a mighty thunderclap interrupted his tale, making them all jump and then laugh.

'He went to fetch his good wife who would have brought the house down, but for her husband, who calmed her, saying, "Why raise your voice and bring shame on our daughter? We like this young man. Wouldn't it be better for them to marry here and now?"' Patrick stopped and looked at his audience, perhaps to gauge their reaction to this twist in the tale, and then went on, 'Thus, when the two young lovers awoke, Messer Lizio put on a gruff manner and threatened Ricciardo with death unless he consented to marry his daughter then and there. He of course agreed and the union was later solemnised before witnesses. Everyone was happy and Ricciardo and his fair Caterina were free to exhaust themselves listening to the nightingales every night.'

The girls clapped at the satisfactory conclusion of the story. The raindrops stuttered singly now and the thunder was more distant. The storm appeared to be abating.

'I believe this story was originally meant to illustrate the guile of Messer Lizio but I think it was the young couple who were the more cunning in getting what they wanted.' Patrick turned to smile at Rose.

Another crack of thunder asserted the last of the storm's dwindling fury. The young people ran out from within their hiding place, across the soaked grass and into the house.

Later, in their bedroom, Rose rubbed her hair dry and watched the storm as it died along the horizon and the sky began to lighten, like a false dawn after troubled night. She stood to the side of the tall window in quiet contemplation and noticed that two people were walking about on the terrace: Patrick and Minnie, underneath an umbrella. They were kicking about in the puddles and twirling the umbrella so that the water flew from it in shining arcs. He handed it to her to hold and shrugged off his jacket. Rose was about to tap on the window when she saw that he put the jacket tenderly around her shoulders and used it as though it were a net to draw her in close to him. Not knowing what to do with her hands, which still held the umbrella tight between her breasts, Minnie was trapped by the coat behind and the umbrella before so that she apparently had no choice but step up close to receive his kiss. Rose saw that Minnie went to him, a willing captive.

# Chapter 48

Rose waited in the cool, unlit room for Patrick to come to dress for dinner. She'd considered going to Minnie but, imagining the scene of retribution and tears, thought better of it. He's made a Veronique of me, Rose thought with surprise, and shuddered at the thought of that crazed and crying woman and knew she could not match her possessive fury. Poor, beautiful Veronique, trained from infancy to sit still and smile and suffer and mend his socks: the perfect muse and helpmeet. How well the adopted family name of Van der Decken suits him, she thought: doomed to sail the seas forever, driven on by the search for the one mortal woman whose sacrifice will rescue him. She lit the lamp hastily, as though to ward off that spectral presence that had crept in with the cold and damp of evening.

When he came he was whistling something jolly through his teeth.

She spoke levelly. 'You shouldn't, you know. She's still very young.'

He was startled by her, unseen among the shadows. 'Rose?'

'Just seventeen.'

He saw her now, upright on the edge of the bed, and went to sit beside her.

'Sweet seventeen,' he mused.

'A metaphor of spring and youth and morning?'

He tried to embrace her but she pulled away. He walked across to the window, so that he could see the wide view of the still-wet terrace and, turning to her, sang, putting on the sentiment, 'When You Were Sweet Sixteen', but because he substituted 'seventeen' had to elide the first two consonants to make it fit the line.

'It was just a little accidental kiss in the rain,' he said at last and held out his hand for her to join him by the window. 'It is you I love, Rose. It's just that when you are not there, sometimes I forget, just for a moment.'

But she would not come to him, saying bitterly, 'It wasn't an accident though, was it? This plan was set in motion by that letter, months ago!'

'Not a bit of it. I couldn't care less for silly Miss Minnie.'

'Liar!' she shouted. 'You lie about everything, I know you do.'

His face turned set and pale and he crossed over to the door, as if to escape.

'The lies you told this afternoon! You as good as told her to go with you, to forget about her duty to her parents, her duty to me, your wife. Her free choice to throw away Charles, who loves her, and her good name and everything. Haven't you done enough harm already?'

'Happy inventions, not lies, Rose darling. Just wait and see,' he said, and left the room.

That night, alone in their room, she wondered how it was that she came to be here, in the middle of Italy, a thousand miles from home. She realised then that Patrick could never mean home for her. He'll never belong, she thought, never feel the journey's done. He really doesn't feel regret for the people and things he loses along the way, because they are always there for him – his whole life captured in a trail of pictures.

Resolving to stay awake and wait for him, she lay down, fully clothed, on their bed and within twenty minutes was asleep. Her dreams were disturbed by babies. They lay crying in hearths among cold ashes, they reached for her from baskets and asked through thin blue lips, 'Mummy?' She was disturbed by them, and yet powerfully moved to give comfort. But when she tried to take them in her arms, the sly nurselings leapt up and ran away on crooked legs. So she was obliged to chase after them, running down corridors, following the quick patter of teasing footsteps that was the drum of the rain outside her window.

Rose was awoken, very early, before it was properly light, by the sound of a wailing infant and realised, with a start, that Patrick had not come to join her in their bed. Though she knew she was now awake, the wailing still came to her, from outside her room. She realised it was not the din of a baby but shouts of blue murder and running footsteps. Patrick had evidently been caught out at last! Terrified that she'd find Charles standing over his lifeless body, slumped in Minnie's bed, she leapt up. The ructions led her to an open bedroom door – surely Minnie's, for she saw that Mrs Openshawe was standing at it, in a state of moral apoplexy, supporting herself upon her husband, and screaming, 'Seducer!'

Rose peeped round the ample obstacle to see Minnie, blushing to the tousled roots of her hair and shouting melodramatically, 'Help, Mama! Help! He intends to ravish me!' and a half-dressed Charles transfixed next to her under the sheets. Surprised in the very act of listening to nightingales, but not exonerated. For Mr Openshawe did not allow Latinate sophistry to muddy his honest, small-town response to an attempt on his property.

'How dare you, sir? I'll wop you, so help me God – I'll murder you!' he bellowed, making as though to take Charles by the scruff. Mrs Openshawe, meanwhile, had half collapsed on the floor and clung to his trouser cuffs so that he was hobbled where he stood.

Dolly and Margaret, both still in their nightdresses, hurtled out of their shared bedroom and Mrs Openshawe rallied herself to scream at them, 'Vipers that I have nursed in my bosom!'

The sisters came to a skidding stop outside the open door of Minnie's bedroom and, seeing what was revealed within, Margaret promptly put her hands over Dolly's eyes.

Minnie only sobbed and said, 'I hate you, Charles O'Grady!'

'Clear out! I said git, you low-down, sneaking bastard!' shouted Mr Openshawe who, despite the dignifying effect of his millions, could still find the stevedore within. 'And take your sorry bitches with you!'

Rollo came careering down the corridor and took up the chant. 'Sneaking bastard, sneaking bastard!' to which he added a war dance of his own.

It was only when Rose escaped centre-stage that she saw Patrick standing with Giovanni Barrili, on the sidelines of that operatic finale. Both were fully clothed in evening jackets, and Patrick was laughing and laughing.

In the hard, innocent, washed-clean morning, Rose packed her bags. Time to go.

Patrick came into the room. He smelled of stale spirits and cigars. He'd obviously been up all night debating and drinking with Giovanni and could produce him to testify to that harmless debauch if required.

He walked over to her. 'What larks, eh, Rosie?'

'You are too cruel!'

'I was getting bored,' he replied sulkily. 'Besides, when it looked as though the democrat was going to put his oar in and postpone my painting until after she was safely a *Mrs*, I had to do something to hurry things along or just get the blasted thing called off.' He opened his hands expansively. 'For the sake of the painting.'

When she made no reply he added, 'In the end, Charles will probably consider I did him a favour.'

She continued packing.

'We may stay,' he advised, flopping down on the bed, indifferent now that the climactic denouement of his trick was past. 'It's the O'Gradys who are banished, not me – for once!' He chuckled and started to hum.

When she did not stop her packing he raised his head quizzically from the bed to look at her. 'I'm to finish the immortal portrait and then the Openshawe circus intends to hang around in Europe until Charles has had the decency either to shoot himself in the head or go for a missionary and get himself eaten by cannibals.' He sighed and yawned. 'If I could just lie here and have a little rest . . .'

She carried on packing, making no effort to do so noiselessly.

Finally he sat up. 'For goodness' sake, Rose, now you've seen how the story ended. It was never meant as a message for Miss Minnie; far too subtle for her little head.'

Rose stopped packing. 'Why are you so cruel?'

'I already answered that one.'

'You plan to destroy Charles, or remove him and his sisters, just so you can finish your portrait?' He said nothing. 'And because it amuses you to do so.'

'They are just little people who don't really matter in the scheme of things. Come and give me a kiss and let's make up.'

She looked at him. 'You don't really care about people, do you?'

'Is that the worst you can say about me?' He smiled, sure of himself.

'Yes, I believe it is.'

A timid knock on their door brought in wan Margart. 'I suppose you know what happened last night. It's not my place to apportion blame. However,' she sighed, 'quite understandably my brother and sister and I must make plans to leave immediately. I would imagine that these circumstances will have an impact upon your continued stay here as guests of the Openshawes . . .'

'I am going home,' announced Rose.

Patrick got up from the bed and, ignoring Margaret, went to her, saying tenderly, 'Darling, don't run off.'

'I'm not running away. I've just recently grown up, you see. And grown-ups don't run away. I'm going home.'

He stood and made to take her in his arms but she dodged away and went back to her packing.

'Yes, you are grown up. So much more grown up than me,' he said mournfully. 'But how will you buy your train ticket?'

'I will ask Margaret . . .' Rose looked at Margaret who was still standing uncomfortably just inside the door. 'Margaret dear, will you help me? I need to get home to my baby.'

Margaret had the straightforward good sense and kindness to answer straight back, 'Of course I shall give you the money.' She did not linger to ask what baby or why Rose travelled alone to be reunited with it, she simply turned on her heel and went to her room for the cash.

'When I have reached Yorkshire I'll wire her the money,' Rose explained matter-of-factly to Patrick and went on with her packing.

He sat back on the bed, his head in his hands, and groaned.

'You're right, I'm not grown up or kind. D'you think the two go together? Perhaps they do.'

She did not reply, so he went on, 'Rose darling, I'm just not ready to give up the game yet and go home. I want to stay out and play just a little bit longer.' Now he seemed to be speaking only to himself. 'Who knows whether I'll ever be ready. Maybe I'm a natural exile. Maybe all artists are and it's settling down, settling for anything, that dulls 'em all in the end.'

Still she did not respond.

'But I know that I do need you,' he went on, explaining it to himself. 'I need you because you are the one to help me make sense of my life.'

At last she spoke, kind and sad. 'I'm not the one you need, Patrick. I haven't got the heart for it any longer. I chose you over

Elizabeth but that isn't the kind of choice anyone should be made to make. Elizabeth needs me and her needs come first, because one must love people over ideas.'

'You think I'm selfish! But you'll happily pour all your love, your everything, into a needy child who will take until it's grown and then cast you off to live its quite unremarkable little life!'

'You're right, of course you are!' she answered him passionately. 'But none of that matters. Loving her won't drive me insane, or make me stupidly jealous, or use me up.'

They both stood and looked at one another, breathing hard, before she continued, in a gentler voice, 'She is the one who will make sense of my life.' Because he looked so hopeless, so lost, she said, 'You can replace me with Minnie, if you can get past Pa Openshawe. As you said, she's just the right age: seventeen is on the cusp of something marvellous.'

He looked gloomily away from her. 'But she'll never do. It's you I need, darling Rose.'

He sounded so heartbroken, she nearly went to him then but steeled herself to reply, 'Patrick, I can't trust you with my heart.'

'We shall send for the baby,' he started, sounding desperate now that he saw she meant it. 'I'm sure that I *can* settle now, find my stroke . . .'

'I don't think you can,' she said simply, 'and I haven't the energy to keep up the search. And, Patrick darling, I'm not *the one*.'

'I know you are,' he persisted. 'You are magic.'

She smiled at that, felt almost sorry for him in his possessive despair. 'Oh Patrick, what was it you called marriage? The longest journey? Well, we didn't quite take it that far . . .' She took off her play wedding ring and put it in her pocket.

'Just think how horrible it will be for me and you when you realise that it's only habit and fear of letting go that shackles us together. Because you would think it, you know. In the end.'

★ ★ ★

Margaret gave her a purse of money and a note of her address in Chicago, saying, 'I knew there was something not right between you two. Good luck, my dear, I hope you find happiness where you seek it.'

Rose did not see Dolly or Charles or Minnie to say goodbye but left a bread-and-butter note of thanks for Mrs Openshawe on a little table in the entrance hall. Placing it there, she saw that a reply had, at last, arrived to her homesick letter. She looked at the Yorkshire postmark and held it close to her chest. Then she put it in her pocket, saying to no one, 'I'm coming.'

As she was leaving by the front door with her bags, she came upon Giovanni who was also dismissed. Unshaven and dishevelled, he looked decadent and knowing. Could a single night with Patrick have been enough to corrupt the proper young man?

He smiled at her and asked courteously, 'May I have the pleasure of giving you a lift? My former employers have allowed me a carriage to Florence, the quicker to be rid of me.'

How hard he has become, she thought.

'Signor Barrili, you are contaminated by association,' she commented and, accepting his offer, stepped into the carriage.

As they rocked and jolted down the chalky roads, they smiled at each other, co-conspirators it seemed, and hardly exchanged a word.

At the railway station in Florence, Giovanni slung her cases on top of a pile of baggage pasted over with European luggage labels and saluted her with a kiss.

And so the lapsed muse retraced her journey back across Europe, all the way to Yorkshire, in the jolly, kindly company of homeward-bound excursionists who had entertained themselves across all the resorts of Europe. She fled the magical, beautiful peninsula and came deliberately home to the wasteland and her daughter.

# Chapter 49

Sheffield!

The anti-climax of drab familiarity: the same trams, the same buildings, the same faceless hordes. It was as though she'd never been away. But, as Rose clipped through the city centre in her cab, she witnessed the uglification that just three years of smoke and fumes had worked upon Sheffield's new town hall and the bright Vulcan who stood atop it; his shiny skin begrimed and pitted, he now wore a mask of murk. Wryly she considered how these last years had blackened her too. No doubt she'd never succeed in washing her name clean again. Perhaps the best she could hope for was that this dirty, dull town would close back over her head and that, in time, her shame would be buried under anonymity and good works. And yet it made her smile to think that the three-year jaunt that had taken her to Paris, Switzerland, Cornwall and Italy had led her straight back here where, she knew at last, her answers lay. Looking out of the cab window at the first signs of autumn she resolved that, this year and ever after, she would not keep her dreary appointment with winter and longing. She would not yearly lapse into mourning for Patrick, cloaked in black and misery, until her death delivered her. This year she'd let her life be lit by her bright baby and look for happiness only at home.

* * *

Once again it was Joan who saw her first as she approached the cottage. Did the girl while away every day in looking out of windows?

'Well, I'll go to my tea!' Joan exclaimed, crossing herself.

'I'm back,' was all Rose replied, through tears and a trembling smile.

Joan and Mapus took her inside and brought Elizabeth to her but this was not the same baby she'd left behind in the spring. To Rose, she seemed to have grown enormous, and how many teeth she'd sprouted! Starved for lack of her, guilty for the absence that had seen her baby turned into a toddler, Rose thought that she would never be able to let her go and put her down again. It broke her heart that Elizabeth struggled and screamed and pushed herself away from this unfamiliar mummy.

That night she and Mapus sat uneasily together.

'Can I trust you not to run away after him, Rose?'

'I've learned to be satisfied with what I have, here.' Rose said this trying to make her tone resolute, sensible.

'And when he comes for you again, to drag you off gallivanting?'

'You're right, Patrick will never surrender, ever, because he's driven by the conviction that life should be only wonderful and beautiful.'

Mapus sniffed at the foolery of this.

'Naturally, he'll be disappointed,' Rose acknowledged, 'Idealists always are. Though I sometimes think they are braver than we, to risk beating out new paths rather than just follow along the old ones.'

Her mother huffed her disapproval, 'I shan't be bamboozled into admiring him!'

'Marpus, you do better to feel sorry for him, just imagine: never to be easy in one's own skin.'

'What should I care, so long as that's an itch you're cured of ?'

'It is,' she reassured, 'And, Mapus dear, I believe he is cured of me – I grew too opinionated in my old age.'

And, though she smiled and patted her mother's hand, Rose sounded almost sad to acknowledge that fever had cooled. She'd settled. Home was where she would remain, most probably to the end of her days, with no larger expectation from life than that when she was happy she would recognise it.

The reunited household eventually found a way of living together again in harmony. It helped that Elizabeth and Robert resided at the core of their lives, for child-rearing gave all a routine and a shared purpose. Rose tried not to speculate where Patrick's quest might have led him: Istanbul, the North Pole, Morecambe? She tried not to imagine him with seventeen-year-old houris in veils, or seal-fishing through ice holes, or sharing a meaningful existence with Bedouin camel drivers, while here she was stuck in South Yorkshire with an old lady, a truculent maid and two demanding toddlers. Not an ideal creative life, not an adventure, but it did have its satisfactions and its pleasures and there was laughter and sometimes real joy in the everyday business of getting by. So Rose kept a rein on her imagination and counted blessings.

A week after she returned home she received her first caller, Guy. He'd recently returned from London, where he'd left his sister in their rented flat in South Kensington, trying to make a success of her flower and fairy paintings.

Guy was heavier, Rose noticed, and had developed even more of a hump.

'Have you heard from him?' was her first question, despite herself.

She did not have to elucidate further, for he drily replied, 'Not a word. He's passed on, I surmise, like a tropical hurricane, uprooting all as he passes through.'

They were silent for a moment, thinking of wreckage left behind.

'You could say he had a propensity for displacing people,' she conceded.

'Makes you wonder why, in the face of the evidence, so many are pleased to put themselves in his way, don't it? But then, who am I to talk? Ever drawn to the eye of the storm, generating no electricity of my own.'

Rose laughed and patted his knee. 'Guy, your tranquillity is what I love most about you.'

'You and few others,' he replied sadly. 'I, who admire all that sparks and flashes, am unfortunately considered something of a wet blanket.'

'Guy,' she said, with a sudden inspiration, 'are you unhappy in love?'

He looked dolefully back at her. 'Eternally.'

'Who is she?'

'*He* is a poet I met on a train. The two-thirty down from Cambridge,' he said flatly. 'Wonderfully talented, of course.'

'Oh Guy,' said Rose sympathetically.

He went on, 'I had to stop him from throwing his latest canto out of the window, followed by himself, and that is how we made our introductions. His name is Nigel but I call him Percy – after that other poet . . .'

Rose waited for him to continue but he seemed to have stalled. 'And what became of Percy after you arrived at your station?' she prompted.

'Well, I took him home and fed him on buttered toast.' He paused again and looked glum. 'Why does genius have to be quite such hard work?' he inquired at last, apparently of the bookshelf.

Rose said nothing.

'The number of times I got there, just in the nick: to dash the prussic acid from his nerveless lips, or stop him from kicking away the chair . . .'

'Goodness! He seems to have had a powerful death wish.'

'A powerful sense of drama. If only he'd been able to inject some of it into his poetry. Anyway, he got bored of me always being on hand to save him – ever the housekeeper,' he said wryly. 'Met a critic on the omnibus (it was the number nine going to Barnes) and now he's making some other dull dog unhappy.'

'And after you'd been so good to him and tried so very hard!' she said, trying to sound scandalised but holding down the giggles.

'Of course, he might not be a genius at all,' he said, as though the idea had just occurred to him, and cheered a little.

'As a general rule, I think it safer to avoid genius, real or imagined,' she said, trying to sound judicious and sensible, though the surprising notion that she was advising her older male cousin on affairs of the heart was rather unexpected.

'I'm sure you're right, Rose dear.'

'Artists are selfish monsters.'

'*Marvellous* selfish monsters,' he corrected. 'Anyway, the great ones have no need to apologise for any of it. It's my belief it is the eccentric individuals who offer the only hope of salvation.'

'Goodness,' said Rose.

'I mean to say, they are brave, or mad, enough to draw our dreams for us.' He smiled at her gloomily.

'We can't all be artists. I know I shouldn't want to be one!' she said boldly.

'But that's just the thing, d'you see? I know I'm a nobody but I have the vaguest glimmer of what it would be to be great and I know, absolutely, I can never attain it. I will leave nothing wonderful behind me of my own.'

'You're just sad about Percy,' she said.

'Ah, the boy! Ever the boy, borne aloft on his wings of poesy!'

Rose patted his hand consolingly.

'Rose,' he sounded thoroughly squashed now, 'the best I can aspire to is to be a footnote.'

'A footnote?'

'Haven't you ever wondered about those obscure names that appear in the index to a great man's life? Those fading inky footmarks left by characters he passed by along the illustrious route, the only evidence of otherwise unrecorded and inconsequential lives.'

'You're not inconsequential!' she said, aware of his large, soft hands, his feminine hips and thighs. 'Anyway, you shall leave your children behind you.'

He raised a sceptical eyebrow at that. 'Darling, I shall live out my days as someone of no significance. And when I'm finally dead and gone, the best that can be said of me will be, he did no actual harm.'

They both laughed and the conversation moved to Edy and her fury at the London art market – worse, apparently, even than the philistines of Cornwall.

Later, after Guy had gone, Rose thought uneasily about what he had said and asked aloud, of no one, 'Has my life, has all that I have felt and thought and seen, been valueless because I can't put it into words or pictures?' It seemed ridiculous, when she felt so full of experience: of love and beauty and ugliness, of life itself. But perhaps Guy was right, that all she could hope to be to history, when Patrick was dead and anthologised, was a footnote. The only evidence that she had lived and breathed and thought at all would be the epitaph, 'Rose Seaton, sometime muse', together with her dates. Worse still, the significant dates would, most probably, be the ones that recorded *his* first and last contact with her. And what of Veronique and Keziah, Dolly, Minnie, even Edy? Would they live on only as the supporting female cast in his life, their names lent a faint glow by association with his immortal flame?

The thought made her furious and she shouted out, 'I, Rose Seaton, exist. I have had my moment in the world!'

# Chapter 50

December 1899 gave way to January 1900 and with it that old, tired land hefted itself into the new century. It seemed to Rose that at that meeting point, epoch ground against epoch, clashing at the fault line like slow, advancing tectonic plates. Perhaps the seismic shudder would topple empires. Perhaps it would shake her own life into its new, contented era.

On a mild May morning, just before Elizabeth's second birthday, her mother came into the garden where Rose was playing with the children, practising games and songs for Elizabeth's birthday party. Bustling around, Mapus looked as though her compressed lips were struggling to hold something in. Something rather bitter.

'What have you come to say, Mapus?' Rose asked impatiently.

Elizabeth-Jane looked both relieved and anxious to be asked.

'Someone is here to see you, pet.'

Rose's heart clenched. Was it Patrick?

It seemed that now that her mother's mouth had opened, it would not shut. 'I mean to say, I can't very well turn him away, since he did us the favour of taking over the old house, and these days he's making such a wonderful go at business . . .'

Rose's expectant face snapped closed again and she linked hands with Robert and Elizabeth.

'Well, I don't want to see him.'

'Nevertheless, he seems very anxious to see you, my love,' insisted her mother.

Crestfallen and embarrassed, Elizabeth-Jane retreated through the open French doors and Rose turned back to the prattling children to resume their dance. She heard footsteps and looked up crossly, straight into the dark face of Harold himself. Seeing him all of a sudden like that, she could not help but notice what a handsome, well-built man he was. It confused her and stopped her from addressing him.

He took the opportunity to speak first. 'I come to tell you that my sister, Marion, has need of you. I mean . . .' His gruff tone had got him through the first sentence he'd addressed to her since she'd slapped his face at her father's will-reading, but now he tried to soften it. 'Marion needs a friend now that she's . . .' Unable to finish, he looked at Elizabeth and Robert, who capered near by. 'You're a dandy pair, aren't you now?'

Rose made no comment and Harold came closer and tried again. 'I only ask for Marion – she has no one she may speak to of her own age. My mother tries to help but Marion is that full of worries and notions . . .'

He stopped again and, with a rush of understanding, Rose burst out, 'Marion is expecting a child?' She was ashamed of herself for sounding incredulous – after all, Marion had married her Sam nearly a year ago and this was a predictable outcome.

He nodded and Rose gestured that they might sit together. She smiled to herself. Marion had learned not to fear the touch of a man's hand. Good for her.

'And do she and Sam carry on at the farm with all their socialist projects?' Her genuine affection for his sister, as well as curiosity, made her feel friendlier towards Harold than she had for a very long time. And perhaps respect, even warmth, grows between old adversaries.

'They do,' he replied shortly. 'For all the good it does 'em.'

'Well I never,' she mused.

'They had some problems to begin with. The land they first chose to build on turned out waterlogged and one of their "settlers" was a wrong 'un and went off with part of the capital . . .' He made himself stop and, since the children had toddled after them, reached out his hand for Elizabeth, who shyly hid in her mother's skirts.

'She has such beautiful curls, the colour of marigolds – just the same as her mother.'

Rose chose not to comment. He looked at Robert, who was now lying on his belly to trap a spider and said, keeping his tone nonjudgemental, 'And this other?'

'Oh, he's not mine,' she answered. 'This one belongs to Joan.'

Embarrassed that he had seemed to suggest that she was single-handedly responsible for every bastard in South Yorkshire, she determined that they should talk only of Marion.

'But now things are not going so well for Marion and Sam?' she asked.

'Oh, well enough, I should say. After I'd bailed them out and given my sister some lessons in book-keeping, things took a turn for the better and now I doubt but they'll make a fist of it – at least for a time.'

Rose smiled.

'I don't see that there's any sense to it meself. It's my belief that human nature cannot be trusted. I mean to say, for everyone to give of his best all the time, for the sake of the community and not for his own benefit, sounds like idle fancy to me. I don't rightly believe people can be depended upon to be that high-minded.'

She smiled to hear how dogmatic he was about human nature, this man who'd never travelled further than Manchester.

'I know what motivates me – my hardest scourge – are my own selfish aims, because I'll make money, whatever it takes, and I don't aspire to be any sort of a philanthropist. No doubt you think me a hard-headed exploiter of man and nature,' he paused to challenge her from under his dark brows. 'It's true that if I do good that's a side-effect of personal ambition.'

'So you don't believe in what they do and how they live and yet you support them?' She wondered that he tried to hide his soft-hearted treatment of Marion and Sam under a cast-iron shell.

'If it keeps 'em happy and they believe in it, I'll help out.'

'But will they be happy living on this socialist settlement?'

'Who's to know? But it seems to me that a happy life is most likely one that's freely chosen.' He stopped for a moment and looked at Robert and Elizabeth, who'd toddled off again. 'I'd say that any baby's greatest blessing must be to have the prospect of choosing their own destiny, not having it dictated by birth or poverty or ill health or . . .' he stopped, and seemed to shake his thoughts clear. 'So, if I have no strong objections to how they live, and I have the means to help, why should I do otherwise?'

She looked at him and said, 'Of course I shall call upon Marion. I am so glad she is to have a baby, babies are wonderful.'

That same week, on another fine sunny day, Rose took Elizabeth in the trap to Eckersby for her first visit to Marion.

She found her friend, not in her sitting room arranged upon a day bed, but feverishly hobbling around the yard, feeding her mother's hens. They took the trap over to look at the building site where the experimental settlement was being built, half a mile from the farmhouse, and Marion led her over the rocked land, leaning on her stick and stumping about over the foundations.

Back at the farmhouse, while Elizabeth helped and hindered Florence and Rosalind with making scones in the kitchen, the two old friends talked with an ease and intimacy that they had not had since they were two damsels swaddled in blankets on the veranda.

'I hope that my baby and your little girl will be friends,' said Marion, unconsciously putting her hand to her belly.

Rose smiled. 'Of course, just as their mothers are.'

'But Rose, I do worry that my poor body won't be strong enough to bear it.' Her voice was trembling and she looked with such beseeching eyes that Rose knew she owed her the comfort of a lie.

'You *will* be strong enough. I know you will! Goodness, just think of all those millions of women who have done it – even me, and you know what a coward I am!'

'I don't fear the pain,' Marion said, her eyes flooding with tears. 'I know all there is to know about that. I'm only feared that I may die and leave my poor Sam behind to cope alone.'

'Oh Marion pet, don't,' said Rose, herself beginning to weep.

'I know that I must be brave and hope for the best,' Marion went on. 'But I do worry so. It seems to me that worrying is the price I must pay, now that I have a future to look forward to.' She wiped her eyes. 'It does seem dangerous to live in expectation of even quite ordinary love and happiness.'

Rose often visited Marion at Eckersby and watched the progress of the settlement which, by the end of the year, was beginning to look more like a hamlet than a spoiled field. Sometimes she would bring Elizabeth and Robert with her to tease Brock, William's sheepdog, or help William milk his prize cow and lark with Marion's little sisters and hunt down bantam eggs. Sam she rarely saw because he was so busily engaged with establishing his little utopia. But she did occasionally meet Harold there. Indeed, he seemed to take every opportunity of getting away from his rented home to sit by Marion's fire and eat his mother's sad cake.

It was no surprise to Rose that the new industrialist avoided the antiquated pile of her girlhood; she well remembered how impossible it was to keep warm and comfortable. It was only a wonder that he persisted in paying rent on it. These occasional parlour teas recalled for Rose those long distant days before Marion had married and she had been ruined and Harold had turned iron master. How the years had altered them and their expectations of life!

As Marion's time drew nearer, Rose was more fearful than ever that her friend's premonition of death in childbirth would prove right. Marion had again taken to lying on her sofa, and was so agitated and uneasy that she seemed to dwindle with every passing day. Sam, distracted by the settlement, apparently did not notice his wife's decline, but her brother spent hours sitting by her side, reading to her or playing music for her.

One night Rose stayed later than normal at the farm, Marion had been very tearful all that evening and had only settled when her mother had given her a few drops of chloral. Rose sat by Marion's side and held her hand until she dropped off to sleep. She was preparing to go home when Harold walked in.

'She's sleeping,' she whispered, pulling on a glove.

He didn't say anything, only took her hands and, pulling off the glove by the fingertips, made her sit next to him on a low bench that stood at right angles to Marion's divan.

'Don't let me chase you away. Won't you sit a little longer?' he asked softly. 'We shan't disturb her, not if we're quiet.'

They sat in the sympathy of silence.

After a while, she remarked, 'Do you remember when you surprised me at her window and told me it was my duty to wake her?'

They both smiled and then looked across to the sleeping Marion, her face haggard in the light of the single lamp.

'Now I think she does best to sleep, long as she likes.' He sounded wretched.

Rose responded by taking his hand in hers and pressing it.

'Do you think that she may . . . succumb?' he asked in a hoarse whisper.

She tried to smile encouragingly at him and shook her head in reply to his question, a little uncomfortable that she was not being straight with him. Then, trying to speak only the truth, she said, 'Even if she does, Harold, there's comfort in knowing that she has had a life, in the end.'

He gave a repressed sob. 'Is that enough? Is it enough to have had just one shot at happiness, and lost it so soon?' He was so moved that he found it difficult to keep his voice low.

'She loves and is loved by someone kind and noble, who is her companion and friend as well as her husband,' whispered Rose, hoping this would calm him.

His voice, when it came, was constricted by emotion as well as the need to keep it low. 'She *has* had that, hasn't she? And that's more than most can hope for . . .'

She nodded, reassured that he seemed to find some comfort in the thought.

'To be loved for who we are,' he finished. Then he slipped from his seat and knelt before her.

'What are you doing?' She tried to muffle her alarm so as not to disturb Marion.

'Will you never understand that that is what I offered you? Just that.' He spoke in a low voice but his words had the same shocking force as though he had shouted them. Rose was transfixed by his dark, passionate face, laid bare of all dissembling.

'This is old, old business, Harold,' she said, struggling to get up, to get away from him.

He looked away from her and then back, muttering, 'It is unfinished business.'

'Then let it be finished,' she whispered back hotly. 'I am a mother now, some would call me a fallen woman.' She paused, wondering if she had shocked him. 'Even then, back when I was only a foolish girl, I wasn't really what you thought I was, or wanted me to be.'

'I know that I loved you then and I can't be made to deny that!' He breathed through his nose, trying to calm himself. But self-restraint lasted only a couple of words before he was once more trembling with ill-repressed emotion. 'Don't you see,

Rose, I only made myself into what I am today because I thought that was the kind of man you could love in return. I offered you everything!'

Rose was so frightened that he'd wake his sister that she stayed still now, looking levelly into his eyes.

'I didn't deserve you,' she said, full of gentle sorrow.

'No, you didn't deserve me,' he repeated dully, all the fight gone out of him.

She tried again to rise but he swiftly held her by the hands to keep her sitting. Wordlessly he searched her face but did not seem to find what he looked for there. He released her, saying, 'In the end I used up the best part of myself chasing after an illusion.'

She did not attempt to leave, so he rose from the floor to sit beside her again.

'Rose, I can't help myself, despite pride and good sense, I still love you,' he said, his voice cracked by emotions reined-in hard. 'It's foolish but it can't be got over.'

'Harold, you must know that there was no sense and no pride in what I did, throwing myself into the flame,' she said sadly, very moved by his dignity, 'but it has left my heart a burnt out chamber. I don't believe I can love again.'

Seeing that Marion stirred in her sleep, Rose put her hand on his arm, to comfort but also to caution him, though he seemed to read only encouragement in the gesture.

'Rose, when there's a foundation of sympathy and friendship and kindness, there's hope.' He said this very quietly, in command of himself now. 'Hope is enough for me to live on, for the present.'

Then he left her. Soon afterwards, as she drove home, another parting from Harold flashed suddenly upon Rose. She saw him, tall and black and intense, standing in the lane that led from the farmhouse and up into the Seaton woods. He'd said almost the same words to her then, when she was a young girl too ignorant and silly to understand what it was he hoped for from her. And that thought had stabbed her with remorse. How was it, though she'd never meant to, she seemed to have only made Harold miserable? Agitated by that thought, the song that Patrick had sung, over and over, on the Neapolitan hillside, played in her head: about the one who loved too passionately and the other not quite well enough. Rose wondered whether every couple was a mis-match of lover and beloved and if that wasn't the best one could expect, after all. Reaching her own home, she crept upstairs to her bed to consider.

# The Final Chapter

That very evening, 22 January 1901, will see the last of Victoria. She floats heavenward from the little island that lies just off the flank of the mainland as the departing sun sweeps a slow tide of morning westward over a subjugated globe. Each in turn of the nations, territories, dominions, colonies, protectorates and mandates that lie in its path will witness the final day of Victoria, *regina et imperatrix*. Somewhere in the South Pacific Ocean, at the crossing of an imaginary line which separates today from tomorrow, the first dawn of a new age will begin. On that momentous morrow the death notices will be printed in newspapers, the bells will toll, loyal Sheffielders will paint the railings black and put on purple. But now on ice floes and tropical islands, in Mughal palaces, outback telegraph stations and Yorkshire parlours alike the news that the world has changed still waits to be broadcast.

Perhaps the Queen pauses in her assent, attracted by the lights of London, set like jewels in the dark haunch of England. Perhaps she swoops across the water and along the pewter wriggle of the Thames, then bustles north on a final, farewell tour of her kingdom. The moon flashes in rivers and lakes, or picks out the white of a road; the dark and undulating pelt of forest and fen and moor is pierced by lights that pinpoint where a town or village lies. Sheffield passes beneath. She barely hesitates – just another of those black islands of fire and smoke that spot her green land. Over beloved Scotland a cold wind whips off the peaks, the lochs gleam, and she reaches her journey's limit over the final British rock lost in the Norwegian Sea. She looks up into the black of her last night before ascending forever, towards the stars.

As Rose tiptoes in to her sleeping daughter and holds the shaded candle so that she can look at that tranquil face, she has no notion that an era has come to its end. Still preoccupied by her conversation with Harold, Joan's sudden appearance on the landing makes her jump.

Looking anxiously into her face, her friend says, 'I've been waiting up for you!'

'I'm sure you had no reason to, dear. I can see myself to my bed.'

'A letter arrived this morning.' Looking anxiously into Rose's face as she hands it over, Joan adds, 'I thought you'd like to see it afore you turned in.'

The letter has an Italian stamp.

'You're to call if you should have need of me,' Joan says, reluctant to leave.

Trying to keep her hand from shaking, Rose takes the letter and has to resist ripping it open then and there.

'It's only a bill from an Italian milliner. Off to bed with you.'

She puts the letter on her dressing table, won't even look at it, as she prepares for bed. She takes her time over brushing out her hair, folds every item of clothing carefully, says her prayers, and all the while that letter with its Italian stamp shouts for her attention. The gum that seals the flap is all that stands between knowledge and ignorance. She will decide when to cross that divide. Strange to think that this is the first and only time she's had the power to make him wait for her.

She climbs between the sheets, and opens the envelope. She will know at last how far she has really come.

Pisa, 1901
Darling Rose,

I do hope that this letter is not one of those literary devices upon which tragedies turn – sent only to be lost or never delivered. I offered up a prayer to Hymen when I dropped it in the box.

I finished the portrait – it is my best work, although I was obliged to chick it up from memory in the end since Miss Minnie was too busy a-weeping and a-wailing to sit. Seems she really did love Charlie boy. Too late! Too late!

Oh, but I have missed you, Rose. I lie abed in this miserable, cold, wet town and remember the garden where we first kissed. Was it poisonous Edy's? Do you remember? Rose, I can't bear it if you don't come back to me and love me like you used to. I need you so . . .

Patrick leaps up before her, like the genie let out of its bottle. He stands beautiful, desirable, with hands outstretched, and her heart answers, as instinctively as a well-trained dog to the whistle. Perhaps the race is not quite run, perhaps this time she'll be able to catch up with him and keep him.

Then, quite deliberately, she pulls herself back from luggage and train timetables, because the time for mad pursuit is over. Strange to realise that, now she no longer feels the want of a husband, she has two suitors clamouring to love or be loved. There they stand, side by side, the gold and the black – Patrick, glamorous, full of dangerous promise, and dignified, devoted Harold. And, if no husband, well then that is an end to her abortive career as a wife. It makes Rose smile when she considers how much effort was put into fitting her to being one, how she herself had wanted nothing else, had yearned and plotted, cried and chased after that ideal state. Yet she has never been one, and now perhaps she never will be. But she'd regret none of it.

The letter drops from her hand.

No, this little domestic life would unfold, day by day, happy or sad, and she'd let it, find contentment in it. Because there's always hope.

On the edge of the long backward journey into sleep, Rose drifts into her parents' drawing room on a May afternoon. The tall trees sway in the garden, the clock ticks upon the mantelshelf and Patrick comes through a window to start her story.



LIMERICK
COUNTY LIBRARY